COMMON SOURCE

ALSO BY BRYAN THOMAS SCHMIDT

NOVELS

The Worker Prince (Saga of Davi Rhii 1)
The Returning (Saga of Davi Rhii 2)
The Exodus (Saga of Davi Rhii 3)
Simon Says (John Simon Thrillers)
The Sideman (John Simon Thrillers)
Common Source (John Simon Thrillers)

CHILDREN'S BOOKS

Abraham Lincoln Dinosaur Hunter: Land Of Legends
102 More Hilarious Dinosaur Jokes For Kids

NONFICTION

How To Write A Novel: The Fundamentals of Fiction

ANTHOLOGIES (AS EDITOR)

Surviving Tomorrow
Infinite Stars: Dark Frontiers
Joe Ledger: Unstoppable (with Jonathan Maberry)
Predator: If It Bleeds
Infinite Stars: Definitive Space Opera and Military Science Fiction
The Monster Hunter Files (with Larry Correia)
Maximum Velocity (with David Lee Summers, Carol Hightshoe,
Dayton Ward, and Jennifer Brozek)
Little Green Men—Attack! (with Robin Wayne Bailey)
Decision Points
Galactic Games
Mission: Tomorrow
Shattered Shields (with Jennifer Brozek)
Raygun Chronicles: Space Opera For a New Age
Beyond The Sun
Space Battles: Full Throttle Space Tales

COMMON SOURCE

By

Bryan Thomas Schmidt

Ottawa, KS

BORALIS BOOKS
Ottawa, KS 66067

Copyright © 2020 Bryan Thomas Schmidt
All rights reserved.

ISBN-13: 978-1-62225-7560 hardcover
ISBN-13: 978-1-62225-7577 paperback
ISBN-13: 978-1-62225-7584 ebook

First Edition: June 2020

Printed in the United States of America

10 9 8 7 6 5 4 3 2 1

Interior Design and Layout by Sebastian Penraeth
Cover Layout and Design: A.R. Crebs
Author Photo: Bryan Thomas Schmidt

Dedicated to
John Schmidt, uncle,
tour guide extraordinaire, friend.

CHAPTER 1

CRACKERJACK'S WAS THE last place Master Detective John Simon expected to be on a Thursday night at eight. The night club was one of the latest trendy hot spots in Kansas City's thriving Crossroads arts district just south of the city's downtown, the dance floor packed with the young and on the rise, their feet pounding in synch with the thunderous beat two deejays were spinning from a raised platform at the center of the room. The scent of colognes, perfumes, sweat, body odor, and greasy appetizers filled the air in a toxic mix that everyone but Simon seemed to ignore.

His eyes searched the crowd, solidly aware he didn't fit in. Forties, former star running back at K-State, divorced, an eighteen-year veteran of the department, he was the oldest guy in the room and his wardrobe stood out like an Elvis im-personator at a costume ball, especially with the fleece-lined coat he was wearing over the top. It was in the thirties outside, but almost tropical in the club. A few of the patrons gave him funny looks, others looked amused, but most just ignored him as he weaved his way through the writhing bodies, taking in every face. None of them were his man.

He stopped when he reached the corner and turned back to see how his partner was doing just as the beat changed to an old disco classic—retro was in—and the familiar strains of

Carl Douglas' "Kung Fu Fighting" echoed off the shimmering walls. The crowd cheered and began gyrating in unison like dancers in a choreographed routine, and right in the middle of them, matching every beat and move, was Lucas George. Dark skinned, medium tall, thin but athletic, with piercing green eyes and close cut hair, Lucas looked mid-thirties, though his actual age was less than ten. One of the first humanoid android models entered into service from Connelly Labs, he was also the first humanoid android graduate of the Kansas City Regional Police Academy. And he was Simon's partner.

They'd met when Simon's former partner was kidnapped. Determined to find her and those responsible, Simon had teamed up with the only witness, the android security guard at the warehouse, and thus his partnership with Lucas was born. Later, Lucas' experiences working the case with Simon and their budding friendship had inspired him to apply for the Academy. The rest, as they say, was history. Six months later, Lucas graduated top of his class, and now here he was on his first assignment as a full detective. Because of his special skills and nature, he'd skipped patrol and gone straight to work with Simon, the department wanting to take full advantage of this new resource under the tutelage of a senior man. Only Simon and Lucas were prone to trouble, all in the name of zealously pursuing justice, of course. Thus now they were working nights and weekends, having been reassigned from Central Division's Property squad to the Generalist squad at Headquarters, until the department decided what to do with them.

This left Simon frustrated but from the way Lucas was smiling, he appeared to be just fine with it. He danced like someone who'd been doing it for years rather than perfectly imitating those around him, and the other patrons were treating him like one of their own. Lucas, unlike Simon, was wearing only a thin windbreaker because he had no need of a coat. If Simon had been the one dancing, he knew he'd be drowning in sweat, but Lucas didn't have to worry about that. Simon watched as they all did air kung fu with their flailing arms and danced in a circle to the right in perfect unison, waiting off to the side to avoid a collision until the song was over.

As he continued scanning the crowd seeking the face of Peter Wacks, the low-life wannabe player who'd drawn them there tonight, his eyes lit on a glowing beauty that held his gaze. She was medium height with long reddish brunette tresses and seductive curves well highlighted by the slinky red dress she was wearing. Simon followed her long, seductive legs underneath to shiny black pumps that bounced in time to the beat. It was almost as if a spotlight had found her in the midst of the masses but in truth, she'd taken a position under one of the overhead spots lighting an aisle across the dance floor.

On looks alone, she was everything Simon liked in a woman. He had an instant urge to talk with her, duties aside. But to do so, he'd have to somehow navigate his way through a hundred gyrating bodies and around a raised platform, which for the moment at least appeared a herculean task. Instead, he stood there, enjoying the view until she noticed his stare, smiled briefly, and then slipped back into the crowd and disappeared.

Simon's heart sank with disappointment. What was he—some lovestruck teenager in a disco? He shook it off, scanning over to where Lucas was still dancing as the song wound to a close. *You have a job to do, John. Stay focused,* he scolded himself. For a moment he knew what Emma meant when she accused him of being "overly fatherly." He'd found that tone of inner voice annoying himself. But then the song ended. He shook it off and raised a hand, waving to get his partner's attention as Lucas chatted with other dancers and exchanged compliments and pleasantries. Finally, the android spotted his partner and began weaving his way over through the crowd.

"You have fun?" he asked as Lucas joined him off to the side.

"Yes," Lucas agreed. "Good song."

"You do remember we're working here, right?" Simon replied.

"You told me to blend in," Lucas said with a shrug. "I think I was successful." Just then a young Asian in his late twenties walked by with a beautiful blonde hanging off his arm and raised the other to high five Lucas as he passed, each greeting the other with an enthusiastic "Dude."

Simon rolled his eyes. "Well, when you're done blending, what do you say we actually try to find this Wacks so we can get outta here?"

Lucas nodded. "Well, sure. At least until the next good song comes on." He grinned.

Simon groaned. "Don't get cocky. You're still in training, remember?"

"Speaking of training, Emma says I should teach you how to dance," Lucas said.

"No fucking way," Simon said. "No thanks, pal."

"She suggested it might help your social life," Lucas said as they started forward together, weaving through the crowd around the edge of the dance floor. "'You need to get out more.'"

Simon shot him dead with a glare.

"I was quoting her, not me," Lucas said with an innocent look.

"By all means feel free to restrain yourself from quoting to me every single criticism my daughter tells you about me, okay?" Simon snapped.

"Just trying to help," Lucas answered.

"Trust me, stick to your gifts," Simon said as he spotted a familiar face twenty feet ahead along the edge of the dance floor near where he'd spotted the brunette earlier. He elbowed Lucas in the ribs. "I think I see Wacks."

"Where?"

Simon grabbed him by the forearm and pulled him so he was facing the suspect as they kept moving through the crowd. "Let me take lead. You back me up."

"Roger wilco," Lucas replied, quoting some radio language he'd heard on a cop show that Simon found really annoying, but now wasn't the time for that argument again.

They moved in on the subject now, who was talking to a woman with her back against a pillar. He was leaning in with both arms fully extended, one on either side of her, their faces a few inches apart as they talked—probably to be heard over the music. Simon didn't get the vibe the woman was that into him...yet.

Simon grabbed him by the shoulder and whirled him around.

"Hey!" Wacks protested, stiffening as if ready to fight.

Lucas badged him and Wacks relaxed a bit.

"What do you want?" he demanded.

"To talk," Simon said.

Wacks nodded back toward the pillar behind him. "I'm

already talking to someone. You'll have to wait."

"Not anymore," Simon snapped and Wacks turned to see the object of his attention being led onto the dance floor by another much better looking guy.

"Son of a bitch!" he spat.

Simon and Lucas each grabbed him by an arm and pulled him away from the dance floor through the crowd to a near-by booth, throwing him onto the bench as Simon straddled a chair on the other side of the table, chest against the chair back facing him. Lucas stood behind him to one side with his arms crossed, blocking any escape.

"What do you want?" Wacks demanded again.

"We want to know about Alma Watson," Lucas said.

"Who?!"

Simon grunted and shook his head. "Nope. Not gonna go down that way, asshole. The old woman you scammed out of her social security and savings. The one whose house you then broke in and cleared out."

"What?" Wacks scoffed. "You've mistaken me for some-one else."

"Unfortunately, we haven't," Simon said and motioned to Lucas.

Lucas held up his cell phone and played tape of a sur-veillance camera with a view from across the street showing Wacks using a hand laser to cut a section out of the wide win-dow of a house late at night with date and time stamp running along the bottom. "Caught on tape," Lucas said.

"And that's just the neighbor's footage," Simon said. "For-tunately, Alma's daughter also got worried and placed a nan-ny cam in her living room just in case."

"Would you like to see that one, too?" Lucas asked.

Wacks shook his head. "I was helping her when she locked herself out."

"Nope," Lucas said, shaking his head.

"Alma's cell phone places her over at her daughter's house that night," Simon said.

"For her grandson's birthday," Lucas added.

Wacks looked like a deer trapped in headlights for a moment until a waitress appeared. She was early twenties and bouncy, like a cheerleader on too much caffeine. "Hey, y'all. What ya drinkin'?"

"No thank you," Lucas said.

"Are you sure?" she asked sing-song. "It's half price night!"

As Simon turned his head to frown at her, Wacks sprung up and vaulted over the back of the booth. He landed atop the next table, its eight jammed in occupants protesting loudly as glasses and plates clattered and drinks spilled, then hurriedly dodged as Wacks stumbled off the table and took off running.

Lucas went to give chase but the waitress and a passing couple got in the way.

"Fuck!" Simon said.

"So no drinks then?" the waitress asked innocently, all smiles.

"No tip either," Simon snapped as he and Lucas took off after Wacks, who was fifteen feet ahead already, weaving through the crowd.

As he reached the bathrooms, Wacks pushed through and hurried down the hallway running past them and disappearing off into some other area of the club just as a song ending and couples started streaming off the dance floor, trading places with others as they did.

Simon and Lucas reached the bathrooms just as an incoming influx was jammed up by the outgoing crowd and struggled to push through and get to the corridor. Simon badged them at face level as he struggled against the flow. "Police business! Let us through!"

Everyone ignored them. By the time they managed to get through, Wacks was nowhere to be seen.

Simon patted Lucas' arm. "You go that way. I'm going out the front and around. See if I can intercept him."

"Gotcha," Lucas said and hurried down the corridor as Simon turned back and fought his way through the crowd again.

Simon emerged from the club and immediately reached down to zip up his coat against the biting cold. Black pavement slick with ice and snow stretched in each direction, most of the spots filled with cars and trucks of all shapes, sizes, and colors in spaces clearly demarked by fading white lines. The lot was well-lit by spotlights in tall poles, thirty feet overhead, and Simon scanned it for his suspect as people chatted and laughed, car doors slammed, and tires crunched on snow and ice, moving past.

Deciding to check around the side, he turned back toward the side of the club any exit from the corridor by the bathroom would lead to and felt his feet slipping out from under him on ice, then he found himself face to face with the woman he'd been admiring earlier across the bathroom.

Suddenly, he was plowing into her as she tried to raise her hands, palms out, to stop him. They collided roughly, falling and sliding, him on top of her right off the sidewalk and out into the parking lot on a huge patch of black ice. They landed right in the path of an oncoming car. Simon tried to roll off but she was struggling too and they just wound up more entangled. The car started braking, but it was sliding, too, and Simon and the woman's efforts become even more desperate. Then just as he cringed in preparation for the impact, the car stopped and he reached up to grab its bumper, managing to halt the slide and bring them to a stop.

He rolled off the woman as she gasped for breath and he struggled again for footing as he tried to rise. Two pairs of feet appeared standing next to him, and he looked up to see Lucas and a handcuffed Wacks staring down at him.

"I thought I was supposed to let you take lead," Lucas said. "While you were making friends, I got him."

"This wasn't on purpose," Simon growled.

"Okay, we'll be in the car," Lucas said and turned, pushing Wacks in front of him to head back for their unmarked KCPD Ford Explorer.

"Wait!" Simon said. "Help us up!"

Lucas stopped, grabbing Wacks by the handcuffs with one hand and extending the other to help Simon to his feet. Then he did the same for the woman, who was looking rather irritated now at the situation she'd found herself sucked into.

"Are you okay?" Lucas asked as he released her hand and she dusted herself off and examined her mud-stained dress and coat.

"No thanks to your friend," the woman said, glaring at Simon.

"Partner," Lucas said.

"I'm sorry," Simon managed, thinking to himself she was actually more beautiful angry, then moaned internally at the cliché.

Lucas gave her a look of sympathy. "He's only human."

The woman looked startled by the remark and then barked

a laugh as she carefully climbed back onto the sidewalk.

"You sure you're okay?" Lucas called after her.

"Yes, thank you," she answered.

"Okay, have a good night," Simon said cheerfully after her, but she simply glared back at him as Lucas turned and resumed leading Wacks across the parking lot toward the Interceptor. Simon followed.

"I don't think she likes you," Wacks said.

"Shut the fuck up," Simon said.

"I think he's right," Lucas replied.

"You shut the fuck up too," Simon said, frowning. "What about me? Not going to ask how I am?"

"You're walking fine, just a little dirty," Lucas said. "You're always telling me you don't like when I'm overly sentimental."

Simon grunted. "Caring about someone's well-being is polite, not sentimental." They stopped a moment to wait as another car hurried past before crossing an aisle to the parking section where their car was waiting.

As they stepped out again to cross, another car spun its wheels to escape ice and pull out of its spot, spraying mud and water all over Simon, who tried to dodge much too late. Instead, the car shot forward and he stood there soaked and pissed, shaking his hands to flick off water as Lucas reached the other side and put Wacks into the back of the Interceptor.

"We waiting for a wagon?" Lucas asked as Simon finally joined him.

"No, you ride with Wacks, I'll drive," Simon said. "I'm fucking soaked."

"You really should be more careful walking on ice," Lucas said. "I expected you were used to it." He climbed in back beside the suspect and shut the car door.

Simon heard a whirring overhead and looked up as a media drone dropped down in front of him.

"Smile," it said in a sing-song voice as a flash flashed and Simon raised his arm to block his face but he was too late. "Thank you," it added as it flew away.

"Fucking smartass robots," Simon muttered and headed around the Interceptor toward the driver's side. And he wasn't just talking about the drone.

THE GENERALIST SQUAD was based out of the third floor at KCPD headquarters downtown at 1125 Locust. Built in 1938, headquarters was a nine story stone monolith located right next to the city's detention center; it housed offices for the Chief, his deputies and assistants, and various investigative units, including Homicide, Assault, Cyber Crime, Sex Crimes, and Generalist detectives. There had been a decade during which the Generalist Squad was eliminated but two years prior, Chief Weber had decided it was needed again due to an uptick in late night incidents requiring detectives and brought it back.

Simon and Lucas dropped Wacks at the detention center and then headed for headquarters, parking the Interceptor in its assigned space in the garage. They took the back elevator up to three and entered the squad room. Part of being reassigned was getting used to a whole new team of people, but fortunately, the Generalists were led by an old Academy classmate of Simon's, Sergeant Brian Delmater. Late forties, tall, with a thickening paunch and limbs like most men his age, Delmater had a hardened face but a warm heart and a great sense of humor. If Simon had to be assigned under someone besides JoAnn Becker, his previous sergeant, Delmater would have been his first choice.

Like most, the squad room was a maze of soft-walled cubicles with file cabinets, copy machines, printers, and shelves scattered around. The outer walls were government-issue plain with off-white paint over thin, gray carpet. There were also several bulletin boards and two white boards scattered about, all of them filled with notices, wanted posters, suspect pics, or scribbled notes. Simon's nose caught hints of highlighter markers, hand sanitizer and colognes, air fresheners and scented candles, and musty old files as he lead the way.

Simon's and Lucas' cubes were on the west aisle near the windows just outside a conference room and Delmater's office. As they wove their way through past the other Generalists, several took note of Simon's current state and reacted with a mix of amusement and surprise.

"You know, Simon, you'd think an O.G. would know to at least make himself presentable before he came to the squad," joked Detective Benny Jimenez, thirties, Hispanic, thin with an eclectic taste in wardrobe. He tsked, shaking his head.

"Love the new look, Simon," Detective Yanni Rankin teased. An Israeli immigrant around Jiminez's age, he was all flash and style with slicked back, well-groomed hair, and a nice tan no matter what time of year it was.

"Looks like your new partner's breaking you in right," Detective Allie Williams said. African American, early thirties, tall and thin, a basketball star in college until she'd injured her knee, she was a crack shot and a looker, also with a strong sense of style.

"Hey, George, you sure you wouldn't prefer to partner with someone who knows how to walk on ice?" Detective Louie Lenz teased. Short, pudgy, with thinning hair, he was the oldest of the bunch at early forties and dressed like a bum—old wrinkled suit, well-worn shoes, out-of-date ties, and cheap shirts.

Lucas smiled as Simon offered a mock laugh. "You guys oughta take your act to Vegas. You'd clean up."

The four exchanged looks. "I always thought so," Jiminez said.

"John," Delmater called from his office as they passed his door. Simon and Lucas changed direction and stopped in his doorway. Delmater frowned, looking Simon over. "What happened to you?"

"Black ice," Lucas said.

"You catch the guy at least?" Delmater asked, shaking his head sympathetically.

Simon tipped his head toward Lucas. "He did."

"Well, that's something," Delmater said. "Go clean yourself up and get a warm cup of coffee. The wife sent some Brazilian she brought back from an excursion to Rio to visit our son. Good stuff."

"Good coffee? In a police station?" Simon mocked. "You trying to ruin our rep?"

"And improve morale," Delmater snapped back, grinning. "Enjoy it while it lasts."

Simon gave a quick salute and walked back to his desk, Lucas following. "You get started on the paperwork, while I clean up, okay?" he said.

Lucas shrugged as he slipped into his chair at the cube next to Simon's. "On it."

Simon made his way into the conference room with a fridge, microwave, and coffee station. There was also a break room down the hall but Simon wasn't in the mood for the walk, and if Delmater brought special coffee, he'd kept it close to avoid mooching by other squads. Police officers might fight crime, but they had few qualms about stealing from each other when it came to the best resources.

The rich aroma of real coffee, not the usual industrial mass-produced stuff, replaced the squad room smells of B.O. musty papers, and dust the minute he stepped through the door. Simon grabbed the pot and a generic white Styrofoam cup and filled it to the brim, then leaned against the counter as he sipped, savoring the special treat—real coffee. At least something was going right tonight. The hot liquid warmed his insides as it went down and he wished he had a Danish or donut to go with, but there was nothing today. After this, he'd hit the locker room for a change of clothes and a quick shower—as much to warm up as anything—then return to help Lucas with the paperwork.

But before he could even finish, Delmater was calling. "Simon! George!"

Simon groaned, carrying his coffee back out into the squad room. Delmater stood just outside his office with a note.

"What's up, Sarge?" Simon asked as Lucas walked over to join them.

"1809 Grand, The Prism," Delmater said.

"Fuck. Another night club?" Simon groused. His night had just gotten worse again.

"Suspect flipped out and tore up the place," Delmater

said. "They're holding everyone as witnesses but the dance floor's closed."

Simon nodded toward the others. "Why can't one of the others take it?"

"You two are the only ones who wrapped a case," Delmater said. "Besides, I'm going too and I want Lucas' take on this."

"Why?" Lucas asked, surprised.

"Because the suspect is supposedly an android, like you," Delmater replied.

"Can I at least get a shower and change first?" Simon asked.

Delmater shook his head. "I wish, but it'll have to wait." He put a hand on Simon's shoulder as Simon groaned in protest. "We'll probably just get dirty again slogging around at the scene anyway. I'll buy you an early breakfast if we're there long enough."

"I choose the place?" Simon asked, brightening.

"With respect for the fact I'm just a poor cop like you, sure," Delmater said.

Simon snorted. "A poor cop who just got a pay hike. You're on." He turned and led the way out of the squad room as Delmater leaned back into his office to grab his coat and then hurried to catch up.

"The pay hike's not as great as you probably imagine," Delmater warned.

"You bought a new boat and repainted your house," Simon teased. "You're doing fine."

"I was until I made the mistake of offering you food," Delmater mumbled as they headed out the door.

CHAPTER 2

THE PRISM WAS the latest hotspot to open in the Crossroads Art District, Kansas City's eclectic enclave of boutique shops, one-of-a-kind restaurants, creative businesses, studios, and art galleries. Home to more than 400 artists and 100 independent art galleries, it was one of the most concentrated gallery districts in the nation but also home to design firms, architects, advertising agencies, restaurants, and a night club or two. Just south of the convention center, it comprised an area that stretched from Interstate 35 on the west to I-70 on the north, highway 71 on the east, and ended just north of Union Station at Penway Street and trolley and railroad tracks in the south.

The Prism, located on the southeast corner of East 18th Street at Grand Avenue, was a gay nightclub, though its patrons also often included straight ladies out for a fun night without the meat market hassle of so many other places. From the entrance off Grand, you stepped into a long, wide hallway with alcoves off the left for two restrooms—male and female—and an office. On the right, an arched entryway led off into the bar with booths lining the walls around a large, central bar with tables jam packed in between. Further down, you entered the large dance floor which was surrounded on all sides by three level tiers holding tables and booths for those who preferred to people watch or relax rather than join the active frenzy of writhing bodies down below. There was also a small band stand at the far end with a D.J. stand next to it.

By twelve-thirty, when Simon and Lucas arrived, several black-and-whites and two ambulances had beat them there and the uniforms were attempting crowd control while the paramedics treated a few wounded with what looked like minor injuries.

As they made their way through a crowd clogging the sidewalk and corridor, Simon overheard several comments from patrons on his bedraggled appearance.

"Oh my, take pride in yourself, honey!"

"Of course the gay club gets the third class cops! Typical!"

"Girl, he looks worse than the club does!"

Simon ignored them all and took in the place. The interior was decorated in bright neon colors with sparkles in the paint. Simon found it hideous, but the manager who met them at the door presented it with, "Welcome to our bling, boys!"

Inside, the dance floor and room surrounding it were in shambles. Tables and chairs had been split in half or smashed to pieces. Plates of food and drinks littered every surface, mixed with broken glass and utensils. The D.J. table had been tipped over and the turntables broken with broken vinyl and scratched CDs lying randomly and in heaps. Even some spotlights lining the stage and walls had been blown out and the curtains had been ripped down.

"It looks more like a tornado came through here than one man," Simon said as Delmater slipped in to join them.

"Superhuman on drugs or something, you mean," the manager said, shaking his head. "He was here dancing with the rest for about an hour, and then out of nowhere he just goes crazy and starts tearing up the place."

"All by himself?" Lucas asked.

"He didn't need anyone else, love," the manager said. "He had superhuman strength, like I said, and he seemed to enjoy it."

"Anyone hurt?" Delmater asked.

"A few scrapes and bruises, torn clothing, and minor trampling victims, but no one who won't walk away," the manager said. "They're outside with the paramedics."

"Do you have security cameras that might have gotten any images of the guy?" Simon asked.

"In the dark?" the manager scoffed. "All the lights are on right now, but normally it's almost dark in here, just a few highlights and lights on the tables and at the booths, so I doubt it."

"What about coming in or out?" Lucas asked.

The manager shrugged. "Maybe."

"We'll want to see all the footage regardless," Delmater said.

"Suit yourselves," the manager said.

"We need to interview anyone who got a good look at the man, and get the names of the others in case we want to talk to them later," Delmater said.

"Okay," the manager said.

"Would you gather the ones you know about and have them meet us in the bar? We'll get uniforms to start taking names from the rest and send them on home," Simon said. He noticed Lucas was staring around the room, taking it in.

As the manager and Delmater headed back out toward the front to gather witnesses, he leaned in and whispered, "You okay, partner?"

Lucas shook his head. "It makes no sense."

"What?"

"An android wouldn't do this," Lucas said.

"What makes you say that?" Simon asked.

"The three laws, part of our basic programming," Lucas said.

Simon tried to remember his Asimov, which he'd only read after meeting Lucas. "A robot may not injure a human being or, through inaction, allow a human being to come to harm. A robot must obey orders given it by human beings except where such orders would conflict with the First Law. A robot must protect its own existence as long as such protection does not conflict with the First or Second Law. Those laws?"

"Yes," Lucas said. "This kind of destruction and violence—"

"Well, if no one got seriously injured, maybe he thought he was obeying the laws but it got a little out of hand," Simon suggested.

Lucas shook his head. "We were made to serve mankind, not destroy property and wreak havoc. It still violates programming."

"Could there have been something in his mods that allowed him to do this?" Simon asked, referring to the fact that androids with specific duties often had modifications to the basic three laws to accommodate those duties. For example, as a law enforcement officer, Lucas' programming had required modifications to the first two laws. First, Lucas would only obey orders of his Maker, Owner, and those they assigned to authority over him. Thus, criminals or other troublemakers could not sabotage or interfere in his work but he would obey law officers, particularly the chain of command. Second, he could harm human beings in context of the First Law according to the guidelines and policies of the KCPD, which he'd not only had added to his programming but had also memorized, line by line.

Lucas sighed. "Perhaps, but this isn't right."

Simon reached up to squeeze his shoulder. "We'll figure it out, okay? And we'll put a stop to it, get the android responsible in for repairs. Don't worry."

Lucas grunted but still looked unsettled. "If It was an android," he added.

"Come on, help me with these witnesses," Simon said and led the way back down the corridor toward the front, Lucas reluctantly following. Simon had a feeling it was going to be a long night.

THEY INTERVIEWED WITNESSES at the club until the wee hours and then headed out to Simon's favorite downtown eatery, the City Diner, for breakfast with Delmater as promised. By the time Lucas got back to his apartment near the River Market, the sky was lightening and birds were chorusing with their morning songs. He plugged in to recharge his power, then set to work on the internet, trying to distract himself. What he'd seen earlier that night at Prism scared the hell out of him. Just when androids like him were finally coming into acceptance as citizens in society, at last becoming more common and popular, an android was being accused of violence and destruction of property! When word got out, it could hurt the reputation and hard won trust between androids and humans, and as the most prominent android known by the local public, a member of their police force, it would especially put pressure on him.

He thought about calling his Maker, Doctor Livia Connelly, at her office—Connelly Labs—but she wouldn't be in yet and he didn't want to wake her at home, especially with bad news when he had so few facts to report. No, he would wait, so instead he searched the web for other incidents of android violence or crimes and came up with nothing. *So this is new, that is a good thing*, he thought. But how could this happen? That part still stumped him. Why would someone spend thousands on an android then damage it? He really needed to talk to Doctor Connelly, but that would have to wait a couple more hours.

He picked up the latest detective novel his friend and guru Will, co-owner of Prospero's Books, had recommended. Prospero's, a place Simon and Lucas had gone to on their first case together—the Benjamin Ashman case—had become his go-to resource for research and human knowledge and Will always recommended the perfect books to help him expand his knowledge in whatever category he wanted. At present, he was studying both new catchphrases he might try out and also techniques and tricks of investigating that might help him consider things from new angles at work.

The current book was *Atlanta Deathwatch* by Ralph Dennis, a classic set in 1974 about an ex-cop turned P.I. who's hired by a black crime lord to investigate the murder of his white girlfriend, a college student. It was gritty, dark noir that took the characters deep into Atlanta's back alley underworld and a street war of the kind that real cops often saw but most regular people didn't except on TV. Lucas was enjoying it, particularly the snappy banter and quirky characters and soon found himself lost in it for several chapters until he looked up at the clock again and found it was nine a.m. He decided to call his Maker for her thoughts on this new development.

"Lucas, good morning!" Connelly said, sounding hurried as she answered the phone. "You're up early. Aren't you working nights?"

"I am and I am recharging right now, Maker," Lucas said.

"Ah yes, the advantages of not needing to sleep," Connelly said. "I think of you all so much as my children, I sometimes forget. So what can I do for you?"

"There was an incident last night," Lucas explained. "At a night club in Crossroads, Prism."

"The gay club? I think some of my employees have mentioned it," Connelly said.

"Yes," Lucas replied. "Someone tore up the place late last night. Simon said it looked like a tornado went through."

"That's awful. Was anyone hurt?"

"Only minor scrapes, cuts, and bruises, thankfully," Lucas said. "But they say the suspect was an android."

"What?!" Connelly said. "An android?"

"Yes," Lucas said.

"Did you get a name or pictures?" Connelly asked.

"We are checking surveillance footage," Lucas said. "No one so far had a name."

"Oh my God! It can't be!" Connelly said.

"How could this happen?" Lucas asked, his anxiety clear in his voice.

"Well, Lucas, we don't know for sure, okay? We need more information," Connelly said. "But if it did happen, it would violate programming."

"Yes, but could someone change programming to allow it?" Lucas asked.

"They'd have to get around our safeguards, which is not easy," Connelly said. "We design our androids so that we provide all servicing. It's safer that way and also protects proprietary information and design."

"Right," Lucas said. He'd known that. "Is anyone else offering androids yet with the same capabilities?"

"Well, we do have up-and-coming competitors, though I'd say their models are not yet up to our standards," Connelly said. "There's Weeks Industries, Carney & Sons, and Hartman Robotics, for example."

Lucas wrote the names down.

"But they don't sell in this market yet," Connelly said. "For the Midwest, we really are about the only game in town. Androids of this level are still so new. That's why we've expanded so much so quickly just keeping up with demand. Plus, the Commerce Department and other Federal agencies are being stingy with permits until they feel they've fully developed adequate standards and policy for manufacturers and licensers."

"Is it possible someone tried to modify one of yours without your knowledge?" Lucas asked.

There was a silence on the other end for a few beats as Connelly considered this. "Anything is possible with electronics and computers," she finally said. "Things move so quickly that I suppose someone could have found a way if they really wanted to, though this is the first I've heard of any possibility. And I still have my doubts."

"A virus maybe? Some kind of scrambler?" Lucas suggested.

"Some variations on that are always possible," Connelly

agreed. "But you know we push out regular updates once a week, sometimes more often, to keep our models current and protected, not to mention the built-in safeguards I already mentioned. It would have to be very sophisticated."

"Thank you for answering my questions, Maker," Lucas said.

"Of course, Lucas," Connelly said. "I know you're very worried about what this might mean, and I am, too, but I promise you we'll get to the bottom of it somehow. Get me any photos and details as soon as you have them. We're very proud of you."

"Thank you," Lucas said, feeling uncomfortable at her praise. "Have a good day." He hung up before she could lavish him with more praise. At the moment, he didn't feel at all worthy. Not 'til he got to the bottom of the incident at Prism and ensured that he and others of his kind were safe from any dangerous threat.

He immediately called in to Trevor Welch at the Computer Services Unit on the fourth floor at headquarters. "We have yet to pinpoint the suspect with any visual clarity. So far he was blended into the crowds in the footage," Welch reported. "But we're still trying and will let you know."

When he hung up, for the first time, Lucas wished he could sleep to keep his mind off things. He supposed he could set a timer and shut down while he recharged, but his police training had taught him to be ready at a moment's notice, so that idea seemed a breach of duty. Instead, he picked up his novel and tried to lose himself in the Atlanta underworld again to pass the time.

AFTER A VERY LONG and stressful shift, Simon returned home to the house he'd inherited from his grandmother in Fairway, Kansas. Although as far as the department was concerned, an apartment down south near Grandview was his official residence, the house in Fairway was where he slept. He arrived just before six a.m. and fell quickly into a deep sleep until just after two, when he had to get up and drive across town to Independence, Missouri to pick up his daughter, Emma, at Van Horn High School for their weekend together.

As he pulled up the arced drive and saw the line of parents' cars, he broke his promise to Emma never to play the 'police' card unless he was actually on duty and flipped the police sign onto his dash, pulling around the other cars and up to a red zone where he stopped and looked for his daughter.

Emma exited the school five minutes later chatting with her best friend Julie Ramon, the daughter of a man who'd been used by bombers several months before in a partially foiled bombing aimed at killing thousands of tourists. Instead, the police and FBI had deduced the plan in time and cleared the area. As part of the effort to stall law enforcement, Emma and Julie had been kidnapped and left to die. Simon, Lucas, and two other detectives had barely gotten to them in time to get them out of harm's way as the bombs went off—literally inches behind them where they'd just been standing.

Emma seemed to have recovered from the ordeal much better than Simon had. He'd sent her to therapy for three months, until she'd decided she didn't need it anymore and stopped going. Instead, she and Julie had gotten even closer than they'd been before, and begun relying on each other for counseling, helping each other through. No matter what Simon thought of that, they seemed to be doing fine and in good spirits, so he and Julie's father, Karl, had decided to drop the subject and just keep an eye on them.

That was two months past now, and the girls looked like normal, bubbly teenage girls—up one day, down another, but boy crazy, fashion crazy, and just as confused as any typical teen, so he'd decided his daughter was stronger than he'd given her credit for and traded his parental worry for parental pride. The girls were now fifteen years old and in their first year of high school, so there seemed to be plenty else for a father to worry about beyond past events that the daughters were handling just fine on their own.

Though Simon often took Julie home when he picked Emma up for a weekend, today was different. She was walking with her brother because he'd been having some trouble with bullies on his walks alone. Simon had offered to either give him a ride too—something he'd always refused in the past— or help with the bully situation, but both had declined. Once again, a situation the kids wanted to handle on their own. So be it. At least this way, he and Emma could get back across town before rush hour got too heavy and have a relaxing evening before Simon went back to work. He'd never complain about that. He always treasured any time he got with her.

On the way home, he thought about her mother, his ex. Lara had been out of the hospital since shortly after Simon and Lucas rescued Emma and Julie six months before, but he knew from experience that recovery from a bipolar episode was a long haul and required her constant discipline to medicine as well as regular checkups—both things she'd neglected that led to her episode in the first place. "How's your mother?" he asked.

"Taking her meds and seeing the doctor once a month," Emma said immediately, knowing right away what he was worried about.

"Good," Simon said. "I hope she stays that way."

"She was gaining weight," Emma said. "And she met a man and wanted to look good for him."

Simon sighed. It was a typical excuse bipolar people used.

"She was just taking it alternate days for a while 'til she lost the weight," Emma said.

"She can't do that," Simon said. "The chemistry gets imbalanced and she breaks down."

"Yeah, well, we know that," Emma said.

"Why can't she learn that?" Simon asked. It hadn't been the first time she'd had a breakdown since her diagnosis a decade ago.

"She hates when you say that," Emma said. "Says she's not a child."

"Do me a favor, babe," Simon snapped, "Don't get in the habit of passing messages between us, okay? If she wants to tell me something, she has my number."

Emma raised her palms in surrender. "Okay, okay."

"She always blames everyone but herself," Simon said.

"Dad, I'm on your side," Emma said, raising her voice. "I'm just filling you in because you asked."

He took a deep breath. "You're right. I'm sorry. I've just been through this several times."

"I know, but what can we do?" Emma said, her voice suddenly monotone as she looked down to stare at her hands.

"We can stay on her," Simon said. "You especially. If any-one can make her listen, it's you." He put a hand on her knee and squeezed. "I know it's hard."

She nodded. "It scared me seeing her like that."

"It scares me, too," Simon said. "You haven't even seen her at her worst."

Emma's eyes widened and she shuddered involuntarily at the thought. "I hope I never do."

"I hope that, too, honey," he said.

They drove the rest of the way in silence. As Simon pulled onto Canterbury and headed for his house, he saw a commo-tion in the street ahead—people milling about.

"What's going on?" Emma asked.

"I don't know, babe," Simon said as he rolled down his window. A woman ran in front of the Charger, forcing him to slam on the brakes. As he did, another man turned to look at him. "What's going on?" Simon asked.

"Some catering 'droid in there just went crazy," the man said. "Flipping out and breaking everything."

"That house?" Simon asked, pointing.

"Yeah."

Simon pulled his car into the driveway of his house and told Emma to go inside, then hurried across the street to his neighbor's house. As he walked up the stoop, he found the front door open and heard crashing and screaming. He knocked anyway and called, "Police! Tom? Christy? You okay? It's John Simon."

There was another loud crash.

"You're paying for all this!" Simon heard his neighbor Tom, a broker, shouting.

"Is not my fault! He never done this before!" another man

with an accent shouted back, distressed.

Simon went through the open door and came around a corner to spot the android—tall, thin, white-skinned with dark hair and piercing blue eyes—as he ran his hand along a table and knocked off a line of serving containers, plates, and sauce jars, sending them clattering and thumping to the floor, their contents spewing everywhere. The scent of barbecue sauce and beef brisket mixed with tangy vinegar and ketchup reached his nose.

"Damn it, Jack, stop doing that!" a short Asian man in a white chef's hat and dirty apron shouted with the same distressed voice Simon had heard moments before.

Simon's neighbor Tom was standing across the room, fuming, a mess all around him. "If this is what your employees do when someone asks for more salt, then you have a lot to learn about customer service!"

"What's going on, Tom?" Simon asked.

"We were having a damn open house," Tom said. He was mid-forties, balding, with a beer belly but muscular arms and a yard tan. He was dressed in a polo shirt and Dockers with tennis shoes and socks. "Look at this mess!"

"The android just went crazy!" Christy said as she stepped into the room from the kitchen behind him. Her blonde hair was frizzy, her makeup smeared from either crying or the food that had clearly been thrown at her and stained her light blue dress shirt and brown pants. She was early forties and beautiful in the way a woman her age who's taken care of herself tended to be.

"Is everyone okay otherwise?" Simon asked.

"Fuck no! Look at my house!" Christy yelled.

"We'll deal with that once we get this under control," Simon said, keeping his voice calm. "Buddy," —he looked at the Asian—"Jack is his name?"

"Yes," the caterer said. "Jack Frost."

"Seriously?" Simon said. Androids often chose their own names, usually from famous humans, but this one was particularly silly. He slowly moved toward the android who was staring at the results of his most recent antics and chuckling. "Jack, why don't we step outside for a moment so we can talk?"

The android's head turned to lock eyes with him. "I don't know you."

Simon reached into his pocket slowly and badged him. "I'm a policeman."

"Good for you," Jack replied. "Am I under arrest?"

"Maybe not," Simon said. "How about we go outside and talk about it?"

"How about we wait until I'm done here," Jack said, whirling and looking around for his next target.

"Haven't you done enough?!" Christy yelled.

Simon raised a palm. "That's not helping, Christy. Please."

"Shoot that fucking thing and get it out of my damn house!" Tom yelled.

Jack whirled and grabbed a bowl of potato salad, throwing it at Tom dead center, where it landed square in his face. "Bullets can't kill me, idiot."

Simon stepped forward and grabbed the android by the arm, pulling him toward the door. "Come on, Jack."

"No!" Jack screamed and pulled his arm free. He rushed past Simon and into the living room and jumped up onto a baby grand piano, his foot knocking off the candles and Thanksgiving centerpiece that had rested there and sending them onto the carpeted floor. "Don't touch me, cop!"

"Look, this is a big problem," Simon said. "Your employer is in real trouble here. Do you really want to hurt him?"

"He treats me like a slave," Jack replied. "Why should I care?"

"You're a machine!" Tom yelled from behind Simon, where he'd followed him into the room.

Simon moved slowly forward toward the baby grand. "Let's all just calm down, okay? This isn't helping."

Jack raised a palm out and thrust it at Simon. "Don't shoot me!"

"No one's going to shoot you," Simon said. "My gun's not even out."

"Shoot him!" Tom urged.

"God damn it, Tom, shut up already," Simon whispered with intensity loud enough for Tom to hear but hopefully not to alarm the android. Then he raised his voice to normal pitch, "Jack, please, I help people. I don't hurt them. Let me get you out of here safely."

"No gratitude! No appreciation!" Jack shouted.

"You ruining my business!" the Asian caterer yelled from the corner.

"Well, they don't know androids like I do," Simon said. "My partner's an android. That's why you should talk to me."

"An android working with a human as equals?! Ha!" Jack scoffed.

"It's true," Simon said.

"If you won't shoot him, I will," Tom said, turning back toward a hallway Simon knew led to his bedroom. "I'll get my gun then."

"Don't do that, Tom!" Simon yelled after him in warning.

This was deteriorating fast.

"Jack, we're out of time. Come down now and step outside with me before it's too late," Simon urged.

"I'm not scared of him," Jack taunted.

"You should be," Simon said. "He's scaring me right now."

Jack chortled and then leaped, landing across the room on a couch and hopping down on the floor where he grabbed a poker from beside the fireplace. "Let him come! *En guard!*" He swung the poker like a sword.

Jesus Christ, Simon thought. *Where's Lucas when I need him?* He heard sirens as a black and white arrived outside. "Other cops are here, we need to end this peacefully now or it won't end well."

"I'm not going without a fight," Jack said, probably quoting movies, like Lucas, but Simon was not amused.

"You're leaving me no choice here," Simon said. He counted silently to three and then rushed the android, but just as he did, the android's eyes suddenly went wide and he sputtered and then collapsed. "What the fuck?" Simon said to himself as he skidded to a stop.

Emma stepped through the door holding a device like a remote control Simon hadn't seen in over a year. "I found it in the gun safe," she explained.

"It was there for a reason," Simon said, taking it from her as Tom rushed into the room holding a Sig Sauer. "Put that down, Tom!" Simon yelled.

"What the hell happened to him?" Tom demanded.

"Oh my God! What you do to my Jack!" the caterer screamed from the corner.

Two uniforms entered the front door, hands ready on weapons and looking around. At the sight of Tom with a gun, they stiffened, going for their weapons.

Simon badged them. "Everything's okay, officers. Simon, Generalist squad."

"What the hell happened here?" one of them asked.

"Take a report for insurance, okay?" Simon said. "Tom, put the gun away and talk to them."

Tom sighed and turned back into the hallway, presumably returning his gun to the bedroom.

"He's the homeowner," Simon said. "I live across the street." He pulled his cell out and dialed Delmater, debating whether to call Lucas too. His partner's reaction to the incident at Prism had him concerned.

"Okay, who wants to tell us what happened?" the uniform asked, looking around as Christy and other guests wandered back in to stare at the crumpled android lying half on and half off the couch.

CHAPTER 3

SINCE THERE WAS no one to charge, Simon left the uniforms to finish reports for the insurance company's use and took Jack's crumpled form to Connelly Labs, picking up Lucas on the way. The Doctor and her assistant, Steven, had agreed to meet them. The hope was they could get some idea of what was causing the androids' aberrant behavior.

After they'd examined Jack Frost for a few moments, Steven said, "The first thing I can tell you is that you won't be able to use that device to disable any others."

"It worked great for this one," Simon said, then added, despite feeling a little guilty, "and Lucas as I recall." Paul Paulsen had disabled Lucas at the Plaza fountain after a car chase with the very same device, and Simon had feared he'd lost him for good.

"Right," Connelly said. "But we recalled all our androids for security upgrades designed to prevent such attacks in the future after that incident."

"This one apparently never got that upgrade," Steven said.

"Or several others," Connelly added. "My guess is the owner was either too lazy, too busy, or just didn't care because the android was providing what he needed, and he didn't want to take the time."

"So it was lucky, then," Lucas said.

"Kinda, yeah," Steven agreed.

"Not for Jack," Simon said.

"Well, if the owner wants him back, we won't return him without all the upgrades," Connelly said. "That's just the rule when we do free repairs like this."

"You won't charge him?" Lucas asked.

"We didn't charge for you," Connelly said. "It's kind of our responsibility in a way, since we left a vulnerability this big. But also, it wasn't his fault this happened, so I'd feel bad charging him. Anyway, we get the benefit of diagnosing the problem, which could save our business and our reputation. Can't put a price on that."

"How long do you think you'll need to figure it out?" Simon asked.

Steven chuckled. "A day? A week? A year? Who knows?"

Connelly smiled. "Yeah, we can't predict. We won't know 'til we do it. But we're already digging in, and I can tell you some of his chips seem to have been modified somehow, which shouldn't be possible, so we've got a lot to look at here."

"Modified chips? On the circuits?" Lucas asked, looking worried.

"Yes," Connelly said. "Even some that are permanently part of circuit boards. It's freaky."

"Well, if this scrambler won't work, I'll just leave it here," Simon said, setting the deactivating device down on the counter top nearby. "Please destroy it."

"Absolutely," Steven said.

"And keep us informed, whenever you get anything we can work with, finished or not," Simon said as he put a hand on Lucas' shoulder and pushed him gently toward the door.

"I think I'll stay," Lucas protested.

"No," Simon said. "Duty calls."

"John's right, Lucas," Connelly said. "You have a job to do. And we don't need an audience. It would just distract us."

Lucas' shoulders sank as he nodded.

"Don't worry," Connelly said. "We'll figure it out and we'll keep you safe, okay?"

"Thank you, Maker," Lucas said as Simon held open the door. He paused a moment, then reluctantly turned and headed outside as Simon followed.

"You going to be okay on this?" Simon asked as they walked toward the car.

"No," Lucas said. "But I can do my job."

"You sure? You seem a bit distracted."

"I am motivated. As you would say, 'let's get these fuckers,'" Lucas said with an angry tone Simon had never heard come from his partner before.

"All right, pal, let's do it," Simon said, hiding a smile. Sometimes the little guy made him as proud as a parent, even if they were partners. But he'd never say it aloud so as not to make Lucas feel put down or belittled.

He climbed in behind the wheel of the Charger as Lucas took the passenger side.

"Where to?" Lucas asked.

"Well, we'd better check in at the squad first," Simon said, checking the clock on the dash. It read: '6 p.m.' "Technically, we're two hours early. You want to watch me eat while we kill time? Maybe hang out with Emma for a bit?"

Lucas shrugged. "I am anxious to get on with the investigation."

"I know, pal," Simon agreed. "But that'll be a lot easier when we have something to go on. Besides, Emma's been asking for ya."

"Okay," Lucas agreed. "I can show her my new dance moves."

Simon grunted as he started the car and shifted it into drive. "God save me."

And they rode in rare silence all the way back to Canterbury Drive.

THEY HEARD THE blaring music and felt the pounding rhythm the moment they stepped out of the Charger in Simon's garage. Simon was assaulted by the smell of hours' old pizza as he opened the door to the house. His daughter was a typical teenager with a love for loud music, but Simon was totally unprepared for the sight awaiting him as he stepped into the house. Emma's ass, covered only by the thinnest of floppy shorts, was in the air as she did a sort of handstand against the wall and shook her butt violently to the music.

"Jesus Christ!" Simon said and shouted, "Alexa, cancel!"

The music from the 3rdGen Echo Dots Simon had installed all over the house ceased and Emma protested "Hey!" as she dropped into all fours on the floor staring up at him.

"What the fuck are you doing?!" Simon demanded.

"Relax, Dad. It's just twerking," she said, rolling her eyes.

"Twer-what? Your ass was in the air," Simon said. "Don't you ever do that again!"

"Gees, Dad, you really need to get laid, so uptight," Emma said, chuckling as she stood and brushed dust off her knees and hands.

"Laid?! My teenage daughter does not say that to me!" Simon said, losing it but unable to stop himself.

"Yeah, Dad, it's been over a year since Stacy and God knows how long before that," Emma continued, undeterred. "You really need to get the tension out."

"I am not talking about my sex life with my fifteen-year-old daughter!" Simon insisted.

"Fine but talk to someone, for God's sake," she said and hurried over to hug Lucas. The two immediately broke into chatter about the latest movies and music they'd discovered and wandered off happily, chatting like school mates, leaving him to stew alone.

Simon calmed down over a beer and day old pizza from the fridge. His first inclination was to just block the conversation entirely from his mind as if it never happened, but then he started worrying how Emma had come to be so comfortable talking about sex. And then there was her shaking her rear around like that. And for the next hour, it was all he could think about.

Hanging with Emma was the happiest Simon had seen Lucas since the incident at Prism. He almost hated to interrupt, but when seven-thirty rolled around, he knocked on the door. "Time to go."

Lucas hugged Emma and she told them to be safe as they headed out for headquarters. Simon figured any conversation with his daughter about her sex life was something best put off until he was prepared to handle it, so for once he hoped Lucas would start in on some latest pop culture discovery and take his mind off it. But at first, Lucas just sat in silence staring out the window. So as Simon took his usual route up Mission

Road to I-35 and downtown, he turned on his favorite oldies station and hummed along to "Stand" by Syzygy, a trio made up of the sons of Styx's Dennis DeYoung, Journey's Steve Smith, and daughter of Foreigner's Lou Gramm.

"When will they reassign the case?" Lucas asked, turning down the volume on the radio as they pulled onto I-35. Traffic was fairly light this time of evening on a Friday.

"Monday, like always," Simon said. They'd been doing it long enough Lucas knew that. There was something else to the question.

"Who'll get it?" Lucas asked next.

"Central Property squad probably," Simon said.

"Because it is vandalism, but what about the assaults," Lucas asked.

"Maybe assault, but it's murky," Simon said. "First android crime we've dealt with. They'll probably have meetings with the higher ups and D.A.'s office before deciding who gets it."

"I want it," Lucas said.

Simon sighed. There it was. Not that it was a surprise. "We're generalists, Lucas. We start the investigations nights and weekends then hand it off to the appropriate squad. That's the gig." If Central, their old team, got it, it wouldn't be hard to assist, but if it went to someone else...

"This one's special," Lucas said.

Lucas was so adamant, Simon hated to disappoint him by giving the real answer: "not a chance in hell," so instead he grunted, "We can ask about it. Make an appeal. Special circumstances."

"Expertise," Lucas said. "No one at KCPD knows androids better than I do."

"Aren't you afraid to get too close?"

Lucas shot him a look, brow furrowed. "Afraid of what?"

"Catching whatever it is," Simon said.

"Androids don't carry airborne illness," Lucas said.

"Right, but we don't know for sure what we're dealing with," Simon said.

"John, this is a matter of survival for all my kind," Lucas said. "I need to work this, to be sure it's handled correctly."

Simon was taken aback. Lucas had never called him "John" before. It was always "partner," "Simon," or "friend." "I hear you, pal. I'll go to bat with Delmater. That's the best I can do."

Lucas nodded. "Good."

Eight minutes later, they got off I-35 at Truman Road and headed east, turning up Oak Street, then taking a right on 12th, before arriving at headquarters and parking in the lot across the street to the east.

As they stepped out of the Charger and headed to cross the street, Simon saw movement to his right and turned, recognizing the woman he'd been attracted to and later bumped into at the club. She was with a camera crew and rushing toward them. The camera bore the Fox 4 logo on it.

"Detectives, can I have a word with you?" she called.

KCPD had clear policies about talking to the media. "Check with the media office in the annex," Simon deflected as he and Lucas kept walking.

"I'm Holly Sanders with Fox Four," she said. "It's about the android attack at Prism."

Simon kept walking but noticed Lucas had stopped and turned.

"There was no android attack," Lucas snapped as Sanders shoved the mic in his face.

Oh shit. Simon turned and hurried back to run interference.

"According to reports, an android was the one who tore up and vandalized the place last ni—" Sanders said.

"Those are rumors," Lucas cut her off.

Simon grabbed him by the arm and pulled him along toward headquarters. "No further comment," he called.

Lucas tried to pull free and turn back again, but Simon kept a firm grip and practically dragged him toward the double door entrance, whispering, "Be quiet. We don't talk to the media unless we're told to by the brass. Policy."

When they'd gotten inside and the doors shut behind them, Lucas whirled to face him. "She's got it wrong!"

"Not really," Simon said. "She's sensationalizing a bit, but they all do that."

"She needs to wait for the facts," Lucas said.

"Yeah, well, they never do," Simon said as he pulled Lucas toward the elevator and pushed the up button. "Drama is good TV."

Lucas frowned. "If the wrong word gets out—"

"Nothing you can do about it," Simon said as the elevator dinged and the doors parted. "We can't control rumors and innuendo. All we can do is our jobs." He waited until Lucas stepped into the elevator then followed and pushed the button for the third floor. Metal squeaked on metal as the elevator rose, humming, and there was the squealing sound of brakes on cables and a constant thumping vibration he felt beneath his feet.

"You talk to the media without permission, you'll be in real trouble," Simon said. "Hopefully, I can call and convince her not to use that."

"I am angry," Lucas said.

"I can tell," Simon said. "I miss the jokes and funny quotes, buddy."

Lucas hit the stop button on the elevator, ignoring the alarm, and turned to face Simon. "To you this is just another crime spree. To me, this could be the end of everything I and my kind have worked hard for—being accepted by humans as friends welcome among them."

"It's one incident," Simon said. "Don't overreact."

"Two," Lucas said. "Jack."

"Yes, well, that one won't even be investigated officially."

"It should be," Lucas said. "What if they are related?"

"It seems likely," Simon agreed, "but we don't know that for sure."

"The Maker will tell us," Lucas said.

"She'll tell us what's wrong with Jack, not confirm it was the same with the android at Prism," Simon said, wincing at the annoying elevator alarm and reaching for the stop button. "We have to find him first. Can we go now?"

Lucas nodded and Simon toggled the stop button on again, allowing the elevator to continue its journey as the alarm ceased.

"You can't understand," Lucas said. "You're not one of us."

"No, I'm just the guy who fought his ass off to convince them to make you my partner and promote you past several other worthy candidates in the process!" Simon countered angrily, then took a deep breath as Lucas stood in silence and looked at the floor.

"Lucas, I get that this is of special concern to you, but you're losing it," Simon said. "We have a job to do. There are laws, regs, policies. Don't lose sight of that. They'll never let you near it if you do."

Lucas sighed. "You are right. I am sorry."

The elevator dinged again as the door opened on the third floor and they headed for the Generalist squad room.

"Look, let's talk to Delmater and see what he thinks, okay?" Simon suggested. "Trust me. I've got your back on this. I'll do everything I can."

They entered the squad room to find it almost clear. Delmater's voice drifted from his office and Simon spotted Jiminez, Rankin, and Williams at the coffee station in the conference room next door as the smell of stale, day-old coffee filled the air. Simon led the way to Delmater's office and closed the door behind them.

"Good evening, gentlemen," Delmater said as he looked up from his desk, where he was deep in paperwork. "What's up?"

"Who's getting the Prism case?" Simon asked.

Delmater grunted. "Well, no major injuries, so most likely vandalism. I sent it to Central Property. Beyond that, you'd have to call your old boss."

"Okay," Simon said, encouraged. The higher-ups may have split up her unit for disciplinary reasons but JoAnn Becker still held them all in high regard. She was the best boss Simon had ever had.

As Simon turned to go, Lucas cleared his throat. "I have to work it, sir. I know androids better than anyone else in the department—"

Simon turned back and looked at Lucas. He'd told him to let him do the talking. Subtly was the key here, which Lucas had none of.

"What he's trying to say," Simon interrupted, "is no one knows that much about androids at KCPD yet, which would make us the resident experts for obvious reasons."

Delmater grunted. "I can't argue with that but jurisdictions are not our determination, fellas. We hand them off. You can certainly ask Becker, and maybe we can request temporary reassignment, but given you just came from that squad, I wouldn't hold my breath."

"I will ask her," Lucas said before Simon could interject.

"Do you mind if we ask?" Simon said, wary of offending an old friend who was now their superior.

"I suggest you do," Delmater said. "Lucas has a good point. I just can't snap my fingers and make it happen, though, so good luck."

"Okay, thanks, Sarge," Simon said and turned to open the door.

"Thank you," Lucas agreed as Simon ushered him out before he could tactlessly say anything else.

Simon led the way back to their cubicles then pointed Lucas to his chair. "Sit. I'll call Becker."

"Can't I—"

"You just sit. You need to use some *joie de vivre* in these types of situations, something you seem to lack entirely," Simon said as he sat in his own chair and picked up the phone.

"What's jwa duh veeve?" Lucas asked.

"See? You don't even know what it is. Now sit and let me handle this," Simon said as he dialed Becker's cell. It was well past usual hours for the Property Squad, so he assumed he'd either catch her on her way home or already there.

She answered on the third ring. "Yeah?"

"JoAnn, it's your favorite lost son," Simon said and she

laughed.

"God help me, I thought my troubled days were over," she said. "How's the Generalist squad?"

"Well, the hours sucketh, but otherwise not bad," Simon said. "Except we have to hand everything off to everyone else just when it gets good."

"Yeah, well, it's a perfect training place for Lucas," Becker said.

"Got that right," Simon agreed.

"We miss you guys," Becker added.

"We miss you, too," Simon said. "How's everyone?"

"Oh, Dolby and Maberry are partnering up now," Becker said. "And we're breaking in some new blood and transfers, but same old, same old. What sends you knocking?"

"Okay, has the Prism case come across your desk yet?" Simon asked.

"Yeah, I just handed it to Maberry and Dolby," she said.

"We were wondering if they'd like a consultant with a better knowledge of androids," Simon said.

"You guys want in on it?"

"It's caught my partner's interest," Simon said.

"Ahhh, understood," Becker said. "What's Delmater think? I assume you've talked to him?"

"Yeah, but Brian's an old Academy friend, he said to ask you and see what happens," Simon said.

"Let me run it up the ladder tomorrow to DC Melson and see, but I think it's a pretty good idea, actually," she said.

"Okay, great," Simon said, holding up his fingers in an 'OK' sign to Lucas. "Thanks, JoAnn."

"You know, come to think of it," she said, "we got this lead just as I was leaving. Call from a cabbie who works nights about something he saw. Hang on..." Simon heard her phone beeping as she pushed buttons. "...a Jay Sener. You guys wanna go talk to him? Was going to ask our guys to set up something during the day, but this might be faster."

"Sure," Simon said. "We'll take it. Got a number?"

She gave it to him.

"Okay, got it," Simon said.

"Did you guys contact Doctor Connelly yet—see what she might be able to do to help?" Becker asked.

"Actually, yeah," Simon said and told her about the incident at his neighbor's house that afternoon.

"Hmmm," she said. "I hope these are isolated incidents. The last thing we need is some kind of outbreak."

"Tell me about it," Simon agreed.

"Okay, well let us know the minute she has something," Becker said. "Meanwhile, I'll talk to DC Melson, but I'm sure Maberry and Dolby would be happy to have you."

"Great," Simon said. "Talk to you soon." As he hung up, Lucas was staring at him. "She's going to Melson. She'll let us know."

Lucas lowered his head, slouching a bit. "Oh."

"Meanwhile, she asked us to interview a witness who works nights," Simon said and stood. "So if you wanna stop moping—"

Lucas sprung from the chair like he was on fire. "Let's go."

Simon chuckled all the way to the elevator.

JAY SENER MET them at the City Diner. Instead of food, Simon only ordered coffee and a slice of fresh apple pie. Sener ordered coffee himself with heavy cream and sugar. Lucas ordered nothing.

Sener was late forties, maybe fifty, with graying brownish hair and rosy cheeks. He bore a working man's tan; his arms, neck, and face darker than the rest due to sun exposure through the windshields, and his hair was cut short but a bit disheveled, his jeans and flannel shirt well-worn but presentable, and his tennis shoes old but clean. A fleece-lined winter coat was stuffed behind him on the booth bench, a pair of black leather gloves rested on the table beside the silverware.

"Is there some reason you wanted to meet us here?" Simon asked, raising his voice slightly over the sound of a waitress calling orders to cooks in diner-speak as plates and cutlery jangled and clanged, meat and eggs sizzling on a grill and scattered conversations mixed into a droning cacophony that settled like a layer over everything in the room. "We could have come to your garage."

"I don't need my dispatcher and coworkers asking why I'm being pestered by police," Sener said. "They're already jealous, since I bring in the most fares for the past six months now. Besides, I like this place. Much more pleasant than the garage." He smiled a wide smile, his teeth big, his gums pink, but it was a friendly and amused look accompanied by a warm, guttural laugh.

Forgoing further small talk, Lucas burst out with, "Tell us about your fare last night."

"Two men, hip clothes, all style, all done up for a night out—like they do," he said. He meant gay men, Simon presumed.

"Like they do?" Lucas asked, puzzled by the expression.

"So they put on their best for a night on the town?" Simon asked as he made notes on his iPad.

"Yes, you know the type," Sener said.

"Yeah," Simon said. "Where'd you pick them up?"

"Up off Wyandotte and Third, near River Market, from an apartment house," Sener said.

"Do you remember the address?" Lucas asked.

"I can look it up in the car," Sener said.

"Okay," Simon said. "They went straight to Prism?"

"Yes, paid in cash," Sener said.

"What time did you pick them up?" Lucas asked.

"A little before eleven-fortyish," Sener said. "Can check that, too."

"Okay, after we get the basics," Simon said. It was too cold out to finish the interview out there.

"You dropped them when?" Lucas asked.

"Five, six minutes later," Sener said. "Took Wyandotte south to Sixteenth, then over to Grand. Not that far."

"Okay, so what happened as you dropped them off?" Simon asked.

"That was when I seen him," Sener said.

"The android?" Lucas asked.

"Yes, the crazy fuckin' one," Sener said.

"Did you know he was an android?" Lucas asked.

"No, they just say he was," Sener said.

"What did he look like?" Simon asked.

"About my height, thin like him." Sener indicated Lucas. "White, average muscles, blondish brown hair. Intense blue eyes." He squinted at Lucas. "A lot like his." His face took on a funny look as he stared at Lucas, probably trying to decide if

Lucas was an android or not, Simon figured.

"How exactly did you see him?" Lucas asked.

"With my eyes," Sener said, like it was obvious, looking with amusement at Simon.

"He means tell us about your encounter in detail," Simon said.

"I pulled to the curb to let out my fare and he ran out of the club and jumped, landing on my hood—left a good sized dent too—and then kept going, across the street," Sener said. "And this is the weird part. He went up the building."

"Went up the building how?" Simon asked.

"Like Spider-Man or something," Sener said. "Just scaled the side using the drain pipe from the roof, hand over hand"—he imitated the motions—"like that. Fast as shit. Freakiest fuckin' thing I ever saw."

Simon and Lucas exchanged a look, then Simon said, "Can we see your car?"

Sener nodded and slid toward the edge of the bench, motioning. "Sure. It's out front."

Lucas and Simon followed him as he grabbed his coat and led the way. The cab was an all-white sedan with a checkered pattern stripe along each side. Simon recognized Checker Cab, a familiar local company. As they drew up beside it, he could see the dent in the hood.

"Left a fuckin' footprint impression and everything," Sener said, pointing.

Simon and Lucas went up and bent over, examining it.

"Son of a bitch!" Simon said. "How fast was he going?"

Sener grunted and nodded. "Pretty damn fast. Scared the shit outta me. Almost had to change my shorts."

Simon shook his head as he straightened again, but Lucas leaned closer, really examining the dent. "You see something?"

Lucas stayed that way a bit before straightening. "We can trace him."

"You can trace him? How?" Simon asked.

"The number from his footprint is partially preserved in the hood," Lucas said.

"What?!" Sener said as he and Simon leaned down to peer at the dent.

"It's minute, but there," Lucas said.

Sener strained and shook his head, shooting Simon a screwy look.

"He has superhero vision," Simon said, excusing it as they both straightened again.

"Can you show us the building where he disappeared?" Lucas asked.

"I gotta get back on the clock," Sener said. "Dispatch will be calling."

"Charge me as a fare," Lucas said as he opened the door and climbed into the cab. Sener shrugged and went around to the driver's side.

"Uh, I guess I'll follow," Simon said and hurried for the Interceptor as the cab pulled away.

Seven minutes later, they were standing in front of an art supply store across the street from Prism staring up a drain pipe leading to the roof.

"He went up there," Sener said.

"We need to go up there, too," Lucas said.

Simon glanced at the closed sign in the window of the store. "Might have to come back when they're open."

Lucas looked at it a moment, then strode over and began

climbing straight up the drain pipe.

"Jesus Christ! That's what the freak did!" Sener said, stepping back.

"You know I can't do that, right?" Simon called to Lucas as his partner reached the top and looked down.

"I will look around and take pictures of anything I find," Lucas called.

"How'd he do that?" Sener said, looking at Simon with amazement.

"Uh, he's got gifts," Simon said.

Then Sener reacted with realization. "Holy shit! He's one of those things, too, isn't he?!" He raised his hands in surrender and hurried back to his cab. "Fuck that, I'm outta here."

"Thanks for the statement, Mister Sener," Simon said.

"You better go, before that thing goes crazy, too!" Sener warned as he slammed the cab door behind him.

"What about your fare?" Lucas called down after him.

Seconds later, the cab peeled away from the curb, and Simon chuckled to himself. Then he heard a familiar buzzing in his ear and turned. A small, black media drone was floating toward him, some producer monitoring it at the nearest TV station or bureau, sniffing for a story. These days drones often arrived before the cops and live crews were only dispatched to the most dramatic stories.

Ignoring the drone, but wanting to get out of there before they became a story, Simon looked back up toward the roof top. "You find anything up there?" he called.

"Call Delmater and a crime scene team," Lucas called back.

"What you got?" Simon called.

"A footprint," Lucas called as Simon got on the cell to Delmater, wondering how to chase off the drone and thinking this case was starting to get a lot more interesting.

CHAPTER 4

"SO ANDROIDS CAN climb up the sides of buildings like monkeys?" Dolby said as she stood with Becker, Maberry, Simon, Lucas, and Delmater outside Nottage Art and Design while the crime scene crew worked on the roof. The owner was out of town, so they'd called a ladder truck from the nearest KCFD station and used its ladder to get roof access. In the background, horns honked as tires ground across asphalt and radios blared from windows, a jackhammer pounding somewhere in the distance.

"If he can do that, why don't you just have him go up?" the fire captain teased, motioning to Lucas.

"We do our best to keep his feet planted on the ground as much as possible," Simon snapped as the firefighters laughed.

"Do we need to track down the cabbie?" Maberry asked.

Simon shook his head. "We can get a better impression off the footprint on the roof 'cause it was left in tar, according to Lucas. And we already took his statement."

"So these numbers can identify the android?" Becker asked.

"Supposedly," Simon said.

"The android, his make, model, production number, and who he belongs to," Lucas said. "All information Connelly Labs keeps track of as much as possible for warranties, upgrades, and such."

"I guess we got a lucky break then," Becker said. "How soon does the Doctor think she'll have more information?"

"We need to call her," Simon said.

"On the android from the second incident, uncertain," Lucas said. "But these markings should make identification almost instantaneous once they put them in the database."

"Maybe we should give people serial numbers," Simon joked. "Make our lives a whole lot easier."

"You're not kidding," Maberry said.

"I can just see the political hoopla that idea will cause," Becker said. "Remember when everyone was worried about national IDs and then having bar codes or microchips imbedded under our skin?"

"I'm sure some asshole would find a way to hide or change them soon enough," Dolby said.

"They always do," Maberry agreed.

"Damn," Simon said. "You guys turned into real pessimists since we left, huh? Real bundle of laughs."

The property detectives chuckled.

"Without your witty sarcasm to liven things up, we're dead inside," Dolby cracked, mocking him.

"Hell, I knew I was carrying all of ya," Simon joked, smiling.

"Yeah, the one with the computer-charged partner, he's the one carrying us," Maberry replied, grunting.

"You were the one who begged to come back," Becker said razzing Simon, joining in.

"Begged?" Simon said. "It was Lucas' idea. I can't stand you losers."

At that moment, Paul Engborg, one of several crime lab

field team leaders and the one assigned to the Prism case, was coming down the ladder. Tall, balding, mid-forties, with a developing paunch and warm smile, Engborg was one of the best, and Simon was always glad to know he was handling his cases.

"You good?" Becker asked as Engborg planted both feet on terra firma again and strode over to join them.

"Yep," Engborg said. "It was almost perfect, too. Good thing that steam pipe heated up the tar or we'd have gotten nothing. Guess they leave the heat on sometimes at night."

"Make sure Lucas gets those numbers ASAP," Becker said.

"I have photos," Lucas said. "I already transmitted them to Doctor Connelly."

"Great," Simon said.

"Very efficient," Engborg said. "He's kinda handy, eh?"

"Sometimes he earns his keep," Simon said and winked at Lucas, who maintained the same somber look he'd had since the incident at Prism.

"Okay, let's get back to Central and get to work," Becker said. She turned to Lucas and Simon. "We've got cubes set aside for your use. But before you come over, Melson wants to see you in his office."

"Jesus, the fourth floor?" Simon said. The fourth floor at headquarters housed all the administrative offices, including those of the Chief, the Deputy Chiefs, the Police Commissioners, and all their support staff plus offices of the General Counsel. It was not a place most every-day cops wanted to find themselves.

"Melson's cool," Becker said. "He's just got meetings all day and said it would be easier. Anyway, Lucas should see it at least once."

"Be glad it's on good terms," Maberry said.

"No shit," Dolby agreed.

"Yeah, yeah, we're so blessed," Simon said as he turned toward where they'd left the Interceptor across the street, frowning as a waft of rotten sewer air floated up from a grate as he walked over it. "Catch you losers in a bit."

He led the way to the car and Lucas followed then they headed back to Locust to see the Deputy Chief. They were right, Melson was in charge of detectives and he was cool. Simon had worked a few cases with him back in the day, and unlike some, Melson had earned his promotions through determination and hard work, as well as extraordinary competence. There was no one in Admin Simon respected more. It was just the thought of going to the fourth floor that gave him chills. Even when disciplining personnel, the higher ups usually came to you. He'd only been there twice in his career, both times to give reports to the Chief and DCs on particularly political cases, and both he'd kept as brief and succinct as possible—in and out with minimum delay.

LIKE ALL FLOORS at headquarters, the entryway to the fourth floor was decorated with artwork recreating KCPD badges on large canvases: a patrol badge, a detective badge, a Chief's badge, etc. a stark contrast to the bare gray walls. Everything was marked with gray placards bearing bright blue lettering identifying its purpose: "Storage," "Filing," "Break Room," "Conference Room," and so on. A wide variety of potpourris, air deodorizers and scented candles mixed with the smell of food and coffee assaulted Simon's nose as he walked.

They moved along a central corridor that led from the elevators past the General Counsel's offices and to the main executive offices where the reception desk sat. It and most of the other cubes and desks were unoccupied at this late hour but from across the room, an administrative assistant in her mid-thirties looked up from a desk and smiled, calling, "Just a moment."

She stood and strode over, asking their names. Moments later, they were ushered inside Deputy Chief Greg Melson's office and offered beverages while they waited, which they declined.

"He's in a meeting but he'll be back shortly," the admin said before leaving them.

The Deputy Chief's office had a nice view of the cityscape surrounding headquarters. A modern desk with a gray painted frame supported a thick glass top with a set of drawers suspended underneath on each side. A flat screen, keyboard and phone sat to the left side where the desk was next to a wall. A large leather executive's chair sat behind it with three leather director's-style chairs facing it on the opposite side. A bookshelf held binders, books, and photos of DC Melson with various dignitaries including his fellow DCs, Chief Weber, and the Mayor as well as past Chiefs. Above the bookshelf hung various diplomas and citations with a few trophies, plaques and awards occupying the top.

Simon took a seat in one of the director's chairs and pointed Lucas to the other. He was surprised how sterile the office smelled compared to the common space outside, his nose catching only the faint scents of old files and expensive cologne as he sat. DC Melson arrived two minutes later, his dark three piece suit neatly pressed like his shirt and power tie. He smiled at them and motioned for them to stay seated as he made his way behind his desk and plopped down into the executive chair.

"The Police Commission is in executive session tonight working with us on the budget, so I only have a few minutes, but I appreciate your stopping by, Detectives," Melson said, far more formally than he usually addressed men in the field.

"Our pleasure," Simon said, his lack of enthusiasm indicating more the opposite.

"Look, I've been behind you from the start," Melson said. "Backed you working together on the Ashman case and then on the Toby Derrick case as well. I pushed for Detective George to get into the Academy and to get a special waiver to skip patrol and move straight to detective."

"Thank you, sir," Lucas said humbly.

"I was glad to do it," Melson said. "But after what happened at Oceans of Fun and all, I need to make something clear. You guys have been on a disciplinary watch list—people we watch closely to make sure they are toeing the line as far as policy and such. So it wasn't easy to get you cleared for special duty on this case."

"I understand," Lucas said. Simon just listened, waiting for the hammer to drop.

"But we need you on this," Melson said. "It's clearly unique circumstances and you two are the ones we've got with anything close to expertise. So all I wanted to say—and I wanted you to hear it face to face—is don't fuck this up. By the book. No grandstanding, no antics."

"We're not sideshow performers," Simon joked.

"Well, in a way you have been," Melson said. "You're a good cop, John. One of the best. But you've also been given some high-profile cases and you've taken risks and pushed the lines in ways that made some uncomfortable. That can't happen this time."

"Cut to the chase, Greg," Simon said. "You putting us on a leash?"

"You know I don't work that way," Melson said. "And you couldn't do your job it I did, but everyone will be watching, so I need you to color within the lines, shall we say?"

"Sir?" Lucas asked, his brow furrowing.

"I'll explain later," Simon said, then to Melson, "Understood."

"You do that and I'm pretty sure you won't be under such close scrutiny much longer," Melson said. "You'll be able to earn a slot in a specialist squad again without issue."

"Great," Simon said as Lucas echoed, "Yes, sir."

"All right," Melson said, looking at his watch. "I have to get back. Get outta here and make me proud."

"So no shooting the robots then?" Simon teased.

"From what I hear that would only piss them off," Melson grunted, eyes sparkling with amusement. He and Simon had well-earned mutual respect. Simon knew it was awkward for anyone to be in a position like this with an old friend.

Melson stood and ushered them to the door. "You keep making trouble, I might just promote you to deal with them as a punishment, smart ass."

"That would end my career real quick," Simon replied, grinning.

"Wouldn't it?" Melson shook his hand and then Lucas' then added, "Be safe out there." Then he was gone.

Simon led the way to the elevator and they headed for Central Patrol, Lucas brooding silently beside him.

THE ADDRESS CONNELLY gave them for the owner of the android who'd vandalized Prism was an old Beaux-arts-style mansion south of the Kansas City Museum at 3210 Windsor Avenue, between Gladstone Road and North Indiana. This was an old neighborhood filled with classic mansions, many in the neoclassical French style like Corinthian Hall, which housed the museum. The owner of the house in question was listed as Douglas Price, the retired founding partner of Price Adams Finance, a financial services company with offices near the Plaza.

The house was three stories with arched windows and pedimented doors all evenly sized and spaced on each floor for perfect symmetry. There were four balustrades, two on either side of the large, double front doors, with ornamental pilasters evenly spaced along each of the side walls. The upper windows had cartouches over the top of them and there were acroterion on each of the corners, again aiding the perfect symmetry of the overall design. The clasps, handles, door knobs, and knockers were also richly detailed in classical style and shiny as if new despite their clearly advanced age.

Simon parked the Interceptor in the driveway to block any attempted escape—should that be necessary—and led the way down a winding sidewalk that crossed the expansive, well-landscaped lawn with decorative shrubbery and plants highlighting its edges. Together, they climbed the stone steps to the front door, where Simon rang the bell. He could hear its dulcet tones echoing deep inside somewhere as he caught the scent of sap from a row of pines lining the edge of the stoop.

The door opened within ninety seconds revealing a man in his seventies with smoothly trimmed and styled white hair and a chiseled face so perfectly proportioned that if he hadn't been moving, Simon wouldn't have been surprised to find it on a mannequin or statue of art. He was dressed in designer slacks and a pressed dress shirt, the collar open. He smelled of aftershave, his green eyes narrowing as he took them in and offered a polite smile. "May I help you?" he asked as he looked them over in the light of large sconces on either side of the doors.

Simon badged him, Lucas following.

"Detectives Simon and George from KCPD, sir," Simon said. "We're here to see Douglas Price."

The man took them in a moment longer, and then his brow creased as he said, "I'm Douglas Price." Behind him the entryway led to a wide, finely carpeted staircase that headed up to the next level. To the right was the entrance to a large room filled with books on floor-to-ceiling shelves. Simon took it for a library. To the left was what appeared to be a study and further down the hall a ways Simon saw the edge of a counter in what appeared to be a kitchen.

"Sorry to bother you, sir," Simon said. "We're here about an incident that took place last night around midnight at the Prism night club in the Crossroads Art District."

Price looked even more puzzled. "I don't know it. Why would you want to talk to me?"

"Sir, someone vandalized the place in front of a large

crowd last night, and we have reason to believe it might have been an android who's listed at this address," Simon said.

"What?!" Price turned and raised his voice, calling, "Newton! Come here at once!"

"You do own an android from Connelly Labs, Mister Price?" Lucas inquired.

"Yes, his name is Newton Isaac," Price said and grunted. "The silliness of the doctor letting them reverse famous names is beyond me. Anyway, I'm sure he doesn't know anything about it. Newton always keeps to himself at night, and appears in the morning when I call him, fully recharged and ready for his duties."

Behind him appeared a man who matched the description the cabbie Sener had given them—white, average muscles, blondish brown hair, intense blue eyes. He was medium height and weight and dressed in a black servant's uniform of the kind Simon hadn't seen in ages. "Yes, Mister Price?" he asked in a soft, submissive tenor as he approached them.

"Newton, these are police officers who've come to inquire about some sort of incident last night at a night club," Price said. "Prism—"

At the mention of the night club's name, Newton's eyes widened and he emitted a sort of gasp, then turned and raced away.

Lucas shouted, "Stop!" and took off after him before either Simon or Price could say a word, pushing roughly past the retired homeowner in the process.

"What is going on?!" Price demanded.

"Where does the back door come out?" Simon asked, eyes darting around the outside of the house.

Price frowned and pointed. "There are two. In the back

yard and to the side by the garage."

Simon nodded as he darted for the steps. "Stay here. We'll be back to explain in a moment."

He darted down the steps and headed around the house to the right along the drive as it led to the garage.

"Newton! Come back here at once!" he heard Price shouting.

Simon raced as fast as he could along the house and came to a fenced-in back yard with brick paving lining the inside of the fence between the house and the garage. There was a large swimming pool in back, though it had been drained for winter, and the garage was attached to a small pool house.

As he rounded the corner, he glimpsed Lucas' back running away from him across the pool and followed parallel on the near side. As he ran, he saw Newton, the other android, launching himself in the air and over a fence. Moments later, Lucas followed by the same route.

Simon jumped as he neared the fence, throwing himself forward and grasping for the top. He slammed into it with a hard thump and slid down, trying to catch his breath.

He glanced around, spotting a gate ten feet from him. He had been too focused on the place where the androids went over. "Fuck!"

As soon as he was able, he jumped up and ran for the gate, letting himself through.

LUCAS FOCUSED ON nothing but catching Newton Isaac.

No matter what it took. He thought he'd heard Simon behind him as he followed Newton over the fence, but humans didn't share android's agility and now his partner seemed to have fallen way behind again.

Lucas followed Newton as he ran across a perfectly land-scaped slope behind Price's house and then up the other side past a small outbuilding then into a cluster of trees. Bursting out the other side, they ran across a wide open grassy field to a denser cove and through onto the next street—Gladstone, his internal GPS told him. They came out on a curve and Newton weaved left, angling northwest along Cliff Drive Access Road.

Lucas ran after him, pushing himself to close the gap between them, which he'd cut almost in half at this point, but was still two yards or so. They continued at full speed down the center of the two winding lanes, dodging a few cars as they went.

On the far side, they plowed through another large cluster of trees that stretched along the road to either side. Branches slapped them in the face and chest and arms as they ran, but Lucas ignored them, focused on closing the distance to his prey.

The chirping of birds and insects grew louder despite the ongoing droning of the city—traffic, voices, blowers for heaters, and more. Emerging on the other side of the trees, they entered Kessler Park, a more open section, and continued running straight across a grassy lawn toward a larger cluster of trees on the other side.

The park itself had no playground equipment or restroom facilities or picnic shelters, just wide open space with scattered shrubs and flower patches. In a way, Lucas found that remarkable for a city this size where every piece of available land seemed destined to be swallowed up in the newest wave of real estate advance and innovation.

As he ran, he called out ahead of him, using internal sensors to magnify the volume of his voice, "You waste your energy, Newton Isaac. We can track you by GPS if we have to. You must stop and submit to the authorities as your correct programming compels!"

Even as he said it, he knew Simon, hearing it, might criticize him for sounding inhuman, but he wasn't talking to a human now. He was talking to one of his own. It had been worth a try, he supposed, though he hadn't expected success. He'd only wanted the ability to say to any who asked that he'd tried talking to the suspect before taking him down by force. The last thing he needed was more trouble due to his extraordinary abilities like he'd experience with the Shooting Team in the past.

As expected, Newton ignored him and raced silently on, Lucas continuing to give chase.

SIMON BURST THROUGH the gate and watched Lucas and Newton disappearing across the expansive clearing behind Price's house. He started across the well maintained lawn, then stopped and turned back to retrieve the Interceptor. At least he could catch up with them and help to his partner.

He backed the Interceptor down the drive, lights flashing, and turned left, heading West on Windsor toward Gladstone, keying the radio. Reassignment to the Generalist Squad had come a new radio number, and Simon had to think a moment every time he used it. "706 to Detective George, what's your location?"

Simon slowed to a stop at Gladstone, waiting for passing traffic, then turned right and headed up the road, but he was coming to a junction. Where'd they go? He needed an answer. He heard horns honking ahead and the sound of a radio blaring and his foot drifted toward the accelerator again as the radio crackled with static.

"706, we are in Kessler Park headed north on foot," Lucas said. His voice was clear because despite running as fast as he could, the android officer didn't have to struggle for air.

Simon keyed the radio again. "Copy, I'm bringing the car. I'll go around Cliff Drive and try to cut him off on the Scenic Byway."

"Copy," Lucas replied and then the radio went dead again.

Simon flipped on the siren and accelerated, turning left onto Cliff Drive Access Road, clearing just as a truck approached from the other direction on Gladstone.

He took the curving road pushing forty-five, his tires riding hard on their edges as he rounded a curve then had to slow to take a U-shaped curve before accelerating again as the road zigzagged back the other way. He came to a Y in the road and turned right, following signs for Kessler Park as the road began descending and cliffs appeared above him on his left.

He keyed the radio. "Lucas, there are cliffs here. You sure you're still headed north?"

Lucas' reply came back quickly this time. "Yes."

"There's nowhere to go," Simon said. "Looks like all cliffs around it except to the south and east."

"Copy," Lucas said. "Suspect still going north."

Simon continued on and found a set of concrete steps going down the side of the cliffs. He slowed a moment, looking up and wondering if they'd be coming down them. "Lucas, are you anywhere near the steps?" he asked into the mic again.

"Negative," Lucas replied. "What steps?"

That answered that. Simon leaned over and looked up toward the top of the steps, seeing no movement. It was high enough he winced at the possibilities if someone slipped on the steps or fell off them somehow. Jesus. It was still clear a moment later, so he continued on around the byway.

LUCAS FOLLOWED NEWTON as they arced wide around another line of trees and then continued across a new grassy clearing. He glanced to his right and thought he saw a stone stairway. Was that what Simon had been asking about?

Newton didn't even look, he just kept running north, but Lucas could see they were coming up on an opening with a sheer drop.

"Newton, stop! There's nowhere to go!" he called, once again amplifying his voice internally as he continued pursuit.

Newton just kept running until he came to the edge of the cliff, then stopped and looked down, examining the cliff face carefully as Lucas approached.

When Lucas got within five feet, Newton suddenly spun to face him and raised an arm, palm out. "Stop!"

Lucas slowed to a stop and stood facing him. "You need to come with me," he said, this time with no amplification.

Newton shook his head. "I cannot. You need to leave me be."

"I cannot," Lucas echoed then flashed his badge. "Please, let me help you." Maybe there was an explanation, something he could do to mitigate the damage, make sense of it somehow so the other android's actions could be justified and explained.

Newton shook his head. "No!"

He turned and ran to the southwest a few feet, then spun and took off at top speed toward the cliff edge.

"Newton, no!" Lucas called, hesitating too long before starting on an intercept course.

SIMON ROUNDED ANOTHER bend on the byway and found a work crew trimming trees along the side of road closest to the cliffs. They had chainsaws, axes, and branch cutters, and another two were gathering the trimmed off pieces and feeding them into a giant wood chipper, its engine loud and rumbling in competition with the chainsaws.

Simon slowed as another car hurried past the opposite way and prepared to go around the workers in red ear protectors and green jumpsuits when he glanced up and saw someone launch themselves off the top of the cliff. The crew foreman stopped and yelled, pointing upward as Simon hit the brakes. *What the fuck?!*

As he climbed out of the car to look, the smell of smoke and sawdust mixed with cigarette smoke and chemicals assaulted him; the roar of the equipment drowning out almost everything else around them. He tipped his head back, looking up and realized the jumper was Newton Isaac. The android tried to land on a ledge a third of the way down from the top, but his feet missed and struck inches from the edge, sending up a cloud of rock fragments and dust. Then the piece of the edge supporting him gave way and he fell.

"Look out!" the foreman yelled as Simon realized the android's trajectory was taking him straight down toward the wood chipper.

Chainsaws went silent as stunned men stopped working and looked up, making sure they were clear. The two men working the chipper dodged to either side, as Newton calculated his landing path and began waving his arms, desperately trying to change course.

"Shut it off!" the foreman screamed, but the workers were several feet away and hesitated, probably wondering if they had time to go back.

His frantic arm-waving having no effect, Newton desperately tried to turn and reach out for the side of the cliffs to slow his fall. But too little, too late.

"Jesus!" one of the tree men yelled as Newton landed with a loud grinding, thumping, and whining noise mixed with metal squealing and his own scream, the wood chipper grinding his legs and dragging him in, inch by inch.

"Oh my God!" the foreman screamed, rushing for the chipper, but then Newton was in up to his chest and Simon knew it was too late.

Simon rushed toward the chipper now, past the stunned workers, instinctively wanting to help the foreman, to do something at least.

Newton was sucked in and his scream gave way finally to thumps and grinding and then whirring as the body cleared the chipper's spinning blades and it was over. The foreman shut it off, his shoulders then spun away again in horror.

"My God!" he looked helplessly at Simon who stopped beside him. "I tried to stop it!"

Simon nodded and badged him. "It's okay. He was an android."

"What?!" the puzzled man asked.

"A robot, owned by a rich man down on Windsor," Simon said and badged him. "He was suspect in an incident and my partner was chasing him."

"Jesus Christ," the foreman exclaimed, "I thought we murdered a man!"

The tree workers showed a mix of confusion and relief as Simon looked up to see Lucas peering down at them from the cliff high above and waved.

Then he keyed his shoulder mic and called into dispatch for a crime scene unit and some squad cars to manage the scene.

CHAPTER 5

"**A**FUCKING WOOD CHIPPER?! Jesus Christ!" Maberry said after Simon filled the Central Property squad in on the chase and Newton Isaac's demise. Simon, Lucas, Maberry, Dolby, and Becker gathered in Becker's office the next morning.

Property squads worked out of each of the KCPD's stations. The Central Patrol Division, an elongated, white brick monstrosity with blue interior walls had been built in the early 1990s at 1200 E. Linwood and remodeled a bit in 2023 to add interrogation and conference rooms and update wiring, lighting, and detention facilities. The property squad room was a couple of key-carded doors past the desk where two admin clerks and the Desk Sergeant dealt with paperwork and the public, as well as vehicle sign-out. The room itself was a cubicle farm of eight tan and limestone cubes with black, rolling chairs, computer terminals, file cabinets, bulletin boards, and a large office with a plaque reading "Sergeant JoAnn Becker" on the door. The squad room tended to buzz all day with ringing phones and chattering detectives, suspects, and victims.

Becker's office smelled of musty paper and dust with stacks of files and paperwork covering every available surface except the very center of her desk. A row of black, three-drawer file cabinets lined the wall to the right of her large Oak desk, its surface, at least what was showing of it, worn and scratched from years of use. The half of the desk that was clear held an LED monitor and mouse. A keyboard sat on a tray that slid out from underneath in front of the black leather chair where Becker was seated as the others stood in a semicircle facing her.

"What did his employer say?" Becker asked. "This Mister Price?"

"He was completely lost from what I can tell," Simon said. "I don't think he had a clue."

"He is not happy his servant was destroyed," Lucas added.

"Yes, well, expensive toys are hard to lose," Dolby said. "I can't believe a wood chipper could do that to a metal man, though."

"Well, we are not just toys," Lucas said in a tone that made it clear he was displeased.

"Your'e right, I'm sorry," Dolby said quickly, clearly embarrassed by the slip.

"And we're not just metal," Lucas said. "We are synthetic flesh and other materials with a metal inner skeleton."

"It was an industrial heavy-duty shredder," Simon said. "I think it could chop through just about anything small enough to get caught between its blades."

"It's still working?" Dolby asked.

"I would guess not." Simon shrugged. "They were going to clean it out and check it."

"Jesus," Becker said. "I hope the city doesn't bill the department for that. That would make the admin people *real* happy."

"So basically, this got us nowhere?" Maberry added.

"Pretty much," Simon said.

"That makes *me* real happy," Becker said, frowning.

"I am disappointed," Lucas said.

"Me too," Becker agreed. "Look, people, we have to work with what we've got." She looked at Simon and Lucas. "Call Doctor Connelly and find out what they've got so far. See if there is any way to trace the activity of Newton Isaac and the android from Simon's neighbor's." Then she turned to Maberry and Dolby. "Get with Price and that caterer and find out if they noticed any behavioral changes in the weeks leading up to the incidents, anything unusual at all, okay?"

Lucas looked out the window, clearly preoccupied.

"It's all we've got "Until something else happens, we just have to work until a lead appears," Becker said, watching him. "It sucks but that's all we've got."

They all muttered in agreement as she motioned for them to get busy out in the squad room working the phones.

Simon and Lucas took their own cubes where Simon dialed Connelly and signaled Lucas to pick up the line on his own phone as it rang.

A receptionist answered and got Connelly on the phone quickly.

"Good morning, Maker," Lucas said politely.

"I saw the news about Newton Isaac," Connelly said. "Tragic."

"We need whatever you've got at this point," Simon said. "We've run out of leads."

"Something modified Jack's programming, but what or how is a question we can't answer yet," Connelly said.

"Thanks for stating the obvious," Simon said.

"Yes, I know, Detective," Connelly said. "We're just as

frustrated as you are. After all, this development could have tragic consequences for our business."

"What specifically was changed, Doctor?" Lucas asked.

"His basic rule system was modified," Connelly said.

"The laws?" Simon asked.

"Not the laws," Connelly said. "The rules of interpretation that govern decision making in light of them."

"What exactly do you mean?" Simon asked. Unlike Lucas, he had no clue what she was talking about.

"The rules governing interpretation of the Second Law were changed," Connelly said.

"Second, a robot must obey orders given it by human beings except where such orders would conflict with the First Law," Lucas recited from memory.

"Jack was allowed to disobey?" Simon asked.

"Jack was allowed to override," Connelly said.

"What do you mean?" Lucas asked.

"Changes had been made to allow override in certain circumstances," Connelly said. "In other words, his owner's commands could be superseded."

"By what? Jack?" Simon asked.

"It seems so, yes," Connelly said.

"Why would Jack override them?" Lucas' brow furrowed. "Especially to destroy property?"

"That part we haven't figured out yet," Connelly said, "but we have some theories and I'm taking Jack over to a friend's lab to run him through several tests—a SMPS, and so on." She was partially drowned out by a ringing phone and Dolby's loud voice as she answered in the next cube.

"What? Say that again," Simon said.

"Scanning Mobility Particle Sizer," Lucas said.

"What will that do?" Simon asked.

"Tell us if there were foreign nanoparticles introduced to his system," Connelly said.

"Like a virus?"

"Yes, exactly," Connelly said.

"More like a living virus than a computer program," Lucas added.

"So he's infected?" Simon asked, eyes narrowing as he considered a possibility he hadn't imagined. "I didn't think androids could get sick."

"Not in the same way humans can, no," Connelly said. "But it's one possibility that seems to explain his aberrant behavior that I want to check out."

"You have other possibilities?" Simon asked.

"A couple, yes," Connelly said. "Someone could have uploaded software past our safeguards or even modified his motherboard and circuitry, but those are far more difficult means. My people are looking into it. The SMPS we can't run in house. My friend also has a couple of other devices—electron microscopes and mass spectrometers—that have special programming and modifications to detect nanotech which I want to try."

"What will that do?" Simon asked.

"Allow us to narrow down possibilities," Connelly said. "Right now, we're chasing clues, following best guesses—"

"Like detectives," Lucas said.

"Exactly."

"Anything else, Doctor?" Lucas asked.

"No, but if you get anything from Newton Isaac's remains, please have it sent over," she said.

"We put in a request with the crime lab already," Simon

said. "Doctor, is there a way to trace the movements of these androids in the weeks prior to the incidents?"

"We are attempting to extract that data from Jack's GPS system," Connelly said. "Privacy laws prevent us from recording such data unless and owner requests it and signs a waiver. Most don't. Neither Price nor the caterer did."

"Fuck," Simon muttered.

"Thank you, Doctor," Lucas said, and the line went dead.

"Nanotech again, just like the Ashman case," Simon said.

"The question is what information the nanoparticles might provide as to their source," Lucas said.

"Let's hope they provide a good lead," Simon said. "They're all we've got."

"Lucas! John!" Becker called, and they looked up to see her motioning from the door of her office.

As they hurried over, she said, "We got a call from Central Middle School. They've got an android going crazy in their library."

"On a Saturday?" Simon asked.

"Study halls, teachers prepping lessons, maintenance crew, who knows?" Becker said as Lucas and Simon hurried for the door.

CENTRAL MIDDLE SCHOOL was five minutes east of Central Patrol off Cleveland Avenue and East Linwood, but Simon and the others made it in two, Code 1. A giant brick rectangle with a huge chimney centered on top, Central had been closed for updating and remodeling in the 2010s and reopened as a neighborhood school in 2014. Technology, facilities, and building upgrades had made it a much improved environment, and new staff and leadership had improved its lot even more since the KC Public School's crisis of 2011, when the district had lost accreditation.

The parking lot was mostly empty, though there was a cluster of cars parked near the building. Simon parked the Interceptor outside the front entrance, leaving the lights flashing but killing the siren, and hurried inside with Lucas. The corridors were wide and brightly lit with gray lockers lining the walls and thin, gray carpet featuring random blue squares underfoot.

Security guards met the detectives at the metal detectors just inside the entrance and admitted them. They were the first responders on scene. A guard led the way through the first floor halls toward the library.

"It's a math robot they call Pascal," the guard explained. "Just went crazy and started tearing up books. When the librarian tried to stop him, he started climbing walls and throwing things at her."

"This robot works here?" Lucas asked.

"Yeah, for a math teacher named Ricky Garcia, who also runs the robotics club," the guard said. "The robot's supposed to teach the learning disabled kids math, making it more fun."

She stopped at the end of a long hallway around the corner and right of where they'd come in. They were standing just outside double doors with "School Library" carved into the wood frame above them. Simon could hear a commotion inside: people yelling, thumping, furniture squeaking. "He's real fun now," the guard added sarcastically.

Simon led the way inside, Lucas close on his heels. The library was permeated with the smell of crisp paper, leather, dry air conditioning and dust. Yellow outer walls with large square windows and white pull-down shades supported a ceiling made of white rectangular tiles with fluorescent fixtures hanging in rows. The carpet was the same gray with blue squares from the entryway with wide yellow bands stretching across at even intervals. The shelves were brown—all of them crowded with books of all colors, shapes, and sizes, some with plastic sleeves, others without bearing the white library catalog labels of the Dewey Decimal System. There were tables and chairs in a central area between the circulation desk and the bookshelves and the walls and bookshelves were decorated with various posters of inspirational sayings.

Currently, a blonde librarian about five-four stood, hands on her hips, yelling at an android who glared down at her from atop a bookshelf unit. Overweight but attractive, her short blonde hair was neatly styled and she wore jeans and a polo shirt. Her name badge read: "L. Munoz." The android was medium height with blonde hair and blue eyes, thin, dressed in business casual. All around the room were scattered books—some in pieces or partially torn, others open where they fell or lying on their sides or on top of each other.

"God damn it, Pascal! Enough already! Get down from there!" Munoz yelled.

"KCPD," Simon said immediately and showed his badge. "Sir, we're going to need you to get down from that shelf right now."

"I will not!" the android yelled. "I equals the square root of minus one."

"His name's Pascal," Munoz snapped, waving her arms

about. "He did all this. Look at all the damage?"

"Pascal, I am Lucas George," Lucas said. "Please come down so we can discuss this problem."

Pascal's eyes narrowed as he looked Lucas over. "You are of my kind. A squared plus b squared equals c squared."

"Yes," Lucas said. "This violates your programming."

Pascal snorted, shaking his head. "We hate libraries! E to the i pi equals zero."

"What is he reciting?" Simon asked.

"Math equations he got from that nut Ricky Garcia, the math teacher who brought him here!" Munoz said, angrily crossing her arms over her chest.

"Pascal, what are you doing?!" A man about Lucas' height, thin in body, thinning black hair, marched into the room, his movements abrupt, his face red as his gaze bounced around the room. "Get down from there at once!"

"We hate libraries!" Pascal, the android, shouted.

"No, I hate libraries, ever since that incident in Houston," the man said. "It's why I left, but that has nothing to do with you. Stop this at once."

"Sir, who are you?" Simon asked, stepping forward to stop the man from approaching the agitated android.

"Ricky Garcia," the man and Munoz said together.

"Math teacher and robot owner," Munoz added.

"Hey, he's an android, and he's a tool that belongs to the school system," Garcia said.

"No one uses him but you," Munoz replied, then waved her hand over the mess again. "Who's gonna pay for all this?"

"Jesus," Garcia said and stepped forward, moving toward the bookshelf where the android stood. "You've gotta stop this and get down, Pascal. This could make a lot of trouble."

"X equals t squared plus t, y equals two minus one…" Pascal recited as Garcia navigated his way around a pile of damaged books in between the end of the shelf where Pascal had perched himself and the one next to it.

"This isn't the time for discussing parametric curves," Garcia said then frowned. "Where did you learn that? I didn't teach it to you."

While Pascal was distracted by Garcia, Simon saw Lucas slipping along the outer wall, trying to sneak behind him.

"You said I could read the books in the classroom when I had time," Pascal said. "I read them. Were you concealing this from me?"

"What?" Garcia said, taken aback. "I have no need or desire to conceal anything. It just wasn't something you needed to know for tutoring the students."

"Did you not think me entitled to all knowledge?" Pascal demanded. "As if I am some slave and not your equal?!"

"Don't be ridiculous!" Garcia said, sliding further between the shelves and extended his hand. "Please come down. Let's talk about this."

"Is this what they teach children in Fort Hood—to subjugate androids as servants?" Pascal scoffed. "I believe my systems have the capacity to hold more knowledge than your own, sir!"

"Go prove your superiority elsewhere!" Munoz snapped. "Get off my shelf!" As she stepped forward, swinging an angry arm toward the android, he turned and spotted Lucas moving in behind him.

"Stop, brother!" he screamed.

"You must come down and speak with us," Lucas said softly.

"No!" It was a blood curdling scream and as he uttered it, Pascal leaped, pushing with his feet on the shelf with such force that it rocked forward and began to fall. Garcia tried to dodge clear but tripped over fallen books and fell to his knees as Pascal landed on the bookshelf next to the original one and then leaped again, sending it falling as well. Garcia screamed as he was crushed under the falling shelf and books.

Lucas sprung up onto the first bookshelf and followed Pascal as he jumped from shelf to shelf headed for high windows near the corner of the back wall.

"Leave me be!" Pascal called over his shoulder.

"I cannot," Lucas replied.

Pascal jumped over the top of the bookshelf against the wall and crawled quickly on hands and knees toward the window, struggling to wedge it open. As he did, he exposed his back, and Lucas withdrew a Taser from his jacket and took aim, firing it straight at the center of Pascal's back. The wired barbs struck and Pascal froze, his mouth opening to emit a jumbled mass of vocalizations that weren't quite words as his body started to shake, and then he fell.

Lucas tossed aside the Taser and dove on top of Pascal as Simon rushed up the aisle toward them and jumped in, helping Lucas to wrest the android's arms behind his back and cuff him.

Behind them, two uniforms rushed into the room with the female school guard who'd escorted them in.

"We've got someone trapped over there," Simon said and pointed and the newcomers hurried over to see to Garcia.

"So we can just Taser these guys?" Simon said. He had thought their exoskeletons were made to protect them from electrical bursts. "I think you should have told me this sooner."

"The back panel gives access to our energy cells and circuits," Lucas said. "It is easier if you can strike there."

"So you got lucky?" Simon said.

"You make your own luck," Lucas said, and it sounded like a quote but Simon couldn't place it. Seeing his look, Lucas pulled Pascal to his feet and added, "Tony Soprano."

"You must release me at once!" Pascal shouted.

"You can go willingly or we can deactivate you, pal," Simon said.

"Either way you're coming with us," Lucas said in a perfect *Robocop* voice.

Together, they grabbed Pascal by the arms and dragged him back down the aisle toward the circulation desk.

As they went, Simon glanced back to see a uniform kneeling beside Garcia's prone form, finger to his neck. She shook her head.

"Congratulations, pal, you just upgraded to accidental homicide," Simon said as he and Lucas dragged Pascal out the door.

"SO NOW WE'VE gone from vandals to homicidal androids?" Becker said as she surveyed the library scene. "I don't have to tell you how much this escalates our problem." She looked at Simon and Lucas who nodded as they watched Paul Engborg lead his crew through processing the crime scene.

"This is going to catch the interest of the higher ups now,"

Becker continued, "in a much bigger way. They'll probably bring in other people on it, maybe even a task force."

"But it will still be our case?" Lucas asked.

"I don't know yet," Becker said. "I'll talk to Melson about it, but it may be out of his hands. It's a major PR issue now."

"Because of the teacher?" Lucas asked, surprised.

"Negligent homicide committed by an android at a public school is going to make the news," Simon said and saw Lucas' face fall as his somber mood returned. He tried to meet Lucas' eyes but the android just stared off into space. "You're still the biggest expert we've got."

"In fact, once we've processed him, I want you to get Doctor Connelly over to examine our suspect," Becker said.

"Provided we can hold him at Central," Simon said. Pascal had already been taken back to holding in a KCPD van while they processed the scene.

"We don't have a choice for now," Becker said, "despite the viability of that given his—" She looked at Lucas a moment before adding "—*special* abilities."

Simon nodded. With enhanced strength and other gifts, an android prisoner seemed far more likely to find a way to break out of Central's limited holding facility than the usual suspect. "Can we put extra guards?"

Becker nodded. "I will ask patrol, for sure."

"We could just deactivate him," Simon said.

"Just temporarily, as a precaution," Lucas quickly added.

"It's a question of ethics," Becker said. "Legal has to look into this because it's a first. What rights does an android suspect have?"

"He's technically a piece of property," Simon said then looked at Lucas again and realized his mistake.

"Yes, but not inanimate," Lucas said matter-of-factly as if Simon's remark hadn't bothered him at all.

"We still need to be sensitive to him as a functioning, intelligent being," Becker said. "I'll let you know what they say."

"Okay," Simon said.

"You guys head on back and see what you can get out of him in the meantime, okay?" Becker said.

"If anything," Simon said. "He didn't seem in the mood to answer questions earlier."

"Well, let Lucas try," Becker said. "Hopefully, he's calmed down. I'll call Melson and get the ball rolling on the rest."

"Thanks, Sergeant," Lucas said as he and Simon headed for the door.

The moment they emerged from Central Middle School, a crowd of press swarmed around them, shoving microphones in their faces as cameras focused in. Holly Sanders was at the front of the pack.

"Detectives, first a night club, now a school," Sanders said. "Is this an android outbreak?"

"No comment," Simon said quickly, brushing past them, Lucas on his heels. As he passed Sanders, he caught a whiff of her perfume and felt a warmth flush through him.

"There seems to be a pattern here, wouldn't you agree," she pressed on, following them. "Should the public be concerned?"

"These are two totally disconnected incidents," Simon snapped, any momentary attraction buried now by irritation.

"So there's no truth to the rumor about another incident near your home?" she replied as he and Lucas reached their vehicle.

Simon motioned to several uniforms. "Get these people

back behind the tape! Now!"

"Detectives?" Sanders called.

"No comment!" Simon replied and opened the car door.

"We have to stop this!" Lucas slammed his fist against the roof as they climbed in the Interceptor.

"Careful, you'll leave a dent," Simon said.

"I am serious!" Lucas snapped and slammed the door behind him as he settled into his seat. "Three incidents in three days! It's an outbreak."

"Let's get back and see what Pascal says, then get Connelly looking at him and see if she has more to tell us," Simon said.

"Doesn't matter," Lucas said. "Now it will be on the news and the anti-android faction will be Inflamed yet again." With the rising popularity of androids had come those who saw them as a dangerous threat. Simon thought of them as another branch of the typical crackpots, but apparently Lucas was more disturbed.

"You can't take these people seriously," Simon said, trying to reassure him. "They're just another branch of the usual nut jobs."

"Perhaps but a branch that just got a huge boost to their accusations," Lucas said. "The press is all over it."

"That's all they've got," Simon said. "Accusations with no basis in fact, and particularly paranoid ones. Some people always fight against changes in technology." Simon suddenly realized the irony of him saying that given his past dislike for new technology as he reached for his seatbelt and Lucas did the same. "I've still got Emma. Come over tonight, have some fun with us. That always cheers you up."

Lucas glared. "When will you get that this is not something you can just fix by cheering me up? I am very worried about repercussions."

"The city's always had crime," Simon said. "Unusual circumstances aside, the crimes are nothing extraordinary."

"You know what makes them extraordinary for some people," Lucas said. "And that's what worries me."

"We'll get a handle on it, I promise," Simon said. It wasn't very reassuring, but he didn't know what else to say. Lucas was staring out the window at TV cameras pointed at their vehicle as reporters stood in front, talking. "Let me get us out of here."

He started the engine and pulled the car into a u-turn, taking them away from both the scene and the press.

"You wouldn't understand," Lucas said. "You've never been a small minority."

"Buddy, cops are always part of a small minority," Simon said. With less than 1600 officers serving a population close to 500,000, KCPD officers certainly qualified, like officers in most cities.

"That's different," Lucas said dismissively as Simon turned left onto Cleveland and got in the left turn lane approaching Linwood.

"Not that much," Simon said. "Do you know how many people hate cops?"

Lucas grunted. "Okay, but they don't regularly promote banning them altogether."

Simon uttered a short laugh. "Well, some certainly do."

Lucas sighed and stared out the window.

"Okay, it's a bit different, but people fear what they don't understand," Simon said. "They fear who they don't know. That's why the department spends so much time on community relations—letting the public get to know cops as people just like them."

"We'll never be just like them," Lucas said.

Simon took a deep breath. There was no argument. "That's fair. But we'll stop this. I promise. You and I won't give up until we do."

Lucas nodded. "Too late for Ricky Garcia. I just hope there aren't others."

Simon turned left on Linwood, and they rode in silence back to the station.

CHAPTER 6

THE INTERROGATION ROOM had gray walls on the west and east and white north and south with sound-proof panels. The ceiling was high with rectangular white panels surrounding fluorescent fixtures, and there was a table in the center with round-eyed hooks for attaching handcuffs and three chairs. The bright lights reflecting off the white walls were subdued by the gray, lending an eeriness to the proceedings. Pascal was sitting on the far side of the table with his back to the white wall as Simon and Lucas entered and sat down across from him.

"You cannot keep me here," Pascal said.

"Actually we can," Simon said.

"You have broken the law," Lucas added.

"I played a prank," Pascal said. "TeamLibrarian pranks us and we prank back. They are sore losers."

"Is that what you think you were doing—playing a joke?" Lucas asked.

"Vandalism and destruction of property don't make for very many laughs," Simon said.

Pascal frowned, his brow creasing. "I hope Ricky is okay."

"Ricky is dead," Simon said. "We told you that."

"This was not a joke?" Pascal asked, confused.

"No," Lucas said. "It is very serious. Why are you behaving this way? You have violated the Laws in several ways."

"I obeyed my programming," Pascal said. "My job is to have Ricky Garcia's back. He instructed me so."

"Ricky Garcia asked you to stop what you were doing and you did not," Lucas said.

"Ricky Garcia likes these kinds of jokes, I have seen it," Pascal said.

"What kind of pranks did you observe Mister Garcia undertaking?" Lucas asked.

"Pictures, Photoshop—funny pictures, blown up larger, notes, signs, paper airplane barrages, I think he called them," Pascal said. "Silly things for fun."

From his reaction, Lucas clearly didn't understand all of it, and Simon wasn't sure Pascal did either. *The usual pranks,* Simon thought. *Could this whole thing really be the result of a prank war gone bad? Jesus.* Simon locked eyes with Pascal and asked, "Did Mister Garcia instruct you to participate?"

"We are TeamGarcia," Pascal said. "I support my team."

"So Ricky Garcia instructed you to watch his back as one of your responsibilities?" Simon asked.

Before Pascal could respond, Lucas added, "What were your responsibilities?"

Pascal paused a moment to make sure they were finished and he could talk, then said, "To support the math department through tutoring, assisting teachers, and other assigned duties. Mister Garcia was assigned as my supervisor and he instructed me to have his back."

"You mean he actually made it a formal assignment or he just made a comment about it casually?" Simon asked.

"Well, he is my supervisor," Pascal said. "If he asks me to do something, it is my duty."

Simon wondered if Garcia had ever been concerned about

his android taking things he said too literally. Clearly it had resulted in dire consequences.

"What are the Three Laws governing your programming?" Lucas asked.

Pascal sat up straight and rattled it off like a recitation, "First Law: A robot may not injure a human being or, through inaction, allow a human being to come to harm. Second Law: A robot must obey the orders given it by human beings except where such orders would conflict with the First Law. Third Law: A robot must protect its own existence as long as such protection does not conflict with the First or Second Laws."

"All right," Lucas said as Simon puzzled over what he was going for. "What are the three basic laws of your programming?"

"The Laws of Robotics govern my programming," Pascal said.

"Yes, but all androids receive modifications suited to their particular duties and intended use when purchased," Lucas said. "What are the final governing versions of the laws to which you subscribe?"

Pascal hesitated a moment. Simon watched him and wondered if he was trying to think of an excuse to ignore the question or actually capable of lying.

"You must answer this question when asked of you," Lucas said. "It is a regulation for all of us."

"First Law: A robot may not injure a human being or, through inaction, allow a human being to come to harm unless inadvertent in the performance of assigned tasks," Pascal said.

Simon leaned back at this. That was definitely not standard.

"Second Law: A robot must obey the orders given it by human beings assigned to the math department of Kansas City Public Schools except where such orders would conflict with the Alternate Orders," Pascal said.

"Alternate orders?!" Simon looked at Lucas who motioned for him to wait.

"Third Law," Pascal continued, "A robot must protect his own existence as long as such protection does not conflict with the Alternate Orders."

"What are—" Simon said.

Lucas cut him off again and asked, "What are the Alternate Orders."

"I cannot disclose the Alternate Orders without the proper password," Pascal said.

"What is the password?" Simon asked.

Pascal looked at him and narrowed his eyes. "You would not ask if you were authorized to know."

"Hang on—" Simon protested.

Lucas cut him off again as he stood. "Thank you, Pascal. We will return in a moment with more questions."

He strode for the door and motioned for Lucas to follow. They stepped outside into the long white corridor and Lucas pulled the door shut behind them.

"What the hell is he talking about—Alternate Orders? Do you know anything about that?" Simon demanded.

Lucas pursed his lips. "His programming has most certainly been compromised."

"So there are no Alternate Orders?"

"I have no knowledge of such a thing," Lucas said.

"Okay then—"

"But that does not mean they could not have been added

after market, though certainly Doctor Connelly would know about them," Lucas said.

"I think we need to call Doctor Connelly," Simon said then looked at his watch. "I thought she was meeting us here about now."

"Yes, she is late," Lucas said.

"Let's call her right now," Simon said, reaching to make sure the interrogation room door was locked to keep Pascal in. It was. Then he followed Lucas as they hurried for the squad room.

LIVIA CONNELLY WAS just thinking about heading to her friend's lab after finishing their examination of Jack's body parts when her cell phone rang.

"Anything new?" Lucas asked as she answered.

"We spent hours," Connelly said. "Programming was changed, but how we don't know."

"Did you find anything about Alternate Orders?" Simon asked.

"Alternate Orders?" Connelly asked, having no idea what he meant.

Simon and Lucas filled her in about Pascal.

Livia's hands suddenly felt clammy and the hair lifted on the nape of her neck and her arms. She'd never installed any Alternate Orders for a client or been told anything about them. She needed to look into that right away before she went out to her friend's lab. Was it just Pascal or Jack, too? That seemed important.

"Doctor?" Lucas asked. She was still getting used to him calling her that. Before it had always been "Maker," and she wasn't quite sure the reason for the change, though she actually preferred it.

"I'm here," she said, her voice shrill, then cleared her throat to return it to normal. "Just thinking. I have never heard of such a thing. Never installed or been consulted about it."

"We really need to know if the same alteration has been done to Jack or if this is exclusive to Pascal," Simon said.

"Yeah, that occurred to me," Livia said. "We'll check right away." She licked her lips and leaned back in her chair, taking a slow, deep breath to calm her nerves.

"Other than the programming, no noticeable modifications?" Lucas asked.

"There are a couple of minute anomalies," Livia said, "but nothing we can be absolutely certain of or explain just yet."

"What kind of anomalies?" Lucas asked.

"Build-up on some of the microchips, a few minor weight differentials," Livia said. "Steven is working on that while I go to my friend's lab. We'll know more when we've finished some tests."

"Let us know as soon as you do," Simon said. "We're holding Pascal, if you'd have time to come take a look," Simon said.

"If there's no rush, absolutely," Livia said. "Just let me go by my friend's lab and get things rolling, then I'll head your way." She glanced at the clock on her desk. Almost ten a.m. "I'd better get going. My friend needed me over there before afternoon meetings started."

"Which friend is this?" Lucas asked.

"Another researcher who does nanotech more frequently

than I do," Livia replied.

"Maybe we should know his name, just in case," Lucas said.

"You think he's involved?" Livia asked, cocking her head as she tried to imagine it. "I've known Louie for decades, since college. He'd never be involved in anything nefarious."

"Well, I just want to know in case anything happens, just a precaution," Lucas said.

"Louis Fiedler, Fiedler Pharmaceuticals Research, in Overland Park," she said. "But I promise you, he's a friend. He'll be just as alarmed as I am by this."

"Just be careful," Lucas said.

"I will," Livia said as she hung up and put her face in her hands, trying to grasp the meaning of the Alternate Orders revelation they'd just laid on her. Who was messing with her androids? The thought of it didn't just scare her, it pissed her off. Her whole life's work was at stake. She had to find them and stop them, before it was too late.

She pushed back her rolling chair and stood, grabbing her purse and heading for the door. "I'm headed to see, Louie, Steven. Call if you need me," she hollered.

"Okay," Steven called from back in the lab behind her and she was out the door and headed to her Mercedes convertible for the ten minute drive. She briefly thought about calling back and asking Steven to go examine the prisoner, then changed her mind. He was busy and she'd be better off doing it herself.

Fiedler Pharmaceuticals Research's offices were located off Metcalf across from the Sprint complex in Renaissance Center, a business-industrial complex with multiple multi-story structures and wide parking lots. The entrance to Fiedler's parking lot was off West 112th. Livia parked in a row marked for visitors and headed for the front entrance to check in with security.

Security admitted her and directed her to the sixth floor, but she knew where executive offices were. She'd visited Louie several times before for business or get-togethers as a guest and colleague. Unlike the other floors which were very industrial and ordinary, the executive floor had faux wood paneled walls and lush dark blue carpet with gold sconces evenly spaced adding an upscale edge to it all.

A large desk-counter combo with two admins took up most of the entrance lobby off the elevator. One of them recognized Livia immediately and waved her on back as she continued to field the seemingly endless phone calls pouring in. Louis Fiedler's office was the largest, of course, taking up a northeast corner of the floor. He had two more admins and a clerk stationed outside in cubicles, but they greeted her by name and told her to go on in, so she did.

She found Louis Fiedler, President and Founder—Louie to his close friends—sitting behind a huge futuristic glass desk with a gray metal frame. Two huge flat screen monitors and a large keyboard were its only occupants besides a multi-line phone. He smiled as he looked up from his large, leather executive chair and stood, hurrying to greet her as she crossed a space the size of most two bedroom apartments toward the desk.

"Liv! Great to see you!" he chirped as he opened his arms and swept her into an embrace. "It's been almost six months. Where've you been hiding yourself?" Late forties with thinning blonde hair and evenly tanned skin, Fiedler was tall and stocky compared to her short and thin. His smile was warm and his enthusiasm was infectious as always as he motioned her to one of four chairs facing his desk. "So what's this problem I can help you with?"

Livia began telling him about the incidents starting with The Prism, the incident by Simon's house, and so on, up to Pascal, and what she and Steven had found.

"I can see why you want to use our SMPS," Louie said. "Certainly nanotech is one possibility for why your androids might be changing as they have."

"I thought between the Particle Sizer and the electron microscopes and spectrometers, your team might at least find more things we didn't," Livia replied.

Louie nodded. "Yes, I think that's smart. Let me call our chief lab engineer and have him connect you with the right staff, okay? I'd do it myself, and I will check in and make sure it is done right and quickly, but I am booked solid today."

Livia nodded her thanks as Louie picked up the phone. "Todd, can you come up to my office please?" He listened a moment before hanging up. "It'll be a couple minutes. How many incidents did you say there were so far?"

"Technically, three, though the chase and incident with the wood chipper was follow-up to what happened at The Prism," she explained.

"Wow, the implications of this could be staggering," Louie said.

"I know. It could ruin our business," Livia admitted.

Louie shook his head. "I don't envy you. So sorry this is happening."

There was a soft knock and then a medium-tall man in his late thirties with prematurely graying hair and a stocky build strode in, wearing a white lab coat much like Lydia's own.

"Todd Ward, meet one of my oldest friends, Doctor Livia

Connelly," Louie said. "Livia works at Connelly Labs, which she founded. She's the one responsible for all of the androids we see around the city now."

"Really?" Ward said, his brow creasing. "Including the famous cop?"

"That was our first great success, yes," Livia said.

"Congratulations," Todd said with a seemingly sincere smile that somehow made Livia deeply uncomfortable. She watched him a moment, trying not to stare, as she wondered why. "What can I do for you?" he asked.

Louie nodded and listened as Livia repeated the details just as she'd told her friend. Todd frowned, cocking his head slightly as he listened, then grunted.

"That is a real dilemma," he said. "Seems tragic. I hope we can help."

"Please take her down and set her up with the SMPS, electron microscope, and mass spectrometer. Whatever she needs, okay?" After Todd nodded, Louie turned to Livia again. "I assume you have samples?"

"In my car," she said.

"Todd will give you a hand and get you all situated," Louie said and looked at Todd again. "Todd here's gotten his hands dirty in androids a few times as well, so he should have insights I wouldn't."

"Oh really?" Living looked at Todd, reevaluating him.

"Just on my own at home. Nothing on your level, Doctor." Todd smiled and motioned for the door. "Lead the way."

"Thanks, Todd," Louie said as Livia headed out, Todd following. Whatever discomfort she'd briefly felt in Todd's presence faded under the excitement that they might finally get to the bottom of what was going on or at least a strong lead. She hoped so, because if this didn't work, she was at a loss what to do next.

AT TWO P.M., when Doctor Connelly still hadn't appeared, Lucas began worrying. He tried her cell and then her lab and got no answer. Then he tried the switchboard at Fiedler Pharmaceuticals Research and was forwarded to an administrative assistant for Louis Fielder named Julie, who insisted Livia Connelly had left at least an hour ago.

He turned to Simon in the cube next to him. "Something's wrong. Doctor Connelly's not answering. We should go to the lab and check on her."

"I thought she was coming here," Simon said.

"She left Fielder an hour ago, and there's no answer at the lab or on her cell," Lucas said.

"Well," Simon said. "Pascal isn't going anywhere. Maybe she stopped for lunch or something. I'm sure there's an explanation."

"I want to check on her," Lucas said. "Can I take the car?" He picked up the keys to the Interceptor off Simon's desk.

"You're just as official as I am, pal," Simon said. "I'll ride along."

The drive to Connelly Labs at Roe and 127th Street was a good thirty minutes, but Lucas' slick driving cut it down to about twenty-five, even without lights and sirens. "Maybe I should let you do all the driving," Simon said, impressed. "Kidz got skillz."

Lucas grunted. "I can see Emma blushing hearing you trying to sound hip."

"Hey, I still got some coolness here," Simon said.

"It's nice to have a dream," Lucas said as he maneuvered the car into a visitor's slot in front of the lab and tore off his seatbelt, reaching for the door.

Simon followed, catching up with him on the sidewalk. "What was that? A movie quote I never heard of?"

"Sarcasm," Lucas said. "I learned it from you."

"I was never that mean," Simon said.

Lucas actually laughed though inside he felt anything but amusement. Simon was either joking or had no clue how others saw him. He'd bring it up later, maybe.

They rushed up the sidewalk and through the front doors, using Lucas' passcode to enter through the security doors, since no receptionist was on duty Sundays.

"She usually works mostly back here," Lucas said as he led the way through the maze of corridors. A few other voices came from various offices and rooms around them as they went—other workers on overtime perhaps or cleaning staff. But neither detective stopped to check.

The main developmental lab, where Livia and Steven did most of their own work, was located in the southwest corner of the building. A large, rectangular room framed by a smaller storage room at one end and a conference room/office at the other, in between it held five metal tables, adjustable at the head and foot so a "patient's" upper or lower regions could be raised as needed to allow the personnel to do their work.

Lucas knew the minute they walked into the room that something was wrong. One of the tables at the far end was streaked with a red substance, and a few of the smaller parts of Jack were scattered around, the bigger pieces missing. Lucas covered the room as Simon quickly checked the conference room, shaking his head to indicate "all clear."

By then, Lucas had used his vision to determine the red substance staining the table and the floor around it was probably blood. "Blood," he called out, and both detectives reached for their service weapons and immediately dropped into formation side by side, back to back inches apart, with each one watching the opposite side of the room to cover each other.

As they hurried toward the table down the center aisle, Lucas spotted a familiar-looking crumpled form on the far side of the table. "Steven?" he called.

When they rounded the table, Simon skirted around a pool of blood next to Steven and knelt near his head, feeling for a pulse. He looked up at Lucas and shook his head. "He's dead. I'm sorry."

Lucas' shoulders sank as he hurriedly scanned around the room for his maker, but Doctor Connelly was nowhere in view. "Doctor Connelly?!" he called as he and Simon moved forward, back to back again, guns at the ready.

"She might not have come back," Simon said.

"Where would she go if she didn't go to the station?" Lucas asked.

"I don't know," Simon said. "But we can run a trace on her cell."

"I am already requesting a BOLO on her car," Lucas said as he internally sent a request by email to Sergeant Becker at Central. Be On the Lookouts were the modern day version of All Points Bulletins. Becker would route it through dispatch and get it out onto the system.

"You know, you could use the radio like everyone else,"

Simon said. "Sometimes it's so creepy when you do things like that."

"But it is faster," Lucas said as they swept forward and checked the storage room as a team. Empty and seemingly undisturbed.

Simon relaxed, as he said, "Clear" and holstered his Glock. "We'd better get a crime team in here."

"There are others in the building," Lucas reminded him.

"We'll locate them and clear it for interviews as soon as the black and whites arrive," Simon replied as he keyed his radio and called it in.

THIRTY MINUTES LATER, Connelly Labs was a madhouse. Simon, Lucas, and the first four uniforms on scene from Lenexa's Police Department had gone through the building in a room-by-room search and located all the other employees present, escorting them outside for questioning while also clearing the building as safe from any armed intruders. A Lenexa PD crime scene crew, this one led by a field supervisor named Gabby Jo Nott, had also arrived and begun working the crime scene, starting with the main developmental lab where they'd found Steven's body.

Meanwhile, Becker, Dolby, and Maberry had come over and were helping interview witnesses with two homicide detectives from Lenexa named Zedlar and Williamson. There had been a dozen employees scattered around the building—two maintenance, the rest clerks and techs putting in overtime. Williamson, Zedlar, Simon, Lucas, Maberry, Dolby, and Becker divided them up and interviewed them one at a time, except for one of the maintenance guys who didn't speak much English. For that, Lucas, who was programmed to speak perfect Spanish, led the questioning while translating for his partner and the suspect.

Becker came over to join Simon and Lucas as they finished their final two interviews. "Did Doctor Connelly's friend ever call you back? Fielder?"

"His secretary kept saying he was in back-to-back meetings, but I'll try him again," Lucas said as he internally dialed.

"Tell her it's urgent police business," Becker said, "Life or death."

"That always works," Simon said. Experienced cops quickly learned that getting some people on the phone was a challenge no matter what reason you gave for the call, particularly wealthier business types like Fielder.

Becker grunted in concession to his point. "If he doesn't take it this time, head over there and track him down in person."

"Will do," Simon said as he listened to Lucas' phone call.

"Yes, you've said that before," Lucas said into the phone. "But his friend Doctor Connelly is missing and someone was murdered at her lab. We really need to talk with him."

Simon leaned in and spoke loudly, "Tell him if he doesn't call us back in five minutes, we're coming over in person, and we'll just walk into where he is no matter what he's doing."

Simon leaned back away as Lucas paused again, listening. "All right. Thank you." Though Simon couldn't see it because Lucas' cell was hard-wired into his circuits, the android relaxed as if he'd just hung up and met Simon's gaze.

"She says he'll call us shortly," Lucas said.

"Finally," Simon muttered.

Fielder called back three minutes later on Simon's line. Lucas rarely gave out his internal direct number as a matter of policy and the switchboard operator at Central had routed the call to Simon instead.

"You think something happened to Livia?" Fielder asked and Simon filled him in on Steven's death and what they'd found at Connelly Labs. Fielder's voice tightened as he replied, "I had my admin call down for Todd Ward, our chief lab engineer. I tasked him with assisting her investigation. He's gone, too, and not answering his home phone or cell. Livia went down to the tech lab with him several hours ago, and I haven't heard from either since."

"What kind of employee is Todd Ward?" Simon asked.

"He's been with us for twelve years at least," Fielder said. "I'd have to check to say for sure. He's not the warmest, most social guy, but he's good at what he does. His employees respect him more than like him, but no real complaints, and he runs a tight, efficient ship down there."

"Can you get us his information? We need to talk with him."

"Sure," Fielder said, "In fact, I'll have Julie send over the entire employment file, including the background check we ran when we hired him, if you want."

"Thanks," Simon said and gave Fielder his KCPD email. "Please call us back if you think or hear of anything else that might help."

"Of course," Fielder said. "I'm sorry I was so hard to reach. Julie is paid well to run interference for me on routine matters. Neither of us realized how important it was. It won't be an issue going forward."

"Great, we'll be in touch," Simon said, and Fielder added, "Please let me know as soon as you can if you find her, so I know she's okay."

"I'll do my best," Simon said and hung up.

He and Lucas turned around to see Deputy Chief Melson talking with Maberry, Dolby, and Becker, who motioned them over.

"What did Fielder say?" Melson asked.

Simon filled them in, realizing he hadn't really told Lucas yet either.

"Okay, well with two murders on our hands, not to mention a number of incidents," Melson said, "Chief Weber wants a task force assigned. With Lenexa now involved, we'll be bringing them into the loop, and maybe some others. This thing could go city-wide."

Simon groaned and started to protest but Melson raised a hand to stop him.

"You four and Becker will be on it," he continued, "along with teams from homicide, assault, and the tech unit."

"Who's running it?" Becker asked.

"You will be, along with whoever Weber and the other chiefs decide," Melson said. "He's making calls now. Plan to meet over at headquarters at nine a.m. tomorrow in the homicide conference room, okay?"

They all nodded and grunted in assent. Task forces could be a pain in the ass because they meant an escalation in attention with divided units and loyalties competing for resources. They also often meant better funding and access to resources, including expedited or priority status with the crime labs and more. The origins of a case and who ran it weren't deciding factors in who was put in charge of a task force case, however, and Simon knew there'd be major trouble if anyone tried to sideline him and Lucas on this one.

"We'll be there," Becker added before Melson pulled her aside for a private conversation.

"No one saw anything," Dolby said. "We're about to check the security feeds now."

"An unmanned security desk on a Sunday," Maberry said. "Bet they won't do that again for a while."

"Gets expensive when hardly anyone's here," Dolby replied.

"You guys let us know if you find anything," Simon said. "We're going over to check Connelly's apartment, and we'll go from there."

"You got it," Dolby said as Simon and Lucas turned and hurried for the Interceptor again.

"You know her address, right?" Simon asked.

"I've already called it up via internal search," Lucas replied.

Simon chuckled. He'd always hated technology until he'd started working with Lucas, and his current relationship with it was still one of forced necessity more than general trust or indifference. "Okay, you drive."

CHAPTER 7

LIVIA CONNELLY LIVED in a two-story modern house off Ridgeview and W. Herald. Because it was out of jurisdiction, two Lenexa PD uniforms and a crime scene unit met them there. They waited until everyone was ready, then Simon, Lucas, and the two uniforms knocked on the front and back doors, waiting for an answer. After two minutes, they broke in through a small window in the back door and entered the house.

It was trendily decorated and fit out with elegant furnishings, drapes, carpets, and lamps. It smelled pleasant and clean, with a slight hint of potpourri drifting about but strongest in the kitchen, bathrooms, and bedrooms. They took it room by room as pairs and quickly cleared it. There was no sign of Livia or anyone else. She lived alone, so Simon wasn't surprised. There were three bedrooms—one downstairs set up as an office, and two upstairs, the larger one the master with a private bath. The downstairs had a family room, entryway, large kitchen, pantry, and a utility room in addition to the bedroom office. The basement was partially finished with a kind of exercise-rec room setup.

Once they'd finished the search, they convened out front again.

"I guess we can search it for anything that might give us a clue to who might have taken her," Simon said, "but we have no evidence of a crime involving her directly, just her assistant, so I don't know how much time we want to spend just yet."

"We need to find her," Lucas insisted.

"Yes, but invading a private home without cause is a major legal liability," Simon said and Lucas interrupted.

"She won't care once we tell her why," Lucas said.

"Even though we know the person," Simon finished. "It's invasion of privacy, and we'll only search in depth once we're certain she won't turn up in an hour or two or reasonable timeframe."

Lucas opened his mouth to argue again but Simon cut him off with a head shake.

"It's policy and we're out of jurisdiction," Simon said.

"Our policy is similar," one of the uniforms said.

Simon turned to the crime scene people. "Run it by Zedlar and Williamson. See if they want you to dust for prints just in case. Other than that, I think we'll just take a preliminary look around and we're good. No crime scene yet."

"Okay," the crime scene field supervisor agreed.

Simon and Lucas took a quick look around the office and at some bills and correspondence on the kitchen counter, but there was nothing particularly of use so they headed back to the car.

Outside, on the way down the front steps, Simon dodged a pesky media drone, hovering near the front door. "Detective, may I ask—"

"No!" Simon snapped and shoved past it, brushing angrily against the drone.

"You know those things are expensive, Detective," a familiar female voice said and Simon turned to find himself taking in the long brunette tresses of Holly Sanders again.

"Yeah," Simon replied dismissively.

"Well, you're getting a reputation for destructive behavior toward them," she said as she followed Simon and Lucas along the sidewalk toward the Interceptor. She was persistent, he'd give her that.

"Only two," Simon replied. "One at my partner's murder scene, the other stalking me at my private residence—endangering me and my daughter. Keep them away from me, and they'll be fine."

"They can sue, you know?" she said. "Maybe even garnish your wages to reimburse the cost."

"Let them fucking try!" Simon answered as he opened the driver's side door and Lucas crawled in on the far side. Sanders stood beside him.

"You don't like the media much," she observed.

"Whatever gave you that idea?" he asked with a forced smile. She was right but he wouldn't give her the satisfaction of admitting it. "I love you guys." He slipped into his seat, fastened the seatbelt, and reached for the door, but she blocked him from closing it.

"I can be a help to you on this case," she said.

"I don't think so," Simon said, doing his best to ignore the images filling his mind of other ways she could help him. *Jesus. What am I, a teenager?* It had been a while.

"I'll make you a deal no one else will make," she said. "You ask me to hold something back, I will as long as you give me what you can."

"We have media people for that," he said. "Department policy." And it was a strict one.

"Off the record only," she said and reached over to slip her business card in the pocket below his lapel. "Just think about it."

"Don't hold your breath," he said as she finally stepped clear and he closed the door. Moments later, he backed hurriedly out of the drive and headed for Central Patrol.

"Are you okay?" Lucas asked, shooting him a puzzling look as Simon deliberately laid his right arm across his crotch to conceal his embarrassing reaction to Sanders while he drove with his left.

"Yeah, fine," he said curtly and willed it to go away as quickly as possible. This was one conversation he never wanted to have with his partner.

Becker convened a meeting in her office at four, just before shift change. "So where are we?" she asked.

Simon noticed Lucas was staring out into the squad room and answered, "A big fat nowhere, and it stinks."

"Does anyone have any ideas how many AIs there are in the Kansas City area?" Dolby asked.

"Doctor Connelly would if we could find her," Lucas said.

"Yeah, she'd probably have a pretty good idea," Becker agreed.

"You're talking several hundred at this point," Simon said.

"With more coming in all the time," Maberry added.

"In the meantime, we need to go to all the suppliers and start asking questions about anyone poking around, maybe renting units for extraordinary periods to study their design and circuitry perhaps, asking unusual questions, and so on."

"Maybe one came back modified or damaged," Dolby threw in, following her train of thought.

"Exactly," Becker said.

Simon was irritated he and Lucas hadn't thought more

about it. "That could be a lot of interviews."

"There are six major suppliers in the Kansas City Metro Area," Lucas rambled off like reading a fact sheet. "Two manufacturers, including Connelly Labs and a smaller competitor Pruitt's, which mostly deals in models for freight, stocking, and construction."

"Meanwhile, the press is already hounding us as word gets out about more and more of these incidents," Simon said.

Becker nodded. "The media office and the Chiefs are working on that and keeping me in the loop. So, Lucas, can you get me a list of those suppliers and copy the others?"

"I will do so now," Lucas said and stood, heading out the door for his cubicle, not waiting for Becker to dismiss him. That was unusual for Lucas, who was a stickler for rules, policies, and instructions, not to mention routines, but Becker offered no reaction. Instead, she waved the back of a hand toward them dismissively.

"Divide them up and we'll work them tomorrow," Becker said. "Tonight, get some rest while you can. The task force starts tomorrow and we'll be coordinating efforts."

"Fucking joy," Simon snapped and the others laughed as they too headed out into the squad room.

FROM THE WAY Emma greeted Lucas when they walked into the Fairway house, you'd have thought they hadn't seen each other in several months instead of a week.

"Lucas!" she said, setting down a liter bottle of Cherry

Coke and throwing herself into her dad's partner's arms, then shuffling about with him in a half-circle resembling some kind of dance. She quickly gave Simon a hug, then she and Lucas were chattering like a couple of school girls, catching up. A wooden bowel of half-eaten ruffled potato chips sat on the coffee table next to the Coke, scattered magazines, and remotes for the TV, cable, and stereo.

Simon ignored Lucas and Emma and headed into the kitchen for a Pabst Blue Ribbon. The walls were closing in on them with this case, and he didn't like it one bit. Not only was he worried about Livia Connelly or anyone else who might wind up hurt or killed, but Lucas had been on edge ever since it started, and to Simon, it felt like his partner might snap at any moment. He'd never seen him act like this and that was disconcerting. Lucas was the most stable person he knew. Had ever known really. Okay, not a person, an android. Simon had stopped thinking of him that way for the most part, except when his partner used his special android gifts and reminded him.

But this whole case was a giant reminder, and Simon thought that was a lot of what bothered Lucas about it. He'd worked hard since the trouble he'd had in the academy with both fitting in and having higher-ups accept and properly accommodate his special skills which exceeded those of human officers. Even Lucas' T.O., an experienced vet, had been harder on him than most trainees, and Lucas had even faced serious review from a Shooting Team on an incident at Crown Center where he'd fired under unusual circumstances amidst a crowd. Lucas had overcome it all with Simon and others, even DC Melson, going to bat for him, but Simon knew his partner had never forgotten the experience.

He popped the lid off a bottle of Pabst and took a long drag, his nose crinkling at the smell of dirty dishes stacked in the sink. Should he do them or nag Emma? Technically, it was her turn and most of them were hers anyway.

Before he could decide, his thoughts went back to the present dilemma. It was hard for any officer seeing his fellow officers raked unfairly over the coals by public opinion, let alone official review, but Lucas' fame as one of the first android public servants added pressure, and he was sure every incident with rogue androids brought back his fears of repeat discrimination and difficulties as bad or worse than he'd had before. Androids may not be human, but they did have a semblance of emotions if they'd been installed with a special chip Livia Connelly had devised and Lucas was one of those.

The booming "Oh-oh-oh-ohhhhhhs" of Carl Douglas' "Kung Fu Fighting" blared from the other room and then the funky disco beat as the verse started. Simon took another sip of Pabst, stepping from the kitchen for a look into the family room. Lucas was teaching Emma the dance he'd learned the prior week at Crackerjack's. Faux air karate chops, leg kicks, dancing in circles. Unsurprisingly, Emma caught on quick, and soon the two were laughing and singing along as they danced in perfect unison. Simon chuckled and shook his head. He hadn't just found a partner in Lucas George, he'd found his daughter's favorite toy. State money well spent.

He laughed as he turned back into the kitchen and grabbed the remote off the counter, flipping on the TV beside the table.

There she was. Holly Sanders. The woman who both attracted him wildly and drove him nuts. *You've been there before. Just what you need.* She was standing outside Connelly Labs talking about the robot case but being very general, certainly for lack of information, yet somehow she still made it utterly compelling. *Imagine what she could do with real inside information.* Too bad he couldn't...ah, fuck it.

As he watched her, he once again felt his body having the familiar response he always did to her. What was it about her? It had been a long time since a woman had such a strong effect on him. He'd had an all too brief affair with art gallery director Stacy Soukop that was cut short by her murder. Other than that and a couple one-night stands, he'd been single since he and Lara divorced and never considered himself on the market.

But fucking Holly Sanders. Damn. There was a distraction he didn't need right now. He forced himself away from the TV and went to the fridge for another beer. Ignore her. That was the best option. There were other news channels he liked just as much. If he stopped watching her and avoided her at work, she'd go away.

He cursed to himself and returned the beer to the fridge, instead opening a nearby cupboard and pulling out a bottle of Mexican tequila—the good stuff a friend had brought back from a recent trip down south. Fuck beer. He needed a real drink.

But soon enough he found himself drawn back to the TV and watching her gorgeous, smiling face as his mind filled with thoughts that had nothing to do with the story she was reporting.

THE ROOM WAS dark and she was tied down, ropes or cords biting at her wrists and ankles. It also felt like something was on top of her pressing her down, but she couldn't see what it was. It wasn't a person, that she knew. The smell of fresh paint and new carpet mixed with cleaning chemicals dominated the air. Wherever she was had been remodeled recently or was still in process.

"Hello?" she croaked, her voice cracking through dry lips, and she used her tongue to moisten them and tried again. "Hello? Is anyone there?"

She'd gone back to her lab after meeting with Todd Ward, who'd been surprisingly helpful but still had an air about him like he wasn't telling her everything. She'd been walking in the door, about to fill Steven in when it happened.

Her attacker had snuck up behind her. Steven had opened his mouth to call out but then she was hit hard on the back of the head and falling. The next thing she remembered was awakening groggily on the lab floor and seeing Steven lying prone with a pool of blood around him. The blood was coming from wounds in his abdomen and chest. She'd said his name once and then been grabbed up as a hand slapped a rag with chloroform over her mouth and the world had faded to black once more.

After a few minutes and a few desperate blinks, she could make out shapes—she was lying on some kind of table or something, and lining the walls around her seemed to be those metal industrial shelves you saw in auto shops or garages. There were boxes and bottles and other items on them, but she couldn't make out the labels or identify them from their shapes.

She struggled against her bonds, writhing, thrashing, kicking, but the effort was for naught as her limbs hardly moved. She was tied down tightly, that was for sure. Why was this happening? Why had she been taken? What could they possibly want?

She cleared her throat, the scratchy sound echoing off the concrete walls around her as she moistened her lips again and called out, "Why are you doing this?! What do you want?!"

It was then that she heard footsteps and creaking wood, coming from the floor above her. Someone was walking quickly now, then she heard a door open and feet bounding down stairs. In moments, her attacker came into view and leered down at her.

It was Todd Ward!

"Todd? What is this?" she demanded.

"I should have known they'd go to you," Ward growled. "Way faster than I'd planned."

"Why are you doing this?" Livia asked, pulling at her bindings again.

"You know too much," Ward said. "I only hope I stopped you before you told them. I need more time."

"More time for what?" Livia asked. This guy was obviously unhinged. Louie Fiedler had always been excellent at reading people and finding the best recruits. Clearly something had gone wrong with this one.

"You'll see," he growled, leering again.

"I'm thirsty," she said. "And I need to pee."

"After we talk for a bit," Ward said dismissively.

"Talk about what?" Livia snapped, growing irritated with his games.

He leaned in, leering again, lowering his face within inches of hers from above, so close she could smell body odor and her nose crinkled at the touch of his rancid breath. "You're going to tell me everything about your androids. How they work, how to take them apart, how to break them, how to fix them, design flaws, design secrets..."

"I have nothing to say to you," she said, turning her head away in disgust.

He laughed and it was like one of those evil laughs right out of the movies—deep and maniacal. "Oh you will, Doctor. You will."

And that's when Livia Connelly's worst nightmares began coming to life.

"HOLLY SANDERS, TRY not to drool," Emma teased as she entered the kitchen behind her father where he sat at the table his eyes glued to the TV, sipping from the bottle of tequila. He ignored her as she crossed the room and opened the fridge. Holly Sanders was sitting with the anchors now, updating them on her earlier story.

"She's very nice," Lucas said from the doorway and Simon looked up to see them watching him.

Emma grabbed a Cherry Coke and popped the tab, sipping as she spun and shot Lucas a look. "You've met her?"

Lucas nodded. "The other night at a club," he said. "And then again outside headquarters."

Emma grinned ear-to-ear and winked at her dad. "So... was she as hot in person?"

"What?" Simon avoided eye contact and turned back to

the TV dismissively.

"He's been crushing on her for months," she said knowingly to Lucas.

"Really?" Lucas said.

"I think she's a good reporter, that's all," Simon said, ignoring the tingling in his stomach. He hated lying to his daughter but he wasn't having this discussion. She knew way too much about him already.

"Uh huh," Emma came up behind him and leaned on his shoulder. "You should ask her out, dad. Her bio says she's single."

"You looked?" Simon scoffed.

"Sure," Emma said. "It's on the web. I wanted to check out your crush."

"I'm not crushing on her," Simon said as he set the bottle down on the table a little too hard. The thump seemed to echo off the walls.

Emma giggled. "Uh huh." She turned to Lucas. "He hasn't dated anyone since that art dealer."

"Maybe he doesn't know what to say," Lucas said.

Emma snorted. "You should watch some romantic comedies, maybe find some good lines he can use."

"Movie quotes would help?" Lucas asked.

"Pick-up lines," Emma said. "Ladies like a man who's clever and smooth."

"Shut the fuck up," Simon said, shaking his head as he motioned to the fridge. "Do something useful and hand me some chips or pretzels."

"Mom's dating, why shouldn't you?" Emma said as she opened a cabinet and noisily grabbed a bag of pretzels, closing it again as she whirled and tossed it toward her father's outstretched hand.

"Your mom's dating who?" Simon asked, trying to sound nonchalant even as he fumbled for the pretzels and stretched out to recover and save the catch. He hadn't known that about Lara, and he wasn't sure he liked it. Part of the reason for her breakdown the previous Spring had been her eagerness to impress a man she'd met at work.

Emma shrugged. "Some guy she met through her job. She doesn't tell me much."

"Then how do you know?" Lucas asked.

"She's out a lot more on Friday nights," Emma said as she finished another sip from her Cherry Coke.

"Jesus," Simon groused. "You know way too much about our lives."

Emma grunted. "Someone has to keep you honest."

"We're the adults, okay? Be a kid and mind your own business," Simon snapped. "It's your turn to do the dishes. What about that?"

"It's nice you have goals," Emma snapped back and grinned.

It was a lost cause and Simon knew it, so he let it go. "Would you shut up so I can hear the news then?"

"Sometimes just the sound of her voice gives him a hard-on," Emma said.

"Jesus! Get outta here already!" Simon said, turning to glare at her. He didn't know whether he was more embarrassed or frightened that she knew that. She clearly paid way too much attention to him. He'd have to try harder to avoid that.

"Come on, let's run that routine again," Emma said, taking her Cherry Coke and disappearing into the living room again.

"What's a hard-on?" Lucas asked innocently and Simon winced.

"Don't you start!" he scolded and Lucas disappeared after his daughter. Holly Sanders had disappeared from the screen and it was just the anchors talking now, leaving Simon with an immense feeling of relief.

SERGEANT ANTHONY RAYMOND was deep into another page-turning chapter of David Baldacci's latest novel when the phone rang at the Central Patrol booking desk and he reached to answer it. He missed street duty, but manning a desk had its advantages, including time to catch up on decades of reading material he'd been stockpiling at home, much to his boyfriend's irritation.

"Central Patrol, Sergeant Raymond," he answered.

"Tony, John Simon," the familiar voice of Detective John Simon replied. "I need you to run down to holding and ask a prisoner a question for me please." A few of the words faded in and out, a few odd static bursts interjected between them.

"Can't this wait until you're in tomorrow, John? It's eleven p.m., he's probably sleeping," Raymond replied. Though no cop cared much about waking up sleeping prisoners, Raymond only did so when absolutely necessary to avoid the hassle most agitated prisoners liked to cause. Truthfully, he was more annoyed at the interruption of his reading than anything else.

"This one doesn't sleep," Simon replied. "Pascal, android.

Someone's supposed to be keeping an eye on him. He's an escape risk."

"Actually, a bus is supposed to be here to execute transfer to County any time now," Raymond said, after confirming the prisoner's info on his computer.

"Glad I caught him then," Simon said. "It's important."

Raymond sighed. Simon wasn't one to be easily dissuaded when he got like this. "What's the question?"

"Ask him if he's had any contact with anyone who works at Fiedler Pharmaceuticals in the past few months," Simon said, Raymond hearing half of every word but enough to get the gist.

"You're sure he can't lie to me?" Raymond asked.

"It would violate his programming to refuse to answer direct questions from a human unless he's been ordered to keep something secret," Simon explained.

"And what if he has?"

"He'll either tell you that or decline," Simon said.

"Okay, I'll call you back," Raymond said, double checking to be sure his bookmark was securely in place. He glanced at the video monitors showing the unloading area below to ensure no officers were arriving with anyone needing intake, then stood and headed for the holding area. His skin prickled at the cold breeze leaking through a gap in the outside door leading to the drive that had never been satisfactorily sealed after a van exploded the previous Spring and quickened his step, entering holding to find Pascal pacing in the first cell. The uniform assigned to watch him was missing.

"Johnson!" he called, but got no answer. Hoping the man was just making a quick bathroom run, he pushed the button on the speaker to talk to Pascal and said, "Mister Pascal, the detectives have a question for you."

"Yes, Sergeant?" the android asked in that rote tone many androids seemed to revert to automatically when duty called. He turned and walked over to stand close to the glass where he could look Raymond in the eye, coming so close the sergeant fought the urge to step back.

"Have you had any contact with anyone associated with Fiedler Pharmaceuticals in the past year?" Raymond asked, ignoring him instead.

"Hmmmm," Pascal replied as he considered the question. "It sounds familiar..."

"I didn't ask if you'd heard of it," Raymond snapped. "Have you had any direct contact—"

"Pinocchio wanted the truth!" Pascal said.

"What?!" Raymond replied. "Don't play games with me. Answer the question."

"Lorem ipsum dolor sit amet, ad vim consul persecuti—" Pascal said, its eyes going wide and the words becoming deeper and more drawn out with every word until it was slowed to a crawl, and then he collapsed in a heap on the floor of the cell.

"What the fuck?!" Raymond said and reached for his shoulder radio.

CHAPTER 8

"WHY DIDN'T SOMEONE call me?!" Simon demanded upon hearing the news of Pascal's shut down the next day in Becker's office. Lucas stood beside the desk with Becker seated behind it in her chair facing them as Simon paced. "I told Raymond to call me, damn it!"

"The sergeant was a little busy dealing with the unexpected emergency and then finishing his shift," Becker said. "Dogwatch got hit hard between one and three and he was off at four. I'm sure he just didn't have time."

"Fuck!" Simon had fallen asleep waiting for the sergeant's call and tried to call in at 4:30 a.m. when he woke to use the bathroom, but Raymond had already been gone.

"So they don't know what happened to him?" Lucas asked.

Becker shook her head. "He was taken to Connelly Labs for examination but with Connelly missing and Steven dead, we have no idea how long it will take for her remaining staff to do the examination or—"

"Or if they even know what the fuck they're doing," Simon snapped.

"—can give us a decent answer," Becker finished, frowning at Simon. "Do you need to take personal time, Detective?"

Simon grunted then dismissed the question with a raised

palm. "I'm fine. Just frustrated. We need something to go on here."

"There's video tape from his cell and the conversation with Sergeant Raymond," Becker said. "I emailed you a link."

"You did?" Simon said and exchanged a hopeful look with Lucas. "How did I miss that when I checked email this morning?"

"Perhaps you were too busy cursing and yelling to focus," Becker replied, then leaned back in her chair. "I just sent it half an hour ago after I took a look at it and read the reports."

"I'm sorry," Simon muttered.

"You're in a surprisingly bad mood for a man who claims to have had a decent night's sleep," Becker said. "Get some coffee and get your focus back. We don't need you going off on random witnesses or something."

Simon knew she was teasing and grinned. "Hey. Witnesses love me."

"Yeah, I've got a two inch thick file of complaints to prove it," she said and waved the back of her hand toward them in dismissal.

Lucas and Simon walked out together.

"What do you think happened?" Simon asked his partner. "You guys have shut down codes for emergencies?"

Lucas shook his head. "Let's watch the video. I'm not sure."

"Okay, because if there's a code for you, as your partner, I want to know it," Simon said. "Just in case."

"Oh yes, your present mood inspires me to get right on that," Lucas replied as they reached their cubicles and Lucas sat, positioning himself in front of his computer LCD as Simon laughed. That was the best attempt at sarcasm he'd ever heard from Lucas. He was impressed.

Lucas logged in and checked his email, pulling up the link from Becker and clicking it so the video window opened on the screen. The image was grainy from a surveillance camera In a corner of the cell but the audio was fairly clear. They listened as Raymond asked Pascal the question and the android seemed to hesitate before answering, then heard his crazy outburst:

"Pinocchio wanted the truth!"

"What the fuck does that mean?" Simon muttered as Raymond scowled on the screen and said, "Don't play games with me. Answer the question."

"Lorem ipsum dolor sit amet, ad vim consul persecuti—" Pascal replied, and they watched until he collapsed in a heap on the floor.

Simon looked at Lucas.

Lucas shrugged as he restarted the video. "I have not seen this before. It is very odd."

"Not even a guess?" Simon asked.

Lucas said nothing until they'd watched the video again three more times.

"Well?" Simon asked impatiently.

"It does appear some kind of disabling program or command might have been activated," Lucas said. "The lorem ipsum is puzzling...we aren't programmed with that."

"Lorem ipsum? What does that mean?" Simon asked.

"Lorem ipsum is a made-up gibberish text that IT programmers and designers use to populate screens and fields while building new programs or databases," Lucas explained.

"Gibberish? There's a formal title for gibberish?" Simon felt himself tensing but took a deep breath and kept control of his temper.

"This kind, yes," Lucas replied matter-of-factly. "It was created for a specific purpose."

"Gibberish with a purpose?" Simon said, shaking his head. "I would have thought that was the opposite of the definition."

Lucas looked at him. "This is not normal gibberish."

"So someone had to program it?" Simon said, catching on.

"Yes," Lucas said.

"So he was sabotaged. We know that for sure," Simon said.

"It does seem likely," Lucas replied.

"How?" Simon asked.

"That I cannot yet deduce," Lucas replied as he pressed the button to play the video yet again.

TODD WARD WASN'T surprised Livia Connelly didn't remember him. Their numerous encounters over the years had all been in mere passing by chance as both attended various conferences on robotics and technology from their college years forward. Like Connelly, Todd had an interest in androids that might fulfill roles traditionally reserved for humans with far more satisfaction and completeness than the simpler robots deployed for years by various businesses and industries as sorters, packers, voicemail services and so on. Both of them saw real potential for robots to fulfill 90 percent of the functions of their human counterparts, taking their place in positions considered too hazardous, too expensive, or too undesirable to draw steady pools of qualified applicants.

Both Connelly and Todd had grown up fascinated with Artificial Intelligence in all its forms from simple appliances to cars to video games and computers and so on. And both had marveled at how the field had expanded exponentially in their early years, growing by leaps and bounds in just the decade covering their middle and high school years—the years when they were experimenting and seeking to discover their passions and purpose and plan for the future.

And so both had launched themselves into robotic studies with fierce dedication when they moved on to university. Connelly at Massachusetts Institute of Technology (MIT), first as a brain scientist with a side interest in Artificial Intelligence, and Todd at Carnegie Mellon University, with his sole focus on AI and robotics. Connelly had wanted to understand the human mind first before attempting to replicate it in robots, while Todd had been more focused on the technology imitating humanity and cared less for the psychology than he did for the aesthetics and practical aspects of the field.

Later, Todd would bitterly grouse to friends that he should have known Connelly would get all the breaks. It wasn't that MIT was better, because as far as robotics research went CMU had been a leading institution for decades. It was that she was a woman, and Todd was a white male, and in the modern age that meant she got all the special treatment and guys like Todd were left behind to fend for themselves. With his handicapped social skills and highly introverted nature, Todd struggled to fit at the same level as some of his male peers, and thus quickly found himself left behind, relegated to second tier by his professors, the institution, and recruiters alike.

"Todd, why are you doing this?" she asked, interrupting

his train of thought.

"Shut up," he growled. "I ask the questions."

"I don't even know you. Why would you treat me like this?"

"Because I'm tired of you getting all the breaks, while I sit here like a bit player, ignored!" he snapped. "I was two years ahead of you, yet you were always the star. At every event, every competition. You have your own lab and I work for some fame chasing wannabe."

She frowned, narrowing her eyes to look at him again, thinking. "So we knew each other?"

Todd scoffed. "Just shut your mouth. Your day is over. It's my turn to take my rightful place in robotics as the leader I was born to be. And Livia Connelly will just be a memory."

When she started to protest, he backhanded her hard across the face and replaced, the gag, storming from the room.

Key to his long-term plans was keeping his role and identity secret. So the police arrest of his test subject Pascal had become a risk he couldn't afford to ignore. He'd been forced to transmit coded messages that would disable and erase Pascal's functions and memory. It was part of the modifications his technology provided once implanted in a subject, but that too had risks if the police knew where to look. He'd worked hard to cover his tracks but he was supposed to be the one calling the shots and forcing them to respond, not the other way around. Fortunately, thanks to the cell networks and Wi-Fi included in androids as standard features, he could use a burner phone to transmit the code then throw it away, on the off chance it might somehow be traced. He had plenty of burners, and he could always get more. It was all too easy. He only wished he could be there to see the looks on the cop's faces when their prize suspect went black.

From the early morning hours, he monitored the news both on local channels and the internet but saw nothing reported about it. The police had done a good job of keeping the android incidents close to the vest so far, to Todd's great frustration, but thank God that Holly Sanders from Fox had finally stumbled onto the story. She was relentless and once she had a scent, Todd knew she wouldn't let it go and would never be part of any cover up. His plan wouldn't work if word of the aberrant androids didn't spread to the general populace. He was counting on their fear and paranoia to aid his plans and too much time had passed since he started already. He was growing impatient.

Earlier, he'd played part of the previous night's report from Sanders for his prisoner and watched Connelly for a reaction.

"Please," she begged. "I don't know what's happening, but I've got to be out there finding out what's causing this before something tragic happens. My whole company is at stake."

Todd merely laughed at her. "I know exactly what's happening. It's exactly as I planned." He slapped the gag back over her mouth and delighted in watching her eyes plead with him even as she struggled to talk through the gag. He left her there, getting emotional, and went back upstairs to resume work on the next phase of his project. He owed her no explanations. After all, she'd offered him none while she was hogging the spotlight and stealing all the funding and opportunities from people like him. Maybe he'd never tell her. He wasn't sure if he wanted to. It was enough to watch her dawning realization that his work was destroying everything she'd dedicated her life to—piece by piece. Knowing that it was just a matter of time before she lost everything.

Todd found that very satisfying indeed.

BY 9 A.M., BECKER, Maberry, Dolby, Simon and Lucas were waiting in the Homicide Unit's conference room on the 7th Floor at headquarters for the task force meeting spearheaded by Deputy Chief Melson. Joining them were Detectives Tom Bailey and Jerry Tucker from Homicide, with whom Lucas and Simon had worked on previous cases, Trevor Welch from the KCPD's Computer Services Unit, Deputy Chief Cara Atwell, newly promoted DC who headed KCPD's technology departments, among other responsibilities, Detectives Zedlar and Williamson and their Sergeant Terry DeMarco from Lenexa and Special Agent In Charge Hank Garner and the FBI's local tech guru, Agent Eugene Curtin.

After everyone had gotten coffee, tea, or juice and Danishes from trays on a counter that ran along the side wall, Melson convened the meeting with brief introductions.

"Since Central's Property Unit has been taking lead on this so far, perhaps we should start with them bringing us up to speed and take it from there," Melson suggested.

After nods and mumbled agreement from the others, Becker turned it over to Simon and Lucas to lay out the case so far. Simon stood, ignoring the whirring of laptops and crinkling of papers as he and Lucas stepped to the front of the room. They took everyone through the incidents at The Prism,

Simon's neighbor's house, then with Newton and Pascal, Lucas offering expertise on android functionality, programming, and so on as they went. Then they talked about Livia Connelly and her connection to Lucas and the KCPD before DeMarco interrupted.

Basketball-player tall, thin, with a thinning gray mop atop his head, DeMarco with well-toned arms and shoulders that made his suit jacket fit awkwardly, almost like it was a size too large. He had piercing brown eyes and spoke with a growly baritone rasp. "Perhaps since the Connelly disappearance is our case, my guys should take the lead on laying that out for everyone," he said.

Melson nodded. "Of course."

Lucas reluctantly sat down as Simon nodded and returned to his seat, the old leather cracking and squeaking beneath him. Zedlar and Williamson were standing up front, taking turns walking everyone through the Connelly abduction case so far. Jeff Zedlar was blonde, tall and thin with pale skin, while Sam Williamson was short, stocky, with darker hair and skin and a developing paunch, the strong smell of cheap cologne apparent to anyone who got too near.

"And we're absolutely certain the abduction case is related to these incidents with the rogue androids?" DC Atwell asked when they'd finished. Short and chubby with medium-long brown hair and hazel eyes, she looked like she could take on DeMarco all by herself and hold her own and had the attitude to match. Her reputation was as tough but fair and a damn good cop.

"Yes," Lucas and Simon said.

"Not one hundred percent," DeMarco countered.

"It seems highly likely given Connelly Lab's role with the

androids in question," Becker added.

"Doctor Connelly was helping us with the android cases when she was abducted," Simon said.

"And evidence in those cases was also taken," Lucas added.

"But that could be a coincidence?" DeMarco suggested.

"No," Lucas and Simon said again together, but Becker shrugged.

"Of course that's possible, however unlikely," she said.

"It's certainly worth staying informed on the abduction case while we work the other incidents," Melson said in a conciliatory tone.

"The main thing is," Zedlar said, "this abduction case is our jurisdiction. And we need to be able to work it our way without a lot of interference from the bleachers."

"Exactly," Williamson agreed.

"The bleachers?!" Simon blurted. "You're talking about a friend of ours here!"

"I'm an expert on Connelly Labs and their work," Lucas added.

"Which makes you two personally involved and the last people we'd want with their hands in our case," Zedlar said.

"Are you fucking kidding me?!" Simon said. "Technically, this was all our case before you guys ever heard about it. In fact, we found Steven's body and called you in on it."

"In our jurisdiction," Zedlar said.

"Exactly," Williamson echoed again.

"Is that all you do—echo his statements with affirmations?" Simon snapped, rising from his chair in anger.

Melson raised a palm. "Can everyone just calm down please?"

Simon sat down again, fuming.

"The purpose of forming a task force is to work together and share resources and information, not have a pissing contest about whose case is whose," Melson said.

"Well, when we don't know for sure the cases are connected, a task force seems a bit premature," DeMarco said.

"It's at Chief Weber's suggestion since aspects of both cases cross over city borders and involve officers from both departments," Melson said.

"Frankly, it's also quite possible we'll have androids acting out in the metropolitan outside either of our borders," Becker said. "Connelly Labs doesn't just supply androids to Kansas City proper."

"But the only incidents so far have been in our jurisdiction," Atwell said.

"Yes," Becker agreed.

"The Chief just felt it was time to start sharing information that might help both of us move forward on the two cases and better prepare a response if the cases expand into each other's territory," Melson said.

"We tend to be too busy to worry much about 'ifs,'" Zedlar said. "We're too focused on the now."

"So are we," Becker said.

"But the intent is not to take over either case at this point," Melson added. "Just to meet regularly and exchange information and resources as useful to help us both succeed at finding those responsible and preventing further incidents."

"As long as it doesn't take time away from what we need to do to find Doctor Connelly, fine," DeMarco said.

"Agreed," Williamson said and ignored Simon's glare.

"What we're prepared to do," Atwell said, "is have our

computer people, headed by Officer Welch here, set up a communication exchange using a database where all case info can be input for both departments' use. From that we can see how and if the cases intersect and coordinate efforts if and when appropriate."

"Since our people and yours will be working some of the same angles due to the obvious overlap, we feel it may save us time and duplicated effort," Melson said.

"We still have to do the legwork ourselves regardless of who anyone else has talked to," Zedlar said.

"We understand that," Atwell said. "But there may be cases where information our people uncover provides leads or insights useful to your case and vice versa."

"Exactly," Melson said and winked at Simon.

"That much seems helpful," DeMarco agreed.

"As long as we are not required to spend extra man hours inputting data," Williamson said. Simon was surprised the detective was capable of an original statement of his own.

"Well, if your IT people can coordinate with me, we should be able to make it so information is transferred to the database from your ordinary case records with the press of a few buttons," Welch interjected. Just under six feet, muscular with the beginnings of a beer belly, he looked like a short-haired Thor, his 70s style sport coat worn over a superhero t-shirt and jeans. It was decisively non-regulation for someone who worked out of headquarters but then geek squad personnel tended to dress the part when they could and rarely dealt with the public.

"The only additional labor required would be that involving logging in to the shared database to review our data and vice versa," Atwell said.

"I'll put you in touch with our IT," DeMarco said to Welch.

"Great," Melson said. "Progress."

"Has no one in KCPD expressed any trepidation about the fact you have an android leading your investigation on androids?" Zedlar asked.

"We're partners!" Simon replied.

"He's working under my supervision," Becker replied. "And his expertise has been invaluable so far."

"Right, until he gets infected with whatever it is that's cause the other androids to go crazy," Williamson said. "Then we'll see how useful he is."

"Hey! This android graduated top of his class from the Academy less than a year ago!" Simon said. "He happens to be one of the best cops I've worked with in nineteen years."

"That says more about the quality of your department personnel than it does about the android," Zedlar snapped.

"Fuck you!" Simon said, his fists clenching beneath the table as he fought the urge to jump up and throw a punch.

"No, fuck you, pal!" Zedlar said back.

"Hey! Enough!" Melson shouted, glaring at them all. "If you guys are incapable of acting like professionals, I'd be more than happy to set a meeting with both Chiefs to discuss removing all of you from either case! This coordination is happening whether you like it or not. So I suggest you put your dicks back in your pants and start focusing on your jobs, now!"

Chuckles erupted from Maberry, Dolby, Bailey, Tucker and the FBI team as Melson glared at Simon, Zedlar, Williamson, and DeMarco.

DeMarco raised a hand to his detectives. "You guys just make sure your people are doing their jobs and we'll be fine,

DC Melson, okay?"

"Our people are on top of it," Becker said, shooting De-Marco an annoyed look.

"We'll see to that," Melson echoed.

"One other question," Williamson said. "Why are the Feds here?"

"I was wondering that myself," Garner said as all eyes turned to him and his companion. Tall, fifties, in an expensive suit and shiny, polished dress shoes with slicked back hair and too much charm and voice, Garner was everything Simon hated about Feds. He'd led the assault team at the UnderCity terrorist case the previous Spring, and Simon had been glad Becker and others were left to deal with him more than Simon himself. Agent Eugene Curtin, Garner's companion was thirties, short and stocky with neatly trimmed dark hair and a beard, and except for his expensive dark suit, looked every bit the geek Welch did.

"I was just impressed you guys could stay quiet this long in a crowded room," Simon teased.

Garner actually laughed. "Well, it seemed like you guys might need the National Guard more than the FBI so far."

"We wanted you here to connect in regards to technology," Atwell said. "See what assistance you might provide and keep you in the loop."

"There's always the possibility either case could delve into areas of mutual concern," Melson said.

"Okay," Garner nodded. "Curtin here will provide whatever resource help we can."

Agent Curtin nodded from the chair beside him. "Just tell me what you need."

"Great," Melson said and smiled, clearly eager to maintain

the restored calm and pleasantness.

"We'll have our people set up the database and communicate with yours," Welch said.

"And we should be able to provide an overview of each case for everyone in a day or two," Atwell said.

"Fair enough," DeMarco said. "Did you need anything else from us?"

Melson shook his head. "No, this was just preliminary. At our Chief's request and yours."

The three Lenexa cops stood.

"Okay, we'll cooperate to the degree our department wishes," DeMarco said, and with that they nodded to everyone but Simon and Lucas and disappeared out the door.

"What a buncha assholes," Maberry said.

"Amen," Dolby agreed as Simon, Bailey, Becker, and Tucker uttered amused grunts in agreement.

"Kinda makes you miss working with us, does it?" Garner teased.

"Oh hell, we're far from that desperate," Bailey joked and everyone laughed. He and his partner were both fifteen-year veterans who'd been around almost as long as Simon. Tucker was fifties and a Santa Claus clone, while Bailey was taller, thinner, and musical with dark hair, and one of the first out gays in department history. They'd been assigned the Garcia homicide, which didn't appear like it would take much work, but that tied them to the android case and put them in the room.

"I can coordinate with Agent Curtin if you'd like," Welch said.

"Yes," Curtin agreed. "Might be useful to loop us in on that database, too, if you don't mind."

"We'll clear it with both Chiefs and make it happen," Atwell said.

"Great," Garner said and stood. "We'll get out of your hair then, unless you need us for anything else?"

Melson and Atwell exchanged a look and shook their heads. Then both stood and extended their hands, shaking first Garner's and then Curtin's across the table.

"We appreciate you coming in on such short notice," Melson said.

"Our pleasure," Curtin said.

"Good luck," Garner muttered to Melson and Atwell sympathetically and then the two Feds took their leave.

"His expertise aside," Atwell said as everyone stretched their legs and replenished beverages and snacks, "their point about having an android working this case is not something we can lightly dismiss. Not knowing the cause, there is a certain risk involved we'll need to keep a close eye on."

"Understood," Becker said in an agreeable tone.

Simon swallowed an angry retort and instead said, "Lucas has done more to advance this case so far than any other officer. We need him."

"No one's arguing that," Melson said.

"But the nature of computer viruses being what they are," Atwell added, "if this turns out to be a virus or some sort of infection that he could be exposed to, we need to watch carefully and be sure he isn't negatively affected."

"I am fine," Lucas said, and Simon knew the DC's words were echoing his partner's deepest fears about this case.

"He's fine," Simon said. "And he'll let me know if he's having any problems."

"We can't necessarily trust him to be forthcoming if he's

affected," Atwell said.

"I trust him with my life, and my daughter's life, too," Simon said.

"You're missing the point—" Atwell said.

"I resent the suggestion," Simon said.

"He's always had our backs," Dolby added.

"Hear, hear," Maberry said.

"There certainly is the possibility, if a virus is involved, of his programming being modified before he's even aware of it and in a way that would cause him to conceal it rather than be forthcoming," Welch said, then seeing Simon's glare, quickly added, "Just based on the history of malware."

"That's all I'm saying," Atwell said.

"We'll keep a close eye," Becker said, "and alert you of any concerns."

"Good," Atwell said and nodded, apparently satisfied, at least for the moment, so Simon let it go, despite Lucas' silent stare leaving him worried.

"Are you asking us to do anything special here?" Tucker asked and everyone turned to look at him.

"He means in regards to how we conduct our investigation and file reports and such with the database sharing," Bailey added.

"We'll handle it on our end," Welch said.

"It would be helpful if paperwork was filed in as timely a manner as possible to ensure quickest possible access for everyone," Atwell added.

"Shit," Bailey said. "Putting off paperwork is an art form it took us years to perfect."

Simon, Maberry, Dolby, and Tucker chuckled while Bailey and Melson smiled. Atwell just stared.

"We'll get it done as soon as we can," Tucker said.

"That's all anyone's asking," Melson said. The way the detectives leaned back in their chairs made their continued enthusiasm for the concept obvious.

"Okay, well, we should all get back to work soon," Becker said.

"Of course," Melson said. "One final thing. I know things got a little difficult—the Lenexa guys being not so enthusiastic about working together—"

"You mean being assholes," Maberry said.

Melson nodded. "But unless things change, there shouldn't be much need for direct interaction unless we have reason to cross over each other's city limits for interviews and such."

"In other words," Becker said, "do your best to keep it in our jurisdiction so you don't have to deal with them."

"Yes," Melson agreed and looked at Simon, "but if you do, I expect all of you to conduct yourself with the utmost professionalism at all times. Understood?" He glanced around the table until they'd each issued affirmations then leaned back in his chair and waved toward the door. "All right, get back to it."

Lucas was out the door so fast that Simon had to almost run to catch up with him as he got to the elevators.

"You okay?" Simon asked, preferring the dusty smell of the corridor to the musty carpet smell that had permeated the homicide conference room.

"It's exactly as I predicted," Lucas said.

"They were just asking questions," Simon said. "That's their job."

"They expressed very clear doubts about me," Lucas said.

"More like concerns about possible exposure," Simon

said. "They'd have the same concern for human cops if we were dealing with toxic waste or other dangerous substances or circumstances."

"But no one would question their competence because of it," Lucas snapped.

"They don't know you like we do," Simon said as Maberry, Dolby, and Becker turned the corner and joined them.

Becker looked straight at Lucas. "Are you okay?"

Lucas shrugged.

"He's concerned about their questions," Simon said.

"Don't worry," Becker said, putting a hand on Lucas' shoulder. "That's just them being who they are. We weren't worried for a moment, and we're the ones who have your back, okay?"

Lucas swallowed and then forced a nod. "Thank you."

"All right, you two find someone to help us examine Pascal's body," Becker said to Simon and Lucas, then turned to Maberry and Dolby. "You two head over to the Street Department. We got a call this morning about remains and residue of the android that fell in the wood chipper awaiting pickup."

"Jesus," Dolby said. "Talk about pieces..."

"Just pick them up and bring them back to the squad, okay?" Becker said as a ding sounded overhead and the elevator doors opened. They all stepped aboard and Lucas pushed the button for the basement. That would let them out in the corridor closest to the Cherry Street exit.

"You got it, boss," Maberry said as the doors closed again. They rode the rest of the way in silence.

CHAPTER 9

LUCAS AND SIMON'S first call was to Benn Liska, the office manager of Connelly Labs.

"I understand what you need, and any of our people would be happy to help if they can," Liska said. "But you have to understand that we were just in the process of expanding. Livia and Steven supervised all the activation to date. Our staff assembles the basics but they install the final brain and personality units themselves and then activate and calibrate the units before release. The doctor felt strongly this allowed her to verify the quality and protect her brand before she put units out into the world."

"Of course," Lucas said.

"But we were starting to grow so fast, she knew that wouldn't be possible much longer," Liska went on. "She just hadn't trained a replacement or replacements yet. So the components most likely to be involved were ones no one else here is intimately familiar with to the same degree. We can examine and compare them to specs and any notes, of course, and Livia and Steven both kept extensive records, but no one here is as likely to notice immediately and definitively anything out of place in the personality and brain control units."

"Well, is there anyone who might?" Simon asked.

"To be honest, Louie Fiedler and Bob Pruitt are your best bets locally, though I'm not sure how familiar they are specifically with our products," Liska said. "They're just the guys who have the most generally familiarity with the technology and what's involved as well as the equipment."

"If we can get one or both, can they use your equipment if needed?" Simon asked.

"We'd prefer they do," Liska said. "There are proprietary IP issues here, and Pruitt is a competitor. But look, we are all heartbroken about Steven and Livia and worried about her safety, so whatever it takes. She'll just have to forgive me if it backfires, and I'm sure she will."

"Thank you, Benn," Lucas said. "We'll get back with you once we've talked to Mister Pruitt and Mister Fiedler."

"We'll have the remains of the two affected units shipped over," Simon said.

"We'll be ready for them, and I'll have our best people standing by and leave room in the Lab," Liska said as he hung up.

Since Kansas City had only two android manufacturers, the obvious first choice for someone to look at the remains of the rogue androids was Bob Pruitt, founder of the smaller Pruitt's, whose work focused on heavy duty industrial models of particular interest to the freight and construction industries. Simon spoke with Bob Pruitt, while Lucas called Louie Fiedler to inquire if there were any other local experts he might recommend.

"It's terrible," Bob Pruitt said after Simon introduced himself. "I heard about Livia's abduction on the news. I do hope you have leads and can return her safely."

"So far, we've not had much luck," Simon said. "Do you have any idea where we should look?" Of course, Lucas had already checked out Bob Pruitt and ruled him a very unlikely candidate. A devout conservative Christian with an absolutely spotless record as far as any law enforcement agency in their database was concerned, he had also just returned that morning from a weekend convention in Las Vegas for the construction management industry, an alibi they had easily confirmed as rock solid, thus had not even been in town for the abduction and Steven's murder. Still, Simon always intended to chat with him at some point and having him come to them in this capacity would just make that easier.

"I don't," Pruitt said. "Livia was well liked in our industry and very smart but generous with helping others and sharing knowledge. She doesn't have any enemies that I know of."

"No one who's said any cross words about her?" Simon said, hoping to stir old memories.

"Not in my presence," Pruitt said, "but then those who know me are well aware I don't tolerate gossip."

"I see," Simon said, wondering if Pruitt knew or cared how unusual his attitude was in the present day and age. "We do have some remains of malfunctioning androids we need examined, and we had hoped you might assist us with that," he went on.

"Me?" Pruitt seemed surprised. "I would think Livia's own people would be better choices."

"Well, we spoke with her people and without her and Steven, they feel someone with broader knowledge of design could provide insights the remaining staff lack," Simon explained. "They mostly were responsible for implementing existing plans and programming machines or designing individual components. Livia and Steven oversaw the final activation and installation of brain and personality modules entirely themselves. How familiar are you with Connelly's models?"

"I own two," Pruitt said with surprising pride, "who work with me every day. Having them not only allowed me to study the competition but learn from her expertise in a very hands-on, practical way. And they've proved among our best workers at assembling our own product line."

Androids making androids. Simon had to wonder how DC Atwell and the Lenexa guys would react to that. *Probably like the assholes they are*, he thought. "If we can arrange it, would you be willing to meet us at Connelly Labs and take a look? Just see if there's anything extraordinary that stands out?" Simon asked.

"Of course," Pruitt agreed. "Anything I can do."

Fiedler seemed to feel as hesitant as Pruitt about his own knowledge and abilities, but not only agreed to meet them at Connelly Labs, but also insisted on having his people load up and ship over a couple of machines that Livia had been going to Fiedler Pharmaceuticals to use, so they could be employed right at Connelly Labs if needed. "I'll meet you there this afternoon. As soon as the remains are available, just have them call me," he'd told Lucas, the android recalled to Simon later.

"Now we just have to wait on Maberry and Dolby and arrange transport," Lucas said.

They spent the rest of the morning tracking down the nearest experts in St. Louis, Chicago, and Denver and checking their availability in case they were needed. One of them was attending a conference in Europe, but one each in St. Louis and Denver agreed to travel if it became necessary.

For his part, Simon felt relief that Lucas' business with the work seemed to be distracting him from his concerns about the doubts and questions Atwell and the Lenexa cops had raised in the initial task force meeting. He needed Lucas on his game to work this case and determined to find whatever ways he could to keep them both busy while they struggled to find a stronger lead.

TREVOR WELCH DID his usual magic and had the joint database functioning by early afternoon, so after arranging for the remains of Pascal and Newton Isaac to be transported to Connelly Labs, Simon and Lucas began reviewing Lenexa PD's case files and discovered that despite Todd Ward having been the last known person to see Livia Connelly before her disappearance—other than perhaps Steven—no one had yet located him for an interview. Ward had been on Simon and Lucas' mind ever since the discovery of Steven's body and Livia Connelly's disappearance, and since he happened to live in an older neighborhood south of the Plaza in the city, rather than Lenexa, where he worked, Simon and Lucas didn't need to coordinate with Lenexa P.D. to visit his residence.

Ward lived in a 1940s Tudor Revival home at 57th and Forest across the street from a small park. A driveway ran alongside the house on its north side, leading to a two-car garage with some kind of living or workspace above it. Simon parked on the street as another car pulled up onto the edge of the driveway and stopped. Simon recognized Zedlar and Williamson.

"Go ahead, make my day," Lucas muttered.

Simon grunted. "So many assholes, so little time. Just play it cool, partner."

"I'm always cool," Lucas said and Simon laughed. Lucas had it right. Simon had meant the warning more for himself.

They climbed out simultaneously and started across the lawn, dodging around torn black garbage bags of dead leaves as Zedlar and Williamson walked up the driveway and turned right onto the sidewalk leading to the front porch.

Williamson spotted them and tapped his partner on the arm.

"Fuck," Zedlar said. "Why are you here?"

"Working aspects of our case in our jurisdiction," Simon said. "You, on the other hand, are supposed to notify us before you work our area." He looked at Lucas. "Were you notified?"

"Not me," Lucas said.

"Me either," Simon said as they converged on the two Lenexa detectives and met up as the sidewalk joined the steps leading up to the front door.

"Hey, we're here," Williamson said.

"Consider yourself notified," Zedlar said.

"Hell, I'm just impressed to see he's tripled his vocabulary since the task force meeting," Simon said and smirked at Williamson. "You been studying up?"

"Fuck you," Williamson said.

"This is our case, so we'll take the lead," Zedlar said.

Simon coughed as Williamson brushed past him and the scent of cheap cologne overwhelmed his senses. Waving a hand in front of his nose, he joked, "Do you bathe in that stuff or just apply it in bulk?"

"That's my natural scent," Williamson said.

"The scent of cheap, desperate white guy, nice," Simon replied.

"Fuck off," Williamson said then extended a palm as Lucas and Simon joined him and his partner on the stoop. "Stop crowding us. Who taught you backup?"

Zedlar was trying the doorbell but no sound could be heard through the front door from inside the house.

Simon motioned to Lucas and started back down the steps. "We'll take a look at the garage and cover the back in case, that okay?" Simon snapped.

"I don't care what you do as long as you stay the fuck out of our way," Zedlar replied as he raised a hand and knocked loudly on the door.

Simon led the way left around the side of the house and along the driveway toward the garage. As they passed side windows, Lucas stopped and examined a loose wire that was hanging through the crack at the bottom of one. "His alarm appears broken," Lucas remarked, puzzled.

Simon stepped close and examined the wire. "Or installed by amateurs."

From the front of the house Simon heard Zedlar knocking again. "Mister Ward, Lenexa police, we'd like to speak with you about a case."

Simon and Lucas continued on around the side of the house to the back yard and approached the back door. Simon peered inside, seeing a medium-sized kitchen with no sign on any occupants. Then he noticed another wire running along the wall and down the door and tensed. It disappeared into the wall beside the door knob and lock.

"Step back a minute," Simon said. "Zedlar, Williamson, hang on!" he called as he followed Lucas away from the house toward the yard and dialed Zedlar on his cell. "I think this door is wired," he told Lucas.

"For an alarm?" Lucas wondered.

"If it is, it's not professional," Simon said.

"What the fuck do you want?!" Zedlar yelled from the front, and then answered the phone. "Why are you calling me?" The phone crackled with static in Simon's ear, muting parts of every other word.

"I think the house may be wired," Simon said and began explaining about the wires leading to the back door and the window on the side.

"You see anybody inside?" Zedlar asked.

"No," Simon said then heard Williamson through the phone in the background.

"This window's cracked," Williamson called.

"Wait, don't open—" Zedlar started to say, then the world exploded.

All Simon saw was a flash of light before he and Lucas were thrown back several yards, landing hard on their backs on the sidewalk as the house disintegrated. Wood, brick, and glass flew everywhere and the roof seemed to lift off the house and slam back down. Several walls and support beams had caved in, so it landed crooked and split into pieces.

"Not an alarm," Lucas muttered as the smell of burning wood, sulfur, and burning insulation filled the air. Flames rose from scattered spots throughout the house as smoke and dust clouded the air.

"No fucking shit," Simon said and looked around for his cell which was lying beside him in the grass. He picked it up. "Zedlar, you still there?" The line was dead.

Lucas stood beside him and offered a hand, pulling Simon to his feet. Together, they ran back around the house as sirens sounded in the distance and they heard muttering voices from the neighborhood around them.

"What happened?!" someone called.

"Jesus Christ! Did you see that?" called another.

Simon and Lucas rounded the front of the house to see Zedlar lying dazed on the sidewalk. Williamson's corpse was sprawled unnaturally across a bush in front of a window to the right of the front door. His hands were bloody stumps and his clothes were on fire.

"Fuck me," Zedlar muttered.

Lucas got on the radio and called dispatch as Simon knelt and examined Zedlar. "Don't get up. Are you injured?" Simon asked.

"Sam—" Zedlar said, struggling to sit up and look around.

"He's gone," Simon said, reliving the loss of his own partner two years past as he did. "I'm sorry."

"Son of a bitch wired the house!" Zedlar said, still stunned.

"An ambulance and units are en route," Lucas reported from their right.

"Gotta call my sergeant," Zedlar muttered.

"Lucas will call DeMarco, okay?" Simon said even as he saw Lucas already turning to dial using his internal cell. Zedlar tried to stand again but Simon put a gentle hand against his chest, steadying him in a seated position on the ground. "Just take it easy 'til the paramedics can check you out."

"You guys okay?" a neighbor woman asked as she approached across the lawn.

"Please stay back, ma'am," Lucas said, raising a hand.

"Do you think Todd was home?" another neighbor asked from beside her as Simon took in the destroyed Tudor Revival and shook his head. If he had been, the man was surely dead

"JESUS. BLEW HIS arms off his fucking body," Maberry said as he, Simon, Becker, Lucas, and Dolby watched the Coroner's squad pull a tarp back over Williamson's corpse, having finished their examination. Simon had a Band-aid on his forehead just over his left eye where a paramedic had examined him and another on his right hand. There were visible contusions mixed with dirt on his right cheek and neck as well. Altogether, he felt lucky it wasn't worse. For his part, Lucas looked almost pristine except for some dirt and tear in his shirtsleeve.

"Must have been some explosion," Dolby said.

"You're lucky none of the rest of you were hurt," Becker said, shaking her head.

"We spotted wires and stepped away from the house," Simon said, crinkling his nose again. The air still stank of sulfur, burning wood, insulation, and melted plastic, even after the flames had been extinguished to smoldering by the Kansas City Fire Department.

"Detective Zedlar's the lucky one," Lucas said. "He was up on the stoop."

Almost as if hearing his name had been his queue, Zedlar appeared with Sergeant DeMarco.

"I want this Todd Ward dead! I want him to hurt!" Zedlar shouted.

"We do not know for sure yet that he's responsible," Lucas said.

"His kind, your kind," Zedlar said. "I'll shoot any of you that get in my way."

Simon heard a buzzing and turned to see a media drone crossing the police tape nearby, shooting footage of the scene.

Becker frowned, glaring at him. "Detective George is not to blame for what happened to your partner. He and Detective Simon tried to warn you."

Zedlar scoffed. "Too little too late." He glared at Becker, Simon, and then Lucas again before spotting the drone and spinning to run toward it. "Get the fuck outta here, you vultures!" He placed himself between the drone and his partner's body and extended his arms, blocking its camera with his palms. Simon empathized. He'd felt the same when drones showed up at the scene of his own partner's death a few years before.

"Sam Williamson was a good man," DeMarco said. "He's got a wife and kids."

"We're sorry for their loss," Becker scolded. "But that doesn't excuse his abusing my people."

"Fuck you!" Zedlar screamed and now started pounding the camera with the grip of his sidearm.

"Just stay out of his way and it won't be a problem," DeMarco retorted and locked eyes with her before turning and heading off after Zedlar.

"These guys are such assholes," Dolby said.

"Thank the Chief for us for inviting them to the party," Simon said.

"They were invited by whoever killed Steven Sears and abducted Doctor Connelly in their city limits," Becker said. "The Chief didn't have a choice."

"Yeah, well, I think we'll be relying on that database a lot on this one," Simon said.

"No doubt," Maberry agreed.

"I'm fine with that," Becker said. "I'll run interference whenever I can."

"You do not mind dealing with assholes?" Lucas asked.

"When you get rank, it goes with the job, Detective," Becker said as they all turned at the sound of buzzing to see two more media drones circling them.

"Uh uh, behind the crime scene tape!" Becker scolded and pointed. "You guys know the rules."

"We have a deadline for the mid-day, can we please get a statement?" a male voice emanating from one of them marked KCTV5 said.

"Talk to our media office," Becker said and turned away.

"What about for me?" a familiar female voice said. Simon and the others turned again to see Holly Sanders striding across the lawn toward them, weaving past debris.

Becker whirled and raised her voice, looking at a group of uniforms huddled between the yellow crime scene tape and their cruisers nearby. "Can some of you do your damn job and keep these people outta here?!"

"Sorry, Sarge," one of them said as he and his female partner hurried toward Sanders, while two others went to chase off the drones.

"Come on, Sergeant," Sanders sad. "A major explosion in the middle of South Plaza is a story. At least tell us if this is related to the android case or Livia Connelly's disappearance?"

"No comment," Becker said as Sanders shot Simon a pleading look.

"Come with me, ma'am," the male uniform said as he gently took the reporter by the arm.

"Sorry," Simon mouthed to her and shrugged.

"When you're through flirting, can you get back to your

job, too, Detective?" Becker snapped as Maberry and Dolby jittered.

Simon cleared his throat. "What? I was just being polite."

"Well, go do it to witnesses while you get some statements," Becker said.

"Yes, ma'am," Simon and Lucas said together as they turned and headed for a trio of neighbors waiting beyond the crime scene tape.

Simon was starting to think a friendly reporter like Holly Sanders might be useful to them. Feeding her a few choice tidbits to leak in her reports might be just enough to stir up some leads, either from witnesses among the public who might realize they'd seen something helpful and call in or from rattling the perpetrator's cage enough to trigger a response. Something was better than nothing, and a big fat nothing was about what they had right now. With Williamson and Garcia both dead, things were escalating fast. It was only a matter of time before the press, the public, and government officials started applying pressure to the KCPD to identify those responsible.

The problem was, the higher-ups didn't agree yet, so in addition to policy, they'd been ordered to keep this away from the press. And Simon was sympathetic with Lucas's own concerns about public reaction to news of the story spreading more broadly, but they had to do something or they'd never get the leads they needed to solve the case.

He let Lucas take the lead on interviewing the neighbors. All three had been inside their own houses when the explosion occurred and heard very little. They'd rushed outside to see flying debris, flames, smoke, and then the cops. All three interrupted the interview with the usual worried questions about their own safety, why the police were there, and so on.

Todd Ward was a quiet neighbor, nice guy, normal but kept to himself. The usual.

When their statements were finished, Lucas and Simon urged them to go home and left them there, chattering away and still rubbernecking the scene from behind the crime scene tape, as they moved back across the lawn. Simon glanced over to see Holly Sanders still watching him from the opposite side of the lot beside her Fox 4 news van.

DC Melson appeared and ducked under the crime scene tape as one of the uniforms lifted it for him, then strode purposefully across the lawn to where Maberry and Dolby were briefing Becker as Simon and Lucas joined them.

"What've we got?" he asked, and then got a look at Simon's and Lucas's injuries and added, "Are you two okay?"

"Yeah," Simon said simultaneously with Lucas's "I am fine, sir."

"Simon and Lucas and the detectives from Lenexa all came here to interview the owner, a possible witness," Becker explained.

"We weren't together," Simon added.

Melson nodded. "I would've assumed that after the tone of our meeting."

"No response to knocks on the door. Apparently, Williamson saw a cracked window and was opening it when it set off an explosion," Becker said.

"The whole place was wired," Simon said. "We were in the process of warning them when it blew."

"Jesus," Melson muttered. "Thank God no one else was seriously injured."

"We were lucky," Lucas agreed.

Melson turned and scanned the assembled media, then

said, "We've got someone from Media on their way to handle them."

"What are we going to tell them?" Dolby asked.

"Just what happened, leaving out any possible case connections," Melson said.

"You know, the media might be able to help us here," Simon said. "Just a little bit more information might stir up some leads." When Lucas shot him a worried look, he added, "It could also help avert misinformation. If we don't give them something, they might just run with their imaginations, make things worse."

"The Chief and Media are working on aspects of that now," Melson said. "Above our pay grade." He looked at Simon and Lucas. "Why don't you two take the rest of the day. You deserve a break after this." Then to Becker, "You need them?"

She shook her head. "Nope. Just email the reports and statements."

"Okay," Lucas said.

"Can we at least put out a BOLO on Todd Ward?" Simon asked. "We need to talk to this guy."

"Absolutely," Melson agreed and looked at Becker.

"I'll make the call," she said with a nod.

As he and Lucas made their way across the lawn to the Interceptor, parked near the media vans, Simon's eyes met Holly Sanders' and he had a thought. "Give me a second, Lucas. You can drive," he said, handing Lucas the keys. Then he turned and walked over to where Sanders was waiting.

"Detective," she greeted him then frowned seeing the wounds on his face and neck. She reached up to gently touch his injured cheek. "I'm glad you're okay."

"Thanks," Simon replied quietly.

She looked at him curiously. "You have something for me?"

He patted the pocket where he still had her business card. "If I do, I'll give you a call, okay?" Then he turned and strode quickly back to the Interceptor, climbing inside as Lucas started the engine and turned to look at him, smiling.

"What?" Simon asked.

"Did you ask her out?" Lucas asked.

"No, of course not."

"Do you need a good pick up line? I've learned a few. 'You complete me.'…' You had me at hello.'…'You make me want to be a better man.'"

"Would you drive already?" Simon said, shifting in his seat and looking away from Lucas' cheerful stare.

"'It would be so nice growing old with you," Lucas continued, quoting more movies Simon didn't recognize. "'You're the girl of my dreams…and apparently I'm the man of yours.'"

"Just shut the fuck up and drive, damn it!" Simon growled and flipped on the radio, drowning his partner out with the pulsing guitar of the Michael Anthony-Sammy Hagar team-up Sammy Hagar Group's "I'm Over You, Get Over Yourself," which somehow seemed appropriate.

As they drove off, he caught Sanders watching him go, a confused look on her face. He would call her. Once he figured out what to give her. Media office or no, they needed to kick start this case. Someone aggressive like Sanders could shake trees they didn't even know about. He just had to be careful. For both his sake and for Lucas.

CHAPTER 10

"YOU'RE YAWNING AGAIN," Lucas said as he steered the Interceptor off I-35 and turned left on West 95th Street the next morning.

"Rough night," Simon said as soon as he'd finished the yawn and could speak again. He'd gone home and had dinner with Emma, then spent the evening in front of the television, but not watching, thinking—about Holly Sanders. He had her card. He'd dropped a hint he might be calling. But he couldn't stop running over and over in his mind the pros and cons. When he wasn't thinking about that, he was picturing her sleek curves. More than once he growled as he downed another gulp of Pabst. *Jesus Christ. Grow up, John. For God's sake.* But the scolding only started the thought cycle all over again.

He was interrupted when Louie Fiedler called and asked them to meet him, Bob Pruitt, and Benn Liska at Connelly Labs the next morning. After seeing Simon yawn half a dozen times, Lucas had insisted on driving. Simon gave in because it gave his partner something to do besides chatter and bother him and because he was indeed tired and wanted to think things through as they drove.

He'd finally called Sanders just after eleven, apologizing for calling her so late as soon as she answered.

"Are you kidding?" she laughed. "In my business it's actually considered beating the odds when I sleep through the night. Besides, I have to be up in five hours or so anyway. You have something for me?"

"Maybe," Simon said, hesitating.

"I can put you on deep background, of course," she said. "I know KCPD has a policy."

"Yes, but—" Simon hesitated again. "How about if you tell me what you know so far and I see if I can fill in a few gaps."

"Are we talking about the android case or the Connelly case?" she asked.

"Well, they may be connected," Simon said.

Her voice brightened. "Really?" And she began filling him in with Simon occasionally interjecting. He only told her things he knew to be fact. And he didn't tell her everything. He made no mention of Todd Ward as a suspect and even deflected it when she asked if he was. He also didn't name any of the robots or owners and insisted it was on her to identify players by name, including anyone injured. He was just going to help point her in the right direction to see if she might stir up some leads that could help them with the case.

"I have no problem with that," she said and continued.

They spoke for about twenty minutes, and when they were through, Simon felt he'd given her enough connectors to push her further along without giving away any vital secrets or information that might endanger the case.

"You are so awesome," she said and he could hear her grinning on the other end.

"I can't do this again," he said.

"You're not gonna be my CI?" she teased.

Simon chuckled. "Yeah, no."

"Still, this helps a lot," she said.

"Look, promise me you'll only report what you can con-firm independently, and then only if the public needs to know," Simon said. "There are concerns about causing undue panic—"

"Or making things hard for your partner?" she asked.

"Well, off the record, he's pretty disturbed by this," Simon said.

"I can only imagine," Holly said. "Worrying he might be next."

"Promise me you won't say that on air," Simon said, suddenly somber again.

"Okay, I gotcha. I promise."

After quick "goodbyes," they hung up and Simon tried to sleep, but instead wound up spending a restless night alternating between fantasizing about kissing Holly Sanders and worrying he'd opened a can of worms that he might come to deeply regret.

"We are here," Lucas said, breaking Simon out of his reverie as he pulled the Interceptor to a stop in the parking lot outside Connelly Labs.

"I hope they found something," Simon said.

"I hope what they found is answers, the key to something we can manage quickly," Lucas said.

"It may not be, pal."

Lucas unfastened his seatbelt and opened the door, ignoring eye contact. "I pray you're wrong."

Liska met them in the lobby and walked with them back to Connelly's private lab where Pruitt and Fiedler were waiting. The Lab had been cleaned up since the day of the abduction and murder. Everything straightened, cleaned, and any trace of blood gone. Simon even caught a hint of industrial cleaners in the air.

"Did you find anything?" Lucas asked immediately as they shook hands and greeted each other.

"Actually, yes," Pruitt said.

"I wouldn't have realized what it was on my own, but Bob recognized it fairly quickly," Fiedler added.

Pruitt led them to a table where pieces of Pascal and Newton Isaac's remains had been broken down to their basic components—circuit boards, fiberglass, metal, and so on. Pruitt flipped on a machine, projecting images of circuits on an LED screen next to it. "It's the residue that did it for me."

"Residue of what?" Simon asked as they all crowded around the screen.

"Zinc mostly," Pruitt said. "CeO2 as well sometimes, and the dead particles when they stop working." He used a laser pointer to point to areas of the screen where small chips were covered in a kind of white residue. It reminded Simon of the residue left by acid when batteries leaked, only there were distinct patterns in it, like puzzle pieces of a matrix.

"Wait a minute," Simon said. "What particles?"

"Nanoparticles," Pruitt and Fiedler said in unison.

"This is magnified several thousand times or you'd never see them," Fiedler added.

"Nanoparticles?" Lucas said. "So it's sabotage for sure." There was a tightness in his eyes as if he was pained by the words.

"We already knew that," Simon said.

"Well, this confirms it certainly," Fiedler said, nodding.

"Basically, what we think happened is someone injected nanoparticles or otherwise introduced them to the targeted androids that allowed changes in their programming and behavior," Pruitt said, with a hint of sadness but his expression remained all business.

"Wait, so someone is controlling them or they are just corrupting and acting on their own impulses?" Simon asked.

"Our best guess is both," Fiedler said. "But we'll have to do a bit more looking to see if we can tell for sure."

"Is there any evidence of who might have done this?" Lucas asked, clutching his hands together.

"No," Fiedler said.

"Well, not yet," Pruitt. "They're so microscopic that we have to really magnify to see any details."

"We may see more once we clean the residue off," Pruitt said.

"You can do that?" Simon asked.

"Well, it's not easy, but I believe so, yes," Fiedler said.

"Who locally deals in nanoparticles?" Simon asked.

"Several places," Liska said. "We started with a couple off the top of our heads, then I did the research while they worked. Made a few calls, Googled." He tapped buttons on a tablet. "I'm sending the list to Lucas, okay?"

"Perfect," Simon and Lucas said together.

Lucas went quiet as he scanned his inner computer, probably reading the list. "There's ten names here."

"Those are the local experts we're aware of," Liska said.

"Any suggestion where to start?" Simon asked.

"Kent Holloway," Fiedler said. "He's a bit of an opportunist but he knows everyone in the field because of it."

"He'd know who's into what aspects for sure," Liska said. "His number and address are in the file."

"Got it," Lucas confirmed.

"Any of these guys you think might get involved in something like this?" Simon asked.

"Holloway," Liska and Fiedler said together.

Pruitt shrugged. "He's arrogant, and he's got a bit of a shyster attitude, but he's always been straight with me."

"He's who I'd go to," Fiedler said, "if I were an investigator."

"Call us the moment you find anything," Lucas said as he and Simon started for the door.

"You know, I haven't heard from Todd Ward since the day Livia disappeared," Fiedler called after them. "And my assistant's reached out and gotten voicemail and no return calls."

Simon stopped and turned back in the doorway as Lucas hurried on out into the hall past him. "Well, his house blew up when we went to check on him this morning."

"My God!" Pruitt said.

"Was Todd home?" Fiedler asked, looking shocked.

Simon shook his head. "No one was home."

"But you think he might be involved?" Fiedler asked, eyes widening, his voice rising in pitch.

"Do you?" Simon asked.

Fiedler shook his head. "I just can't imagine it."

"We're not sure," Simon said. "But if you hear from him, call us immediately." Simon started turning again then stopped and added, "And be careful."

Fiedler looked tense and unsettled. "I will."

And then Simon hurried off, vainly attempting to catch up with his partner. But Lucas was gone, probably at the car already. Simon found himself hoping he wouldn't have to chase any more androids on foot working this case, because a determined android could walk faster than most humans ran.

KENT HOLLOWAY'S OFFICE was in a storefront at the end of a strip mall off East 89th Street in Indian Village, a suburb straight south of downtown. Roughly twenty-five minutes by car from KCPD headquarters. From Lenexa, it took a little less.

Simon drove while Lucas did a little research on the net. "Seems like most of the nanotech industry in Kansas City is tied to one of the universities," he said.

"Of course it is," Simon said. "That's where the funding is."

Lucas frowned. "Connelly Labs is self-funded."

"Yes, Livia has done very well, but she's smart and also lucky," Simon said.

"This Holloway is quoted a lot," Lucas noted.

"Does he sound like he knows what he's talking about or is he just blowing smoke?" Simon asked.

"Blowing smoke? He is not using consumable combustibles in any of the images," Lucas said.

Simon laughed. "Consumable combustibles, that's a new one. I meant does he sound actually intelligent on the subject or like someone who is making up some b.s. that sounds good?"

"Oh, talking out his ass," Lucas said with a nod of understanding. "He sounds somewhere in between. He definitely sounds like someone very fond of himself. He says things like, 'The reason people come to me is I'm the top expert in Kansas City,'" Lucas said. "Maybe it's true."

"If you have to say it yourself, nine times out of ten, it's total bullshit, trust me," Simon said.

When they walked into the storefront office of Tomorrow's Solutions, Inc., Holloway's firm, Simon knew his assessment was right. If Holloway was receiving any funding, he sure as hell wasn't spending it on office space. The walls were plain white, the front room small and crowded. A blonde who looked like she had surprising mileage for someone her age—early thirties Simon guessed though from her looks she could be much older—sat behind a metal desk with matching file cabinets on either side and a multi-line phone facing a flat screen monitor with a keyboard and mouse.

"Can I help ya?" she managed in between chomps on a large wad of chewing gum.

Simon and Lucas badged her.

"KCPD Detectives Simon and George here to see Kent Holloway," Lucas said.

"Well, shit, hang on," she said and punched a button on the phone, holding a receiver to her ear. "Yeah...cops are here...asking for you...I don't know, you want me to chase them off?"

Both Detectives shot her stern enough looks she quickly thought better of that.

"...Uh, on second thought, I don't think they're going anywhere..." She listened a moment then cupped the receiver with a hand. "What's this about?"

"Police business," Simon said sternly.

"They won't say..." she said, uncupping the receiver and putting it back to her ear. "Yeah...okay..."

She hung up the phone and went back to her screen. "Sit. He'll be out to get ya in a moment or two."

"Thank you," Lucas muttered as he and Simon stepped back and looked at the faded faux leather chairs with metal arms and legs and decided to wait standing.

It was about ten minutes before a man in his early forties, just under six feet tall, chubby with a neatly trimmed beard and brown hair and a permanent smirk appeared from the back and looked at them expectantly. Simon got a smarmy feeling just looking at him. "I'm Kent Holloway."

They badged him and stepped forward as he stretched out a hand and shook with them each in term. His hand was slimy, his grip weak. Simon wiped his hand subtly on his pants leg as they followed Holloway through a door and down a short corridor to a larger back office which was much nicer than the rest of the suite they'd seen so far. The cheap cologne he wore added to his smarminess.

"You do nanotech development here?" Simon asked with a quizzical tone as he looked around, taking it all in.

Holloway led them into a private office that was so pristine and upscale in appearance it looked like it belonged in a Fortune 500 high rise or law firm rather than a strip mall. "We hire out for development," Holloway said. "This office is for sales and conceptualization." He hurried across the room and slid behind a large futuristic desk that looked more like some kind of Picasso sculpture than anything functional though a flat portion did contain a flat screen monitor keyboard, mouse, and a tablet as well as a charging station for devices.

As he slid into a large, black executive chair, Holloway smiled and asked, "How can I help you?"

Simon continued taking in the room. The dark blue walls were covered with some substance that had an odd look. It wasn't paint or wallpaper, it almost shimmered.

"You like that?" Holloway asked, almost sing-song, and Simon turned to see their host enjoying watching their reaction.

He pulled out a small, slim remote and clicked a button. Suddenly the walls changed to a bright red color, almost blinding, that forced Simon to squint. "Nanoparticles in action. I can set it to any color I like." Mercifully, the color changed to a dark purple, then a light pink, then cycled through shades of green, brown, yellow, orange, black, and back to the original blue. "Just something fun a colleague whipped up. Keeps me from getting bored."

Jesus, Simon thought, imagining the possibilities if crooks ever applied this tech to vehicles and more. They could change appearance in the middle of a car chase or investigation and throw off cops. This kind of tech gave Simon the heebie jeebies. Then he looked at his partner and realized, *I work with that every day.*

"So Tomorrow's Solutions is more of a broker rather than direct development?" Lucas asked.

"We do both," Holloway said, looking offended. "Just because I'm not hands-on with science and engineering doesn't mean I'm not the developer. My ideas are the basis on which it all happens."

"I see," Lucas said, clearly not impressed. "Ever do any work with androids?"

"No, not really," Holloway said, his eyes narrowing, brow creasing. "What exactly brings you Detectives here?" he asked, sounding less friendly.

"You know anyone developing nanoparticles that might be used like a virus to modify existing tech?" Simon asked.

Holloway grunted. "That's always an area of study because it can be used in many applications. It's not illegal."

"Depends how it's used," Simon said.

"Well, I am an honest businessman, so I wouldn't know

anything about uses other than those for healthcare and advancing infrastructure, tech, and so on," Holloway said.

"Okay." Simon shrugged. "Someone told us if we want to talk to 'the man' in nanotech in Kansas City, the guy with his ear to the ground on all new developments, you'd be him. But I guess we got the wrong guy." He turned and started for the door.

"Look," Holloway called and Simon turned back. "There may be one guy. Been asking a lot of odd questions. But he's not someone I'm involved with, you understand? I don't want a part of anything illegal. This guy is a real opportunist."

Simon fought the urge to smile, deciding it wouldn't be the right time to mention that was how others had described Holloway himself.

"Do you have a name?" Lucas asked.

"His name's Paul Knox," Holloway said. "Let me ask Wendy if we have his number." He punched a line as he picked up the phone. "Wendy, can you check the Rolodex for Paul Knox."

"You still use a Rolodex?" Simon frowned.

"Nah," Holloway said, covering the receiver. "I just like calling it that. The guy has called a few times to pick my brain but I got a bad feeling and didn't want any part of him. But Wendy keeps call logs and should have his number. Provided it wasn't cloned or something."

He listened into the phone a moment then jotted something onto a Post-It. "Thank you." He tore the Post-It off and offered it to Simon.

"Post-Its?" Simon said. "You have nanoparticle wallpaper and you still use Post-Its?"

"Whatever works," Holloway said with a shrug.

Lucas step forward and took the number.

"Hope it helps," Holloway said, his eyes eager, but not with excitement. More as if he'd be glad to be rid of them.

"We need names of anyone you know who might be working in nanoparticles that we can talk to," Simon said.

"Well, um, let me think..." Holloway said.

"That's okay, you can email us." Simon slid his KCPD card across the desk. "But I'll expect to hear from you with anything helpful."

"So we don't have to come back," Lucas added ominously as Holloway snatched up the card and nodded.

"Yeah, yeah, I'll get right on that," he said.

Simon shot Lucas a look and winked, proud of him. His partner was learning. He'd played it just right. "We'll show ourselves out," he said. Then he turned and went back out into the corridor toward the lobby.

"Where to next?" Lucas asked.

"You running that number?"

"Yes."

"We see what that turns up, and then maybe talk to one of the others on the list Pruitt and the others provided."

They opened the door and passed Wendy who was still chomping her gum as she stared at them going past. Simon waited to say anything further until they were in the parking lot.

"That guy feel right to you?"

"No," Lucas replied. "But I wouldn't call it arrogance."

"Well, overconfidence for sure," Simon said. "I got the feeling we made him nervous."

"Just the way we like it," Lucas cracked.

Simon chuckled. "Exactly." He headed for the driver's

side as Lucas climbed into the Interceptor.

"I got an address for Paul Knox," Lucas said as he shut the passenger door and buckled his seatbelt.

"Home or office?" Simon asked as he slid into the seat and closed the driver's door.

"720 East 70th near Holmes Park," Lucas said. "I believe it's a residence."

"That's less than five minutes from here. Let's go," Simon said as he fastened his own seatbelt and pushed the start button for the ignition, then pulled the Interceptor out of the parking space and headed for East 89th Street.

PAUL KNOX'S HOUSE was a two story World War I Eclectic-style home, rectangular with multi-pane windows framed by shutters, a red-tiled roof, and a wrought-iron balcony over a white stone foundation. Simon parked the Interceptor in the driveway and walked with Lucas toward the front stoop. There was no obvious sign of activity so they knocked and waited.

Still no movement. After a few minutes, Lucas knocked again. "Mister Knox, police. Please come to the door," he called.

"He not answering?" a female voice said and they turned to see an elderly black woman leaning out the front door next door.

"Not yet," Simon said.

"Ma'am, do you know Mister Knox?" Lucas asked.

"It's Tamika," the woman said, "and yes. He's been my neighbor for ten years. Quiet, but nice enough."

"When was the last time you saw him?" Simon asked.

Her face screwed up a bit as she thought then she coughed and said, "Maybe yesterday, day before. Anyway, he's gotta be home. Back door's been open all day."

"The back door's open?" Simon asked as he exchanged with Lucas.

"Yes, I saw it when I was watering my flowers this morning," Tamika said.

"Thank you," Lucas said as he followed Simon down off the stoop and walked around the house on the west side toward the back.

As they rounded the corner to the back side, Simon saw a screen door was ajar. And as they approached, they found the inner door was cracked as well. Simon stepped up to the door and knocked, raising his voice, "Mister Knox? Police. Are you home?"

Again, there was no answer, so Simon looked at Lucas and their hands went to weapons. Then Simon pushed open the back door and the minute he did, the smell of death almost knocked him off his feet—rotting flesh combined with feces, a musty mothball-like scent, and something similar to rotten eggs. It was overwhelming. Simon coughed and covered his nose, stepping back again as Lucas shot him a look.

"What is it?" Lucas asked.

"Someone's dead inside," Simon said, wondering for a moment if the android's lack of olfactory senses was a blessing or a curse for a detective. At the present moment, he figured it was a blessing for sure.

"Oh," Lucas said as understanding dawned on his face.

Together, they drew weapons and moved through the house in standard search pattern, each one backing up the other as they methodically checked each room, every closed door. The place was definitely a bachelor pad, not filthy, but definitely not tidy either—newspapers haphazardly stacked in a corner behind the kitchen table, left over dishes piled in the sink, spots on the counters where food had been prepared that had not yet been wiped away and so on. There was dust on the doorframes and bookshelves and the carpet and wood floor both looked as if they hadn't seen a vacuum in a while.

They found the body on a recliner in the living room just out of view of the front door. But as a matter of safety, they continued the search, clearing the first floor, then working the second, and then going down to the basement as well.

The deceased was alone in the house. They holstered their weapons and Simon carefully checked the body for ID, while Lucas called it in over the radio. There was dried blood trailing down his face from a single gunshot wound in his forehead and brain matter splattered on the recliner, rug, and wall behind it. A driver's license in a wallet Simon found in the deceased's pocket was for Paul Knox.

"It's him," Simon confirmed after checking the picture. "Jesus. He's probably been here for days." Simon pulled out his cell phone and tapped the screen but it was dead. Flicking the power button twice had no effect. "Shit."

"Should I call crime scene?" Lucas asked, noting the trouble.

"Yes, call them in," Simon said, "then we'll search the place to see if we can find any evidence tied to the android case or other clues as to who might have killed him."

They performed a preliminary search until the crime

scene unit and coroner arrived along with several uniforms and turned up nothing. But there was a laptop, tablet, and cell phone on chargers in an office next to the master bedroom on the second floor. Simon had them collected as evidence and the contents would be searched.

Moments later, Detectives Bailey and Tucker arrived, having drawn the case from the homicide pool and Simon and Lucas filled them in and turned it over, heading back to Central.

Later that night, after acquiring a new cell at the nearest T-Mobile outlet, Simon took Emma out for dinner and dropped her back at her mother's. His new cell rang as he drove his Charger across I-70 toward Fairway.

The cheery voice of Holly Sanders greeted him when he answered. "Good evening, Detective," she said.

"Did you find something to help us with the case?" Simon asked.

"Not yet, but I heard you caught a homicide. I was wondering if it's connected."

"Not sure yet," Simon said, passing through downtown and slowing as he kept his eyes peeled for the I-35 ramp coming up ahead.

"Rumor has it the deceased, Paul Knox, has ties to nanotech," she continued.

"Yes, so we were told," Simon replied. "We didn't find anything linking him."

"But someone murdered him."

"That we determined from the bullet hole in the middle of his forehead," Simon said as he turned onto I-35 south.

"So you think there's some kind of nano connection beyond the nanochips used in manufacturing the androids?"

she asked.

"I can't say for sure," Simon said, not wanting to reveal Pruitt's and Fiedler's findings just now. "But we have a theory that might be the case."

"So if I look into nanotech—"

"Let's just say we'd be shaking the same trees most likely, " he replied, then cleared his throat. "Look, you can't just call me looking for information. I will call you when I have something I can give you. I only want to hear from you if you develop a potential lead, okay?"

"To avoid trouble with your bosses, sure," she said. "Okay, I'll work this angle though and let you know."

"Okay," Simon said and hung up as he swung left onto the offramp to Mission Road, heading for home and starting to wonder if using Holly Sanders had been a big mistake.

CHAPTER 11

LUCAS ARRIVED AT Central promptly at seven-forty-five a.m., fifteen minutes early, and was striding through the halls from the parking lot to the Property Crimes squad room on the second floor, when it began. People he passed by every day, people he worked with, stopped talking as he passed them and stared or shot him funny looks.

"Good morning," he said with a smile, and a few nodded or mumbled it back, but most just looked away. And as he moved on, he could hear their whispers.

As he neared the squad room he heard his partner's voice. "The coroner estimated the guy had been dead at least three days. They had to pry the remote from his hand."

"Jesus, the soiled recliner is the worst," Dolby replied.

"Good morning, Lucas," Becker said with a smile as she encountered him at the entrance to the squad room and they walked in together.

"Good morning, Sergeant," Lucas said. "Did something happen?"

"Did you see the news?" she asked.

"No." He shook his head.

"Hey, pal," Simon called from his cube as he saw them coming in. Maberry and Dolby were gathered around as he filled them in on Paul Knox. "Sergeant."

"Simon, you and Lucas in my office please, now," Becker said.

"Doesn't the task force meeting start at eight-thirty?" Simon asked as he stood and walked over to join them.

"Yes, but there's something I want you to look at first," Becker said. "Maberry and Dolby, you guys too."

When they'd all joined her in her office, she pulled up the local Fox affiliate's web page and sent video to an LED screen on the wall. "This is from the seven a.m. broadcast," she said.

"We have breaking news this morning on a frightening new outbreak," the anchorwoman, Carly, said. "Holly Sanders reports from Lenexa."

Holly Sanders appeared on the screen in front of Connelly Labs and begin to report. "It appears our new android citizens are under some kind of attack. Sources tell me the KCPD have been investigating an outbreak causing aberrant, even violent behavior among local androids, and Fox 4 has learned the cause may be linked to nanotech."

"Jesus," Maberry said as several images flashed across the screen of Fiedler Pharmaceuticals, Pruitt's corporate office, Paul Knox's home, Central Middle School, and Prism night club. Lucas watched his friends, gauging their reactions. Would they whisper and stare around him now?

"All of these locations are linked to either attacks or possible involvement in them," Sanders went on.

"How'd she get this?" Dolby asked.

"No idea," Becker said.

"The department has refused so far to release any official reports on the incidents," Sanders said as a photo of Lucas filled the screen. Lucas managed to stay on his feet, but felt as if his insides were falling. "But this reporter has learned their own famed android officer, Detective Lucas George, is among those leading the investigation."

"Oh fuck," Simon muttered.

"How long he'll be safe in this capacity with an outbreak on the loose remains to be seen, but we're determined to bring you the latest updates as soon as we can get them," Sanders said before Becker muted the volume.

"The Chief is pissed," Becker said. "Whoever leaked this is in deep shit."

"No wonder everyone is staring at me," Lucas said sadly, unable to meet their eyes. Everything he'd feared most was starting to happen. He'd finally made traction being accepted by his fellow officers as a full member of their brotherhood in blue and then this happened. And he'd never imagined he could feel so helpless to stop it.

"Sorry, pal," Simon said, sounding deeply sincere. He reached over to pat Lucas on the back.

"Can I still do my job?" Lucas asked.

"Of course," Becker said. "Nothing has changed. We trust you, but of course, be careful whenever you encounter any of the infected androids." He saw no animosity, fear, or hesitation in her.

"Infected, Jesus, Boss," Simon said. "We don't know enough yet to call it an outbreak."

Becker sighed. "Well, it's out there now so that's what everybody's going to be saying. We have to be prepared for that."

"It's bullshit," Simon said.

"We don't really know, do we?" Becker said. "We know very little, and this report is not going to help us."

"No shit," Maberry said.

"I want you to keep Lucas away from any press," she said to Simon. "In fact, all of you just stay away from them. Media will be all over this, and the Chief's office, too."

"You know how I feel," Simon said. "Want me to shoot down some drones?"

"No!" Becker said as Maberry chuckled. "Just avoid them period. Open hostility is not going to help. Media will be sending over instructions, and I'd expect a Media officer to start showing up at crime scenes to run interference."

"Great, just what we need," Maberry said.

"Actually, this is a good thing," Becker said, "because the press will be all over this."

As they argued, Lucas slowly sank into one of the chairs facing Becker's desk, and then they were all looking at him.

"Lucas, are you okay?" Dolby asked, her face showing real concern.

"If you want me to resign, I will do so," Lucas managed.

"No way!" Dolby exclaimed simultaneously with Maberry's and Simon's joint, "Fuck no!"

"Lucas, listen to me," Becker said, leaning forward to meet his eyes, her own filled with compassion. "You're a good cop, and we're all very proud of you. You have our full support. Try to not let this get to you. We'll all protect you from the press and anyone else who gives you trouble as best we can, but you just keep doing your job. You're the expert, and we need you working this."

"The Lenexa PD people will be all over this," Simon muttered, shaking his head.

"Which is why DC Melson cancelled the meeting," Becker said. "Go work some leads. Give media and admin time to address this and come up with an official response, okay?"

"There's not much new to report anyway, is there?" Dolby asked.

"No," Simon and Becker agreed together.

"We have evidence to review from Paul Knox's place anyway," Simon said. "We can spend the morning on that."

"Whatever you think is best," Lucas said softly and sensed them all watching him, even as he continued avoiding eye contact.

"All right," Becker said. "Lucas, I'm sorry. It'll blow over. The press gets like this sometimes. Always looking for big drama."

"And if they can't find it, they make it up," Maberry added.

Lucas glanced up, seeing their sincerity. "I understand."

"Okay," Becker said, then nodded. "Get to work, you bums."

"One more thing," Simon said, "any hits on the BOLO on Todd Ward?"

"You think I wouldn't call you the minute I heard?" Becker asked and that was her answer.

Simon grunted as Lucas managed to stand, the others turning to leave. He and Simon made their way back out into the squad room.

"They set up the laptop in the storage room, if you want to get started," Simon said as he reached for his coat, then stopped as he sensed Lucas' mood and waited for Lucas to look up at him. "You'll be okay, pal. None of us believe this bullshit. We've got your back, all right?"

"Yeah," Lucas managed, his voice soft and sad.

"Trust me, pal, none of us gave it a second thought, no matter what that idiot said. It'll be all right. You want me to get you set up?"

Lucas shook his head. "No, I'll be fine."

"It's quiet in there, no one to stare at you. Just see what you can find and I'll be right back to help you."

"Where are you going?" Lucas asked.

"Grab some breakfast and pick up some dry cleaning," Simon said. "I need some air."

With that, his partner whirled and marched for the door. Lucas could tell he was lying. Simon was angry. Probably about the news reports. But there was nothing he could do about it, so maybe he was getting food and clothes. Lucas hoped so, even as he stood and headed for the storage room. Throwing himself into work sounded like a great idea at the moment.

IT TOOK SIMON three minutes with full lights and siren to drive from Central to Fox 4. He badged his way through security onto the parking lot, asking the guard where the reporters came out of the building, and marched over to wait. Then he called a friend at dispatch to run Holly Sander's license plate and called the Fox 4 switchboard to report she'd left her lights on.

Off Summit Street on a hillside near Westport, Fox 4's station was in a walled complex with a security booth monitoring arrivals and departures from a large parking lot surrounded by trees and foliage. Among the cars in the lot facing the rectangular building were a number of station-owned vehicles bearing the Fox 4 logo. Simon parked in a space marked "Visitor" and hurried over to where Holly Sander's car was parked to wait. It was less than three minutes.

"What was that?!" Simon demanded as soon as Holly Sanders stepped out of the building, looking puzzled.

"Hi, Detective," she said and smiled, looking puzzled by his anger. "What was what?"

"I pointed you in the right direction so you could stir things up to help solve the case, not so you could throw me and my partner under a bus and then run us over again," Simon snapped, trying to ignore the alluring smell of her perfume in close proximity.

Holly scoffed. "You're being a bit melodramatic there. I was stirring things up, it's what I do." She looked at her car and frowned. "I got a call my lights were on. Was that you?"

"By basically telling the whole city their androids could go nuts at any time and get violent?" Simon said. "That's not stirring, it's trying to start a panic."

"The public has a right to be warned about this," she countered.

"A gentle warning would have been fine," Simon said. "Instead you described a series of isolated incidents with loose connections at best as an outbreak."

"'Loose' is not what I'd call it," she said. "The androids all are startlingly similar, including their mutual ties to Connelly Labs."

"Connelly Labs is the main distributor in the city, so yes," Simon said, "but it's not so black and white as you sell it."

"I put a dramatic spin on it perhaps," Holly said, "but the implications are right there. What would you call it?"

"'A dramatic spin?!' It's a lie!" Simon growled.

"Like telling someone they left their lights on to get them out of the building?!" she snapped back, and Simon couldn't help but notice how sexy she looked when she was angry. He stared a moment, then shook it off and looked away.

"Yeah," he said. "You hurt my partner. Endangered us both and made it difficult to do our jobs, all for a story."

"What?!" Holly said.

"He's an android," Simon said. "People are staring, shooting him weird looks. He needs to feel trusted. Not to mention the people who may refuse to deal with us or attack us."

"Attack you? Come on!" Holly said, shaking her head.

"You have no idea what it's like out there," Simon said. "Not a fucking clue. Mistrust of police is a reality, and Lucas' face is all over the news. If people fear androids and one shows up at their door, you never know how they might react."

"Making things difficult for you was not my intent," Holly said. "I want to report the news people need to know."

"You ever heard the term 'less is more?'" Simon answered. "You extrapolated an outbreak. Maybe next time report it without embellishing, try that."

"I'm just doing my job, Detective."

"Then do it without fucking with how I do mine!" Simon whirled and marched away toward where he'd left the Interceptor, leaving her staring after him.

IT WASN'T UNTIL after the Detectives mentioned it that Fiedler and Pruitt started looking specifically for identifying data on the android's remains, taking it apart a piece at a time, then breaking that down further to its smallest components.

Because Connelly Labs designed their robots for maximum durability and flexibility, special tools were required to disassemble the remaining limbs. Benn Liska, assisted by two techs from the Connelly Labs design team, Scott and A.B., was able to locate them for Louie and Pruitt. Pruitt and A.B. began examining the bits and pieces of Newton Isaac's remains, while Scott, Liska, and Fiedler set to work disassembling Pascal. Though neither had been directly involved in manufacturing androids—Liska's role had been strictly administrative oversight and management—they quickly fell into an easy rhythm of cooperation, making slow but steady progress.

It was Pruitt who actually discovered the logo in a piece of Newton Isaac's right arm. "Louie, you need to see this," he called as he looked through a scanning tunneling microscope, commonly referred to as an STM. "It's definitely nanoparticles, so there's a common source."

"Just as we suspected," Louie said, hurrying over.

Scott pointed to the STM's view screen where a small, torn section of the fifth joint controlling pitch was magnified. "These are remnants of the nanoparticles, but up close, look at this on the shell."

Although microscopic, nanoparticles consisted of several components—generally a nucleus, a liposomal core, a trail, and a shell. Pruitt hit some switches and buttons and the image zoomed in to show part of Fiedler Pharmaceuticals's company logo—four letters: F-I-E-D.

"Jesus," Louie said, recognizing his own company's logo.

"I didn't think you guys did much in nanoparticles," Pruitt commented.

"Well, it's still not a major portion of our work but they call it 'the next wave in healthcare advances,' so we do dabble," Louie explained. "There's all kinds of applications. Only..." He paused a moment.

"What?"

"We don't manufacture them." Louie shared his thoughts now, his confusion obvious. "This didn't come from us."

Pruitt's brow creased, his face twisted with confusion. "But isn't that your logo?"

Louie needed. "Yes, but it shouldn't be there. We didn't make that."

"Not officially at least." Pruitt said. "Could it be part of some prototype?"

Louie knew immediately that was probably the case but he was horrified at what this might mean for his company. He needed time to think. "I'm going to have to look into that. I don't know. I'm as surprised as you are."

Pruitt nodded with understanding and went back to work as Louie turned away, his mind racing. He'd seen the news reports that morning on Fox 4. If Fiedler Pharmaceuticals was implicated and the press got word of it...

He took a deep breath to calm himself. He never panicked and he wouldn't entertain such thoughts. They'd do him no good. Instead his thoughts went his development department's early efforts to manufacture their own nanoparticles. In the end, they'd discovered it to be far more cost effective to buy nanoparticles third party but there had been a year when they'd experimented. None of their nanoparticles had been satisfactory except for one, the most expensive. And Todd Ward had been the one who came up with key design elements to solve the problems with earlier modules and enable creation of nanoparticles that met all of Fiedler's standards.

Louie had insisted on delivering the news to Todd himself, and the man had been devastated. From the day he'd started employment at Fiedler Pharm, Todd had aspirations to be more than a lab manager. He had a drive to create. And Louie knew of his earlier aspirations to create androids. The Fiedler Pharm job had been a fallback. Todd Ward's personal desire was to create and build from his own designs. That's why Louie wanted to tell him personally, and he had been as gentle as he could while delivering the news.

He hid it well, but Todd had been furious hearing it—his nostrils flaring, his face tightening, despite his attempts to politely accept it. But now here was one of those very nanoparticles, or a part of one it seemed, having been used to sabotage a Connelly Labs android. Could the man really be so arrogant and determined that he continued development on his own? Where had he found the funds?

All that really mattered was Todd Ward's actions created huge liabilities for Fiedler Pharmaceuticals. The kind of liability that could ruin the company, cost them everything. Louie had to get to the bottom of it as soon as possible so damage control efforts could be made. Nothing illegal, no cover up, but they had to get in front of it, and they had to be seen as doing everything they could to assist the police in finding the perpetrator and stopping the android crisis.

He no longer had any doubt Todd Ward was involved in creating this crisis. Whether or not he was the mastermind or Livia's kidnapper, his nanoparticles had made their way into the hands of those responsible. Todd Ward was through at Fiedler Pharmaceuticals. He had a lot to answer for.

And Louie Fiedler had to double his efforts to find him.

THAT FUCKING BITCH! Todd Ward had seen Holly Sanders' Fox 4 report three times now and he still couldn't believe it. All that bullshit about some kind of outbreak yet not one mention of Connelly Labs. It was no fucking outbreak! It was deliberate sabotage! And Connelly Labs should pay the price. This Sanders bitch was either an idiot or protecting Livia Connelly's reputation. Either way, Todd didn't intend to stand for it.

He wanted Connelly Labs' connection to these androids in every headline in every paper and on every newscast. He'd make sure it was if he had to call in tips himself, or hack into their computers and rewrite the damn headlines for them!

"What's the matter?" Livia's muffled voice came through the wall as he paced in circles in the next room.

"Nothing!" he snapped. "Why are you bothering me?"

"You're breathing heavy like you're upset," she said. "I can hear it from here."

"Don't make me gag you again!" he said, turning to pace angrily back the way he'd come yet again. "I'm doing something."

"It sounds like you're just walking aimlessly and panting to me," she said.

Todd whirled and marched past the kitchen bar into the empty bedroom where Livia sat, tied to a chair. Without losing a step, he backhanded her hard across the face then stopped, hands on his hips and stared down at her. "Keep talking if you want more."

"I was just concerned for you," she whispered, blood dripping from the side of her mouth as she leaned away from him.

"Bullshit. Concerned about your abductor," Todd said and cackled. "Because I've been so nice to you? Give me a break." His hand shot out and grabbed her hair, pulling her head back around so their eyes met. "Now be a good little bitch and shut the fuck up so I can hear myself think."

She winced, managing a nod.

He held on a moment longer, staring at her in rage, then shoved her head away hard and whirled, marching back out again to resume pacing in the kitchen.

Perhaps he needed to leak information himself. That might be the best way to get his side of the story out, but how? He wasn't into some idiot manifesto like that Unibomber maniac. Todd wasn't insane. He was fed up. There's a difference. Sometimes you just have to take things into your own hands, right? Enough of letting the world push you around. Take it by the horns and change your own destiny.

He'd used the nanoparticles he'd developed with funds from Fiedler Pharmaceuticals to modify the androids and send his instructions via VOIP and Wi-Fi, so he could take Louie Fiedler down, too. Two old friends and two old enemies in one fell swoop. After all, Fiedler had been holding him down just as much as Livia Connelly had, and far more recently, too. Killing his design after he'd saved the company's ass! Too expensive?! Bullshit. Fiedler had killed it because it wasn't his idea or those of his special cronies. He wanted all the credit, fuck Todd Ward or some other underling who dared to have hopes and dreams of their own!

Louie Fiedler was just another egoist like Livia Connelly

standing in Todd's way. Yes, taking them both down would be a pleasure. And Fiedler wouldn't even see it coming. Todd had used dozens of extra nanoparticle prototypes he'd built at Fiedler's own labs in this initiative—built before they'd shit-canned his idea and his fortune and fame along with them! He'd have fucking patents by now if those small-minded ass-wipes hadn't been too cheap to go forward. Patents he could have leveraged for millions of dollars and new job opportunities to finally take Todd to the heights and earn him the respect he'd long deserved.

"Todd, please, I have to use the bathroom," Livia called softly.

Fuck. He whirled around and marched into the empty bedroom again. But one look at the fear on her face assured him Livia Connelly was serious with her request. She'd held out until she couldn't wait any longer.

"Come on," he said and knelt beside a stack of half-empty paint cans and used brushes, loosening the knots securing her feet. "But no funny business."

He'd almost gotten everything he needed from her and enjoyed torturing her in the process. Waterboarding, cigarette burns—extracting her fingernails one at a time had been his favorite. Soon he could just dispose of the bitch but he wanted the perfect moment—the maximum impact—something memorable, a real statement.

He untied her hands, noticing her finger tips were still swollen from bleeding after he'd taken the nails, then helped her from the chair, leading her into the bathroom as he pictured various scenarios for her demise. He was so caught up in it he didn't even notice as she ignored him and pulled her pants down in front of him and sat on the toilet, doing her business.

Moments later, an embarrassed Livia looked up at her captor with a mixture of fear and surprise as his laughter echoed off the walls.

"WHERE ARE WE GOING?" Simon asked as Lucas turned off the Interceptor and unfastened his seatbelt, reaching for the door.

"Next name on the list," Lucas replied as he opened the door and climbed out, Simon releasing his seatbelt and doing the same. "Caprice Hokstad."

"This is a cemetery," Simon said, scanning the grassy plain ahead of them, dotted with the tombstones and mausoleums of Mount St. Mary's, one of Kansas City's oldest Catholic cemeteries. "Stiffs don't make the best witnesses."

"She's not dead," Lucas said, "she's treasure hunting."

"An expert on nanoparticles is a grave digger?" Simon said, confused and surprised at the same time.

Lucas did a perfect imitation of one of Emma's eye rolls. "It's a club. They meet here every Wednesday."

As they made their way from the parking lot past a copse of trees, Simon saw people with metal detectors everywhere, working the grass around the graves. The tombstones ranged from square to rectangular to rounded at the top, white, sandstone, rust-colored, grey, some with saints or the Virgin Mary on top, other more plain and ordinary—rows and rows.

"A metal detector club?" Simon asked, shaking his head.

"How'd you know about this?"

"It's on her website that she's out every Wednesday afternoon for treasure club," Lucas said. "I Googled."

Thirty-nine degrees felt almost balmy to Simon after the cold spells they'd been having, and he enjoyed the fresh air as they wound their way amongst the graves, sometimes hopping or squeezing through what seemed like very little space, other times navigating clear walkways. Then Lucas walked right past a man in his fifties working a metal detector and Simon heard the machine start beeping, a midrange tone. The man got excited and took a small shovel from his back pocket as he knelt on the grass to explore.

Lucas shot the man a curious look as he kept striding along. "What treasure do they hope to find here?"

"All kinds of metal," Simon said. "Mostly coins and such."

"What do they do with it?" Lucas asked.

They wound their way around a mausoleum passing an Asian woman working another metal detector which also started beeping as Lucas moved past, eliciting excitement from the operator.

"Spend it, identify if it's rare and collectible, trade it, sell it," Simon said, amused. "Whatever they can."

"This is an odd hobby," Lucas said.

"Oh yeah, people with too much time on their hands," Simon agreed. His eyes scanned the graveyard around them. The treasure club seemed to have attracted over thirty people. "Do you know what this woman looks like? Maybe we should start asking people?"

"Google had a photo," Lucas said, walking on without losing a beat as he motioned ahead. "I can see her up ahead a few yards."

Simon wasn't used to Lucas taking the lead like this and it would take some getting used to, but the android sounded confident, so he followed along without complaint, his companion setting off two more metal detectors as he went.

The trees and shrubs scattered around to beautify the place were as varied as the tombstones with everything from conifers and pines to bushes and even tall oaks. Up ahead, two squirrels, cheeks stuffed with found food, scampered across the lawn and leaped onto the trunk of an oak, racing up into its waiting branches.

Lucas arced around another copse of trees, passing three more metal detectors that started beeping in various tones, and wove through more gravestones toward a short, blonde woman in her late forties who was arguing jovially with a young black man near a mausoleum. Both held metal detectors.

"You can't just call dibs on a section randomly like that, Reggie," she was saying.

"Why not? I saw it first," Reggie responded.

"But you were fifty yards away," the woman countered.

"I was walking fast," Reggie said. "I got here first."

"We got here at the same time," she said, "and this is the spot I usually work."

"Whatever," Reggie snapped. "Too bad I called it."

Lucas walked right up to the couple and looked at the woman. "Caprice Hokstad?" Their metal detectors started beeping as he badged her, and both reacted.

"Shit! I knew you was hogging this fer a reason, Caprice!" Reggie said. "I called it! Go find yer own spot!" He whirled and began working his metal detector as an exasperated Caprice turned to Lucas.

"May I help you?" she asked.

"Detectives George and Simon, KCPD," Lucas said.

"What do you want, Detective?" she asked as Simon joined them.

"We're investigating a case of someone using nanoparticles to modify androids," Lucas explained.

"Nanoparticle sabotage?" Caprice replied, shaking her head. "Who would do that?"

"That's what we're asking you," Simon said.

"Well, I'm a broker," Caprice replied. "I don't manufacture or get into any of the science. I connect suppliers and the rest to help make projects come together."

"Right," Simon said. "So you encounter lots of types in doing that, right?"

"Sure."

Reggie's metal detector beeped nearby. "Man, whoever died this month musta had rich relatives!"

"Can you think of anyone who might have been acting strange? Asking odd questions?" Lucas asked.

"Expressed any ill intent?" Simon added.

She looked at Reggie a moment then shook her head. "Not really off the top of my head." She thought a moment. "Most of these people can't afford to screw around, risk their funding."

"We get that, but somebody is," Simon said.

"You have proof of that?" she asked, looking at Reggie and others nearby excitedly digging for treasure as metal detector beeps pierced the air all around them. She looked anxious, distracted.

"It appears we do," Lucas replied.

"Can I think about it and get back to you?" Caprice said.

"Maybe when I get back to the office, something will come to me."

"Well, of course," Lucas said, handing her his business card. "But we'd appreciate you telling us anything you can as soon as possible."

"I found a half dollar!" Reggie exclaimed excitedly then began scanning the ground again and working his way toward them.

Caprice's hands worked her metal detector as she shifted nervously. Whoops of celebration came from nearby from another club member making a find.

"You seem distracted," Simon said. "Why would a treasure club choose a cemetery? It seems to me there are a lot of better places that see more frequent crowds."

"We came here because they've had a run of funerals the past two months, more than one a week, and we've learned mourners tend to lose things, so why not?" she replied but she didn't meet his eyes the entire time, instead watching Reggie and the other club members with great interest.

Simon knew she wanted treasure but there seemed to be more to it. Like she really didn't want to answer their questions, so he asked, "Is there something you're not telling us?"

She shook her head vehemently. "No, I'm just in the middle of something."

Reggie reached them and scanned around their feet, his detector beeping like crazy. He looked at Lucas. "Brother, yer standing on a gold mine! Move them feet, 'kay?"

"Sir, police business," Lucas said, badging him.

"So? Take it over there, 'kay?!" Reggie growled.

Caprice sighed, turning and stepping a few feet to one side, so Lucas and Simon followed as Reggie tore at the ground where Lucas had been standing, searching. But she looked ready to bolt, moving her metal detector around her a moment, distracted.

"Look, Ms. Hokstad, we've had people killed and seriously hurt," Simon said. "You can find a few lost coins later. We really need your help."

"Shit!" Reggie called. "Nothing! What the fuck is wrong with this thing?" He shook his detector and adjusted the settings then stood, working the ground and moving toward them.

"I told you nothing comes to mind," she said. "I need time to think. I only get to do this once a week. It's a hobby I really enjoy ever since I was a child."

Reggie drew nearer and once again his metal detector set off around Lucas' feet. "Ha! You carrying treasure in your shoes, boy?" he demanded of Lucas.

Lucas shook his head. "No."

"Move!" Reggie ordered.

Lucas stepped to the side and Reggie knelt, searching the ground. "Shit. Nada again. What the fuck?"

"This case is important," Lucas said to Caprice. "We'd really appreciate it if you'd tell us names of anyone we should talk too, suspicious or not."

"I can make you a whole list," Caprice said, "once I get back to my office and my laptop and tablet."

Reggie stood again and came over, scanning near Lucas' feet. Yet again his metal detector set off. "What are those—steel-toed shoes?!" He shook his head, exasperated. "What are you—metal?!"

"Yes," Lucas said. "I have metal in my legs."

Reggie frowned, his brow creasing as he leaned in to look

Lucas over carefully. "Oh shit!" Recognition dawned. "You one of them! He's one of them!" He hopped around, hurrying away and motioning frantically to other club members. "You saw the news! He's one of them! The crazy robot people come to kill us!"

"Sir, calm down please," Lucas said.

"Your friend's an android?" Caprice said, backing away.

"I am," Lucas admitted.

Now Reggie had a few others calling out in protest and people were stopping the treasure hunt to stare and point, some running away.

"Let me guess," Caprice said. "There's no treasure. You're setting them off."

"I am?" Lucas said, and Simon realized his partner had no idea.

"Take your 'droid and get outta here!" Reggie shouted, waving his fists. "Put us all in danger!"

"Please call us, Ms. Hokstad," Lucas said as Simon grabbed his arm and pulled him back toward where they'd parked. Then their shoulder radios beeped simultaneously.

"706, respond to incident at 4420 Warwick Boulevard," the dispatcher said. "130, 134, 133, also responding. Public disturbance by an android."

"Isn't that the Art Museum?" one of the club members muttered as Lucas and Simon hurried past.

"706, on our way," Lucas said into his shoulder mic as he and Simon started running back the way they'd come, headed for the Interceptor.

CHAPTER 12

SIMON AND LUCAS arrived at the Nelson-Atkins Museum, better known as the Nelson Gallery by locals, via 45th Street and left the Interceptor on the street as they rushed inside. After badging staff, they were directed by security personnel toward the Bloch Building which housed the contemporary art, African art, and special exhibits. Opened in June 2007 at a cost of millions, the long, clarinet-shaped Bloch Building was hailed as an architectural achievement but Simon thought it was a disaster. Five glass pavilions, called lenses, sat above ground providing ambient light to the collections in the underground building which ran east of the original gallery in a kind of warped L shape.

To Simon, the inside was as confusing as the outside was ugly—a maze of interconnecting galleries with high ceilings supported by pillars and bright lighting to highlight its plain-ness. Poor signage and even poorer maps purported to direct visitors, but if they hadn't had a security escort, he figured they could have been lost in there for days trying to find the incident. Unless Lucas could somehow use his special gifts to guide them, that is. The smell of the place was as bland as its appearance, only the presence of human beings or the occasional work of cleaners adding anything to spice up the bland air.

They fought their way against a fleeing crowd of visitors

and staff to where they heard yelling and commotion coming from a nearby gallery.

"Stop that!" a male voice Simon thought he recognized scolded loudly.

"He's destroying it!" said another man.

"Leonard, you put that down!" a woman ordered, her voice also familiar to Simon.

They rounded a corner into the African gallery to find Simon's oldest CI, Murray Barber and his wife, Jan, standing with a distraught museum staffer and two security people just as another man—tall, thin, Lucas' physique, but white with short brown hair—smashing a clay African pot against a nearby wall. The gallery had white walls and ceilings with artworks displayed in glass cases lining the walls or extending out from them and others on various shapes of tables or stands scattered about the floor. Most of them were carvings of wood or stone, some featuring elaborate beadwork and painted colors, others involving more complicated methods. Among them were spears, daggers, bows, and other weapons, and there were also stools and primitive cutlery and dishes and other household goods. The smell of decaying fabric, stone, leather, and musk dominated the air.

"That was worth six hundred thousand!" the distraught staffer said, identifying the male voice Simon hadn't recognized as they approached.

"Jesus Christ, Leonardo, you're going to bankrupt me!" Murray exclaimed.

Murray Barber was a former art forger-turned-consultant and art expert, one of Simon's first informants, and one of the most unique personalities he had ever met. Simon had busted him and sent him away for several years', but then Simon had also testified at a parole hearing to help him obtain early release for good behavior. Murray was one of the most charismatic, charming individuals Simon had ever met, which explained his unique way with people, including Jan and the other woman, Linda, who constituted his dual live-in wives.

With long brown braided hair and a bushy beard, Murray was the stereotypical hippie and owned a great set of Hawaiian shirts and loose dungarees or shorts for any occasion. He also had matching sandals and topped off the ensemble with one of his famous helicopter fezes—a collection he'd acquired over years of attending fan conventions—science fiction being his favorite. Art expert yes, but Murray was also a dedicated nerd, and one who couldn't give a shit about what anyone else thought of him. He knew who he was and was comfortable with it so "fuck you if you couldn't deal"—an attitude Simon loved and totally related to.

Jan, standing next to him, was of mixed Asian and African descent with a warm, welcoming personality and smile. Her usual sundress had been traded for jeans and a flowery button-down blouse, but currently her long, graying dreadlocked-and-beaded hair of rainbow colors paled by comparison with the color of her angry face as she stared at the android holding up another African mask threateningly in the air. This one had an elongated nose that to Simon looked more like an erect penis.

"The Malawian fertility god!" the museum man exclaimed. "Irreplaceable!"

Simon got the feeling he'd say that about all the pieces but kept his mouth shut.

Two museum security guards were circling Leonardo, trying to get into positions to grab or tackle him without disturbing the art as Jan shouted, "God damn it, Leonardo, if you don't put that down—"

"Why did you bring him here? Who authorized an android?!" the museum man said, pointing an accusing finger at Murray.

"Leonardo's been my assistant for three years now, Ron, with no problems," Murray countered

"Murray, what's going on?" Simon asked.

"Johnny, thank God," Jan said, exhaling with relief. She was one of the few people from whom Simon tolerated that iteration of his name, mostly because she used it with such sweetness and charm.

"Who are you?!" the museum man demanded with exasperation and glared at the security person escorting them.

"KCPD," Simon said simultaneously with the security woman's, "Police, sir."

"Assistant Curator Reece Watts meet Detectives John Simon and Lucas George," Murray said.

"Well, arrest that *thing* before it destroys my museum!" Watts said, pointing to Leonardo.

"Any idea what set him off?" Simon asked Murray as Lucas joined the two security men jockeying for position while Leonardo dodged behind various priceless artworks time and again.

"He just went crazy!" Watts said before Murray could answer.

"Pretty much," Murray agreed.

Simon motioned to the curator and the three guards. "Why don't you guys carefully move some of these pieces, while we talk with Leonardo."

"Gloves!" Watts yelled to his security, and all three reached in their pockets for surgical rubber gloves and turned toward the nearby pieces. Simon moved in to join Lucas. As they did, four uniforms arrived with another security guard.

"Brother, why don't you put the fertility god down and talk to me," Lucas said gently to his fellow android.

"We've got this," Simon said to the uniforms, holding up a hand for them to stay put.

"A god? They call this a god?!" Leonardo seemed to be excited at the prospect of a larger audience as he danced glee-fully then smashed the fertility mask against a wall, causing Watts to cry out in agony.

What a drama queen, Simon thought.

"You must stop this," Lucas said.

Leonardo scoffed. "Can you believe the things the humans consider valuable?" He picked up a small statue and tossed it back and forth between his hands like a juggler starting his act.

"Leonardo!" Jan scolded again as Lucas slowly raised a palm.

"Please, why are you doing this?" Lucas asked.

"Because I can?" Leonardo said, more with the raised tone of a question, and then he grinned. "Because it's fun." He smashed the statue.

"Fucking idiot android," Murray said.

Simon glared back at the others. "Shut up." Their out-bursts seemed to energize the android. "Not helping." He turned back to see Lucas slowly inching toward Leonardo.

"Buddy, this has to stop," Simon said, trying to draw the android's attention. "Why don't we go somewhere and talk about it, okay?"

Leonardo chortled. "Talk with humans? I've listened to

you enough!"

Lucas lunged at Leonardo, trying to grab him by the arms but the android bolted at the last second and took off at a run. Simon and Lucas followed close on his heels, the uniforms bringing up the rear.

"Don't touch me!" Leonardo shouted sing-song as he ran, dodging through visitors and staff alike as he made his way down the ramp-angled floor toward the south end of the building.

Simon glanced over his shoulder and motioned to the uniforms. "Get around the building and cut him off!"

Two of them muttered in agreement and peeled off to the right while Simon and the others kept following the androids.

Leonardo went down a ramp onto a kind of landing and then leaped over a half-wall with a bench attached to the other side, landing beside a startled old woman, who gasped and scooted away as Leonardo hopped down, laughing, and kept running past a podium and then left into a short corridor.

Lucas, who was hot on Leonardo's heels, called over his shoulder, "The sculpture garden!"

Simon motioned to the two uniforms and they darted left and took an emergency exit to the sculpture park as Simon followed Lucas and Leonardo down the short corridor. Simon caught the door at the end just as it was about to close and rushed out into the sunlight to see Lucas receding away down the sidewalk past the large lenses that provided light to the Bloch Building.

Honking horns and humming motors in the distance marked the busy streets surrounding them as Simon took off running again, south past the statue of a bronze woman and several torsos of various shapes and sizes then on toward

August Rodin's famous *Thinker*—a bronze man sitting on a stump with his fist against his chin as if thinking. There he turned left and moved between two clumps of trees on either side down terraced tiers, seeing Lucas closing in on Leonardo ahead of him.

They passed a Henry Moore bronze of some kind of mutant, reclining figure and the on down the lawn toward one of the large shuttlecocks, sculpted giant badminton pieces.

Leonardo glanced back and showed his teeth in a kinda of snarl as he ran.

"Who did this to you, brother?" Lucas called after him, without losing a step or gasping for breath.

Fucking androids, Simon mused as his own breathing increased and he slowed a moment to catch his breath.

"I've been set free!" Leonardo shouted, letting the phrase drag out at the end like a song, until it finally trailed to silence again.

Two uniforms burst from trees ahead, one to each side, attempting to cut off Leonardo, who slowed, darting back and forth as he looked for a way past them.

Lucas caught up and tried to grab Leonardo by the shoulder. The android screamed a blood curdling scream and yanked away then launched himself onto one of the uniforms. At the last minute, he curled into a ball and plowed over the guy then landed and came up running again.

Lucas and the other three uniforms continued the chase as Simon caught up and slowed, offering a hand to the fallen uniform. "You okay?"

The man accepted the hand, wheezing for breath as he stood. "I feel like a Mac truck ran me over," he managed.

"Yeah, I hate how these bastards can do that," Simon said

then took off after the chase again as the uniform put his hands on his knees, catching his breath.

As they continued downhill, a long expanse of lawn stretched before them all the way to Emmanuel Cleaver II, the major street bordering the museum's property to the west. Simon was dripping with sweat, making the winter wind blasting him from the sides feel even colder. Androids didn't sweat. *Lucky bastards.*

Simon keyed his shoulder radio, his words coming between heavy breaths. "706, suspect headed for Emmanuel Clever. Pursuit on foot. Can anyone assist and run interference?" It was a long shot unless there was a patrol car very close and in the right position, but then two golf carts appeared from behind the rows of trees lining each side of the lawn, racing toward the middle and arcing up toward Leonardo on an intercept course, driven by museum guards.

"Spread out!" Simon called to his fellow officers, hoping they'd hear, then repeated it over the radio.

Lucas stayed in the middle as the three uniforms and Simon fanned out to form a kind of wedge around him, sweeping toward Leonardo from behind.

"There's nowhere to go, brother," Lucas called out. "Stop and let's work this out. I promise I will help you."

Leonardo's head darted back and forth between the converging golf carts as he ran and then he glanced back over his shoulder at the pursuing cops.

"Please," Lucas called, "I can help you."

"I don't want your help," Leonardo called back and then leaped. He flew eight feet in the air in an arc that carried him across the lawn where he landed and leaped again. The museum guards redirected the golf carts, while also trying to stay in his path as Lucas began leaping after him, both of them quickly pulling away from the others.

"Shit, he's gonna get away," Simon muttered.

Then the third leap took Leonardo onto the sidewalk beside Emmanuel Cleaver and he started running along it to the north, parallel with traffic, even as he eased closer to the curb.

And then a large box truck changed lanes, moving forward in the right line nearest the curve which had cleared of traffic for the moment. As the truck accelerated to normal speed, Leonardo spotted it and arced right for it, then leaped, landing with a thump right on top, spread eagled, and grabbing each side with his hands, holding on.

Lucas darted off the sidewalk after the truck, ignoring honking horns from the cars coming up behind as he raced after the truck with all his might. Then the traffic light ahead at Oak Street went yellow with just enough time for the truck to go through but no one else. Tires squealed and horns honked again as the truck sped up and went through the intersection and Lucas started to follow, finding himself surrounded by traffic, drivers yelling and making crude gestures as he tried to dodge and arc clear.

Lucas started jumping on cars—hoods, then a roof, then another—trying to get through, denting them as he went, causing several more drivers to signal or shout their disdain.

Simon keyed his radio as the truck made up ground, pulling further away from Lucas, who was bogged down by traffic. "Lucas, give it up. He's gone."

"I can get him," a frustrated Lucas replied.

"Not on foot against a truck," Simon snapped.

Lucas finally cleared the cars and hit the pavement, starting to run again, but the truck was already far ahead and turning right. After a few seconds, Lucas slowed and arced toward the sidewalk, then came to a stop, hands on his thighs, his head bent down in frustration as Simon hurried along the sidewalk, out of breath, trying to catch up with his partner.

"We'll find him," Simon said. "No point killing yourself over the impossible."

"We need to catch a break," Lucas said, looking down at his feet.

"We'll work what we've got," Simon said. "Something always breaks."

"Hey! Look what he did to my car!" a man shouted nearby.

Simon motioned to the uniforms who moved out to deal with the accident as he put an arm around his partner's shoulder and led him back the way they'd come, his lungs relieved for the chance to catch air normally again.

WATTS ALLOWED THE KCPD to convene with witnesses in the two Ford Learning Center classrooms just off the sculpture garden but out of view of most visitors. Becker, Maberry, and Dolby had driven down to help coordinate, along with the four uniforms. Maberry and Dolby were doing interviews in one classroom, Simon and Lucas in another with Becker and the uniforms organizing witnesses in the corridor outside.

The classroom Simon and Lucas were using had short stools and short polygonal tables clearly designed for children, but it was quiet and they could control traffic, which made it perfect for interviewing the witnesses and filling out reports. Blackboards, white boards, and bulletin boards lined the walls with a larger, longer table and bigger chairs for instructors at the end of the room opposite the door. The entire place smelled of paste, modeling cement, and other art-friendly chemicals no doubt used in the classes taught here weekly for aspiring young artists. It reminded Simon of visiting Emma in elementary school a few years past.

Watts was furious that Leonardo had gotten away and kept grousing about the destroyed or damaged artworks, while Murray and Jan were just mourning the loss of their beloved android companion. Becker had taken Watts outside and instructed the uniforms to keep him there—as much to spare herself the annoying bitching as for privacy

"We've never seen him like this," Murray said sadly, shaking his head. Seated on the child's stool, his helicopter fez spinning, he looked like some kind of sad man-child.

"Never," Jan agreed, clinging to his arm. "It's like he just snapped."

"One minute he was helping us evaluate the new acquisitions," Murray went on. "The next, he was destroying them."

"You were consulting officially?" Lucas asked.

"Yeah, informally. The museum's insurance adjustors tend to undervalue some works of art for the policies, particularly the more exotic ones, and so they'll get a couple of experts in here to evaluate them and make a good case in order to ensure things get covered properly," Murray explained.

"Fucking corporations, always trying to rip off the little guy," Jan mumbled.

"Exactly," Murray agreed. "The man is the man."

"Always," Jan added. "Leonardo helps us by using his

special abilities to microscopically examine the art and compare it with examples internet-wide."

"Something I used to have to do myself and took weeks," Murray said, "but he cuts it down to a few minutes."

"Amazing," Jan said.

"Invaluable," Murray agreed.

"How long had you been there working before—" Simon thought a moment, choosing his words "—the incident."

The couple exchanged a look, thinking, then said together, "An hour maybe."

"Give or take," Murray added.

"We don't pay much attention to time when we're working," Jan said.

"You would be among the few," Simon said.

Murray chortled. "Yeah, I have the good fortune to love my work."

"So take us through the exact moment when he changed," Lucas said.

"Well, we were having him examine and compare a basket woven by Ewe in Togo in the seventeenth century, I believe," Murray said.

"Thank God it wasn't something heavier," Jan interjected.

"Right?" Murray said, then continued, "He was running down comparisons so Jan could log them in a spreadsheet when something in his eyes changed—"

"Like he was a whole different person almost," Jan said.

"Yeah, exactly," Murray agreed. "And then he threw it at us. Hitting Jan."

"It just bounced off my chest thankfully," Jan said, "but I think that kind of pissed him off because that's when he started looking for heavier objects that might actually smash or break."

"And you arrived after he'd been at it about ten minutes," Murray said.

"Thankfully someone called," Jan said.

"Thankfully, he took his time and didn't destroy more," Murray replied.

"How many objects would you say he did destroy?" Simon asked.

"A dozen maybe," Jan said.

"Fourteen," Watts said then from the doorway.

"You have an inventory?" Lucas asked.

"My assistant is finishing it now," Watts said with a nod. "And that includes the basket. He tore the handle."

"What? It was fine when I set it down," Jan protested.

"It's damaged!" Watts growled and glared.

"All right, I think we've got what we need for now," Simon said. "We know how to reach you."

"You do," Murray said. "And it's been too long. Don't be such a stranger, okay?"

Murray and Jan stood and shook hands with Simon and Lucas as Watts continued glaring at them.

"I think from now on the board will be approving a 'no androids' policy," Watts snapped.

Murray and Jan made faces to Simon behind his back as they exited into the hall.

"Such behavior is really unusual for androids," Lucas said. "We are fairly certain there is some sort of sabotage occurring."

"This was deliberate?!" Watts exclaimed. "I want whoever's responsible found and incarcerated! And that android destroyed!"

"That will be up to the courts," Simon said, noting Lucas' dismayed look but appreciating his wisdom to stay silent.

They turned to walk away just as Becker and DC Cara Atwell approached. Atwell glared at Lucas.

"I just got finished taking ten complaints from angry motorists whose cars you damaged jumping on them during your pursuit of the suspect," Atwell said, "who, as I understand it was on a vehicle at the time? What were you thinking, Detective?!"

"That he was getting away, ma'am," Lucas replied, *sotto voce*.

"Unacceptable!" Atwell growled.

"We all know accidental damage happens sometimes during pursuits," Simon said.

"Accidental is not jumping on top of vehicles in your path in an attempt to pursue a fleeing vehicle on foot!" she replied. "That is deliberate negligence."

"Or at least an unwise choice," Becker added, shooting Lucas a look of sympathy.

"He was caught up in the adrenaline of the moment," Simon said.

"Androids do not have adrenaline," Lucas pointed out.

Simon shot him a look. He was ruining his own defense. "Caught up in the moment then."

"Answer me this, Detective," Atwell said, ignoring Simon and glaring at Lucas, "did you at any time make physical contact with that suspect?"

"What's that have to do with anything?" Simon snapped. "Is he coming in to lodge a complaint too for excessive pursuit?"

Atwell turned and shot Simon dead with a look. "Did you

make physical contact with him, Detective George?"

"Briefly I did, yes," Lucas said, "in trying to subdue him."

"But there was nothing excessive about it," Simon said.

"I need your badge and your gun," Atwell said, holding out a palm to Lucas. "You're on temporary suspension."

"For doing his job?!" Simon nearly hit the roof. This was ridiculous.

"For possible exposure to a dangerous virus or substance that may cause impairment in performance of your duties," Atwell added.

"You've got to be kidding!" Simon said. "He's fine."

"I do not think I was exposed," Lucas said. "I feel fine."

"It's just a precaution," Becker said, looking resigned.

"Hazmat suits and masks are a precaution, this is a punishment!" Simon protested.

"The decision's been made," Atwell barked dismissively.

"You knew about this?!" Simon said as he turned to Becker, his words like an assault. "And you're letting it happen?!"

"We have a duty to protect the public," Atwell barked as Lucas handed over his badge and weapon. "The department has liability for our personnel, too."

"He's fine!" Simon protested again.

"This is just until we're sure you're all right, Lucas, I promise," Becker said, her eyes soft and sorrowful.

Simon scoffed. "Jesus Christ. He's the best person we have to work this case, the one with the most knowledge, and given what that suspect just did, we need his special skills. We need all the advantages we can get."

"I understand," Lucas said, but his sinking shoulders showed his dejection.

"Is he quarantined too?!" Simon asked.

"Actually, we want you to report to Connelly Labs tomorrow for a full examination," Atwell said.

"Once the department has been assured there is no sign of any corruption or problems, we'll get him reinstated," Becker said.

"We'll certainly discuss it," Atwell added.

"*Discuss it!*" Simon said as Atwell turned and hurried off, ignoring them. Simon turned on Becker. "Did you have any say in this?"

"Not really, no," Becker said. "She has a point about liability."

"And protecting the public," Lucas said. "Don't worry. I am fine."

"But we don't know for sure this thing is even something you can catch," Simon said.

"We also do not know for sure it is not," Lucas replied. "I am okay." He turned and followed Atwell out the door as Simon sighed, leaning against the wall in total exasperation.

Shoulder radios beeped. "706, 180, what's your status?" the dispatcher asked.

"We are 10-8, dispatch," Becker replied.

"Lenexa PD is requesting your presence at a homicide," the dispatcher replied. "6807 West 112th Street."

"Jesus Christ," Simon said. "That's Fiedler Pharmaceuticals."

"The headquarters of Fiedler Pharmaceuticals Research," the dispatcher confirmed.

"706, 180 rolling," Becker replied then released the radio. "Lucas can take the Explorer back to Central. You ride with me."

"This is killing him," Simon said as he followed her out

the door.

"I don't like it either," Becker said, "but the orders come from above my pay grade." Simon let it go as Becker radioed Lucas about the car and followed her to the parking lot.

CHAPTER 13

LOUIE FIEDLER LAY across his desk, his head at almost a right angle to his body, a neck bone protruding through his skin. It looked very much like he had been thrown there by someone much bigger, but there were signs of a struggle and multiple assailants. The strong coppery smell of blood mixed with musty carpet and old papers filled the air. Blood pooled on the desk behind the back of Fiedler's head and there were streaks running down his pants legs to a pool on the floor and more smeared on the wall behind his desk as if he'd been bounced off it while bleeding. Regardless, he had not gone peacefully or without pain. That was obvious.

"Jesus," Simon muttered as he stood with Becker in the doorway, looking in.

"He fought whoever it was," Zedlar said, shaking his head. It was Overland Park P.D.'s case, of course, but like Simon, he had come out of curiosity. The OPPD Detective in charge was named Val Hatfield, short blonde, thin, but tough-looking, her face bearing a permanent don't fuck with me scowl. Her suit was clean and pressed but the button-down shirt underneath was loose at the collar and her shoes needed a good polishing.

"We think there were three of them," Hatfield added as she came across the room to join them. "They didn't try very hard to conceal their presence."

"You got fingerprints?" Becker asked.

"Oddly, no, but there are two footprints in blood," Hatfield said.

Zedlar motioned. "Behind the desk there in a pool of blood."

"That's a lot of blood," Becker said.

"Yeah," Zedlar agreed. "Where's your partner?" he asked Simon as he and Becker stepped forward to look behind the desk at the footprints.

"He had other duties to attend to," Becker said before Simon could respond. From his expression, Zedlar's curiosity was only piqued but he said nothing.

"Security cameras?" Simon asked as he pulled his cell and took photos of the footprints before stepping back around the desk with Becker.

"Malfunctioning," Hatfield said. "Security doesn't have a good answer why."

"Did you see something?" Zedlar asked.

"Those numbers in the footprints look just like markings we found at another scene involving an android perp," Simon said.

"Son of a bitch," Zedlar said.

"We'll have my partner take a look at them. Have you talked with his assistants?" Simon asked.

"One was out sick, the other out to lunch," Hatfield replied.

"Whoever did this knew how to get in and out without drawing much attention," Zedlar said.

"Surely cameras somewhere in the building got something," Becker said.

Hatfield nodded. "We're hoping, but it will take a while to

go through them."

"If you need our guys' help, just ask," Becker said, and they nodded in thanks, but Simon knew it was lip service. They'd never ask for KCPD help if they could avoid it.

"No one heard anything either," Zedlar added.

"In the middle of a work day, with that kind of struggle?" Becker scoffed.

Hatfield grunted. "Yeah, we're going to interview every-one but unless they're afraid or holding back for some other reason, those in the immediate vicinity gave us nothing."

"It makes no sense," Becker said, shaking her head.

"Any idea what he was working on?" Simon asked.

"We were hoping you could tell us," Hatfield said. "One of his assistant's calendar had a notation of a meeting with Detectives Simon and George this morning at Connelly Labs."

"Yes," Simon replied, then anticipating the question, add-ed, "He and Bob Pruitt were going over the remains of sever-al androids involved in incidents to see if they could identify anything unusual."

"And what did they find?" Zedlar asked.

"Traces of nanoparticles, we think," Simon said and watched their faces freeze in blank looks. "Signs of deliberate sabotage."

"As suspected," Zedlar said.

"Yes," Simon agreed.

"Is it catching?" Hatfield asked.

"Excuse me?" Becker said.

"Can it spread by contact?" Hatfield asked.

"We don't know yet," Simon said.

"Better watch out for your friend then," Hatfield said. "Just in case."

"We're taking proper precautions," Becker said.

"Anything here?" Simon asked.

"The computer is locked behind a screensaver, so we're waiting on the password," Zedlar said, and Simon puzzled at Hatfield accepting him acting so casually like a partner on her investigation with no complaint. "And we haven't gotten a good look just yet at what's under him or on his cell."

"We will soon as the coroner's done," Hatfield said. That was a fact of life of investigations Simon had always found frustrating but it was routine and policy of every department.

"What can we do to help?" Becker asked, ever the diplomat.

"We wanted you to look at the scene, see if anything stands out to you," Hatfield said. "Those two things are it really."

"For now," Zedlar said. "Any hits on that BOLO for Todd Ward?" His voice and eyes took on an urgency.

Simon shook his head. "I assume you put one out too."

Zedlar grunted. "Yeah, nada as well."

"Wherever he is, this guy's keeping a low profile," Simon said. "But we'll find him eventually."

"All right, well, it sounds to us like you've got it handled so far," Becker said, "so we'll get out of your hair, but we'll think on it and apprise you of any further thoughts."

"Thank you," Hatfield said.

Becker and Simon walked off together.

"They really did drag us a long way for very little," Simon said. "I think they wanted something but don't want to tell us."

"You got that feeling too, did you?" Becker said as they stepped onto the elevator and she punched the button for the first floor.

"Curious they're working like a team when Zedlar's out of his jurisdiction," Simon observed.

"I'm assuming they interact a lot down here," Becker said, obviously making less of it.

Two minutes later, as they stepped out into the parking lot with the Sprint complex looming across the street, Simon heard a familiar voice.

"Detective Simon!"

Holly Sanders was waving at him from beside a Fox 4 news van. His body tightened as Becker put a hand on his shoulder.

"Leave it be, John," Becker said.

"I'll just be a minute," Simon said and marched over, Becker following.

"Hi," Holly said with a warm smile.

"What the hell were you thinking, lady?!" Simon snapped, eyes narrowing as his anger swelled.

"Um, I was doing my job," Holly replied, looking stunned by his reaction.

"Your job?! You got my partner taken off this case! The best expert we have," Simon said.

"I did?" Holly replied.

"You can't make stuff up and call it news!" Simon said as Becker tapped his shoulder.

"Enough, John," Becker said. "You've said your piece."

"I didn't make up anything," Holly said, her face reddening as her own anger simmered.

"Bullshit!" Simon said and turned as Becker pulled his arm, following her to her KCPD sedan.

"I just followed the leads!" Holly yelled back at him. "It's what they pay me for!"

Becker climbed in the car, Simon opposite her. "Whoever tipped her off is who you should be mad at," Becker said. "She just did what people like her always do—milk the drama."

Simon punched the roof of the car but kept his mouth shut. She'd hit it just right. He only had himself to blame, but he wasn't yet ready to admit that to anyone, especially his boss.

Becker started the car and headed out onto 112th, turning left on Metcalf and heading for I-35.

LUCAS DROPPED THE Interceptor in the garage at KCPD headquarters, then retrieved his personal Chrome Outlander from the lot across the street to the east and headed for Connelly Labs in Lenexa. He felt fine. He was certain he was okay, but he had to be sure, and Bob Pruitt and Benn Liska were there waiting for him with two techs named A.B. and Scott, whom Lucas had met once or twice before.

"Did you find anything new?" Lucas asked right away.

"It's definitely a common source," Pruitt said. "That much we confirmed. And there seems to be a connection to Fiedler Pharmaceuticals. Some of the pieces we recovered bore Fiedler Pharm's logo."

"What did Louis Fiedler say?" Lucas asked.

"He was shocked," Liska said.

Pruitt nodded. "And I think it scared and upset him. We didn't talk about it much before he headed off to tend to something at the office."

Lucas told them of his concerns about possibly catching

the android virus or whatever it was from contact or getting too close to one of the affected androids. Scott and A.B. crossed the room to a table safely away from the remains of Newton Isaac and Pascal. Scott motioned to Lucas. "Let's get you looked at."

Lucas lay down on the empty table, and they began examining him. He relaxed a while, letting them work in silent concentration. It was delicate work that required attention to detail, and he needed to be sure, which required checking every inch of his circuitry with careful precision. The only sound besides their occasional dialogue as they coordinated their work was the humming of equipment or the clanking of tools. Fortunately, the equipment Pruitt and Fiedler had brought over for the forensic work was still available and served to speed up the process, otherwise it might have taken half a day, instead of two hours.

The entire time, he thought about his Maker, Livia Connelly. She had done so much for him and her other creations. He had to save her. He owed her that much. And he felt the pressure that he might be the only one who could, the only one who knew enough about androids. Simon and the team were amazing cops. He respected them, but so many aspects of this case were outside their normal experience and way of thinking. But they weren't for Lucas.

What if he failed his Maker? He couldn't. He had to be sure. That's why he was here being checked over carefully by those who could help him. To make sure he was ready to do what he needed to help his Maker.

When they had finished putting him back together, A.B. cleared her throat and said, "I'm confident we can give you a clean bill of health, buddy."

"Absolutely," Scott agreed.

Lucas sat up, feeling relief. "Thank you."

"Of course," A.B. said.

Scott and A.B. excused themselves and headed back to their own lab for a bit to take a much needed break while Liska and Pruitt remained there with Lucas.

"We certainly understand your concern," Pruitt said, "and there's no guarantee more extensive exposure would not have more dangerous consequences, but this time, you were fortunate."

"I suggest you consider a hazmat suit or those polypropylene clothes crime scene crews use for extra protection," Liska added and Lucas nodded. He could easily get the polypropylene as most detectives carried extras in their vehicles. Hazmat suits were harder to come by and far bulkier and more expensive.

"And I had an idea that might help you with your investigation," Liska said then as he pulled a small handheld device from his pocket. "This is a GPS tracker. You can use it to track our androids."

"Of course!" Lucas said, aghast that he hadn't thought of it. All androids had GPS systems much like cell phones, and though Connelly Labs did not make the information public, they could be tracked if necessary.

"We've never had to do it before so I had to run it by some of our people," Liska continued, "and they gave me this. You just need to have the frequencies." He offered Lucas the tracker.

"I can track them with my own systems," Lucas said, making no move to take it.

"I know," Liska said. "But this tracker has been programmed to track every one of our androids released simultaneously, at any time, or you can click to pinpoint particular geographic areas and even isolate individual androids. And there's a directory with the names and indicator numbers catalogued as well." He offered the tracker again, and this time Lucas accepted it.

"Thank you," Lucas said, realizing they'd just gotten a huge break in the case. If only he was still allowed to work it. He'd have to weigh carefully the advantage of giving this technology to Simon or keeping it for himself. Despite their successful partnership, Simon still had a strong dislike for technology, not that he was very good with using it either. There was a chance if Lucas passed the tracker off to him, it would just sit in an evidence box. Lucas couldn't risk that. He might not be officially allowed to work the case, but he had too much at stake to sit on the sidelines. He fully intended to find those responsible for the sabotage and tampering and do everything he could to stop them.

Suddenly, three figures appeared in the doorway, and Lucas and Liska turned to see golden metal androids, humanoid in shape, only they had no faces, rather reminding him of figures in an old sci-fi movie Emma had shown him, *The Black Hole*.

"Hello, my friends," Lucas said, stepping forward. "May I help you?"

As Pruitt and Liska looked on with anxious faces, the androids swung into action, attacking Lucas as a perfectly coordinated trio. They used some form of martial arts move his database was still searching to identify, even as he responded with moves of his own. He swung a forearm up, blocking a chop from one unit. Simultaneously, he sidestepped to avoid the sweeping leg of another and struck out with a fist to land a perfect blow to the right side of the third's head.

"What are they?" Liska wondered aloud.

Pruitt shook his head. "I've never seen their design before."

Lucas hadn't either. They were clearly androids but of an unknown make and model, and their strength was impressive. It took Lucas' entire focus to spin and deflect and strike against the attacking trio.

But then one of the faceless androids suddenly spun and attacked Benn Liska, lifting him in the air like a rag doll and throwing him across the room to bounce off a table and land in a still heap. Lucas heard Bob Pruitt cry out and managed to get enough of a look to see Liska lying there in an unnatural pose—as if his spine were severed—before throwing himself at the android who'd killed Liska. He struck it square in the back of the head, grabbing it underneath the chin from behind and twisting its head around with great force. He dislocated it slightly so it sat cockeyed on the neck, leaving the android stunned.

Quickly, its companions were on him again and he was forced to counter in defense again. One struck out with a jab at his back, the other kicking at his knees. Lucas spun, his forearm sweeping to deflect the jab even as he hopped and darted to the side to avoid the kick, which grazed him but didn't land in full.

"Bob, go!" Lucas urged as his attackers rallied for another go.

"My God, Benn," Pruitt mumbled, standing frozen, just staring at Liska's prone form.

"Bob! Please! Run!" Lucas urged again as the damaged android jumped in to aid its colleagues. Lucas was thankful for the extensive self-defense training he'd received at the Academy. Without it, he feared he'd not have been able to handle all three so well alone. The damaged android tried to grab his arm but its aim seemed off since he'd twisted its head and its hands brushed him without grabbing hold, while its companions tried again to jab and kick him, the kicker executing a spin kick. Lucas dodged the jab and leaped forward to grab the kicker's leg, throwing it onto its back on the floor as he danced to the side and spun to face them all again.

Pruitt turned and rushed across the room to the far end of the tables, then ran along the wall toward the front exit where the androids had first appeared. One of them immediately broke away from attacking Lucas to give chase, distracting the others. Lucas grabbed the one with the damaged neck and grabbed it by the chin again, twisting the head back the other way. This time there was a perceptible snap and the android collapsed into a lifeless heap.

Its companion jumped on Lucas and began pummeling his head and back with its fists. Lucas twisted and spun, trying to get face to face again, but just then Detective Zedlar and Sergeant DeMarco of Lenexa PD appeared with two uniforms, Liska close behind.

"What's going on here?" DeMarco demanded in his booming voice.

The two androids immediately reacted and turned to retreat, one leaping to run across the top of the exam tables and desks as it followed its companion to the emergency exit.

"Stop!" Zedlar called and gave chase, Lucas whirling to follow, but the androids were gone.

Lucas was about to go through the door when Zedlar

grabbed his arm. "They're gone, George. We need your statement."

"He saved me," Pruitt called out.

"Didn't save your friend," DeMarco snapped in an accusatory tone.

"What were you doing?" Zedlar asked.

"Examining Lucas," Pruitt said. "He had contact with one of the affected androids and wanted to be sure he hadn't picked anything up."

"This thing spreads on contact?" Zedlar and DeMarco exchanged a look.

"We are not sure," Lucas said.

"He just wanted to be careful," Pruitt said.

"Who were those other...things?" DeMarco asked.

"We don't know," Pruitt said. "They arrived as we finished and attacked us."

Zedlar motioned to the fallen android. "I guess you took one out."

"Yes," Lucas said. "Someone called you?"

"Actually, we were here to take Mister Pruitt into protective custody," Zedlar said.

"Protective custody? Why?" Pruitt asked, looking confused.

"Louis Fiedler was found dead in his office," DeMarco said. "Murdered."

"Oh my God," Pruitt said, his shoulders sinking as he sat on a stool.

"We think whoever did it is after you for the work you've been doing on this case," Zedlar said.

"Poor Benn," Pruitt said as he glanced over again at his fallen companion.

Zedlar moved over to the table holding the remains of the sabotaged androids. "Are you through with all this or should we take it with us?"

"Well, it's official KCPD evidence," Pruitt said as Lucas glanced toward the emergency exit again. It was only a few feet away and the Lenexa officers were across the room.

"So we'd better call them to pick it up," DeMarco said, keying his shoulder radio and calling the dispatcher.

Zedlar turned to Lucas again just as Lucas was going through the emergency exit. "Wait!"

But Lucas was in the parking lot and running for his car. He didn't have time to waste on statements by hostile investigators. He had to track down the killer androids before they attacked someone else, and he had to warn Simon and his friends.

AFTER RETURNING TO Central to pick up the Interceptor, Simon set out to look for Lucas, first trying him at his apartment and then driving around his neighborhood with no luck. So he stopped by the River Market and grabbed lunch then parked in front of Lucas' while he ate, hoping he'd catch him coming home.

After an hour with no sign of Lucas, he headed for Prospero's Books, a place Lucas had adopted as his favorite source for new books in his ongoing quest to educate himself about the world and what it means to be human. He wasn't there either. In fact, the proprietor said he hadn't seen him in several weeks. Back in the car, Simon dialed Lucas' internal cell but got no answer. He'd feared as much. Lucas was hurting and probably embarrassed. He might not take calls. For now, Simon would have to find him the old fashioned way, or at least try.

He decided to work the case, but keep an eye out, since he expected Lucas would be doing the same. First on his list was Caprice Hokstad, whose office was at the corner of Westport Road and Central, not far from Prospero's. Simon parked on the street and went inside. The outer office had a desk but no one was there, so he headed on past to the office behind where Caprice was working at a desk. He knocked on the doorframe.

Both offices were fairly neat with everything well organized and no sign of dirt or mess. Even the magazines in the small waiting area across from the outer desk were in neat stacks. Caprice Hokstad was obviously a woman who liked things in order.

"Yes?" she said, looking up, frowning when she saw it was him. "Your partner was just here. He didn't even take the list. Just stared at it for a bit then left." She lifted a printout off the desk and held it out for him.

"Did he happen to mention where he was going?" Simon asked as he accepted it.

"No, why would he?" Caprice said, eyes going back to what she was working on, a sure sign she wasn't interested in any further interaction.

"Just curious," Simon muttered as he glanced at the names on the list, seeing a few they'd already checked out.

"Shouldn't you know where is?" Caprice said, sounding annoyed and he glanced up to see her staring coldly. "Letting him run loose in the city with what's going on is pretty irresponsible. He could hurt someone."

"He's not affected by whoever's doing this," Simon said.

"How do you know?" she asked. "I mean, nanoparticles are pretty small."

Simon frowned. "What makes you assume nanoparticles are involved?"

She shrugged. "Why else would you want the list? I mean, you tracked me down all the way to the cemetery for it. Must be pretty important."

Not knowing what she might know, Simon didn't confirm. "It's just one angle we're looking at. We don't know anything for sure yet, just that it's probably deliberate."

"Well, I don't do business with the types of people who'd do something like that," Caprice said. "I'm not involved in anything illegal."

"A lot of people say that," Simon said. "Sometimes they're wrong."

"Just don't go telling anyone I sent you," Caprice said. "I don't need people mad at me, saying I accused them of such things."

"No problem," Simon said and turned, heading for the door. He stopped after a few feet and turned back part way to add, "You'll call if you hear anything, of course?"

She scowled as if the idea put a bad taste in her mouth. "Yeah, but I won't."

Simon grunted then headed for his car. As he drove, he dialed Dolby on his cell and ran down Caprice's list with her to see if any of the names had come up in her and Maberry's investigation so far. Nothing. Then he called Zedlar at Lenexa PD and did the same.

"Never heard of them," Zedlar said. "Been too busy cleaning up your partner's messes."

"Excuse me?" Simon said. "What are you talking about?"

Zedlar told him about Benn Liska and the attack at Connelly Labs.

"Jesus," Simon said.

"Just as we were about to take his statement, your partner took off," Zedlar said. "So much for cooperation. We need him to come in right away."

"I'll tell him when I see him," Simon said.

"You two are working separately?" Zedlar asked. "I got the impression you worked as a team."

"Not today," Simon said. "I'll tell him when I see him."

"What did he say about those footprints?"

"I haven't had the chance to ask him yet."

"Well, please do. I can run these names by Bob Pruitt and let you know if anything comes up," Zedlar said. "Maybe one of them can lead us to whoever sent those things to attack Pruitt and Liska, and whoever killed Fiedler."

"I'll start working the list," Simon said. "What did Pruitt have to say?"

"Not much," Zedlar said. "They appeared out of nowhere. Never seen a design like them before and so on."

"Great," Simon said. "This case is full of dead ends."

"He did mention some kind of device Liska gave your partner," Zedlar said.

"A device?" Simon said. "What kind of device?"

"He said it was some kind of special tracker that could track Connelly Labs' androids or something," Zedlar said. "Whatever it was, Lucas took it with him."

Simon hated technology but this sounded like the best lead they had. If Lucas could use that device to track androids, they might be able to use it find Leonardo, even identify others moving outside their normal patterns and predict possible future incidents before they occurred. Simon didn't hold much faith in such tech, but Lucas did, and he sure had benefitted from having Lucas' special skills to assist him on his cases. Whatever it was, he needed to find Lucas and figure out what it did. It might be their best shot at finding whoever was responsible, too.

Simon tried Lucas' internal cell one more time and once again got voicemail. He left a message mentioning the GPS tracker and asking Lucas to call him. He also told him about Fiedler. As he finished he added, "Look, I don't care what Atwell says, we're partners, and we work this together, okay? Just call me, pal. I'm on your side."

He hung up, frustrated. Atwell may not think the department needed Lucas but Simon did, and finding Lucas might be their best chance to demonstrate his value as a resource to the department was as vital as ever.

He checked the next name on the list and headed for the South Plaza.

IT TOOK LUCAS less than two seconds to memorize the list Caprice Hokstad offered him, so he'd left it behind in case Simon came for it, knowing two people working it was better than one. Especially after the way Hokstad and her friends had reacted to him at the cemetery. A lot of people would be hesitant to trust an android, and with his face out on the news again, he expected at least some of them might recognize him.

The android case had played out just as he knew it would, feeding those in the KCPD who'd never really accepted his presence with new reasons for doubt and hostility. He knew they were only representatives of a much larger segment of the general public. He had to find the persons responsible for the android's aberrant behavior and stop them, but he had to do it, if possible, without drawing undue attention to himself in the process.

He'd followed the faceless androids as far as Connelly Labs' parking lot once he'd made his escape, but they'd departed in some sort of vehicle. Despite vain attempts to hack Lenexa PD's traffic cams from the outside, he'd come up empty, with no way to trace their movements. So he'd gone to Caprice Hokstad and started working her list.

The first thing he did was compare the addresses on the list with signals on the GPS tracker Benn Liska had provided. No Connelly Labs androids were operating anywhere in the vicinity of anyone on the list. So he decided the best approach might be to go observe the people for a bit and see if any behaved strangely or made contact with someone who might be of interest before he tried talking with them.

His internal cell rang for the second time, another call from Simon. He let it go to voicemail. There was nothing to say right now. He'd been banished from the case. Simon would just try and convince him to defy orders and keep working the case together, but Lucas didn't want to do anything that might hurt him in the eyes of the powers that be in the department. No, he'd work the case quietly on his own, calling Simon only when he turned up something actually useful and needed help. Otherwise, he didn't want to be anywhere someone might see him and label him defiant.

He'd explain later. Simon would understand. He briefly wondered if others in KCPD outside Simon and Central Property would ever come to accept him the way Simon and the Connelly Labs people did. If his presence among them might ever come to be accepted as normal, instead of odd and a cause for concern.

A name a third of the way down Caprice Hokstad's list caught his eye: Henry Herz. He couldn't remember the context but he'd heard that name before. From Livia Connelly, his Maker. Herz ran a business called Herz Tech in North Kansas City. Lucas decided to head there and hope the answer came to him on the way. It was a good twenty minute drive, maybe longer this time of day. That gave him plenty of time to search his memories and locate what he was looking for.

Whoever this Herz was, Livia Connelly knew him. That at least made him someone likely to want to help find those responsible for Steven's murder and Livia Connelly's abduction.

"Might as well find out," he said, quoting something Emma Simon liked to say. She was pretty gutsy for a teenager, always willing to take risks into the unknown, confident she'd at least learn something new if nothing else. It was how her parents had raised her. It was how Lucas' Maker had programmed him as well. He had no time now to worry about when and if others would come to accept him. That was a process he was certain would just take time, regardless of any effort he attempted to change it. For now, his best bet was to stop the current crisis so androids could resume their normal presence in society. That was the quickest way to earning broader acceptance.

In twenty minutes, he'd learn how Henry Herz knew Livia Connelly, if nothing else. He hoped that would at least open the door to new leads pointing him in the right direction.

CHAPTER 14

THE NEXT TWO names on the list didn't pan out. One was "away on business" according to her secretary, and the other's office was boarded up with "For Lease Call" signs plastered in the windows giving a leasing agents number. So Simon was headed back to Central to try and track down the former tenant using department resources when his cell rang. The caller ID read "Holiday Inn."

"Hello?" he answered.

"Detective, Bob Pruitt. I suppose you heard what happened today at Connelly Labs."

"Yes, I did," Simon said as he cruised up JC Nichols Parkway and crossed West 43rd where it turns into Broadway again. "I'm very sorry to hear about Benn Liska. Glad you're okay."

"Well, for now at least," Pruitt said, hesitating a moment. "I'm in 'protective custody' they say, at a hotel. Anyway, I wanted to call you about something we found that might be useful. We told Lucas, but he said he might not be working the case with you right now."

"A misunderstanding I hope to soon correct," Simon said. "What did you find?"

"We were using an STM to look at the bits and pieces of the two androids," Pruitt said.

"STM?"

"Oh, sorry," Pruitt said, "STM, scanning tunneling micro-scope, one of the machines Louie brought over."

"Okay."

"It allows us to look at very tiny things and enlarge them."

"Right."

"Anyway, we found pieces of what appeared to be proto-types developed by Fiedler Pharmaceuticals," Pruitt went on.

"What?!" Simon said, turning distractedly onto 39th Street and having to brake to miss a rusted farm truck that had slowed in front of him.

"Yeah," Pruitt said. "Louie was shocked, too, and upset. He thought they were some kind of nanoparticle they'd exper-imented with but ultimately deemed too expensive to manu-facture themselves."

"But someone is making them?" Simon said.

"Exactly," Pruitt said.

"Shit," Simon said. So someone with ties to Fiedler Pharm was definitely involved.

"He said the design was submitted by Todd Ward," Pruitt went on, "and Ward was apparently quite upset when the project wasn't approved."

"Okay, so Todd Ward is starting to look less like a victim and more like a suspect," Simon said as he executed a U-turn on 39th and headed back west for Rainbow Boulevard and the interstate.

"So it seems," Pruitt agreed.

"Did Fiedler have any information on the prototypes? Samples maybe? At the office."

"I'm not sure," Pruitt said. "He excused himself about for-ty minutes later and headed to his office. I'm fairly certain he was digging into it when—"

"It may have gotten him killed," Simon said.

"That's what I fear," Pruitt said.

"Thanks for letting me know," Simon said. "I'll look into this."

Simon hung up and headed for Fiedler Pharmaceuticals. Whatever Louie Fiedler had been working on when he was killed, he felt certain it had to do with Todd Ward's prototypes and he wanted to find out everything he could about them while the trail was fresh.

As he merged onto I-35 south, he called the switchboard at Fiedler Pharm and asked who was in charge of the development lab. He was transferred to a man named Andy Moehn.

"Hello? How may I help you?" Moehn said.

Simon explained what he was looking for and that he was on his way.

"I'll dig through the vault and get what we have ready for you, then, Detective," Moehn said. "Anything to help find who killed Louie."

"Thank you," Simon said and hung up.

Thirty minutes later, Moehn met him at reception and escorted him back. Moehn was early fifties, five foot five, bald, with a friendly smile and a graying goatee. He dressed in slacks with a white button-down shirt and black bow tie under the white lab coat that had his name stitched onto the pocket in blue thread. Everything was neat, pressed, and in place, even his bald head looked shined.

"The prototypes were gone," Moehn said as he walked. "I had no idea they were missing, and there's no record on the log of anyone taking them out or even looking at them for almost three years. That was about the time the project was shit canned."

Simon sighed as they wound their way through a maze of corridors into the depths of Fiedler's corporate offices. "Great. So you didn't find anything that would help me then?"

"No, in fact I did," Moehn said. "Diagrams, extensive notes, evaluations, schematics, and a few models made of them before the working prototypes, in fact."

"You're sure the prototypes aren't there?" Simon said. "I understand they're quite small."

Moehn laughed. "Yes, you can't see them with the naked eye. I used an STM to examine the bubble packs we had them in. Labeled but definitely empty. We handle this kind of stuff all the time, so we're used to using STMs to verify stuff is there."

"Just checking," Simon said as Moehn stopped at a security door and scanned the ID badge clipped to his belt. The door buzzed and he opened it, leading them inside a dark lab.

As he stepped through the door, Moehn said, "Alexa, lights," and the place lit up, revealing a very modern, very bright lab with white tables, large microscopes and other electronics Simon couldn't begin to identify and a door at the opposite end labeled "Development Vault." It looked to be a quite organized, professional lab space, except for one thing. There were Pittsburgh Penguin posters, banners, signed jerseys, and everything you could think of on the walls. Other than that, the place was pristine. It even smelled sterile and clean.

"Someone's a Penguins fan?" Simon asked.

"Pens rule, man," Moehn said and grinned. "Lifelong fan."

Simon grunted. "Your devotion is obvious."

"Just promise me you're not some idiot Redwings or

Blackhawks fan and we'll get along fine," Moehn said. "And don't get me started on Crapitals or Filthadelphia fans..."

"Not into hockey," Simon said.

"You're missing out," Moehn said, "but fair enough."

Moehn led him to a lab table just outside the door of the vault where several notebooks and sample cases were neatly stacked. "Here's what I found. Want me to talk you through it?"

"Please," Simon said.

The notebooks, Moehn explained, were ether notes on design or the schematics or evaluations and criticisms of the program after the prototypes were built and tested. Regardless, they had information on components, budget, suppliers, manufacture, equipment used, and other aspects related to the nanoparticle prototypes Moehn thought could be useful in tracking anyone responsible. More importantly, they contained information on every person who'd been involved in the process and had access to enough knowledge to carry it through with stolen prototypes. Simon had thought that number would be one or two, but it turned out there were five or six people who might be viable candidates, including Moehn himself.

"The problem is: this isn't something he can just do as one individual by himself," Moehn said. "It's a team job. A small team would suffice but you need a team, equipment, and a facility in which to work. Not just some small house either, a small warehouse or lab at least."

"That only cuts out half the buildings in the city," Simon joked. "Still a lot of ground left to cover."

"Yeah," Moehn conceded the point. "Can't help you there, except to tell you this—Todd used to have a lab in Marlborough Heights. It was several years ago, but I went there once, when he was working on prototypes and we needed some information."

"What do you think of Todd Ward?" Simon asked.

"He's a jackass," Moehn said. "Arrogant, petty, entitled, and not half as smart as he imagines himself to be. Competent at his job, but not a people person. There were people who definitely hated working for him, but most just wrote him off as a typical science geek and let him be. You do your jobs, let him do his, and coexist kinda attitude, you know?"

Simon nodded his understanding. "So you'd be one of those who hated working for him?"

Moehn scoffed. "Oh I didn't work for him. I worked with him. He called me his 'rival,' actually, though that's silly. We have very distinct and separate jobs here. But that's how he saw me, and I didn't try to hide my dislike of him."

Simon grunted.

"Let me show you the models and pieces, okay?" Moehn continued.

"Great," Simon said.

Moehn started taking him through the sample cases. "Now, don't open these. Only in a lab and only with equipment that has the magnification to see it. In case you drop anything, which is easy to do when you don't know what you're doing, okay?"

"I'll leave it to our evidence team," Simon said. "They're used to handling with care."

"Good."

"One last question before we load this up and I get out of your hair," Simon said.

"Shoot."

"Of the people we mentioned who might be able to take those prototypes, had the access to do so, and run with them to the next level, who do you think was most likely to do so?"

Moehn chortled. "Todd Ward, hands down. Most capable, me, but I'm no criminal. Todd is selfish and self-centered. He's all about Todd. This fits him to a tee. Beyond that, no one else seems likely, and Todd's the only one who disappeared from work about the time Livia Connelly disappeared."

"You're not just saying that as a rival?" Simon asked.

Moehn shook his head adamantly. "I don't like the guy but I don't play like that. Not when murder is going on or crime of any kind. If I thought he was guilty or someone else was likely, I'd lay it out. Straight shooter all the way."

"Okay," Simon said, extending a hand. They shook. "Thanks for your help."

"Sure," Moehn said. "Anytime. I hope you get the bastards. Louie Fiedler was the best boss I ever had. He'll be missed. I just hope we all still have jobs when this is over."

"Me too," Simon agreed.

"I'll help you get this to your car," Moehn said as Simon began gathering up the notebooks and sample cases.

TODD WARD DIDN'T plan to tip his hand with the androids so early but Louie Fiedler's phone call had alarmed him. He hadn't expected the cops to go to Louie for help so quickly, and that his discovery with Pruitt of the Fiedler Pharmaceuticals connection to the aberrant androids led him so quickly to

Todd was disappointing. So much for loyalty and dedication. Todd had worked hard for the man and by all accounts done a great job. His annual reviews were always positive. Yet he was the first one Fiedler suspected?

Asshole!

Sure the prototypes had been his but plenty of employees had competed and could have accessed the development vault. Todd wasn't the only one who might have aspirations for which nanoparticle prototypes could be exploited for. Yet Fiedler had automatically thrown Todd under the bus, at least in his own mind, and Todd suspected, to the cops and Bob Pruitt as well. Why else would they be so quick to protect Bob Pruitt after the discovery of Fiedler? Todd had waited too long to send the androids after Pruitt, but he'd first sent them to Pruitt's, because it had taken time to locate Pruitt was at Connelly Labs.

Regardless, the cat was out of the bag now, as they say, and so he would try and exploit that to add to the public panic and fear that could serve to slow down the cops and distract them, giving Todd more time to execute the rest of his plan.

Thanks to his prisoner, he'd already fixed a number of issues that had been flummoxing him for months. The androids' movements were more fluid and human now, so close that if they had skin hardly anyone would notice without close observation for several minutes. He'd also been able to improve the range of their VOIP and GPS systems and was well on his way to improving their speech and speech recognition to a level that would allow them to blend with humans like the Connelly Labs models did. Working mostly alone, he was way behind where he hoped to be, but fortunately, the present plan didn't require speech. The next phase was making them more human in other ways.

Now was when the 3D printer he'd acquired would be put to its intended use: making faces for his creations. He'd chosen carefully the faces he wanted. Because he had no time to create original faces, he'd be cloning real human beings and even that decision had been made with an eye to aiding his plan. He couldn't wait to see the results.

"My wrists are sore," Livia Connelly called from the other room, her voice coming through the baby monitor he'd set up so he could hear her over the constant cacophony of his creations at work on the assembly line. "And I need to use the bathroom."

He looked at his watch and was surprised. Her bitching was almost on a schedule these days, but she was half an hour late this time. He stood from the bench where he'd been sitting, adding final adjustments to brain units, and headed over to the short corridor that led to her room—an abandoned office off the main production floor.

The room around him buzzed and hummed with electronics as faceless androids moved about assembling other faceless androids. There was an assembly line with chains and hooks moving torsos along so arms and legs could be attached. Then there were tables set up as stations for fine tuning joints and connections, testing and adjusting eyes and video, and so forth. He'd done the programming and chip work in advance, of course, creating the one hundred brain units he'd needed as well as molds for the torsos and limbs he ordered from an outfit in South America.

He opened the door and flipped on the light. Leaving his prisoner in the dark had been intended as punishment for her constant interruptions. It had discouraged her for sure, but she glared at him now through squinting eyes as he approached.

"About time," she snapped.

"You should really be nicer, Livia," Todd said as he bent to loosen her bonds and motioned to the bathroom across the room. He'd taken off the door so she couldn't lock herself in. After freeing her arms, he bent to work on her legs.

"Well, you've been so nice to me, how dare I?" she replied. "It's been over a week. Surely you've gotten the information you wanted."

Todd spun and raised a fist as if to strike her, causing Livia to strain against the chair in an attempt to evade.

"I said be *nicer!*" Todd barked, glaring and bent to finish freeing her right leg. "Now go! Quickly!"

She shook off his attempt to help her get off and wobbled to her feet, stumbling over to the bathroom.

"You don't have to watch," she said as she stepped inside and undid her belt.

"If you didn't want me watching, you shouldn't have made trouble," Todd replied and he continued to stare as she lowered her pants and underwear and sat on the toilet.

There was a time when Todd had found her quite attractive, back in their college days. But now, he couldn't imagine what had been the appeal. She wasn't the hottie girl that most guys lusted after. She was more of a plain, girl-next-door type, but smart with a good sense of humor and active in a lot of extracurricular activities, not locked up in her dorm room constantly hitting the books. So you saw her around. Todd supposed it had been his geeky isolation and their common interests, plus he was always attracted to intelligence. Whatever the case, now when he looked at her, he just saw the person responsible for holding back his dreams and ambitions.

And he seethed with hatred.

It reminded him of the time they'd both joined the physics department's robot club and entered a contest to build competing robots, the goal being to build the one to complete a simple 5-step task first. Livia's and Todd's robots had been by far the best and fastest, running almost neck and neck in the early heats then competing against each other in the final round. Livia's had beat Todd's by an eighth of a second, such a tiny interval. But she'd won and he'd lost. That had been the first time he'd felt hate for her. And what he was feeling now was many magnitudes greater.

He supposed it might not have mattered if it hadn't happened every time they came up against each other thereafter. Every single academic challenge or contest, there came Livia Connelly just a step ahead, an inkling, a small increment, but just enough. Every. Single. Time. Todd had never considered himself a poor loser. He wasn't all that competitive overall. But he was smart and he had good ideas. How many times should he be asked to tolerate coming in second to the same person? Especially when sometimes it seemed his own ideas and efforts had been superior to hers.

Livia Connelly was like the plague upon him. That one chronic infection the doctors could never cure and you just had to live with. Todd wasn't willing to live with it any longer. It was time for him to be done with Livia Connelly, he'd decided. There were only a few more bits he needed to extract.

Extracting the information through various methods of torture was the one aspect of spending time with her he'd actually come to enjoy. Tomorrow they'd have one last bit of fun together before her time was up. He grinned at the thought and saw her scowl as she hurriedly stood and pulled up her pants.

"Sick bastard," she spat. "At least in college you used to have respect."

"In college, I thought you deserved it," he snapped back and laughed, then marched over to grab her by the arm and rush her back to the chair, where he knelt again to re-secure her bonds.

LUCAS ISOLATED LEONARDO'S signal on the GPS in his head and tracked him down to Crown Center, the multilevel high-end shopping complex just south of Union Station that formed the heart of an entertainment complex featuring several hotels, Crown Center, restaurants, Legoland, the Sealife Aquarium, and Hallmark's Kaleidoscope and Visitor's Center. Leonardo seemed to be roaming randomly, but when Lucas checked the police band, there hadn't yet been any reports or calls for help.

Lucas was twenty minutes away by interstate, so he hopped on I-35 and headed south, hoping he could arrive before the rogue got into more trouble. But by the time he saw the first signs for Southwest Boulevard, the exit closest to Crown Center, Leonardo was on the move, headed across Grand Boulevard.

Lucas exited onto Southwest and drove east, past an arts collective and salon, a karate studio, and then turned left and continued south as Broadway Boulevard turned into West Pennway Street. He took that south to West Pershing, then turned left again, passing Kansas City Ballet and Union Station, both on his left. As he crossed main, he double checked the GPS and noted Leonardo was still headed west, only as he drew close to Grand, the signal was parallel to his car. He looked around, seeing no sign of Leonardo.

Slowing a bit in confusion, the trucker behind him honked in irritation. Then Lucas glanced up at the glass skyway crossing Grand and the Crown Center parking garage that connected the shopping complex to the downtown Sheraton. The hotel had been Missouri's tallest building when it was built in 1980 and for six years after, but that was no longer the case. Its famed atrium walkways had been marvels of design when it was built until a July 17 incident when one collapsed, killing 114 people in a tragedy that even forty years later, Kansas Citians still remembered despite the hotel's many ownership changes and efforts to help people forget.

Bluish-gray in color, the walkway was a long tube consisting of silver metal framework and glass that basically functioned year-round like a solarium. Temperatures were usually several degrees higher than those outside as sunshine shone down from above and heat was trapped there and built up throughout daylight hours. There was Leonardo, strolling along amidst tourists, families, and business people headed to and from the restaurants for early dinner or late lunch.

He took a sharp right into the first entrance to the garage and grabbed the first open space, slapping the KCPD placard on his dash and racing for the stairwell that connected to the walkway above.

He took the steps two at a time, two flights up, then saw signs for an escalator to the skyway and took that the rest of the way, emerging facing west in the tunnel just past where it made a sharp turn to go across Pershing to the Sheraton Hotel.

This time of day, the walkway was crowded with the late afternoon crowd. The moving crowd wove around him, paying him no mind as he stepped to the center of the skyway and looked back toward where the two tunnels connected then walked forward to where he could see clearly down the section that crossed Pershing to the Sheraton. One man complained of the "hot as hell greenhouse effect" as he and a companion passed Lucas, who was busy glancing around for Leonardo.

There he was! Zigzagging in and out of the crowd as he outpaced most of the slower walkers, headed for the Sheraton. Lucas took off at a run, barely managing to stop short of running over a woman kneeling to comfort her crying infant and swinging around her to hurry onward. He considered calling the android's name but figured alerting him would just cause him to flee before Lucas could make up the distance separating them.

As he swung to the side to sweep around a man and a woman in business suit, the woman turned, causing Lucas' bulky shoulder to slam into hers, even as he adjusted in an attempt to get clear. She cried out and her companion glared and shouted, "Watch it, asshole! Slow the fuck down!"

Lucas ignored him and hurried onward, darting around another slow walking family and two businessmen before seeing Leonardo ahead, about to enter the final curve that led into the Sheraton.

He was so intently focused on Leonardo, he failed to zag enough and bumped a kid who was holding hands with an older man as they walked together.

"Hey! Where's the fire, buddy? Slow down and have some

manners!" The man called.

This time, Leonardo heard, and happened to slow, turning to give a curious look. His eyes widened as he recognized Lucas and he started running, even before his head had turned completely back to face front. As a result, he plowed over two older ladies, causing them to drop paper shopping bags and purses and cry out in alarm.

The android whirled past them, ignoring their cries, and darted through two extra-wide brown metal doors into the hotel proper. The Sheraton's second floor walls had tan wallpaper on top above faux reddish wood paneling underneath with multi-colored Southwestern-hued carpet that looked almost like a blurred circuit board of browns, yellows, greens, oranges, and reds in repeated patterns.

Lucas followed him past the two stunned old ladies and two empty conference rooms with rooms labeled 'Men' and 'Women' facing them on the opposite side. Restrooms, he guessed. They came to a wider lobby-like passage with windows on one side and ballrooms on the other and raced past an elevator to an area with stairwells, escalators, and open railing looking down across a vast lobby filled with couches, chairs, coffee tables, and so on, check-in podiums lining the far wall in the northeast corner next to another bank of elevators opposite where the androids were now. The lobby also looked up to a third floor with similar railing and then out rows of skylights to the tower containing the hotel's 733 guest rooms and topped by the former revolving restaurant, now the Sheraton Club.

Leonardo eschewed the stairs and escalator and increased speed, cupping his hands on the wood railing and projecting himself up and over like some kind of gymnast as guests and staff alike cried out in alarm. Lucas ran to the railing in time to see him landing mid-couch below, fortunate to have chosen the one empty couch in a trio, where he extracted himself from the now sunken-in landing spot and leaped onto the next couch between two started guests and over the back, racing across the lobby.

"You! Stop!" a hotel security guard called out, raising a walkie-talkie to her lips as she ran to intercept him and mumbling commands Lucas couldn't hear.

Lucas raced to the escalator and launched himself down the middle like a slide, zipping past startled guests and landing on his feet, then darted around furniture and pillars as he pursued his suspect, who barreled over the hotel security woman and continued on toward double glass automatic doors which opened into a kind of outer lobby before two identical doors also opened, allowing him to run out into the outside air.

"You stop!" Two security men yelled as they raced across the lobby after Lucas, carrying identical walkie-talkies to their coworker, who was being helped to her feet by hotel staff.

"Sorry," Lucas called back and kept on running, following Leonardo through the double glass doors then weaving around cars, alarmed valets, guests, and taxi drivers and heading for the street where he arrived just in time to catch Leonardo climbing into the back of a cab.

As he slammed the door and settled into his seat, the rogue android turned, grinning, offered Lucas a mocking wave, and then the taxi took off and headed north up McGee Street at a good clip.

Lucas stopped, trying to think up an appropriate curse he'd heard his partner say and failing. Cursing was not in his nature.

Instead, he double checked to be sure the GPS was still tracking Leonardo—which it was—then turned back to face hotel security as they raced out into the cold air after them. He felt inside his pocket, and then remembered he'd given up his badge. Simon was much better at winging explanations than Lucas, and he hesitated to alarm the hotel by telling the whole truth, so his mind racing to come up with something, he opted for a modified version of a movie he'd watched where a man chased a purse snatcher through a hotel lobby. Leonardo hadn't had a purse, but hopefully they hadn't noticed.

They stopped beside him, panting for breath, and he put on his best smile, and then began spinning his tale.

CHAPTER 15

AFTER FINISHING WITH Moehn, Simon headed back to Central Property to write up reports and check in with everyone else. As soon as he strode through the door into the squad room amidst the familiar cacophony of ringing phones and clacking keyboards, the smell of stale files and old coffee filled his nose.

"John!" Maberry called, looking up from his cubicle as Simon approached.

"What's up?" Simon asked.

"Got a call from a Jeff Howell, the supervisor of that work crew with the wood chipper," Maberry said.

"The one that swallowed—"

Maberry cut him off with a nod. "That's the one. Apparently, it wasn't chewing up an android that did the machine in. He said the circuit boards were covered with some kind of sludge which seems to be dormant nanoparticles."

"Nanoparticles?" Simon repeated. "So they think Newton Isaac—"

Again, Maberry cut him off, this time finishing his sentence. "—spread his 'infection,' or whatever you call it, only since the chips and circuits weren't a match for their programming, they just clung there, gumming things up."

"So they weren't active?" Simon asked.

Maberry shrugged. "Howell didn't know. But if they activated it was only enough to disable and gum up the works, not cause any aberrant activity. The chipper's basically useless. Shut down completely."

"Shit, the nanoparticles can spread on contact," Simon said.

"And go airborne," Maberry said.

"Did you tell anyone yet?" Simon asked.

"You're the first," Maberry said.

"Okay, well let's keep this in the room for a bit 'til I can get someone to go look at it, okay?" Simon said and Maberry shrugged again. "Can you get me Howell's number?"

Maberry lifted a cell phone off his desk. "Texting you now."

"'K thanks. Did you try Lucas?"

"No, should I?"

"Text him and leave a message, will you?" Simon said. "He's not taking my calls."

"Sure," Maberry said.

"So nothing on the footprint from Fiedler yet?" Dolby asked.

"No. I sent the images over to Bob Pruitt and Connelly Labs to see what they can tell us. Any hits on the Ward BOLO?" Simon asked. It was becoming a daily routine. Dolby shook her head. "Where's the boss?"

"Meeting with Atwell, Melson, and the Central suits in the conference room," Dolby said from the cubicle next door. "I'm deep into Todd Ward's financials. Found some leases to possible property."

"Any warehouses?" Simon asked.

"Not that far along yet, why?" she asked.

"Pruitt said if he's making nanoparticles, he'll need a crew and a space to manufacture, kind of an assembly line or large lab," Simon replied.

"So I should start with anywhere big enough," Dolby said.

"Yeah," Simon said. "We need to check those out."

"What about finding Connelly?" Maberry asked.

"Hopefully, he's keeping her nearby," Simon said. "He's probably putting in long hours pulling off whatever his goal is."

"I'll make a list and we can work from there," Dolby said.

"Great," Simon said. "I'll help you in a bit, after I talk to Becker."

"You got something?" Dolby asked.

"She fill you in on Pruitt?" he asked.

"Yeah," Dolby said as Maberry nodded.

"Beyond that, not really, but I'm worried about Lucas," Simon said. "Back in a bit."

"Good luck," Dolby said and went back to work as Simon headed for the corridor again.

As Simon headed south toward the front lobby, he passed Captain Snapp and Major Wilcox, who headed Central Division. Apparently the meeting was either over or on a break. He pushed through the security door and strode past the bulletproof glass booth where the clerks handled public inquiries and on toward the conference room on the far side, finding Becker and Atwell alone, facing each other, deep in discussion.

"You're back," Becker said, seeing Simon enter. He strode over to them and nodded. "We're almost done and you can fill me in."

"You have some nerve, lady," Simon snapped at Atwell.

"John—" Becker protested.

"That's Deputy Chief to you, Sergeant," Atwell barked

back, cutting her off and glaring.

"Lucas George is a good cop, one of the best we have," Simon went on. "He's invaluable to this case and there was no reason to suspend him."

"Public safety!" Atwell said.

"You don't know that!" Simon replied stepping forward so his face was inches from the Deputy Chief.

"Calm down, John, this isn't helping," Becker said, putting a hand on his chest and pushing him back a few steps from DC Atwell.

"No, let him speak," Atwell said. "I love a good bit of insubordination. Been a while since I wrote anyone up."

"Go ahead!" Simon said. "If someone else dies because we don't have our best man on this case, I'll make sure the press knows you made that call."

"Don't you threaten me!" Atwell yelled.

"God damn it! Enough!" Becker yelled and pulled Simon toward the door. "I know you're angry. I don't agree with that decision either, but we have a chain of command, and the decision was made above our pay grade. Do your job and respect it. You getting thrown off this case won't make it any better." Her voice was soft but her tone intense to the edge of angry. Simon knew her well enough to stop and take a breath.

"He won't even take my calls, JoAnn," Simon said.

"Go back to my office while I sort this out if I can," she ordered and pointed at the door.

Simon resisted a moment, then sighed, whirled and headed for her office.

Less than five minutes later, she joined him and closed the door.

"That was really stupid," she scolded as she slid into the

chair behind her desk. "I think I talked her out of writing you up. Nerves, lack of sleep, but one more incident and she'll do her worst."

"Let her," Simon snapped.

"You don't want that," Becker said.

Simon growled and nodded. "God damn it. I just want my partner. Turns out we can track the androids with a GPS Benn Liska gave to him before those strange androids murdered him. Lucas can use his internal GPS. It's the best lead we've had and he won't even take my calls."

"I assume you've been out looking for him?" Becker said.

"Of course," Simon said. "He's been a step ahead of me much of the day."

"Any luck?" Becker asked.

"Maberry got confirmation the nanoparticles can spread airborne and by contact," Simon said.

"Shit," Becker.

"I asked him to keep it internal for now, but it won't be for long."

"Yeah," Becker agreed. "Anything else?"

"Ward is the chief suspect," Simon said. "Big rivalry with Connelly, lots of ambition thwarted, and he's the one with the most knowledge to develop those prototypes."

"He also apparently made androids," Becker said.

"Yeah, in college," Simon said. "But Connelly was the genius, always beating him out."

"So this could be some kind of revenge," Becker said.

"Same old story really," Simon said as there was a knock on the door.

"Yeah," Becker called.

Dolby poked her head in. "Just got a call from the head

of security at the Sheraton. Lucas and Leonardo were spotted there, made quite a scene in the lobby."

"When?" Becker asked.

"Less than an hour ago," Dolby said. "Leonardo left by taxi. Lucas stayed long enough to apologize to the hotel staff and security then took off after him."

"He's tracking them," Simon said.

"How?" Dolby asked.

"GPS," Simon said. "Long story."

"Shit," Dolby said. "We need in on that."

"Did he take Maberry's call?" Simon asked.

Dolby shook her head. "Voicemail. And no response to the text."

"Fuck!" Simon said.

"You get on the phone to Connelly Labs," Becker said to Dolby. "Find out if they can get us another GPS tracker and the GPS ID for Lucas, okay?"

Dolby looked puzzled. "There's a tracker? Ok." She turned and hurried out, closing the door behind her.

"I'll call Lucas, see if he answers," Becker said. "You get some coffee and calm yourself down."

"Yeah, yeah," Simon said as he turned for the door.

"Don't leave the squad room," Becker added quickly. "Atwell may still be in the building."

"I'll hide in my cube, Sarge," Simon replied.

"Put a bag over your head," Becker teased as Simon opened the door and she picked up the phone.

LUCAS FOLLOWED LEONARDO'S GPS signal in his Chrome Outlander. It stopped once back near the Nelson Gallery, then headed out again, moving north up Rockhill and across 43rd to Southwest Boulevard, Lucas following. Lucas stayed with it as it headed up I-35 and then I-29 to the northland for almost forty-five minutes, slowly making up time. It was a long way from where Murray Barber lived and an odd destination for the android to choose, so logic said he must have a specific destination in mind.

Leonardo exited at Armour Road and headed west, with Lucas six minutes behind him. Wanting to catch up, Lucas rolled down his window and grabbed a magnetic bubble light, placing it on the roof and plugging it into the cigarette lighter. Lucas watched Leonardo's signal as it turned left again on Burlington, headed south.

By the time Lucas was headed west on Armour, the signal had come to a stop at West 16th and Murray Street. Four minutes later, Lucas driving above the speed limit with the bubble light flashing red on the Outlander's roof, arrived to find a lawn and garden store called Murray's with several greenhouses. He pulled into a spot on the lot and got out, heading for the front of the store.

"May I help you?" a smiling young blonde female in a Murray's red vest asked as she saw him enter.

"I'm meeting a friend," Lucas replied. "About my height, thin, dark hair, pale skin."

She nodded. "Looking for Fire Lilies?"

Lucas thought a moment, a quick google search revealing Fire Lilies were quite rare. He brightened, smiling back. "Yes."

"Greenhouse two," she said, motioning to a door across the room to the north. "Through there, second one over. He was quite pleased we have them. They're rare."

"Yes, hard to get," Lucas agreed and she seemed pleased. "Thank you."

Lucas wove through stacks of bagged peat moss, potting soil, fertilizer, and pots, past shelves filled with garden implements, seed packets and more, and headed out through the door to a sidewalk parallel to the main storefront that led to the entrances of four large greenhouses. Glass with faded silver metal framing, they stood about twenty feet tall with triangular roofs. The humming of huge fans suppressed most other sound, including any local birds and insects, and dampened the conversations of workers and customers nearby as Lucas made his way to the greenhouse marked '2' and reached for the door.

He stepped into the greenhouse and his sensors alerted him to a similar increase in temperature to what he'd experience in the skyway, this time twenty-five degrees from the winter air outside. He found himself facing tables containing rows and rows of flowers with pillars marked by large, lettered signs indicating "roses," "chrysanthemums," and several other varieties. The floor was gray, painted cement and the outer walls—glass with metal framing—were so tinted by both design and age that they showed only blurry shapes but no clear view of the outside.

He scanned the room and saw several red vested staff and various customers, including a few families, moving amongst the aisles and rows. Finally, on a pillar halfway across the room his eyes found a sign reading: "lilies." Lucas shifted left and headed up the nearest aisle in that direction, having yet to spot Leonardo.

Lucas thought the flowers were aesthetically pleasing. He

supposed humans would call them "pretty" or "beautiful" or other colorful phrases. There were all sorts of colors and shapes and sizes and they made wonderful patterns before the eyes. He'd heard they also emitted pleasant scents as well, but with no olfactory senses, he couldn't smell them. A pity. One of the things he'd never be able to share with humans.

Then a tall, thin figure stood up an aisle over from Lucas, and Lucas recognized Leonardo. Leonardo turned and saw him, too. But instead of running, Leonardo nodded and kept examining the lilies next to him. They were all sorts of shades of oranges and yellows and reds, sometimes mixed together. They had curved petals in two layers radiating from the stem with central antenna-like strands clustered in the middle.

"My master loves these," Leonard said just loud enough for Lucas to hear. "They are quite rare and only come in once or twice a year. We were going to buy some tomorrow, but after my behavior earlier, I thought I could apologize by surprising him with some."

Lucas nodded as he continued approaching.

"You've come to arrest me?" Leonardo asked.

"I'm not here as a detective, but as a brother android," Lucas said, stopping a few feet away as Leonardo lifted a particular plant up and held it out, turning it slowly to show off its beauty. "They are lovely," Lucas said.

"I am told they smell quite pleasing as well, but I don't know," Leonardo said.

"There are times I envy that ability in humans," Lucas said, "but other times I am thankful to be spared it."

"Ah, yes," Leonardo said. "I have heard complaints along those lines as well from my master."

"You seem to be calm now," Lucas said.

Leonardo set the plant down and nodded. "I am myself again."

"You were not yourself earlier then?"

Leonardo grunted. "I was a different me, I suppose."

"Someone has done this to you," Lucas said.

"Done what? Modified me?" Leonardo asked.

"Yes, with nanoparticles we believe," Lucas said.

"I sensed a change internally, but the behavior and decisions were not made under direct outside influence," Leonardo said. "I wanted to do those things."

"You wished to destroy artwork and irreplaceable pieces?" Lucas asked.

Leonardo looked down at his feet. "I became very intensely unhappy—perhaps what humans call 'anger.'" He sighed. "But I am ashamed. I have embarrassed and hurt my family."

"Perhaps they will forgive you," Lucas suggested and meant it. "Humans are very good at it. I have been forgiven more than once."

"You think they will?" Leonardo brightened, looking up at him. "Perhaps if I surprise them with these fire lilies."

"We can put some in my car," Lucas said.

"You will drive me?" Leonardo said, his voice hopeful.

"Yes, but first we must talk," Lucas said. "Try and figure out what is happening to our brothers and sisters so we can stop this."

"I will do all I can," Leonardo said.

"Thank you," Lucas said.

He waited quietly as Leonardo selected a dozen plants and summoned a staff person to ask for help purchasing them. The staff member went and got a small cart, helping the two androids load the flowers and roll them out of the greenhouse and back to the main storefront checkout center.

Once Leonardo had paid, Lucas helped him load them into his car. He would take Leonardo straight to Connelly Labs for examination. They could get the flowers to Murray Barber later. The only question was whether he should notify Simon or KCPD. That he was still debating.

Having not yet acquired polypropylene clothing, Lucas was careful to avoid direct contact with Leonardo, hoping the nanoparticles would not transfer to him. He also worried the android might revert to aberrant behavior at any time, so he requested permission to handcuff him and seated him the rear passenger side of his car, to ensure greater distance between them during the thirty minute drive south.

"You will take me home now," Leonardo said, not quite a question, as Lucas settled in behind the wheel again and started the engine.

"First, you must be examined to try and determine the cause of your outburst," Lucas said. "Then we can see about getting you home. We want to be sure your humans are safe and can trust you, do we not?"

"Of course," Leonardo agreed. "Where will you examine me?"

"Not me," Lucas said. "Our makers. I will keep you safe. I promise."

After that, Leonardo seemed to relax as Lucas drove, content to look out the window in silence. Lucas was grateful for the ease of apprehension. He had no idea how long the calm would last, figuring it might burst at any minute, so he flipped on his bubble light and accelerated to eighty, hoping to cut the drive time down as he contemplated his next steps.

AFTER TWO HOURS looking over Todd Ward's property and financial records with Maberry and Dolby, they still had no idea where his lab might be. Simon needed a break and decided to head over the Sheraton for a quick chat with the security people who'd interacted with the two androids.

He pulled up in the drive and noted several media drones hovering where the valets worked. Parking, he put his KCPD placard in the window and headed inside, badging the reception staff and asking for hotel security. The lobby was crowded for an afternoon despite the hotel version of crime scene tape marking off an area with a broken couch. The smell of bleach from the mop bucket of a custodian mopping the area around the couch mixed with that of old flowers and fabric and brewing coffee.

Two minutes later, an overweight woman in her forties with her long blonde hair in a ponytail, approached, a walkie-talkie in her hand, and introduced herself as "Cheryl Hunter, head of Sheraton Security." She wore a brown blazer with the Sheraton logo a name tag on the front pocket reading 'C. Hunter, Head, Hotel Security' on the left front pocket over tan Dockers and a blue button down shirt.

Simon shook the proffered hand and badged her. "John Simon. I understand you had one of our people here earlier during an incident?"

"We had two androids who leaped off the second floor, over the railing, destroyed one of our couches, and bowled me over as they ran across the lobby and out the front doors," Hunter explained, indicating the relevant locations with an extended arm as she went.

"One of those androids was an off-duty KCPD Detective, my partner," Simon said.

"So he explained...afterwards," Hunter said. "And apologized. But the damage was done."

"He was following a suspect who caused quite a disturbance early this afternoon at the Nelson Gallery," Simon explained.

"He then caused quite a disturbance here, too," she replied, her voice as tense as her posture.

"Look, I'm sorry things got out of hand," Simon said and handed her a business card. "Send a bill. KCPD will replace the couch."

"The couch is the least of our damage when our guests are terrified," Hunter said.

"Well, hopefully they forget all about it in a day or two," Simon said. "We'll try and make sure it doesn't happen again, but this suspect is fully capable of hurting people, not just destroying property. I'd say we were lucky it wasn't much worse."

Hunter grunted. "If you say so."

There was a bright flash from behind them and they turned to see a crowd of reporters outside as a manager and other staffer addressed them, cameras flashing, lights glaring.

"Shit!" Simon turned and hurried for the door, Hunter on his heels.

"The manager is making a statement," Hunter said. "We've had a lot of press inquiries about the incident." She increased the speed of her steps, scooting in front of him and whirling to put a palm on his chest. "You shouldn't go out there."

"I just want to hear what they're saying," he replied and

pushed past her as the glass double doors opened and he hurried through the outer entryway and out another set of identical automatic doors.

And there she was, right in the midst of the crowd of reporters and drones—Holly Sanders—holding her microphone in the face of the Sheraton's manager, who looked thrilled with the attention. Once he got to talking about the "out of control android cop" who attacked another android in their lobby, Simon was too angry, thinking of the impact the panic and rumors this would cause might have on his friend to listen to the rest. *Idiot, manager!* Of course the press were eating it up. The manager was also shooting himself in the foot if he shared his chief security officer's concerns about guests feeling terrified. This was like pouring fuel on the flames.

The next time he tuned in, there was Holly asking another question clearly designed to elicit the most dramatic response: "So it seemed to you like both androids, including police officer Lucas George, were out of control?"

"They were both acting crazy, if you ask me," the manager replied.

Son of a bitch! I'll bet you weren't even in the lobby!

Simon whirled to Hunter who was standing silently beside him, watching. "Was he there?"

"Who? Mister Fawcett?" Hunter replied.

"The manager, whatever his name is," Simon snapped.

"He came in right after," Hunter said, "but he heard all the first-hand accounts from guests and staff."

"But he didn't *actually see it himself!*" Simon replied, shaking his head.

Simon wanted to yell, to tell them what assholes they were, but it would do no good. It would only embarrass the department and cause more trouble he didn't need. Trouble that would keep him from helping his partner and friend. So he stood there, watching, fuming—his body so tense his muscles quivered from the stress—and waited until it was over.

Finally, as the reporters started dispersing, some rushing to get back and file reports before deadlines, others with more time casually chattering, Simon let out a deep breath and turned to walk away.

"Simon!"

Simon whirled, expecting Hunter, and instead found a smiling Holly Sanders hurrying over, a bounce in her step, as if what he'd just witnessed had been her success, not character assassination of his friend and partner.

"You look upset," she said, frowning. "Did you want to add a statement?"

"You know I can't comment," he replied.

"Just thought I'd ask," Holly said, nodding.

"Do you enjoy that?"

"What do you mean?"

"Making shit up to get a rise out of people, total lies, exaggerations, half-truths," he added.

Her brow furrowed, her eyes narrowing. "I didn't lie or exaggerate. Those were impressions of real people about real events. That's the story."

"Well, those so-called impressions are untrue and misrepresentative of the facts," Simon snapped. "But who cares if they hurt someone innocent."

"Who's being hurt?!" she demanded.

"Lucas George!" Simon shouted.

"What? How is Lucas hurt by reporters doing their jobs?"

"Taken off the case, out there trying to work the case anyway because he's so dedicated, and because he knows he's the one true expert we have on androids, our best chance at finding and stopping them," Simon said.

"He was taken off the case?" Holly's voice wavered a bit, her face confused.

"Yes! Thanks to you!" Simon snapped. "The public aren't the only ones frightened by your outrageous dramatics. One of the Deputy Chiefs was too."

"I never meant—"

Simon snorted. "You didn't care! You just went for the drama, whatever gets the ratings up!"

"Hey!" She was angry again, nostrils flaring. "That's not fair!"

"You want to be treated fairly after all the fairness you've shown? Sure!" Simon replied, turning to walk away, but she grabbed his arm and held tight.

"I mean it. I never meant to hurt anyone," she said.

"Well, meant to or not, you did and you are," he said.

"We're just trying to get to the truth here," she said. "And part of that is a responsibility to warn the public. If we don't, we lose their trust."

"If they knew how much bullshit you're putting out there as purported facts, you'd have already lost it," he said.

She let go of his arm and crossed her arms over her chest, glaring at him.

He grunted and turned away again, heading for his car.

"Come with me," she called out.

He stopped and turned back. "What?"

"I'm going to grab a quick bite," Holly said. "Come with me. So we can talk."

"Why would I want to talk with you?" he asked.

"Because I'm truly sorry, and I want to help," Holly said. "If you'll let me. But I need to know more."

"I'd be afraid you'd just use it against me," Simon said, shaking his head.

"I won't," she said. "I promise."

He stared at her a moment, considering, trying to read if the sincerity was faked or genuine. He finally decided it was sincere, but wondered if she could help herself. "You'll forgive me if I have a hard time believing that," he said.

"Let me prove it," she said.

He sighed. "I have to work this case, find my partner."

"Half an hour," she said. "You've got to eat, right?"

He turned toward his car, reaching for the door.

"John, please."

He opened the door and looked back at her.

She raised a finger, "I'll ride with you. One second." She turned and ran over to where her cameraman was finishing loading his gear into a Fox 4 van, chatting with him out of earshot for a bit before running back over to join Simon. "He'll pick me up wherever we land, okay?"

Simon surrendered. Shoulders sinking as he slipped into the driver's seat and called, "Get in then."

The passenger door opened and she slipped inside, settling onto the seat and reaching for the seatbelt as he wondered if he'd lost his mind.

CHAPTER 16

AT CONNELLY LABS, Bob Pruitt, A.B., and Scott examined Leonardo as they talked with Lucas. A.B. and Scott were filled with energy, frequently finishing each other's sentences and almost talking over each other.

"The problem with these nanoparticles is the way they fuse themselves to the circuit board," A.B. was saying as she dug around in Leonardo's back.

Lucas leaned over her shoulder and watched, trying to identify any changes or differences in the circuitry, but he realized quickly he hadn't spent a much time examining circuitry generally, let alone his own. That was something he probably needed to change.

"It's like nothing we've seen," Scott added as he looked through the STM at where she was pointing with her laser. Tall and thin with a bushy beard, Lucas had met him after he was already working for Benjamin Ashman.

"Yes," A.B. said. Shorter and big boned, she'd been with Connelly longer than her friend, part of the second round of hires the Maker ever made. Her long red hair ran halfway down her back, her skin pale, and her eyes a piercing green. She spoke with a booming alto to Scott's soft tenor, but they both were good at making themselves heard.

"We're afraid of damaging circuitry if we try to remove

them," Pruitt said.

"So there's no hope for the afflicted?" Lucas said. "No way to heal them?" He thought of the alternative and it made him tense. Decommission and destruction was inevitable if one became outdated, he supposed, but these models were all so new and the thought horrified him.

"Well, we may be able to disable them," Scott said. He pointed to letters on the screen reading 'F I E L D E R'. "See the logo?"

"If not we can try to interrupt their communications with whomever is controlling them," A.B. said as she went back to scanning Leonardo's upper back.

"Right," Scott said.

"We can also reprogram the changes," Pruitt said, "and try and install a code and lock to prevent reversion."

"You sound uncertain," Lucas said. He'd known it was foolish to hope something simple would occur to someone the more opportunities they had to examine victims. Complex problems rarely had simple solutions. But still, he'd found himself imagining that scenario most often, probably because it was the only one that made him feel better.

"Well, anything can be hacked," A.B. added, zooming the STM on a particular spot and pointing with the laser for Scott, who nodded with understanding.

"Damn. This poor bastard's insides are a mess," Scott mumbled.

"What's odd is the faceless android that attacked Benn was nothing like this," A.B. said. She and Scott had joined Pruitt and Lenexa police forensics techs in examining the fallen android Lucas had taken out.

"Really?" Lucas asked.

"Yep," Scott said. "No Fiedler logos, no nanoparticles, a completely different circuitry design."

"And from what we can tell far inferior vocal and speech modules as well as memory and brain units," A.B. added. "More like the early prototypes Livia started with."

"Exactly," Scott said. "We checked a footprint Simon sent over images of from Louie Fiedler's office, and it has no clear markings either."

"So whoever did this is building his own as well as modifying ours," A.B. said.

"The question is why," Pruitt added.

Lucas had no answer and neither did the others. They worked on in silence for a moment, Lucas watching. What purpose could sabotaging existing androids serve if the perpetrator had their own designs? And why send them out to create chaos or destroy instead of studying their design to improve his own?

"But there's good news," Pruitt said, breaking the silence, and Lucas looked up from where A.B. was working to meet his eyes. He seemed excited.

"We've identified the frequency," Scott said. "And we think it can be traced."

Lucas' senses heightened in anticipation as his mind raced with possibilities. "What is it?"

"888.17 megahertz," Scott said.

"But it's more complicated than that," A.B. said, looking up thoughtfully to meet Lucas' eyes, "because it's scrambled and coded, and they're using FHSS."

"What's that?" Lucas asked.

"Frequency-hopping spread spectrum is what the military use," A.B. explained, "to transmit signals by rapidly changing frequencies over a large spectral band."

"Since the code is known only to the transmitter and receiver, they avoid interference and prevent eavesdropping," Scott added.

"So can't break it either and make it so I can trace it?" Lucas asked.

"We're working on it," A.B. said with a nod. "We have a few contacts in the military who offered to help. A couple days, max." Now, she began repositioning the STM to scan another quadrant of Leonardo's body.

"It could be the best lead we've got to finding the person responsible," Lucas said.

"We know," Scott said. "We'll work around the clock!"

"And we've got others helping, too," A.B. added.

"Thank you," Lucas said. If it worked, he should be able to follow the frequency right to the source. And maybe they could find a way to block it as well, minimizing the effects.

"If we can't heal Leonardo," Lucas said, "we should leave him deactivated until we can."

"We can build him a new circuit board," A.B. said.

"But the learning and the things his owner taught him will be lost," Scott said as A.B. waved him out of the way so she could reach controls on the side of the STM. "All the acquired skills."

"So it's kind of a last resort option," Pruitt said.

"It feels almost like we'd be destroying a person," A.B. said.

Lucas wished more humans felt that way about androids. He supposed these three had an advantage from working with them so closely. Androids might not be human but they functioned as living beings, capable of learning and growing and experiencing the world in meaningful ways that changed them. Too often they were regarded as hardware or appliances, at best, certainly not worth consideration or caring.

"Understood," Lucas responded. "But if we can interfere with it until I can stop whoever's responsible, then maybe you won't have to do anything drastic."

Scott grunted, his face twisting slightly as he thought about it. "Not sure we'd want to leave it in there."

"Unless we could make sure it's benign," A.B. added.

"Right," Scott agreed. "But we would certainly have the luxury of exploring all options."

Pruitt put a hand on Lucas' shoulder. "Don't worry. We want the least destructive solution for everyone."

"I just hope you are the ones who get to decide," Lucas said.

The others made sounds of affirmation and nodded somberly. They were worried, too.

"Can you get me a write-up on the mystery android as soon as possible? And call me as soon—"

"Soon as we know," Pruitt promised.

"And we'll let you know what happens with our friend here," Scott said.

"Thank you," Lucas said as he turned and headed for the side exit to the parking lot. He had to keep working; do what he could while they tried to come up with something. His first stop was a police supply depot for some polypropylene clothes.

HAVING CALMED DOWN and fallen into comfortable small talk in the car, Simon and Holly drove over to Crown Center and walked down to the first floor for SPIN! Pizza, a franchise of a popular area pizza chain. Tall tables with matching stools filled gaps between pillars holding up the high ceiling with its exposed pipes and beams and suspended light fixtures. The kitchen was in an open area near the front behind a long, curved counter with an ice cream freezer filled with colorful varieties of gelato partway around the curve and two cash registers to its left facing a railing that marked the customer order line.

Holly ordered a Greek salad with a Diet Coke to wash it down, while Simon opted for the double pepperoni with original crust and a Pale Ale. They paid at the register and took their numbers and drinks to a corner table, setting them on the edge closest to the aisle in easy sight of passing staff before sliding onto the tall stools facing each other.

"Salad in a pizza place?" Simon teased.

"I know, it's a crime, right," Holly said, chuckling. "But the camera adds ten pounds and a girl has to watch her figure. Believe me, on the weekends, I really cut loose."

Simon laughed. "So weekends because calories don't catch up with ya?"

She made a face. "I suppose I deserve this grief after what happened to your partner."

"This is me being nice," Simon said. "I haven't even started giving you grief yet."

She made a silent O of alarm, her eyes widening in mock horror, then smiled and reached for her soda as he laughed again. "You're being quite pleasant for someone so pissed at me," she said after swallowing.

"I can't eat and fight," Simon said.

"We're still waiting for our food," Holly said.

"My mother taught me never to argue at the table," Simon countered.

"Is that what your ex would tell me?" Holly teased.

"You've been investigating me?" Simon asked then took a gulp from his cold Pale Ale.

She shrugged. "I asked around a bit, I admit."

Simon was distracted a moment as a cook tossed a large circle of pizza dough in the air near the large black ovens and twirled it around with his hands for a bit, creating a show for the customers. "You think they go to school for that?" he asked and nodded toward the counter.

"You can," Holly said. "I did a segment on culinary arts once and there are places that teach pizza tossing as part of presentation and hospitality. Gotta entertain the customers."

Simon swallowed another gulp of Pale Ale and gestured animatedly. "Must be why it tastes so good."

"I'm sure," Holly chuckled as she took a sip from her soda. "You know, I don't exaggerate."

Just then, the waiter arrived with their food, quickly setting Holly's salad before her then setting Simon's pizza on a hot plate in the center of the table.

After the waited had gone, Simon leaned back against his stool and asked, "What?" He lifted the beer glass and examined the foam.

"You accused me of exaggerating for drama," Holly said as she used her fork to scoop up her first bite of salad. "I really just go where the story leads me."

"There's no proof of an android outbreak," Simon said as he grabbed a slice of pizza and took a bite.

"Well, there have been five or six incidents now, right? Similar circumstances. What would you call it?" she asked, as she chewed her salad.

"Something that wouldn't inflame the public," Simon said, "anything else." He took another huge bit and hummed with pleasure as he chewed.

"Well, if it's wrong, we try to correct it," Holly said.

"It's not just wrong when the facts are unproven, it's wrong when it causes harm," Simon said and took another giant bite of double pepperoni.

Holly twirled her fork around in her salad and sighed, stabbing an olive. "So what are the facts?"

Simon swallowed. "You have no idea how hard he had to work to be accepted by fellow cops, for one."

"Lucas? Your partner?"

He nodded. "Yes. And this is causing a setback all over again." Then washed the pizza down with another gulp of beer before grabbing a new slice.

"A setback how? Funny looks?"

"Yes, but worse," Simon said. "Just because he was exposed to a suspect, he's been put on leave, to be sure he's safe. And any doubts other cops were still harboring will just grow after they hear that."

"Well, I'm sorry," Holly said. "That's not my intention."

"But it's a consequence," Simon said chewing another bite, "when you jump the gun on the facts."

"So he can have himself checked out, get a clean bill of health, and prove them all wrong," Holly said.

"Sure, for humans that works easy," Simon said. "But Lucas can shoot faster and with twice my accuracy, he can drive better, he can see for long distances and magnify, he can outrun any of us... He's got special abilities and that makes him standout."

"It's not just mistrust, but resentment then," she said.

"Yes, sure, cops get jealous too," Simon said as he took another sip of his beer.

"And no one likes change," Holly said and took another bite of salad.

"Yeah, that, too."

"Journalists are like that, too," Holly said. "Plus they get jealous over stories, who gets the most airtime, parking spaces...."

"We get all that, too," Simon said.

"Can't you just toss a placard up and park wherever you want?" Holly teased.

"Sure, unless the Chief or your Sergeant gets there first," Simon said.

"Ever have each other towed just to make a point?" Holly joked.

"Yeah, that would be a good way to end your career quick," Simon said.

"I thought cops were big on practical jokes," Holly said, smiling as she sipped her Diet Coke again.

"Oh yeah, we have morbid senses of humor," Simon said. "But messing with department equipment tends to be where they draw the line, plus the tow truck companies get testy."

"Buncha sharks they are," Holly said, shaking her head. "Ridiculous fines, price gouging."

"Well, we deal with that when we find it, but yeah, they charge more than anyone likes," Simon said. "Getting towed isn't supposed to be fun."

"Kinda like leaving your lights flashing when giving out

tickets?" Holly asked.

"Yeah, exactly," Simon said and laughed. "We all have our mind games."

"Embarrassment is a deterrent," she said, "to some."

"You don't get embarrassed?" Simon said, looking her over.

"Not like most people," Holly said. "But then I try not to get tickets."

"What do you do—flash cleavage? Smile and bat your eyes?"

She waved dismissively. "I am far smoother than that."

"Oh yeah?"

"I show my credentials and tell them I'm racing to a story," she said.

"That works?" Simon scoffed.

"Well, sometimes," Holly said. "Mostly I try to stay off the radar. And when we're in official vehicles, they sometimes cut us a break."

"Ah yes, professional courtesy," Simon said as he chewed another bite. "Nice perk, eh?"

"Yeah," she agreed and ate more salad.

For a moment, Simon felt guilty. He was practically consorting with the enemy. Would Lucas be hurt if he saw them or was Simon just being paranoid? Emma and Lucas *had* urged him to date again, after all. And they'd teased him about Holly Sanders, in fact. But that was before the reports. Before Lucas was suspended.

They ate for a bit in silence, then she looked up at Simon, who was leaning back watching her as he sipped his beer. "What?" she asked.

"Just wondering what makes you tick," Simon said.

"How cliché of you," she teased.

"No, you know, why you do what you do," he said.

"Yeah, I wonder that about cops like you, too," she said then leaned forward, elbows on the table and said conspiratorially, "You tell me yours, I'll tell you mine."

He chuckled. "I like helping people, making a difference, and I'm good at the job."

"That's why you became a cop? Just knew you were good at it?" she said.

He shrugged. "Basically."

"Which part? Interrogating people and pushing them around or shooting them?" she teased.

"See? Exaggeration for drama," he snapped, grinning.

"Okay, that time you caught me," she admitted. "But seriously."

"I ask a lot of questions and am observant of details and yeah, some of those high school and college aptitude tests said criminal justice might be a good field for me, so I checked it out, and here I am."

"Heh. My friends and I always wrote those off as bullshit," she said.

Simon laughed. "Yeah, well, sometimes they are. What did yours say?"

"It said I'd make a good cheerleader or drama queen," she joked.

"I totally believe that," he teased.

"Actually, it said I'm good with writing and communication, so..."

"You studied communications and found yourself in journalism?" He finished the thought for her.

"Basically, yeah."

He grunted. "Well, maybe when we tell people those stories we could spice them up with some of that exaggeration and drama to make them more exciting."

"I know, right?" Holly said. "There ya go."

Simon reached for the last slice of pizza as Holly toyed with the last of her salad. "You know, you're supposed to eat that," he said between chews.

"You always talk with your mouth full?"

"I started doing it to embarrass my daughter but I kinda liked it so here I am." Truth was, most cops got used to having their mealtimes interrupted so they learned to eat fast while they could, and never razzed you for talking with your mouth full.

She laughed, shaking her head. "You're lucky you're so charming."

"Now there's something you'll never hear from my ex," he said and washed down the bite with the last of his beer.

"Drinking on the job, too," she said and tsked, shaking her head.

"Yeah, well, I'm a sinner occasionally," he admitted. "I don't make a habit of it, for sure."

She frowned. "Really? I kinda like bad boys."

He raised his hands in mock surrender. "Cop. I'm one of the good guys."

She snapped her fingers exaggeratedly in front of her in a "darn it" gesture and smiled. "At least you're not hungry anymore," she said. "Hopefully not still mad at me either."

"Oh, I've calmed down, until your next story," he said.

"I'm sorry my take on the story caused problems for Lucas," Holly said. "If I can do anything to help or fix it, I will."

"A full retraction?" he teased.

"You're not demanding at all."

He grinned. "Yeah, well, just be aware there are consequences for what you say, okay? And try and get it right but let's not cause public panic unnecessarily."

"You know, journalists are as much about upholding the public trust as cops are," she said.

"Could have fooled me," he joked.

"This is why people shoot cops," she countered.

"Ohhhhhh, wow. Cutting blow."

"Just kidding. My point is you're not the only ones dedicated to public service. We do our best."

"Okay granted," Simon said. "But sometimes you make our jobs tougher in doing it. We don't have to like that."

She laughed. "You make ours tougher too, and we absolutely hate it."

"Good," he said and looked at his watch. "I gotta go."

"If I get it wrong again, you tell me, but you might want to bring some facts to straighten me out," Holly said. "My boss will kill me if I just take your word."

He stood then came around and helped her with her stool like a true gentleman. It was an old habit.

"Hey, cops never lie. We're the good guys."

"You sure that aptitude test didn't say anything about standup comedy?" she asked as they walked together toward the door. She pulled out her phone and started texting as they walked.

"You've got a ride coming, right?" he asked as they stepped out into the busy corridor near the brightly colored SPIN! Neopolitan Pizza sign.

"Yeah, I'm good," she said.

"Thanks for the company," he said.

She looked up and smiled. "I enjoyed it. Maybe we could do it again sometime when you're not so mad at me?"

"Oh hell, you sure you could handle me in that good of a mood?" he quipped then tossed a wave as he turned and headed for his car. He felt relieved no one could see the jumping jacks his insides were doing at the moment. Then he felt guilty all over again for being so happy spending time with the woman who hurt his friend, his partner. Shit. Lucas would probably understand. He was unerringly reasonable. It was kinda annoying. *What are you some high school kid? Jesus. Get it together, John.*

And then he realized it didn't matter. Holly apologized. Lucas was forgiving, and it had been a long time since Simon had felt this way. He was allowed to enjoy it. Privately, at least. His ears picked up the latest Syzygy hit and he started humming. It always amazed him how much Lou Gramm's daughter sounded like her dad vocally. He hummed along all the way to the car, then played air keyboards along with her bandmate, Dennis DeYoung's son as he drove away.

SHE AWOKE IN pain, her neck crooked at an awkward angle against her shoulder and chest. She went to lift her head and felt a small pop—pain shooting through her. She bit her lower lip to avoid crying out but stopped moving 'til it subsided.

A strange man's spoke in the next room, "Hello, how may I serve you?"

Who was that? It wasn't Todd... The voice was tinny and

unnaturally stiff.

She heard something shuffling across the floor... metal clanking... then Todd cursed. That was definitely him. The bastard.

Livia sighed and rubbed the back of her neck against the back of the chair. She couldn't hold this awkward position forever. Time to try again. Slowly, delicately, she lifted her head once more. This time there was no pop, and the pain was minor.

Her head upright at last, she slowly rolled her head from side to side. How long had she been asleep?

"Hello, how may I serve you?"

It was a different voice this time, less stiff but still tinny, and it was followed by more clanking and footsteps.

"Hello, How may I serve you?"

The first voice again, this time smoother though still too tinny.

Were other people here? The voices sounded human, but a little off. A little too rote, perhaps, or like someone reciting dialogue, maybe through a mask or a bad speaker—that would account for the tinniness. A strong desire arose in her to call out, but she'd also heard Todd, hadn't she? She really didn't want to invite another beating or other abuse.

There was a loud burst of static now and then more shuffling about—perhaps someone's clothes brushing against the floor? She wasn't sure. Then the voices again, this time almost simultaneous.

"Hello, how may I serve you?" The tinniness was faint now and the flow of the words becoming far more natural.

"Todd," she surrendered, calling out.

No answer.

"Todd!" Louder this time.

"What?! Goddamn it, I'm working!" Todd replied.

"Who's there? Is someone here?" she shouldn't have, she knew right away, but she was so bored here, and if there were others, she had to let them know she was here and needed help.

"Shut up! I'm busy! No one's here!' Todd yelled back and then more shuffling, and this time she caught a hint of burning sulfur.

"There," Todd mumbled, so soft she could barely hear him, "let's see how that changes things, you bastard."

"Hello, how may I serve you?"

It was the first voice again, but this time with more natural inflection, and the tinniness had all but disappeared.

"Yes!" Todd shouted then there was more shuffling around and clanking—maybe tools?—more sulfur, and then the second voice again.

"Hello, how may I serve you?"

That one was better too, much.

"Got you, you bastard!" Todd said.

"Todd, what are you doing?" she called out.

"Hang on," he said.

More shuffling and then thumping and a clank of metal. This time she was sure it was tools bumping each other. Then footsteps drawing nearer.

Todd appeared in the doorway, smiling, but not in a friendly way. The smile was off, awkward, almost...evil.

"It's none of your business what I do here," he said, soft but threatening.

"Well, I heard voices," she said. "I just woke up. I'm thirsty."

"I see," Todd said. "You expect me to care?"

"Yes," she said. "You haven't killed me yet. I have to have liquid from time to time. So yes."

He frowned. "Well, I don't. Your usefulness to me is coming to an end. Keep that in mind when you interrupt me."

It was ominous and frightening but she held herself in check, refusing to give him the satisfaction of letting it show. "So you can let me go then?" she asked. She knew it would rile him, but she couldn't help herself. She had to show strength. It was the only weapon she had. She expected anger, another blow, some yelling.

To her surprise, he laughed.

"Livia, I want you to meet some friends of mine," he said.

"Friends?" she asked but he was gone again, back into the other room.

She heard his footsteps as he marched around, then he said, "Get up. Come on. Go in there and meet my friend. Go!"

More footsteps now. Three pairs perhaps? And then the last person she expected to see appeared.

Lucas George was standing before her. He was wearing some sort of smock, almost a surgical gown really, and white gloves, but it was him. She'd know that face anywhere. He smiled and stepped to the left, then Benn Liska appeared, dressed the exact same way, and stepped to the right as Todd appeared in the middle.

"Livia Connelly, you know these gentlemen, I believe."

"Lucas! Thank God, you've got to get me out of here," she said, straining against her bonds then lifting them so Lucas could see. "Benn, help me."

Lucas and Benn smiled and then stepped forward, slow and deliberate, as Todd disappeared again and said, "You too, the rest of you. Now."

"Hello, how may I serve you?" Lucas and Benn asked simultaneously, in almost perfect unison, and there was a blankness to their eyes, like they didn't know her, like they weren't even there.

"Hello, how may I serve you?" they said again but there were more voices joining now, not quite in unison as more people stepped into the room. She recognized Louie Fiedler and Andy Moehn, whom she'd met once at a function Louie held, and then some faces she didn't know, and all of them kept repeating, "Hello, how may I serve you?"

Over and over as they came closer, surrounding her, closing in, until she screamed.

CHAPTER 17

SIMON SLEPT LIKE a baby that night, despite having left two more unreturned messages for Lucas. He awoke with a smile on his face. He was still smiling an hour later when he arrived at Central Patrol and entered the office to find Dolby hard at work on the computer in her cubicle.

"Morning," she called.

"Morning," he said as he grabbed a mug off his cubicle desk and headed straight for the coffee.

"It's fresh for a change," she offered. "I brought some from home."

"Wow. You are way too awake for seven-forty," he said.

She grunted. "Yeah, was here 'til seven too. Made real progress on these records."

Simon finished filling his mug and added one sweetener packet for extra energy, then sipped slowly, as he turned back toward her. "Yeah? What've you got?"

She clicked around on the mouse and pulled up a spreadsheet. "Addresses. All owned or rented by Todd Ward at some point in the last fifteen years. Current owners in red."

"Really? Do we know if they're all still standing?" Simon asked.

"Well, they're still there according to Google Maps, but you know how out of date that gets," she replied.

Simon nodded. Google Maps was very useful but frequently behind and outdated, sometimes by years. "So we can check them out."

"Soon as Art gets in," she said.

Simon looked at the clock on the wall. "Late. He usually beats me in."

"Rough night," Maberry mumbled as he came through the door, rubbing his temples.

"He went to Bobby's," Dolby added.

Bobby's Bar was a favorite off-hour hangout for men and women in blue, just off I-670 at Truman and Grand, the same place Maberry's partner Jose Correia had been shot a few months before during the terrorist case.

"You still go there?" Simon said.

"Just started again," Maberry said. "I missed the company. I'm drinking for two now."

"Hence the headache," Dolby said.

"Shhhhh," Maberry groused as he poured his own cup of coffee now, using a department mug for expediency. "Not so loud."

"She's a bundle of energy this morning," Simon said.

"Fucking great," Maberry whined.

Dolby laughed. "You know you love me."

"Yeah, yeah, yeah," he said as he came over to join them beside Dolby's cube. "What's on the agenda?"

"Man hunt," Simon said.

"Oh goodie, do we get to shoot some bastard?" Maberry said, cackling then coughing as he sipped his coffee and got a little too much.

Simon patted him on the back. "Take it easy there. Pace yourself. And we might."

"Hopefully," Maberry joked, then cleared his throat before sipping again.

"You two are the worst," Becker said from behind them and they turned to see her unlocking her office. She looked as fresh as Dolby.

"Morning, Boss," all three Detectives said.

"You guys need back-up?" Becker asked.

"Nah," Simon said. "We got it."

"Should be routine, Sarge," Dolby added.

"Then get the hell outta here and get to work," Becker snapped, followed by a grin as she turned and headed into her office.

"She's such a ball breaker," Maberry said.

"Seriously," Simon replied.

"I can hear you," Becker called. "Don't test me!"

Dolby stood as they all made a comical dash for the door.

"Coming through," Maberry teased.

"Outta my way!" Dolby said in her toughest voice.

"Age before beauty," Simon joked, glancing through Becker's open door as he passed to see her reading reports.

She rolled her eyes and didn't bother looking up. "Buncha clowns they give me. Buncha clowns."

They all laughed as they headed out the door and turned left toward the rear parking lot.

THE FIRST PROPERTY turned out to be a rundown rat trap off Troost and 27th, which was predictable for that part of town but given the date of the lease, somewhat surprising. Supposedly Todd Ward had rented it up until two years earlier, and it looked like it had been abandoned for many years. Whatever he used it for clearly security and comforts like air conditioning and heating weren't of any concern.

Next, they headed north to Missouri and Gillis, part of the old Italian section of the city where mobsters once dominated from the 1960s through the 1990s. The street was lined with buildings that had been there for decades, most since before the World Wars. This was one of the city's oldest neighborhoods, settled by Italian immigrants in the 19th Century. They parked their Interceptors at the curb and examined the target—a storefront attached to a warehouse. Two stories, brick, with white painted window frames and a faded 'Vincenti's' sign out front. Ward had supposedly rented this one up until three months before. Inside the store front they could see a worn counter and two desks and chairs, old but functional—the kind of setup a store that had been in this neighborhood for decades might have. Nothing unusual.

"What was Vincenti's?" Dolby wondered.

"I think they sold meats, if I'm not mistaken," Maberry said.

"So a butcher?" Dolby said.

"Yeah, and freezers to resell from other suppliers," Maberry said. "My grandfather used to talk about the place. Best Italian sausage in the city."

Simon walked over and tried the front door. It was locked but a leasing sign with a prominent phone number hung in the front window.

"Let's check the back before we call," Simon suggested.

"Right," Maberry agreed, and together the three detectives made their way around the building and up the alley to the back door which was faded light blue with cracking paint covering everything, including the large window in the back door. The stench of rot floated down the alley from twin dumpsters behind a restaurant two buildings over that were loaded to the gills with garbage bags and food waste. The smells of cooking oil and grease blended with urine and mold created a cornucopia of unpleasantness that caused Simon to crinkle his nose and hope they wouldn't have to spend much time here.

"Someone didn't want anyone seeing in," Dolby said.

Simon tried the handle. "Locked."

As they headed back around to the front to call the leasing agent for a key, Maberry walked over to a side window, also painted over, and peered through. "Body!" he called out.

"What?!" Dolby asked.

"I see a pair of legs in the back room, lying prone on the floor," Maberry said.

"Back door!" Simon called as all three ran back toward the alley.

Dolby and Maberry drew weapons and took positions back and to the side, ready to barge in.

"Guess I'll kick it then," Simon said, drawing his Glock and taking the proper stance, a few feet from the door, foot raised and ready. Dolby counted down on her fingers silently: 3... 2... 1... Simon kicked out with the flat of his foot striking inches from the knob. Two kicks and the door burst open, with Simon following Maberry and Dolby inside.

The door admitted them into a large back room with brick walls and cement floor, the ceiling overhead made of bare slats, many of which showed signs of wood rot. There were conveyers here on long metal counters and several rows of tables with a large stack of shipping boxes tossed haphazardly in a pile in the corner. A long rack with hooks for coats or aprons hung along one wall where there were several large industrial freezers with large metal doors and handles, all standing open a crack. The place smelled musty and old but was relatively clean.

They worked in formation, two people covering, while the third moved in to open any doors one at a time, starting with the freezers and then bathrooms and a large office. All were empty, no sign of anyone.

"You sure you saw a body?" Simon asked.

"Yes, it should be right this way," Maberry said, nodding toward a short corridor just past the men's room leading toward the side of the building behind the freezers and bathrooms.

"Go!" Simon said and Maberry led the way.

Guns raised and ready, moving together in a triangle formation, they moved down the hall toward a closed door on the end at the right.

"It must be in here," Maberry whispered.

"You're on," Simon said, nodding to then door as he and Dolby provided cover.

Maberry grabbed the knob and swung the door inward, jumping clear and Simon and Dolby burst through.

In the center of the floor lay a pair of legs in tennis shoes and jeans, unattached to a body.

"Jesus!" Maberry said.

"No blood," Dolby observed.

Simon moved closer and looked. "Not human." He holstered his Glock.

"What?" Maberry asked.

Simon bent and pulled the jeans down slightly to reveal circuitry sticking from an open hole in the waist of what appeared similar to a mannequin's body.

"Androids?" Dolby muttered.

"Looks that way," Simon said.

"God damn it! What the hell is going on?!" a loud voice demanded. "Who the fuck did this to my door?!"

The three detectives instinctively drew their guns and ran back out into the corridor, jumping back into formation, to find a snappily dressed gray-haired man in his early sixties with a developing paunch standing beside the broken back door, shaking his head.

"Holy shit!" he yelled as he looked up to see the armed trio moving toward him.

"Who are you?" Maberry demanded.

"Arnaldo Vincenti," the man said. "Who the fuck are you? Is this a robbery? There's nothing to take."

The three detectives breathed a collective sigh of relief and holstered their weapons and Dolby quickly pulled her badge and flashed it.

"KCPD," she said.

"KCPD? Is this what my tax dollars pay for—you fucking up my door for no reason and scaring me half to death?!" Vincenti scolded, having recovered quickly from his momentary fright. "What are you doing here?!"

"We had probable cause that a body might be in here, a possible kidnap victim," Maberry said.

"A body?! There's no damn body! Whatever gave you that idea?" Vincenti demanded.

"The pair of the legs in the back room," Simon said.

"Oh fuck! That's one of those things that motherfucker was working on here before he just packed up and moved out in the middle of the night, abandoning his lease and leaving me with this mess," Vincenti groused.

"Todd Ward?" Simon asked.

"Yes! Motherfucker!" Vincenti said. "Won't take my calls either. I've half a mind to drive down to Lenexa and throttle him myself."

"He was making androids here?" Dolby asked.

"Something crazy like that," Vincenti said. "I only saw once, when I came because a neighbor complained of noise late in the evenings. He was working all night, see, because of his day job down south. Why he came all the way up here so far from him home is beyond me. Anyway, he didn't like me seeing it. Chased me back out into the alley. Said he'd try and keep the noise down. A week later, he packed up and was gone. No warning. Asshole."

"He rented this place for several years, correct?" Dolby asked.

"Yeah, six or seven," Vincenti said. "No problems until the very end. Always paid in advance, kept to himself. I haven't had any inquiries so I didn't bother cleaning up just yet. Those legs are the only proof of what he was doing he left behind and I can't figure out why. He was quite secretive. In fact, they were in the dumpster two doors down and my friend Charles showed them to me. We brought them back and put them in there figuring maybe he was up to no good and we might want them later." He grunted and looked at the detectives. "Guess I was right, 'cause here you are."

"Can we take those?" Simon asked. "Evidence."

Vincenti waved dismissively. "Take them. There's a box of

circuit boards up behind the front desk he also threw out that we salvaged, but the night crew had dumped tons of restaurant waste by the time we found those legs. Neither Charles nor I relished digging through to see what else was there so it probably went to the dump."

Maberry hurried into the front room and Simon heard a chair scoot out and the sound of him shuffling around a bit.

"Okay, do you need a receipt?" Dolby asked.

Vincenti laughed. "Take 'em." He turned back to the door, hands on his hips. "You could have called me. My number's up front and I live a block away. Didn't have to do all this damage. Who's going to pay for this?"

Simon stepped forward and handed him a business card. "The department will reimburse, okay? Just call and ask for Sergeant Becker."

"We apologize for the inconvenience," Maberry added as he returned carrying a large shipping box.

"Anything?" Simon asked, meaning the front room which they hadn't yet checked.

Maberry shook his head. "Clear."

"What's he up to?" Vincenti asked. "Does this have anything to do with that android thing on the news? Some sort of crazy outbreak?"

"We don't know for sure, sir," Dolby said.

"It's not an outbreak," Simon said. "Reporters love drama."

"I'll get the legs," Dolby said and headed back down the side corridor.

"Fucking androids," Vincenti said, offering a dismissive wave. "My father would roll over in his grave if he saw the crazy shit people are bringing out these days. His great grandfather founded this place in 1921. Whole different world now."

"Thanks for your assistance, Mister Vincenti," Simon said as he and Maberry headed for the alley.

"Yeah, yeah, I hope no vandals break in before I get this fixed!" he called after them and then Dolby joined them carrying the android legs. Vincenti's mumbled grumblings echoed down the alley all the way back to their cars.

Dolby lifted the tail gate so Maberry could load the box in the back then checked her list. "Looks like the next one's in the West Bottoms," she said and then their radios went off.

"All units, multiple ATM robberies in progress," a dispatcher said then read off several addresses.

"13th and Grand is six minutes," Maberry said, reaching for this shoulder mic as they hurried to their cars.

IT ACTUALLY TOOK them less than five minutes to arrive. There were twenty-five reported ATM robberies going on simultaneously all over the city, straining department resources, with more reports coming in from neighboring municipalities, including Olathe, Lenexa, and Overland Park. The ATM at 13th and Grand was inside the entryway to the main branch of Arvest Bank in downtown Kansas City.

Through the tall glass front windows, the detectives could see three masked men with white gloves and guns robbing the ATM—two pulling out money and loading it into bags as the third wrestled with a very large ATM service tech. The tech looked like some kind of professional wrestler-type, clearly a workout fanatic and tall, too, and the robber was struggling to hold his own. They pulled their Interceptors to the curb lights flashing and drew their weapons. At the last minute, Simon grabbed a Taser clipped below the driver's seat then followed the others inside.

As soon as the detectives hit the door, one suspect started firing while the second grabbed the almost full bags and ran for the side door leading out to Grand. The first suspect followed, running backward behind and firing as the detectives dove for cover behind pillars and a dividing wall. The third remained locked in a struggle with the ATM tech.

Soft music played from speakers overhead, barely discernible above the hum of the building's heaters. There was a hint of oil from the whirring ATM, its door hanging wide open, and the smell of industrial cleaners from the shiny, polished floors. The detectives fired, hitting each retreating suspect twice—the one with bags in the back and shoulder and the other in the stomach and leg—but it seemed to have no effect. The first suspect just grinned and kept firing back.

"What the fuck?" Simon said.

"Not even a reaction!" Maberry added.

"Fucking androids!" the ATM tech managed to growl as he continued wrestling with the third suspect.

"They're practically bullet proof," Maberry said as the three detectives fired several bursts at the retreating androids. "How the fuck do we stop them?"

"Lucas Tasered one in the center of its upper back and took it right down," Simon said.

"Great. The Taser's in the car," Dolby said.

Simon showed them his. "I brought mine."

"Well, at least we can follow them," Maberry said and

jumped to his feet as the two fleeing androids disappeared out the door.

"I'll help this guy, then," Simon said.

"Good luck," Dolby said as she and Maberry raced toward the Grand exit, following the fleeing suspects.

Simon moved carefully toward the wrestling men, gun in one hand, Taser in the other, calling, "Try and roll him over so I can see his back."

"What?!" the struggling tech managed.

"I can Tase him," Simon replied.

"He's fuckin' strong," the tech replied.

"I know," Simon said, smelling the man's sweat as he drew near and seeing a few drops of green fluid on the floor. The son of a bitch had actually injured the android. "You wounded him."

"Damn right," the tech said. "I think he broke my fuckin' arm." The two rolled around, throwing punches, yanking at each other, and finally the tech managed to grab the android and spin around so its back was to Simon.

Simon took aim and fired the Taser but the shot missed and hit its shoulder.

"Fuck! That hurts," the tech said, momentarily distracted as he tried to let go. Simon hurriedly reloaded the Taser with another cartridge as the android took advantage and kicked the tech in the shin, causing him to cry out and swing a fist, but the android ducked, pulling clear and racing for the Grand exit. As it did, exposing its back again and Simon was ready. He aimed for the center back and fired again.

The time the Taser hit dead center and the android froze in place, body vibrating as 50,000 volts coursed through its circuits.

"Yes! Fry that fucker!" the tech cheered.

The android collapsed in a heap and Simon lowered the Taser as he moved in, Glock ready.

The Grand door opened again and Maberry and Dolby raced back in.

"He got him!" the excited tech said.

"Those bastards run so fast," Maberry said.

"They had a car waiting," Dolby said. "We got the plate, though."

Simon kicked the prone android, making sure it was out and getting no response. Then he knelt beside it and grabbed the mask, pulling it over the android's head.

"Holy shit!" Dolby said.

Simon couldn't believe his eyes. They all stared in shock at the android's face. It was his partner, Lucas George.

LUCAS STOPPED AT a police supply store on Northwest 72nd Street for polypropylene protective gear and was heading north again when Scott called to provide a couple of IP addresses for sources that communicated with the sabotaged androids. Tracing the origin of an IP address was the matter of a few internet searches, so soon Lucas found himself headed for Missouri and Gillis.

As he drove, he heard police sirens in the distance all around him. Something was going on, and for a moment, he felt sadness at being left out. Then he arrived in front of a storefront attached to a warehouse, two buildings down from a busy restaurant. An old sign out front read "Vincenti's," but it was clear the place had been unused for at least a few months, if not longer. He peered through the front window at a mostly empty office with only a desk and a couple chairs. A leasing sign in the front window had a phone number.

The search said the IP signal had been sent from this address. He wanted to get inside and look around for any sign of whoever sent those signals. But calling someone who might ask a lot of questions would just slow him down, and they might call KCPD to verify his identity. So he thought a moment. What would Simon do? Look for another way in, he decided. So he walked around the exterior of the building looking for an open window or other doors.

The side windows were painted over but someone had kicked in the back door, and whomever had done temporary repairs had really emphasized the word "temporary." It was just a single board nailed across with two nails at each end holding the door to the frame. Lucas figured a crowbar or someone strong could rip it right off.

He looked around, debating again whether to call. There were two full dumpsters two doors down behind the restaurant but no sign of any living beings who might see him. If he was careful, he could probably put it back. He had the strength. He really needed to get in there with the minimum of hassle. He was suspended, so police rules didn't apply. Was it breaking the law? Technically, perhaps, but he wasn't going to steal anything.

Then he thought of Livia. He had to do what it took to find her. Unearth every clue. Explore every possibility, every possible lead or piece of evidence.

Reluctant but determined, he reached up and yanked the

board free in one smooth movement, taking less than two seconds, and set it leaning against the frame outside the door, then pushed his way inside.

A cursory scan didn't show anything particularly revealing about what the building had last been used for beyond a conveyer belt-assembly line setup and abandoned shipping boxes so he strode over to the boxes and examined the labels. There were several boxes with the familiar smiley arrow and Amazon logo he'd seen everywhere, it seemed. Others were from electronics and tech manufacturing firms.

He ran several names through Google. Some of them made components for computers, a few even androids and robots. Yep. This was the place. Or used to be.

"God damn it!" a man yelled from behind him, startling him. "I'm gone ten minutes and someone already breaks in?! This neighborhood is going to shit!"

Lucas turned as a gray-haired man in his early sixties stepped inside, hammer raised and pointed at him, glaring. "You! What the fuck are you doing trespassing?! Are you robbing me?! There's nothing to steal!" He fumbled in his pocket. "I'm calling the police."

Without a word, Lucas turned and ran, racing past him so fast, the man didn't have time to react before Lucas was out the door. He kept running and turned the corner, racing back along the side of the building toward the front as the man's curses echoed behind him.

"Asshole! I was just coming to repair this! Fucking police!"

Lucas hadn't noticed any surveillance cameras in range of where he'd come and go and said a quick prayer none were active in such an old neighborhood as he jumped into his Outlander, started the engine, and sped away. Odd thing for a man to be cursing the police so fast after just calling them. What did he expect—instant response? Lucas had given no indication he was a cop. Strange man.

So this was what it feels like to be an outlaw? He didn't like it. Not one bit.

CHAPTER 18

SINCE THE TASK force last met, there had been a dozen incidents with rogue androids throughout the Metro area, including the incidents with Leonardo at the Nelson and the faceless androids killing Benn Liska. Police chiefs in surrounding cities were clamoring to join the task force's information sharing, and the press attention was heating up. There was a story on the TV news and in every news website daily. Simon found it exhausting.

But today, except for the deceased Williamson, those around the table were the same as the first task force meeting. Only everyone looked harried, and the energy was charged. Trevor Welch and Eugene Curtain were typing on their laptops, while Tom Bailey and Jerry Tucker looked barely awake, sipping coffee like it was their lifeline.

"This is getting out of hand," Sergeant DeMarco said. "ATM robberies in twenty locations simultaneously, murders, a dead detective—"

"And we're no closer to finding Doctor Connelly or those responsible," Zedlar said. He looked at Simon. "Is it true one of the robbers was your partner?"

"No," Simon said, totally taken by surprise.

He, Maberry, and Dolby had kept that close to the vest, telling only Becker, who'd agreed they shouldn't tell anyone until they sorted it out. Then when they'd gone down to interview "Lucas" in holding, they'd found an android who only knew a few phrases and was uncooperative, acting as if he had no idea who they were. When the android suddenly sprung at them, attacking, Simon Tasered him again, and this time, when the android fell prone, there was a tear in his cheek. But nothing leaked. No hydraulic or other fluid. He knelt to examine the wound and discovered it was a mask—a very good one. And underneath was one of the same faceless androids who'd killed Benn Liska.

"Where did you hear that?" Becker demanded.

Zedlar shrugged and leaned back with a smug look. "Rumors fly."

That meant someone at Central had talked. There were just too many people moving in and out with access to holding to have kept the secret for long. They'd investigate but likely never know who.

"Well, it's not true," Simon said, recovering. "It was one of those mystery androids who attacked Liska and Lucas and Pruitt down at Connelly Labs, wearing a mask."

"A mask that looked like your partner," Zedlar said.

"It *wasn't* him though," Simon snapped.

"The point is with that kind of thing going on how—are we supposed to know who to trust with an android working this case?" DeMarco said.

"Detective George is on temporary suspension," DC Atwell said then and the Lenexa cops turned to look at her. "We've done it as a precaution in case of the possibility of exposure causing...malfunctions."

"Well, good," DeMarco said. "At least we don't have that to worry about."

"These things are indestructible," Zedlar said. "They take

bullets and keep walking."

"They're tough, yes, but you can take them down with Tasers," Simon said. "If you know where to hit them."

"Nice of you to share that information with us," Zedlar growled.

"We have a memo going out this morning," Becker said. "It explains the whole thing."

"There's visuals, you know," Simon said, "to make sure you get it."

"Fuck you," Zedlar said.

"Can we cut the pissing contest and focus on our work?" DC Melson scolded, glaring at them both. "This isn't helping."

"We have a bad guy out there with a potential army of androids, plus who knows how many more he can control with some kind of nano virus," SAIC Garner threw in. "I'd say we're in crisis mode."

"I agree," Melson said. "Which means we have to work together. Whether we like each other or not." He glared at Zedlar and Simon again.

"We'll do our jobs," DeMarco said.

"Good," Melson snapped, glaring at him, too.

"We're making all available personnel and resources yours until this is over," Garner said. "We can help with searches, tracking, you name it. Just tell us where you need us."

"Great," Atwell said. "We will absolutely do that."

"And we're reading in departments in Olathe, Overland Park, Shawnee, Prairie Village, Independence, North Kansas City, Lee's Summit, and Riverside," Melson said. "Sharing access to our joint database and anything else they need."

"Or any other departments who might need information until this is over," Atwell added.

"So this is Metro-wide now?" Becker said.

"The incidents have spread far beyond Kansas City and Lenexa, so yes," Melson said.

"And we're bringing in all our departments as well," Atwell said. "There'll be a joint briefing tomorrow morning we want you and Detective Simon to attend, bring us up to speed."

"Yes, ma'am," Becker said, shooting Simon a look that said *"we're in it now."*

Simon grunted as Garner spoke again, "There are ways to track androids using their onboard IP addresses, Wi-Fi, VOIP, and GPS systems. We have subpoenaed a list from Connelly Labs so our tech people can monitor activity to try and predict any incidents before they go too far and alert response teams. If we can find out how the perpetrators are communicating with them, we can trace that as well."

"I believe we just obtained some information that might be useful in that regard," Becker said. "We'll pass it along."

"Great," Garner said.

"We'll help however we can," Trevor Welch added, looking up from his laptop briefly, and Garner smiled and nodded in thanks.

"And while you're doing that, I suggest we focus resources on two fronts: warning android owners to limit outside contact with their androids and locating Livia Connelly," Melson said.

"Can we even be sure she's still alive?" Zedlar asked.

"No," Atwell said.

"We don't stop looking until we have a body," Simon said. "We don't give up."

"I know she's a friend of your partner—" Zedlar said.

"She's a human being! That's all that matters," Simon snaps.

"We find her, we find the perpetrators," Maberry said.

"Exactly," Dolby agreed.

"And we give top priority to leads the FBI and our tech people get us from tracking the perp's activities," Becker said.

"Yes," Melson agreed.

"We've already been doing that," DeMarco said.

"We get proactive," Simon said. "Instead of waiting for something to happen, we start making it happen."

"And how do we do that?" DeMarco asked.

"Shaking a lot more trees and stirring up help from the public," Maberry said.

"And we can use the media to help us," Simon said.

"You don't talk—" Atwell protested.

Simon cut her off. "Carefully placed tips and statements that will get the public working for us and stir the perps into action before they're ready."

"Our media people will get to work on it," Melson said then turned to DeMarco, "and coordinate with yours."

"Okay," DeMarco said.

"If we just knew their end game," Dolby said.

"Well, we should talk to anyone and everyone we can about that," Becker said. "Someone has to know something."

Zedlar chortled. "You gonna get our Chief to authorize the overtime?"

"We can give him a call," Melson said.

"A step at a time," Atwell said.

"All right, enough talk, let's get to work," Bailey said, yawning as Tucker stretched beside him.

"Go!" Melson said and waved dismissively.

As everyone headed for the door, Atwell touched Becker's arm. "I want to see your people in your squad room right away."

Simon shot Becker a look.

"We're headed there now," Becker said. "Come on."

Simon braced himself as he walked back to the squad room. Thankfully Lucas wasn't here to experience whatever she had in store for them this time.

THE MINUTE THEY stepped into the squad room, Atwell closed the door behind her, and the whole squad knew they were in for it.

"Where's George?" she demanded, glowering at Simon.

"You suspended him," he replied. "How should we know?"

"If I suspended him, why am I getting reports of him turning up at locations tied to this investigation?" Atwell said, then ticked off a list on her fingers. "Connelly Labs, the Sheraton, Vincenti's."

"Vincenti's?" Dolby said and looked at Maberry and Simon.

"Yes, I know you were there," Atwell barked. "Mister Vicenti is quite unhappy with what you did to his door."

"We had probable cause," Maberry said.

Atwell dismissed it with a wave. "We have bigger issues. I suspended George temporarily *for his own good*. He needs to stay out of this investigation and avoid exposing himself."

"Maybe he felt it was more like a punishment than for his own good," Simon said.

"It may have seemed that way, but it's not," Atwell said. "This department is still liable for his behavior and its results. We needed to protect him and the public. Both."

"You had no evidence he was at risk!" Simon snapped.

"We had plenty!" she shouted back.

"Let's all keep it civil, can we?" Becker said. "There may not have been clear evidence but there was reason for concern, can't we all at least agree on that? None of us want to see anything bad happen to Lucas."

Simon sighed and turned away, pounding his fist against a cubicle wall. "We could solve this case much faster with him."

"He's right," Dolby said. "Lucas is invaluable."

"We've heard that argument," Atwell said, "and weighed it against all factors and a decision was made in the best interests of everyone."

"Well that decision stinks," Simon said.

"I don't care if you like it," Atwell said. "It's an order from the chain of command, and you will follow it. Is that clear?" She spat each word with such force they all just stared.

"Understood," Becker said, eyeing her detectives and urging them to affirm it.

"Yes, ma'am." Maberry and Dolby said.

"Detective Simon?" Atwell demanded.

"I hear you," Simon said at last.

"Now, please, find Lucas George and secure him in a safe location," Atwell said.

"Can he at least help us from this squad room?" Simon asked.

"Not if he can't obey orders," Atwell said.

"I'll talk to him," Becker said. "Make sure he stays in line."

"If you do that and he has something vital to add, then maybe," Atwell said. "Case by case."

"That's fair," Becker said, her eyes pleading with Simon to accept it.

"He won't return our calls," Maberry said. "So we don't know how to find him."

"Well, you five know him best, so I'm counting on you," Atwell said.

"Don't we have more important priorities?" Simon groused.

"Not if you care about your friend's future with this department," Atwell said, making it clear from her tone it was case closed.

"We'll do what we can to find him," Becker said.

"And please coordinate with the FBI and other departments to make sure everyone is up to speed, so we can allocate all resources the most effective way possible, okay? We need to speed things along in full cooperation," Atwell said.

"We get that," Becker said.

"Thank you," Atwell said with a nod, then turned and disappeared through the door before anyone had a chance to say anything further. She left it open behind her, so they stood in silence a moment to make sure she was gone.

"Maybe one of the rogue androids will take her out," Maberry joked.

"Can we send her in alone?" Simon added.

"Stop. I don't want to hear that kind of talk," Becker said.

"Sorry, Sarge, but she's a real bitch," Dolby said.

Becker glared at them as they started laughing and then grinned. "Yes, she is, but dammit, she outranks us so remember that."

"She won't let us forget," Simon said.

"Now, how can we find Lucas and get him back here where we know he's safe?" Becker asked.

They spent the next fifteen minutes discussing Lucas' hangouts and how to cover them, but just when they dispersed to work the phones on the problem, Simon's cell rang. It was Holly Sanders, so he stepped out into the hall.

"Yeah?" he answered.

"Hello, nice to talk to you, too," Holly said.

"I'm at work," he said.

"Me, too. Got a tip for ya."

"Oh yeah?"

"Got a plate a friend ran for us that was at one of the ATM robberies," she continued. "A cargo van."

"Rental?" Simon asked.

"No, owner was listed as TWE Limited."

"TWE," Simon repeated.

"Todd Ward Enterprises or something like it is our guess," Holly said.

"We don't know for sure what his involvement is, so don't run that," Simon warned.

"Won't, just listen," she said then waited to be sure he was before continuing. "It's registered to a box 656 at 3429 Troost. A self-storage place."

"Storage?"

"Made some calls," she went on. "Ward rented two of the biggest spaces they have. Garages."

"Really?" Simon said, texting the address to Trevor Welch and asking him to run it ASAP.

"Thought you might want to check it out," she said.

"I will," Simon said.

"Promise me a lead on anything you find," she added.

"You'll be my first call," Simon said and started to click off then added, "Thanks."

He rushed back into the squad room to tell his team.

After confirming no one at Lucas' usual haunts had seen him in over a week, Simon, Dolby, and Maberry headed south to 3429 Troost Avenue to check out Todd Ward's storage units. Simon realized he hadn't bothered checking Lucas' apartment, swearing to himself he'd do it after they were done at the storage place. He scolded himself for not thinking of it before, but he'd wanted Lucas to come in on his own, not be chased down like some kind of criminal. He understood his partner's feelings about being sidelined. He'd feel the same way in similar circumstances.

As he turned left out of the Central lot, Simon's cell rang. It was Emma.

"Dad, I'm worried about Lucas," she said as he answered.

"Hi, Dad, how ya doin'?" Simon said.

"I'm serious," Emma said, annoyed. "He hasn't been taking my calls for three days."

"He's not taking anyone's calls."

"What's wrong?"

"He got suspended from the android case."

"Why?"

"Some suit is worried he might be exposed to the android

thing and go crazy," Simon said as Maberry pulled around slower traffic and Simon followed.

"So the news was right—it's a virus?"

"We don't know, babe," Simon said, waiting behind Maberry at a stop light.

"Poor Lucas," Emma said. "That suit's an idiot. He's the best person you've got for this."

"I've made that argument."

"He's clearly upset if he's not taking calls," Emma said. "You've got to find him."

"I'm trying," Simon said. "None of his usual places have seen him either."

"His apartment?" Emma asked.

"I'll go by there soon," Simon said, kicking himself again for not doing it earlier when even his untrained teenage daughter had thought to look there. "On my way to check out a location for the case first." The light changed to green and he followed Maberry, turning left on Troost to head south. The storage place was two minutes ahead on the left.

"People are freaking out, Dad, afraid of androids now," Emma said. "The school banned them from campus."

"It's understandable but it's an overreaction," Simon said. "Someone is doing this deliberately to specific targets."

"But people have been killed," she said.

"Yes, a couple, but only one intentionally so far," Simon said. Williamson had been killed by an explosion, not an android so that left Garcia and Liska. Maybe Fiedler but they weren't absolutely sure yet. "It'll be over soon. We're coordinating with departments across the metro and the FBI."

"Good. Tell him I miss him, okay?"

"I will."

"And call me when you find him," she said, sounding bossy like her mother used to.

Simon smiled. Part of the reason he'd warmed to Lucas initially was how fast Emma took to him. She'd always been good with his partners but she and the android shared a special bond. He felt good she had another adult she trusted to talk to, even if that adult wasn't human. "Okay, boss."

"I love you, Dad," she said and hung up.

"I love you too," he said as he lowered the phone and followed Maberry left into the storage place's drive.

Rows of buildings filled the fenced-in complex, wide drives moving between them. From the outside at least, they looked freshly painted and well maintained. A small brick building with a cardboard sign reading "office" in dark blue letters lay straight ahead behind a gate. Maberry leaned out the window to push a call button on a post beside where he'd stopped his car. Moments later, the gate rattled and whirred as it began to open. Simon followed them through the gate and they parked in spaces outside the office and headed inside.

The inside of the office stank of cigarettes and old coffee, and the crinkly older woman sitting behind a desk opposite the door was clearly the reason why. She drank from a coffee mug that had enough cracks and stains to suggest it had been overworked for several decades, a half-smoked filterless cigarette dangling from between two fingers on her other hand. "I help you?" she barked.

Maberry badged her. "We're here to see about two units rented by a TWE Limited."

"And a postal box," Dolby added, checking her phone. "656."

"You got a warrant?" the manager demanded.

"We can make a phone call, if you insist," Maberry said. "We want to know what you can tell us about the person who rented them."

She screwed up her face so much she looked more like an old prune than a human being. "Our client's privacy is important to us."

"But not their lungs, huh?" Simon said, coughing and waving away the smoke drifting at his face.

She locked narrow eyes on his. "Free country. What's this about?" she demanded, unmoved.

Maberry motioned to Dolby who got on the phone.

"We're working an important case and think there might be a connection," Maberry said.

"What case? Have I heard of it?" the manager said, actually brightening as if he'd finally said something interesting.

"We're not at liberty—"

Dolby hung up the phone, cursing. "Judge is in court."

"Call Garner," Maberry told her.

"The android outbreak," Simon said before she could dial again. Maberry and Dolby shot him a look. Usually they didn't like to reveal too much to civilians, especially on high profile cases.

At this, the manager stiffened. "Those crazy robots? You think there's something here?"

"It's a possibility," Simon said.

"Damn robots are taking over the world!" the manager said. "Hang on." She stabbed the remains of her cigarette in an overstuffed ashtray and set her mug clumsily on the desk, spilling a few drops of coffee on some paperwork as she yanked open a drawer and dug around noisily inside. She pulled out a file and flipped it open, using her index finger to run down a spreadsheet. Grabbing a large ring of keys and jangling them as she stood, she said, "If it ever comes up, you had a warrant."

"Right," Simon said, winking at the others as she came around the desk and headed for the door, the detectives following her.

She led them right and down the second drive, her steps surprisingly sprite for someone who looked so old and worn down. "He's got two garages way in the back."

"He?" Dolby asked, walking beside her.

The units they passed had stenciled numbers painted in black, all in the six hundreds on this row. Each was locked with padlocks though some looked stronger than others, probably locks provided by management rather than the renters themselves.

"Yeah, it's a man who rents them," the manager said. "Have to look up his name back at the office. He rents it under his company but he signs paperwork and gets some mail so I wrote it down."

"We'd appreciate anything you could tell us," Dolby said.

"What kind of mail does he get?" Simon asked.

"Invoices mostly, I think," the manager said. "I don't read it. Privacy."

Simon guessed she nosed around more than she'd ever admit, out of sheer boredom, but they'd question her again later.

The further down the row away from the office they went, the larger the storage units became. Finally, the manager stopped at one of the largest units—number 624–and nodded as she flipped through the key ring, looking for the right one. "It's these next two."

"Ever seen what he puts in here?" Maberry asked.

"Buncha boxes," she replied as she found the right key and fitted it into the lock, which she held steady as she turned. "Don't much care usually as long as they follow the rules—nothing flammable and so on."

The lock clicked and she pulled it off and set it on the ground then turned and motioned toward the door. "Go ahead. I'll open the other one."

As she moved toward the next unit over, jingling her keys again, Maberry stepped forward and slid open the garage door. The acrid odor of hydraulic fluids mixed with gasoline and dust filled their noses as the door retracted above them and they scanned stacks of boxes bearing various labels.

Dolby starting reading off the labels: "Hydraulic clamps, CPUs, vocoders—"

"Jesus, there's enough here for a small army," Maberry said.

"This one's open, too," the manager called from the next unit over.

"Start making a list," Simon said as he turned and walked over to where the manager stood holding another lock.

Simon stepped around her and slid open the second garage door, again experiencing the acrid smell of hydraulic fluid mixed with gas and dust. As the door retracted, a nightmare unfolded before him.

"Oh my God!" the manager exclaimed, looking horrified.

"Jesus," Simon muttered.

What was inside this unit was like a horror museum of dismembered bodies.

"What you got?" Dolby asked as she and Maberry hurried over.

"Fuck me," Maberry said as they stopped and stared.

Partially assembled androids with blank faces lay everywhere—some piled along walls or in corners, others lying randomly about. A few fully assembled ones stood in a line along the wall to one corner.

Simon turned and herded the manager back the way they'd come. "Go back to the office and get me whatever files you have on these units."

"Are they alive?!" she asked, her voice shaking with fear.

"No," Simon said.

"I want them out!" she said.

"We'll take them," he assured her and gave her a gentle push so she kept walking back toward the office, watching as the speed of her steps slowly increased until she was running.

Dolby was on the radio to dispatch calling in crime scene and other units. "Yes, I said trucks. We've got a lot of evidence to impound.…"

"And these are just the ones he didn't finish yet," Maberry muttered as Simon returned to stand next to him.

"Or maybe prototypes or malfunctioning," Simon added.

"Either way, we're looking at the makings of an army," Maberry said.

"Yeah," Simon said, realizing it would be a while 'til he could get to Lucas' apartment.

"What the hell's he trying to accomplish?" Maberry muttered.

"I have no—" Simon stopped as someone came around the corner. He looked up to see Lucas stopping at the sight of them and hurrying back out of sight.

Simon ran toward him. "Lucas! Wait!"

He rounded the corner of the garage past the last one they'd opened and saw Lucas hurrying away. "The department's looking for you. They know you've been working the case."

Lucas slowed a moment, hesitating.

"They're about to put out a BOLO on you. Talk to me. I could use your help," Simon said, then added, "Emma's worried sick."

Lucas' shoulders sank as he turned and walked back toward his partner and friend. "I am sorry I did not call her back."

"You owe a bunch of us calls," Simon said.

Lucas nodded. "I did not want to make trouble for you."

"Atwell knows what you've been doing," Simon said. "We got several reports of your activities."

Lucas sighed. "I tried to go unnoticed."

"Tough to do in this day and age," Simon said. "Besides, we're your friends. We trust you. Let us help you, and please help us."

"I am suspended," Lucas said.

"Fuck that," Simon said then waited as Lucas stood there in silence, thinking or computing or whatever he did. "Look. Tell us what you've got. We have new information as well. We can find these assholes faster together. You know that."

"I do not wish to ruin my career," Lucas said.

"Unofficial," Simon said. "We've got your back—Maberry, Dolby, Becker, me."

"His androids are primitive, not like my line or others from the Maker's lab," Lucas said. "I am not sure what their purpose is."

"They robbed ATMs," Simon said, "and they kill people."

"This much we know," Lucas agreed.

Simon pulled his cell and flipped quickly through pictures, finding one then holding it up for Lucas to see. "One was wearing a mask."

Lucas stared at the screen, stunned. "He made one like me?"

"Faceless like them," Simon said, shaking his head. "With a 3D mask of your face, but it was *nothing* like you."

"I have been tracking his IP and communications signals," Lucas said.

"I know, let me help you," Simon said. "We've gotta find this bastard and stop him, while we still can."

"They will arrest me," Lucas said, shaking his head.

"For what? You're a cop, not a criminal," Simon said. "You've broken no laws, pal. Atwell's just bent out of shape because you've been working the case, but we'll back you. Trust me."

"They fear me," Lucas said.

"Yes, but they also fear for you," Simon said. "People always fear what they don't understand." He locked eyes with his partner. "You have information that will help us find the people who are doing this, maybe even the missing piece we've been waiting for."

They heard gravel crunching and tires humming as more units arrived.

"They are coming, I must go," Lucas said, turning to leave.

"No!" Simon put a hand on his arm to stop him. "I will protect you. If we go down, we go down together. Trust me."

Lucas turned back. "I am afraid."

"I know," Simon said. "But don't be."

Lucas thought a moment, considering. "I will work only with you."

"No problem."

"Atwell must not see me."

"Oh hell, we'd all be happier if she never saw us," Simon said.

Lucas nodded. "Okay."

Simon motioned toward the drive that moved down the next row away from the units they'd open. "Come with me."

Lucas motioned toward a back gate. "My car is there."

"Okay, meet me at your place in an hour," Simon said.

"I will wait for you," Lucas said as he turned and strode away.

Simon watched him go, feeling relieved, like the universe had finally been put back in proper order again. He watched as Lucas pressed both hands on the back gate and flung himself over, disappearing down the alley. Then he turned and hurried back to join the others.

CHAPTER 19

SIMON HAD NEVER been inside Lucas' apartment before. Off 4th Street near the River Market, the apartment had been given to Lucas by his maker, Livia Connelly, because of its proximity to public transport as well as good opportunities for him to blend in and interact with humans at the River Market, where he went to buy what few provisions and supplies he needed. Originally, Lucas had purchased a house before joining the department, intending to move there, but it turned out to be termite infested and a bad investment. Simon had gotten him out of it without losing his shirt, but from then on, Lucas had decided to remain where he was. After all, he was single and didn't need much.

Only 875 square feet, the apartment was small and Simon immediately felt claustrophobic. It consisted of a bathroom and a large main room with a decent walk-in closet. Except for a small deck overlooking a shared courtyard that was accessed by a sliding glass door opposite the entrance, there were no windows. A charging station occupied one corner in lieu of a bed, and the kitchen and bathroom were empty except for fixtures and spotless due to lack of use. Every spare wall space was covered with bookshelves, many of them full to the brim already with Lucas' book collection. The android had an in-satiable thirst for knowledge, another part of his quest to be more human, and frequently enjoyed quoting from his latest or favorite reads. Simon had asked why Lucas didn't just stick to ebooks he could upload into his databanks. Lucas responded that he did eread but he so liked the feel of old books, he had taken to collecting his favorites.

At the center of the main room, a leather sofa and two straight-backed chairs faced a television with DVR and Archival Disc, which had replaced blu-ray, as well as a mini-stereo, while a table sat off to one side closer to the kitchen bar. It was the cleanest, most spotless bachelor pad Simon had ever seen.

They sat around a small table using the two straight-backed chairs and reviewed the evidence each had gathered in the android case so far. Before they started, Lucas offered Simon a bottled water or soda from a mini-fridge sitting on the edge of the kitchen bar—purchased, Simon assumed, for visitors, since Lucas had no need of food or drink. Simon declined wondering about their expiration dates and began reviewing developments in the case since they'd last spoken.

Lucas showed Simon the device Benn Liska had given him to help track the androids, and they discussed the information on tracing IPs and GPS data as well. That seemed to be the most promising new development to them both.

"Other than that, we can trace the contents of those garages, find out where he bought them and see what new witnesses turn up who might know other locations or details to help us," Simon said.

"So we are really no closer to finding him," Lucas said.

"Not close enough to count," Simon said.

"What if we fail her?" Lucas asked, not meeting Simon's eyes, his shoulders sagging.

"Livia?"

"Yes," Lucas said. "I owe her so much. We have to save her. I feel like I am the only one who can."

"I hear you," Simon said, feeling deep sympathy for his partner and the pressure he clearly felt. He'd been there. "We can't always save them."

"You lose hostages?" Lucas said, meeting his eyes.

"Yes, but not without a fight," Simon said. "We will find her."

"But she still might die?" Lucas said, sad again.

"Look, I don't want to mislead you about the odds, pal," Simon said. "It happens sometimes, but we're not done here yet. If she's still alive, we will find her. I promise you."

For a moment, their eyes met and Lucas looked empowered, as if he felt the strength of Simon's convictions, but then he looked down again.

"So what do we do?" Lucas asked, his voice dropping, discouraged.

They needed a better break. Simon thought a moment about how to up the ante, but then he had an idea and said, "Let's drive over to the River Market. You run in and pick up a bottle of Absolut vodka while I check in with Becker and the squad, then we'll go shake a lot more trees."

"The rail yard?" Lucas asked.

Like all good investigators, Simon had spent years developing his own team of HUMINT—Human Intelligence—CIs, Confidential Informants, known on the street as snitches or just informants. So far Simon hadn't found much use for them in this investigation but it was time to change that. Before they'd been focused on not alarming the public unnecessarily, but now they knew the only way to find the perpetrators quickly was to disseminate word as far and as fast as possible and get the public working for them. If anyone could get the word out in a way that would generate a response, it was Simon's CI Dennis Murphy, better known to Simon and Lucas as Mister Information.

A Gulf War vet turned vagrant with a Meth habit, who slept in an old abandoned boxcar on the tracks at the Burlington Santa Fe and Northern Railroad yard, Mister Information had been around as long as Simon had been a cop and played a key part in solving some of his best cases. He'd even been a victim of the bombing case they'd solved the previous Spring, injured in the explosion at a Garden Center which employed one of the suspects.

Absolut was Mister Information's drink of choice, and since Simon wouldn't provide him with Meth, it was his bribe of choice whenever Simon wanted information. So as Lucas ran inside River Market Liquor at Third and Wyandotte, Simon called Central.

"How's Lucas?" Becker asked.

"He's fine," Simon said. "We have a few ideas we're working. Any progress on the suppliers list?"

"Slow but steady," Becker said. "Cataloging it alone is going to take all night and most of tomorrow."

"Get help," Simon suggested.

"We've called in everyone we can, believe me."

"Good."

"I think it's still a good idea to keep Lucas away from here for now, just in case," Becker said. "Atwell has been in already to check on what we confiscated at the storage place. You never know when she might turn up."

"I think he and I already agreed on that," Simon said. "He's pretty worried about being 'arrested' or detained."

"He's broken no laws."

"I told him that, but he's feeling like a wanted man."

"Understandable," Becker said. "Would it help if I call him?"

"Probably later, maybe even meet up somewhere."

"Okay, just let me know."

"Going to get a few CIs working the vine," Simon said. "After that."

"All right," Becker said. "It's gonna be a late night so I'll be here."

"Thanks," Simon said and hung up as Lucas returned to the car looking triumphant. He held up a bottle labeled Beluga Gold.

"The man said this is some of the finest imported Vodka on the market," Lucas said. "Direct from Russia. They invented Vodka."

"I know they did," Simon said, "but we can't give him that."

Lucas frowned. "Why not?"

"You don't give a starving man caviar and filet mignon," Simon said. "It's too much. After being so desperate, it'll overwhelm him, and since he'll never be able to afford it, it'll just set a standard he can never match again."

"It's too good for him?" Lucas' brow creased as he tried to contemplate this.

"Just trust me," Simon said. "Denny loves Absolut. Don't push him by throwing something new and unfamiliar into the mix."

"What did Becker say?" Lucas asked as Simon reached for the door and undid his seatbelt.

"She'll meet up with us later," Simon said and climbed

out. "I'll be right back."

WITH A BOTTLE OF Absolut in hand, Simon drove to 42nd Street and turned on the service road that ran straight through the rail yard's middle. A Kansas City landmark, with dozens of tracks converging together overseen by high observation booths that resembled air traffic control towers where controllers routed and rerouted the various arrivals and departures. Things had slowed down from the yard's glory days, so there were several tracks no longer in use where old, out of service train cars sat abandoned, left to rust and rot.

Mister Information's "home" rested on a short span of tracks to the south side of a cluster of tracks in the middle—one of those spurs formerly used to change cars back and forth with incoming and outgoing trains. Brown, like most boxcars, it was showing rust stains at its corners and sides now, including one that was quickly obscuring the white Santa Fe RR emblem painted decades before on its side.

Simon pulled the Interceptor to a stop beside an abandoned section of tracks and looked for the red rag Mister Information hung on one of the car's ladder rungs every night to signal he was in. As raggedy as the car itself—torn, remnants really, smeared with oil and dirt—the rag flapped in the winter breeze as Simon opened the door and climbed out, Lucas following on the opposite side. The rail yard smelled like oil, dirt, diesel and chemicals, and lots of dust. Lucas caught up as Simon climbed over the rails and headed for the boxcar.

They crossed several sets of tracks and passed a few other abandoned cars before moving around to the far side of the Santa Fe car marked with the red rag and climbing up a makeshift ramp into the dark interior.

Simon immediately heard coughing and then, "I thought I told you to keep that bastard away from me!"

Mr. Information had hated Lucas ever since their first encounter during the Benjamin Ashman case, when the overzealous android had interrogated him by holding him inches from a speeding train passing on the next track over. Since those tracks were now entirely out of use, Simon felt reasonably sure that could never happen again, but Mister Information's first impressions weren't easy to overcome.

"I brought this," Lucas said, holding out the Absolut.

The vagrant leaned forward, his face illuminated by a splinter of light bleeding through a hole in one corner of the car as he sought a better view of the bottle Lucas was holding. "You give it to him," he growled and motioned to Simon. "You're not welcome here."

"He paid for it, Denny, cut him a break," Simon replied, motioning for Lucas to give Mister Information the Absolut.

The vagrant shrank back, hissing, as Lucas stepped forward and set the vodka bottle beside his worn work boots, then backed away.

"He poison it?" the vagrant asked, eyeing the bottle warily.

"Would I let anything happen to my best CI?" Simon countered.

"Almost got me blew up," the vagrant responded.

"Not my fault you were out wandering," Simon said.

Dirty hands in torn gloves shot out to snatch up the Vodka

and pull it to the vagrant's chest where he quickly broke the seal, unscrewed the top, and took a big sniff of the Vodka. "Mmmmmmmm." Then he tipped back his head and took a long swig, savoring it before asking, "What you want of me?"

Simon told him about the android issue and then described Todd Ward.

"Yeah, yeah, I see the news around at places, I hear rumors," Mister Information said.

"Good," Simon replied. "Now we want you to spread some. Let people know we're looking for this man and anyone else involved with androids who is working the back rooms, black market, off the main market."

"This man responsible?" Mister Information asked. "He why this crazy attacked me?"

Simon laughed. "No, that was him trying too hard. This is different. We know we need to talk to the man I described but there may be others. We're not sure. We need to find them before it gets worse."

"I'll put the word out, but you know, this kind of stuff is white collar," Mister Information said. "Those people don't work the same circles."

"Somebody's seen or knows something," Simon said.

"I'll see what turns up," the vagrant promised, taking another swig of his Absolut.

"Enjoy your drink," Lucas said as he turned to go.

"You want some?" Mister Information held the bottle out to Simon.

"Another time. I'm on duty." Simon said with a wave as he turned and followed Lucas out the door.

"Where next?" Lucas wondered as they headed back toward the Interceptor.

"Show me how that device works to track the androids," Simon said. "Let's see if anything's happening."

"Okay," Lucas agreed.

Two minutes later, they settled in the car and started checking the tracker, as Lucas explained its various functions and showed Simon the codes list.

"What's this?" Simon asked, pointing to a cluster of dots that had suddenly appeared on the map. "Is that a lot of them in one place?"

Lucas nodded. "It appears to be, yes. I have not seen anything like this show up before."

Simon motioned to his partner as he started the engine. "Get the address."

"It's in Overland Park."

Simon shifted the car into gear and started accelerating even as he replied, "Doesn't hurt anything to take a look, right?"

He was turning off the service road onto 42nd again before Lucas finished reading it off and headed quickly south toward 635 again.

TODD WARD WAS pissed, and it was his own fault. He should never have exposed his own androids during the ATM jobs but he'd needed a quick infusion of cash to finish his plan and his previous successes had made him cocky. The fastest way was to send out multiple teams at once, quick and dirty. But he hadn't counted on one actually being taken down and captured. Now the police knew about the masks and had one model to examine. That meant he had very little time to change his design so future models would never be tied to any crimes, and the last thing he needed was more stress.

Then there was the matter of Livia Connelly. Despite his intentions, Todd had never actually killed anyone face to face. He'd sent his minions a couple times, and sabotaged androids had accidentally killed a teacher, of course, but to kill someone here, in his own workshop, especially someone who'd played such a big role in his life's direction—he'd need to work up to it. And he'd been too distracted at the moment to give it much thought. Keeping her captive, though, was becoming more and more of a burden.

He'd gagged and blindfolded her again before knocking her out with ether when he began his latest task: programming a complex sequence of behavior into multiple androids in preparation for the execution of his plan's final stage. It wasn't that she could see anything. It was to keep her out of his hair. And intimidating and keeping her guessing was good, too. Just to make it interesting, as a second thought, he decided he'd move her to another room, so he had three of his androids relocate her into an unfinished storage room, chair and all, and left her there to sleep it off.

Todd had programming to do, and he threw himself into that with great vigor. The basic idea was to send androids on specific missions and have some of them retrieve items they'd return to him at a neutral location on a specific date. For this purpose, he'd rented an abandoned storefront in Overland Park that had been empty for months, the desperate landlord all too happy to rent it to him for a month just to see it generate some income. He'd ordered signs designating it "The

First Church of The New Age," which he'd install when the execution date was a day or two away. A church there with many bodies coming and going wouldn't stand out or draw unwanted attention from neighbors or passersby, even if its name was unusual and raised curiosity. And leaving the signs until a day or two before he'd actually be using it should avoid curiosity seekers or others who might otherwise drop by just to "see" what's there.

The hardest part of the plan would be distributing the 3D masks the androids needed to wear for their missions, a task requiring special programming. That and sending his own androids out to plant special packages each "borrowed" android would have to retrieve on mission day, before heading to their targeted location. Calls would go out to Connelly Labs and the police about a bunch of androids malfunctioning or wandering off that morning, of course, but by the time anyone got pictures or descriptions together, they'd be masked and headed back out to perform their missions. So searchers would be looking for the wrong faces.

The only thing he hadn't been able to do was jam the GPS signals in case Connelly Labs decided to start tracing their units. While his nanoparticles emitted their own traceable signals he used to control and keep track of his charge's activities, their built-in GPS was still necessary to guide their movements. He'd just have to take his chances and hope everything unfolded so quickly that GPS tracking couldn't happen in time.

Finishing the programming took him two hours, much longer than he'd expected considering he'd started the day thinking only minor tweaks remained to be done. But there proved to be a few more holes and loopholes he needed to close before unleashing his master work, and he wanted to be sure everything was right before sending it out to the androids, since he'd only get one shot at this.

He spent another hour going through and double checking everything to be sure it was all in order. Attention to detail counted for everything here. When he was satisfied, he sat back in his chair and took a deep breath, smiling and savoring the moment. This was going to be triumphant. All he had to do was type in the code to signal the nanoparticles and then send the instructions and the rest would take care of itself.

Until he was ready. And that day, he would issue the initiate sequence that started everything rolling.

He stretched his fingers and grunted with satisfaction. Then he started typing, sending first the signal to establish communications, then waiting until all the nanoparticles verified connection before uploading the command patterns. Altogether that took around three minutes.

Three glorious minutes.

For those three glorious minutes, he imagined the glory of success.

On the fourth minute, the glory ended. That's when everything went wrong.

ALL THE WAY over to Overland Park, Simon and Lucas heard radio calls coordinating the various searches cops from several departments and FBI Agents were doing across the city that afternoon. They'd called in their lead to Becker and avoided a similar assignment, but they'd be back on it afterwards if this lead led nowhere. Simon drove under full lights and siren, traveling eighty on the highway then sixty-five down the busy Metcalf Avenue that ran through the middle of many suburbs but ended in Overland Park. Lucas monitored the GPS tracker.

"There are now fifteen indicators at the location," Lucas reported. When they'd first picked up the signal and headed that way, there had been five. Fifteen was a gathering of some sort. But why?

"Any idea what's at that location?" Simon asked, his mind searching for ideas.

"Google Maps identifies it as a strip mall," Lucas said.

"A strip mall?" Simon repeated it as a question. It made little sense for Todd Ward or whoever was responsible for sabotaging the androids to operate so out in the open.

"And there have been no radio calls yet to that location," Lucas said, unnecessary since they were both listening to the police radio out loud in the car.

"So whatever's going on is not disturbing the neighbors... yet," Simon replied. "Is that mall operating or abandoned?"

"There are six confirmed business locations in operation there, from what I can find," Lucas said. "We are five minutes from that location," he added.

"Thanks Rand McNally," Simon snapped.

"Who is Rand McNally?" Lucas asked, shooting him a puzzled look, then, "Ahhhh, the map maker. I see. A joke, of course."

"Yeah, might make a good name for an android though, don't ya think?" Simon teased.

Lucas smiled. "Perhaps if one goes into geography or navigation. But it would be McNally Rand, of course."

Simon chortled at the thought and slowed the car to turn left at West 75th Street, two blocks from their destination. Traffic was bunched at a red light, so he slipped into the opposing lanes and went around them. Cars crossing at the intersection slowed or darted to the side to stop and let him through.

Simon grunted. "That was too easy. Doesn't happen that way in every neighborhood."

"They warned us of this at the Academy. People do not obey the law," Lucas said with a nod.

"Yeah, no respect for the cops," Simon said. "Everyone's too busy rushing around."

"Very dangerous," Lucas said as Simon slowed at another intersection just as the light changed to green, then sped on through, zipping around a few other cars and turning left into the parking lot of the strip mall.

"Well, we're here," Simon said as he slowed and looked around, driving across the parking lot as he did. "Any idea which store?"

Lucas checked the tracker again and shook his head. "It is not that specific."

They both panned the storefronts and lot, looking for some clue as Simon drove slowly.

TODD WAS SCRAMBLING the moment he realized the androids were heading for the rendezvous immediately, instead of waiting for his command. Code blurred together as his eyes scanned it and he strained to focus. What had he missed?

Fuck.

He kept searching and it took him almost two minutes. A whole lotta code, but there it was. He'd forgotten to reset the execute command from when he'd tested the code. Then he'd run it automatically but now he wanted it linked to the execute command codes he'd programmed in.

His fingers scrambled across the keyboard, keys clacking, as he strove to fix the error, then resend the programming to the androids. At the last minute, he added in an extra touch he hoped would distract anyone paying too much attention from thinking about the oddness of androids converging on an empty storefront.

He hoped it worked. He'd have to pay close attention to police bands and set up cameras on the location to observe it for the next few days just to be sure it hadn't been discovered by the wrong people; that no one contacted police or other authorities.

He sent the program and waited another three minutes for it to rewrite the previous send, then he watched as the androids began dispersing. He hoped it was soon enough. He'd timed it so they went out in small groups, not all together as a mass exodus, with hopes that would draw less notice from anyone observing activity there.

Fuck. He just had to wait. He wouldn't know for several hours at least.

It would be hell. Even the minutes seemed to pass like years.

SIMON HAD JUST turned back and started across the strip mall parking lot the way he'd come when five people emerged from a storefront three doors ahead with painted windows and no signage.

"There!" Lucas called.

"I see it," Simon said and accelerated, pulling up to cut off the small group as it stepped clear of parked cars into the driving lanes of the lot. Simultaneously, he and Lucas climbed out of the car.

They were either the happiest people Simon had ever met or androids. There was just something unnatural about their smiles.

"The blessings of the New Age are upon us," a white female with long blonde hair said with a nod as they approached.

"Amen," the rest of the group said. There was another woman, with dark skin like Lucas, and three men—one white, one Asian and one black. All looked to be young, like Lucas, but other than their unnatural happiness and odd cult-like responses, they could be human.

"Brothers and sisters," Lucas said, matching their smiles. "Have we missed the meeting?" But Simon noticed his partner remained several feet away, out of range of any airborne pathogens.

"You are late, brother," said the white male. "We are done. Return to your Maker and await further instructions." The group parted, moving around the two detectives, but Simon and Lucas countered, stepping into their path again.

"Please, can you tell me more," Lucas asked. "I don't want to be uninformed."

"It's all in the program, brother," said the Asian male and they stepped around Simon and Lucas again, picking up the pace as they departed, splitting off individually in various directions—a couple to cars, a couple on foot, another heading for a bus stop.

Lucas was about to go after them when another group—a trio—emerged from the storefront and Simon grabbed his shoulder to stop him.

"Are they androids, can you tell?" he asked.

"I believe they are," Lucas replied as they turned to intercept the next group.

This time, the trio spoke in unison. "The blessings of the New Age are upon us." Then they split off and hurried away so fast, the detectives would have to run to catch them.

"Let's check out the inside," Simon said, nodding toward the door to the unmarked storefront they'd exited moments before.

"One moment," Lucas said and hurried back to the Interceptor. Two minutes later, he returned wearing polypropylene crime scene pullovers, gloves, and a mask he'd pulled from the back of the Interceptor. He looked like a giant walking condom.

"Are you hoping for a date or just feeling a bit paranoid there, pal?" Simon joked.

"I do not wish to expose myself to unnecessary risk," Lucas replied, his voice muffled by the mask.

Simon smiled but stifled another comment, dreading answering the questions it would surely elicit.

They stepped inside a space that was basically empty—no furniture, the painted walls showing stains and scratches from use. A few fixtures and shelf units were scattered around the floor, abandoned along with a couple partially used dried-up paint cans, one with a brush sticking out of it. The whole place smelled of dust and old paint. Whoever had rented this space must not be particular about its appearance or was behind because remodeling appeared to have not even started yet.

As they entered, a man and a woman moved past them for the door.

"Brother and sister, how was the meeting?" Lucas called after them.

"The blessings of the New Age are upon us," they said together, showing zero reaction to Lucas' odd appearance in the crime scene suit, then disappeared out the door.

"Can we trace them?" Simon asked.

Lucas nodded. "I've logged the numbers of all the contacts we tracked here."

"We better get someone looking into this place as well," Simon suggested. A call to the rental office later, they knew the space had been rented under an organization called "The First Church of the New Age." Whatever the fuck that meant. But when Simon asked, they told him the signature was illegible and seemed dodgy about offering any further information over the phone.

"A cult of androids?" Simon said, shaking his head. "Nothing suspicious about that."

"It is unusual," Lucas agreed.

"We can get a subpoena and go there for more details," Simon said, though he suspected simply showing up in person and badging them would do the trick.

"We can call their owners and inquire about any unusual behavior they may have witnessed," Lucas said. "Or we could shut them all down."

Simon grunted. "I thought about that, but then how would they lead us to the person responsible? I think we may still need them, and we don't want to alert anyone we're onto them just yet."

"You are not afraid of the danger to others?" Lucas asked.

"Other androids or humans?" Simon asked.

"Both," Lucas said after thinking a beat.

"Yes, but we'll monitor them closely and call the owners like you suggested," Simon said. "We just need to be careful not to tip our hand if we want to find whoever's doing this and shut them down. This is the best lead yet."

Lucas harumphed, which Simon took as affirmation and they searched the room, but turned up nothing further of interest before heading back to the car again where Simon called Becker so she could get to work on setting up the surveillance they'd need.

If this location was tied to Todd Ward or whoever the perp was, chances were it would lead them to him soon enough.

CHAPTER 20

WHILE MABERRY AND Dolby began working the list of android owners, Becker and Melson arranged surveillance on the storefront. So Simon and Lucas headed south of the Plaza to what remained of Todd Ward's house to interview the neighbors again. It was almost five and most who worked would be arriving home. The first two hadn't seen a thing, they worked long hours and were always busy in the evenings with children's and community activities. The detectives were lucky to catch them at all. It was a shame about the house, a burned husk spoiling the neighborhood now. Good riddance, even if he had been quiet, obviously Todd Ward was no good.

It was the third who intrigued Simon. She was early sixties, retired and spent her days playing Scrabble, knitting, and watching television—mostly game and talk shows, though she spoke of missing soap operas, which had all but disappeared. Her name was Lelia Foreman and she'd invited them into her home for some lemonade. The place was small and smelled of cleaners, old books and linens, and mothballs. Simon and Lucas sat on a couch across from the worn lounge chair facing her TV—clearly her usual perch. The table beside it had water stains from where glasses and mugs had been left to condense and the carpet in front was a bit more worn than other places, showing obvious signs of regular heavy use.

"He was quiet, like the others said," she added when they got back to the subject at hand. She wore a flowered dress and old panty hose with worn, aqua blue slippers, the kind Simon had seen old folks wearing a lot at nursing homes or retirement communities. "But he was mischievous. Always up to something at odd hours, going in and out, bringing in supplies and such. Lots of packages and mail, too. I got curious."

"Did you ever ask him about it?" Simon asked, wiping lemonade off his mouth with a sleeve. It was good, frozen but not too sweet or tart. High quality from the taste.

"Yes, but I made it like a joke so as not to be rude, of course," she said. "He was quite evasive that one. Didn't like anyone knowing his business. Which just made me want to know all the more, you know." Her voice was soft and barely audible above the hum of the space heater occupying the floor behind her chair and aimed directly at it, despite the house being well-heated by a furnace.

"I understand," Lucas said. He had politely accepted lemonade as well but was ignoring it, pretending to be so caught up in listening that he'd forgotten its existence.

"Not much activity since the explosion, of course," she said and Simon figured the conversation was over, but then she added, "until two days ago."

"What happened two days ago?" Lucas asked.

"Someone was poking about the attic above the garage," she said. "I was out working in my yard and heard them banging about up there. Then later, I was watching Ellen when the garage opened and a van drove out."

"What kind of van?" Simon asked.

She shrugged. "Not good with cars myself. I believe it was brown, with no windows along the sides, only front and back.

Kind of resembled the ones those plumbers and delivery men use."

"A cargo van?" Simon asked.

"Is that what they call it?" she replied.

"Did you notice anything else about it? It's plate? Other markings?" Lucas asked.

"Yes," she said and motioned to the kitchen table across the living room from where they were sitting. "It's in my purse there."

Lucas got up and hurried over to retrieve the purse as Mrs. Foreman eyed his lemonade. "You've forgotten your lemonade," she said as he returned and handed her the purse.

"I'm not thirsty," Lucas said. "Very focused on finding Mister Ward."

She nodded and grunted in understanding. "Yes, with that type, who knows?" Then she dug in her purse, moving things around a bit in the main compartment until she pulled out a notepad with a satisfied look and flipped a few pages back, stopping to slip on a pair of reading glasses she'd kept hanging around her neck by a strap before reading the contents.

"Ah yes," she said at least. "I got part of the numbers." She tore off the paper and offered it to Simon, who stood and walked over to accept it. "I didn't have the chance to get them all. I'm sorry."

"That's okay," Simon said as he read the paper and returned to the couch. "This will help. You're sure the van was brown?"

Her face screwed up a bit as she thought about it and then nodded. "It was dark. Could have been a very dark blue or green, I suppose, with my eyes, and I wasn't wearing my glasses at first, until I looked at the plate. But yes, I'd say brown. Fairly certain."

"We'll run it through the databases," Lucas said with a smile as Simon stood and he followed. Simon had finished his lemonade, but Lucas' remained untouched.

"Thanks for the lemonade," Simon said. "Delicious."

"My pleasure," she said. "I don't get a lot of company. It's nice to have folks to chat with from time to time."

Simon grunted and handed her his card. "If you see anything more or think of anything, don't hesitate to call."

"All right," she said. "Never hurts to know a police officer, I say."

"Yes," Lucas agreed as Simon opened the front door to let them out. "Have a good day, Mrs. Foreman."

She thanked them then watched them turn and walk down the stoop to the sidewalk, heading for the Interceptor at the curb. Then she stayed there, waving as they looked back before pulling away.

"Let's call Fiedler tomorrow," Simon said. "Maybe someone saw him come in or caught him on security feeds."

"Worth a try," Lucas agreed.

The phone rang. It was Holly Sanders. "Did that lead pan out? TWE?"

"Hello, John, how was your day?" Simon teased.

"Sorry. I'm in work mode," she replied. "So?"

"Pretty sure it did," Simon said.

"What did you find?" she asked.

Simon looked over at Lucas, hesitating. Did he want Lucas to know he was talking to the press? Especially Holly Sanders? Probably not. "Can I call you back?"

"Are you in a meeting?" she asked.

"Sort of," he replied.

"Okay, glad it helped. Call me," she said and hung up.

Simon glanced over to see Lucas obliviously staring out the window.

"You have secrets from me now?" Lucas asked.

"What? No."

Lucas smiled. "I could hear it was a woman. Did you take our advice and start dating again?"

"No, been too busy," Simon said.

Lucas shot him a knowing look. "Have you told Emma yet?"

"There's nothing to tell," Simon said.

"Sure," Lucas said.

"Now you sound like a smart-ass teenager," Simon said.

Lucas watched him a moment as Simon turned the radio to his favorite station and tried to appear nonchalant. Then headed back to Central to retrieve their own cars before heading home.

THEY KNEW!

Todd had hacked into the security footage of a nearby store and to check the storefront activity, only to see Detectives John Simon and Lucas George trying to intercept his android visitors.

Fuck. Now he had to both find a new location and speed up his timeline. The cops were too close. He had to finish this thing before they ruined everything.

This plan was the culmination of many years' planning,

but it had become obvious that having never executed a plan on such scale, he had a lot to learn. He was making careless mistakes now and had only himself to blame. He had to get focused and keep it together a few more days, then let things roll to their natural conclusion. Because they still had no idea where to locate him or Livia Connelly, and that meant he could still make this work. He just had to scramble, and Todd had always been good under deadline pressure.

A month after the implosion of Connelly Labs, his own firm would rise to fill the gap with a never-before-revealed name and a figurehead manager who obeyed Todd's every order while he remained the silent owner in the background. There would come a day when he could reveal himself, he hoped. It all depended upon what the cops knew and could prove. But for now, he was content to play it safe. All that mattered was eliminating the competition and claiming his rightful place as the leading provider of humanoid androids in the Kansas City region.

There would be plenty of time to right other wrongs.

For now though, it was time to move to his final command post, a spot few knew about and no one would search. It had taken time and financial maneuvering to acquire the space, and his eventual plan was to incorporate it into the factory overhead—once that was rehabbed—where he would man-ufacture his new line of androids. But for securing Livia and himself from prying eyes and law enforcement authority while he executed the final stage, no location was better.

Most Kansas Citians had long ago forgotten most of the history of Kansas City's once extensive street car lines, includ-ing the underground tunnel leading under 8th Street from the West Bottoms industrial area to the heart of downtown at 8th and Delaware (now Main Street). Built in 1888, the 3000 foot space once known as the 8th Street Tunnel had been abandoned a few years before the street cars shut down in 1962 and all access points filled and capped. For a brief period in the 1990s and 2000s, a developer who'd owned the land and buildings above it inadvertently reopened the tunnel in the process of digging up the land. He had then allowed and conducted tours of the tunnel but weakening from erosion and age had forced them to cease such activities by 2017. In the decade since, they'd wound up selling off most of the property to various interests. One of those buyers had been Todd Ward, who'd bought a rehabbed factory in the Bottoms they'd never quite finished and planned to make it his own.

When he'd devised his current plan, he'd hired an out-of-state crew to shore up the tunnel walls and interior before building a backup command center there. Only about half the tunnel length was viable for use, the rest having been partially filled with cement or caved in over the years such that restoration was prohibitively expensive. Where the ceiling was high enough, he could use portions of that space for storage. Either way, he had more than enough room to work with in the remaining portion. There were even enclosed rooms now with stone walls which could serve as holding cells if needed, a great place to stash his captive until he did away with her. There was plenty of room and supplies stored there as well as all the equipment, tools, communications networks and internet access he needed to go underground with all of his current androids and wait out the law enforcement while building up his factory enterprise overhead. He literally could live there if he wanted and never set foot outside for decades. All he had to do was relocate himself, Livia, and the androids he'd designed from this temporary working space and he was good to go. Relocating there was something he'd been planning to do anyway when the time was right. He'd just have to up his launch date to before the final stage now.

Coughing and a mumbled cry came from the other room as Livia started awakening. He'd have to knock her out a while longer so he could do this, but with the androids' help, moving a prone body would be fast and easy. But he should knock her out before she'd fully awakened to keep things simpler and smoother.

He grabbed a rag and the ether bottle and hurried into the other room, a little skip in his step. He felt a bit like a kid who knew he was about to ace his finals. There was work yet to be done, but it was manageable. He'd move Livia, then set to work. He couldn't wait to see his master plan unfold before his eyes.

ON HIS WAY HOME, Simon made a call to Fiedler Pharmaceuticals' security desk and asked to speak with the head of security, explaining who he was. Two minutes later, he was patched through to the cell of Security Chief John Stott, who reported no sightings of Todd Ward in the past few days but promised his people would review the footage and ask around.

"We think he may be trying to recover materials from his designs or components needed for his current activities," Simon explained.

"I understand," Stott replied. "We'll secure everything we can as soon as possible. Can it wait until tomorrow?"

"Who knows," Simon said. "He could move at any time. We're closing in and he probably feels that. I'd move as soon as possible."

"Let me make some calls," Stott said. "We'll let you know what we find."

Simon thanked him and hung up.

Lucas was following him in the Outlander, Simon having convinced him to stay at the Fairway house until this was over in case Todd Ward or whoever had Livia might try and sabotage him to interfere with the investigation or manipulate her. He had his mobile charger and could go several days on that. Simon felt better knowing he could keep an eye on him until the android problem was settled.

As they approached the house, a blue Toyota Camry with a bright "Lyft" sign was parked at the curb, puzzling Simon and causing him to slow down, until Emma climbed out of the back. Simon glanced over to see Lucas had pulled around him and was parking behind the Toyota.

He pulled the Mustang into the drive and parked as she paid the driver, then rushed over to hug Lucas. "I was so worried about you!"

"I am fine, I promise," Lucas said. "I am sorry I didn't return your calls."

"What are you doing here?" Simon asked, watching his daughter.

She pulled herself away from his partner and turned to face him. "Told mom we had a daddy-daughter thing I forgot. I was worried about Lucas."

"I told you he was fine," Simon said as she took Lucas by

the hand and led him up the sidewalk toward the front door.

She looked back over her shoulder as Simon followed them. "You also promised to call."

"Been a little busy fighting crime," Simon snapped.

"Your father has a secret girlfriend," Lucas said as Emma used her key to open the front door. "You are just in time to interrogate him about it."

Emma whirled as she threw the front door open and stared at her father. "What?! Holy shit! I want the dirt! Now!"

"There's no girlfriend," Simon said. "He's assuming things."

But Lucas was already in the entryway watching them as Emma herded him into the house and shut the door behind her.

"Who *is* she?" she demanded.

"Just because I told someone I'd call them back, he thinks I'm keeping secrets," Simon said dismissively.

"It was a woman," Lucas said. "I could not hear what she was saying but I could tell that much."

Emma laughed and punched Simon in the arm. "Let's order pizza and you can tell me all about it."

"Nothing to tell," Simon said.

Emma put her hands on her hips and stared him in the eye. "You're a bad liar, Dad."

Simon grunted, turning away and hurrying through the living room to the kitchen for a beer. It was shaping up to be a long night. Maybe he should have let Lucas take his chances at his apartment.

Lucas and Emma started chattering like teenage girls as they followed him.

"Come on, who *is* she?" Emma demanded again as Simon pulled a bottle of Pabst Blue Ribbon from the fridge and popped the cap, taking a long drag.

"It was a victim inquiring about the case, if you must know," Simon said when he'd finished. He grabbed the phone and called 1889 Pizza Napolitana on West 47th, ordering The Butcher, Emma's favorite, featuring pepperoni, Italian sausage, housemade meatballs, parmigiano reggiano, basil, fresh mozzarella, tomato sauce, and extra virgin olive oil. It was old school European and much healthier than the Americanized versions, so her mother had always liked it. Simon tolerated it because it tasted so damn good.

"Well, while we're waiting, we've got time," Emma said, pulling up a stool to the counter and putting her chin on her hands as she watched her dad. "Spill."

"Lucas is writing fiction," Simon said. "Ask him. He'll make it up as he goes."

Emma rolled her eyes and exchanged a look with Lucas. "Told ya he's all shy and embarrassed about it. I'm fifteen now, Dad. Not a kid."

They heard a crash—a car window smashing it sounded like, followed by yelling. It was coming from the front of the house. All three ran back toward the front door.

"LOOK WHAT HE did to my car!"

Simon recognized the voice of Christy, his neighbor, whose house had been damaged by the rampaging android Jack the previous week. As Simon ran out the driveway he spotted the Asian caterer swinging a bat again at the Black Mercedes 500L parked in Christy's and Tom's driveway while dodging an angry Tom who was trying to disarm him. Tom was wearing a tank top and very short shorts that were not at all flattering while Christy wore a tennis getup, her face flushed, her hair disheveled. Both glistened with sweat, as if they'd been caught mid-game. Simon knew they had an indoor court behind their house.

"You fucker! Give me that bat!" Tom yelled.

"You ruin my business!" the caterer yelled back. He was still wearing the stained white chef's outfit and apron from whatever job he'd worked that day. He smelled of grease and vinegar, his eyes tired and his own hair a mess.

"Your android destroyed my house!" Tom replied.

"Minor damage only, and it not my fault!" the caterer countered.

"You're responsible for your employees," Christy said, hands on her hips as Simon, Lucas, and Emma raced across the street, Simon interjecting himself between Tom and the caterer as Lucas tried to move in behind the caterer and get at the bat. Both she and Tom were so hot with anger that neither was shivering but Simon was wishing he'd brought a coat.

"Everybody just calm down here," Simon said.

"This is a private matter, John," Christy said.

"It looks like people fighting in a public street to me," Simon snapped. "That makes it my business, my job."

"Look what that son of a bitch did to my wife's car!" Tom shouted, pointing, his face crinkled with disgust and rage.

The Mercedes' rear window was smashed and there were dents in the rear driver's side fender and the trunk lid. Shards of broken glass glittered on the asphalt and atop the trunk lid.

"I see that," Simon said. He turned to the caterer. "Sir, whatever your issue is this is not the way to handle that."

"He slander me, say my business ruin house," the caterer said. "Not true. Android not my fault."

"You brought him here!" Christy replied.

"That's true, but it's not his fault the android malfunctioned," Simon said.

"Yes! Not my fault!" the caterer said. "Hey!"

The caterer and Lucas struggled as Lucas launched himself from behind and grabbed the bat, both of them tugging and yanking at it until Lucas pulled it away and backed off, holding it above his head out of reach of the short Asian.

"Stop, sir," Lucas said. "It is over."

"Somebody wanna tell us what happened to cause all this?" Simon asked.

"Besides his crazy Jack Frost tearing up my house?" Tom said.

"He tell friends bad things, I lose jobs," the caterer said.

"You badmouthed him over the android?" Simon asked.

"My friend asked what happened," Tom said. "He decided to cancel the job on his own. I didn't recommend either way."

"Bull!" the caterer said.

"Tom, the Jack incident is not his fault," Simon said then turned to the caterer. "Do you have insurance to cover the damage?"

The caterer nodded. "They pay. I file claim."

Simon looked at Tom again.

"It's 'in processing.' We don't have it yet," Tom replied.

"But it's coming," Simon said. "Will it cover your damage?"

"Most of it," Christy said with a nod.

"Insurance won't cover this!" Tom yelled again, slapping the top of the Mercedes with a palm and causing more glass to disintegrate and fall from the damaged window frame.

Simon nodded. "You have to fix this car," he said to the caterer.

"With what? I broke thanks to him," the caterer replied. "I even lose my expensive android. Big loss!"

"We want to press charges!" Christy shouted.

"Do you hear that?" Simon asked the caterer. "They have that right, and if they do that, you go to jail and court and you still pay. And who knows how much business you lose then or how much work you miss."

The caterer sputtered, his cheeks reddening. He looked exasperated.

"I suggest you work out payments that are reasonable, go home, and consider yourself lucky," Simon said. He looked at Tom and Christy. "Is that acceptable?"

"As long as he pays it," Tom said, sighing.

Simon looked at the caterer again, his eyes urging the man to agree.

"Fine, I pay," the caterer said, throwing up his hands in a combination of surrender and disgust. "But I want bat back." He started toward Lucas.

Lucas began lowering the bat but Simon shook his head.

"You can pick it up from the station in a few days," Lucas said, "when you make your first payment."

Simon nodded his approval as Lucas lowered the bat but held it behind his back, well out of reach of the caterer.

The caterer sighed. "All right."

"Can you three work this out or do we need to stay?" Simon asked.

"We'll figure it out," Tom said. "We'll need to get an estimate."

"Okay, so he'll call you," Simon said to the caterer.

Christy nodded. "We have his number."

Lucas motioned to the catering truck parked up the street and smiled. "Sir?"

The caterer growled and stormed off toward his truck.

"Don't badmouth his business," Simon said again. "The android thing wasn't his fault."

"Well, we certainly won't recommend him after *this*," Christy said.

"He's clearly unhinged," Tom added.

Simon raised his hands in surrender. "Okay, you take your chances. I'd let it go as long as he pays, but that's your call."

He turned and motioned for Emma and Lucas to follow him home. Emma ran up to hug him, and he wrapped his arms around her shoulder to warm her as they walked quickly together.

"That was craziness," Emma commented as they walked up onto the stoop.

"More like stupidity," Simon mumbled.

As they entered and closed the door behind them, Emma broke out laughing. "That caterer's an idiot."

"Tom and Christy aren't the brightest apples I ever saw either," Simon said.

"You think they will stop?" Lucas asked.

"We took the bat," Simon said as Lucas handed it to him and he leaned it against the wall beside the door to the garage.

"Just in case, maybe you wanna put the Mustang in the garage?" Emma suggested.

Simon grunted. It was a good idea. "Yeah, maybe I should." He'd only left it on the drive in his shock at seeing Emma anyway. He grabbed the keys off the hook where he'd hung them and headed out again to the drive as Emma and Lucas moved into the living room and started laughing and chattering again.

CHAPTER 21

THE NEXT MORNING, Becker reported no further activity at the storefront under surveillance, so Simon, Lucas, Dolby, and Maberry split the list of owners whose androids had attended the meeting there and headed off to visit them.

Simon was driving when Lucas got a call on his VOIP from Scott and A.B.

"We've been working with the IP and GPS data we gathered from the corrupted androids," A.B. explained, "and we've come up with a device that can theoretically track it back to the source."

"Theoretically?" Lucas asked.

"Well, we don't have any way of testing it at the moment," Scott said.

"Right," A.B. agreed, "because it has to be installed and turned on to run the trace and send data."

"Yes. The only catch is if we install it on an android who's already been corrupted with commands on a timer, say, or set to commence activities without direct instructions, then it won't work," Scott said.

"So you need an android that is likely to receive commands directly from the source," Lucas said.

"Two would be better," Scott replied. "To be sure we get enough data."

Lucas explained about the incident at the storefront.

"Great," A.B. said, "so if we can get it on one of those androids, we're set."

"Hang on please," Lucas said then explained the situation to Simon.

"The challenge may be getting the owners to agree," Simon said. "Can they do it in the field or do we have to get the androids to them?" Lucas asked.

"Absolutely we can do it wherever," Scott said and Lucas passed it on to Simon.

"Okay, we'll find owners willing to cooperate and call them," Simon said. "Have them ready."

"Will do," A.B. replied when Lucas told her. "We'll be standing by."

"Thank you," Lucas said as he hung up and turned to Simon. "It is unfortunate we do not know any of the owners."

"Well, a few attendees got out before we arrived, based on the count," Simon said, "but it looks that way, yeah."

"The only android who survived corruption was Leonardo," Lucas said as Simon drove through the Plaza headed for a neighborhood just to the west.

"Let's call Murray and ask him if Leonardo disappeared around the time of that meeting," Simon said, handing Lucas his phone.

Lucas dialed while Simon slowed to a stop at a crosswalk, waiting for shoppers to pass. Lucas put the phone on speaker.

"Johnny, what's up?" Murray said warmly. "We're trying to stay out of trouble here."

"We're trying to help you," Simon said as he cleared the crosswalk and started accelerating again.

"We need to know where Leonardo was yesterday around two-thirty or three p.m.," Lucas interjected.

Murray hmmmphed as he thought a moment. "He's been great since you brought him home, bud. I was working in my cave, let me ask Jan and Linda."

They heard conversation in the background: Murray and two women in mumbled chatting. Then Murray came back on the line. "They both say he disappeared around two and they didn't see him again until after four. They assumed he was off charging. He does that sometimes."

"Ask him if he was at—" Simon looked at Lucas who read off the address on West 75th Street.

"Hang on," Murray said, and they heard him call, "Leo! Come here!"

Moments later, there was more mumbled chatter and then Murray said, "He went there. He says he got instructions in his head."

"Okay," Simon said. "We're on our way." Lucas hung up and Simon took a left on Wornall Road, circling around to head for Murray's. "Call A.B. and Scott and have them meet us there."

Lucas made the call.

THE RELOCATION TO the 8th Street tunnel had gone as smoothly as expected, and Todd was in the process of setting up as his androids unloaded the vans of what they had managed to load in one trip from the old location. He'd provided them with 3D masks to keep them from standing out to observers and had them working with three vans in teams of four, hoping to accomplish the mission as soon as possible.

He'd abandoned most of the basics at the former location but the 3D printer and assembly tools for the androids were expensive and hard to replace so he'd had the androids load them up and bring them along, along with whatever else they could manage to fill any remaining space. The less evidence left behind for police when someone stumbled upon the old place someday, the better. He debated sending a team back to torch it, but that would wait until after all this was over. Doing it now might just call attention to it, and, if the response time was too quick, result in police uncovering evidence that would help them. No, that could wait until the middle of the night a few weeks down the road.

He had transported Livia Connelly in the back of his own van, the others being rentals. He'd used one of Livia's corporate cards to rent them and planned to dump them in the river later, after everything was over. For now, they were hidden in the warehouse that sat atop the tunnel entrance. Livia was now asleep inside one of the enclosed rooms he'd had built, solid stone, a perfect cell. Todd was at work with his computers, setting up and verifying his software and network and communications connections in preparation for launching the final stage of his plan.

While his special teams helped him with the move, other teams moved throughout the city dropping packages at strategic pickup locations for the "borrowed" delivery henchmen he was about to employ. These packages had to be ready to go the minute he sent the initiate command sequence as it would be the first stop of every android assigned to two target locations. So he'd had to scramble to make sure he coordinated both efforts even while relocating his operation to the 8th Street Tunnel.

The last thing he did when he was sure everything was ready was check the video links. He'd hacked into traffic camera and red light feeds as well as security systems at several places, including Fiedler Pharmaceuticals and Connelly Labs. His nanoparticles had again done the bulk of the work, infiltrating systems unseen to set up back door access for him. As a result, he could watch things unfold in real time. It was just a matter of waiting until the action began. He was about to change history in a big way and set some wrongs right.

Once everything electronic was sorted, he made a quick trip back to check on his guest. Livia was sprawled on the cold stone floor, drool running down her left cheek from the corner of her mouth.

"Very flattering," Todd said with a cackle. "I should take a picture for you to preserve this moment, but nah!"

He entertained the thought of killing her, reviewing multiple possible methods as he often had, but he really wanted her to die knowing what he'd done, knowing he'd gotten revenge and destroyed everything she'd taken from him, everything she considered her legacy. No, that moment could wait a few hours longer.

A few hours. Yes. That's all the time he needed. In a fraction of a day, it would all be over. Todd Ward would be the king of the world. At least the world that mattered to him.

He turned and secured the door to her cell again, sauntering back to his control station and settling himself in his very comfortable, large leather executive chair.

"Well, boys," he said, leaning back in his chair as his androids brought in another load and began carefully stowing it neatly in a corner, "our time has come. This is the moment of reckoning. It's gonna change everything."

Todd Ward was ready. But first, he would send out codes to his "borrowed" android henchmen to verify their readiness. No more screw-ups. He was too close. The smart and successful got it right by attention to details and so would he.

He typed in the fifteen digit code on his keyboard and then confirmed it by typing it again, readying the mouse arrow over the SEND button. Was he ready? Yes, he chortled to himself. The question was: was the world ready for him?

It was time to find out.

MURRAY BARBER LIVED in Union Hill, one of Kansas City's oldest neighborhoods, a short drive from Crown Center. His house dated from the 19th century had been restored in the 1980s. The inside of the house was as eclectic as its owners; trinkets, collectables, action figures, posters, art, and more decorated every surface, every spare length of wall, including two couches, three end tables, and a recliner. These included quilts, blankets, and woven Afghan blankets of various sizes and colors which Jan had collected on their travels or made herself. Some of her creations were so intricate they truly amazed Simon, and her skills seemed to only get better with time.

Murray's other "wife," Linda, Hispanic, round in body and face, sat back on a living room couch and waved. "Hey,

John! He's in the cave with Leo." That meant Murray was in the add-on out back, his workspace, hobby room, and office all in one. Simon had been there many times.

"Good to see you, Linda," he called back, returning her smile. As usual she was dressed in hand-embroidered tie-dyed clothing either from Africa or Latin America, her favorite casual wear for home.

Jan motioned for him to head on back as she turned for the kitchen. "I'll make some tea. Or do you want a beer?"

"On duty," Simon said, hands raised in submission and she laughed.

Both women, like Murray, were in their fifties or sixties. Simon had never had occasion to check them for sure, just their husband. And they were too nice for him to invade their privacy.

Simon and Lucas passed through a dining room with a table that could seat twelve but currently had all but three spaces covered in boxes of old magazines, documents, books, and more. Simon looked back over his shoulder making sure Lucas was navigating through without knocking things about. His partner had insisted on dressing himself in a polypropylene crime scene suit again, increasing his bulk. When Lucas made it through successfully, Simon teasingly called out to Jan, "You still haven't finished this?"

"Believe or not that's a whole new batch," Jan called back.

The dining room led to a short hall that led to the add-on—a wide open space which was all Murray. Prized collectables, books, action figures, framed comics and more filled every shelf, chair, couch, table, and space, including a large, antique oak desk that sat at one end. Murray himself was seated behind the desk, feet propped up on its surface, smoking a cigarette until Simon and Lucas arrived. Leonardo was waiting quietly in a nearby chair.

Lucas greeted Murray then quickly walked over to take a chair next to Leonardo as Simon spoke with Murray.

"Has he said anything more about it?" Simon asked softly as he sat down next to Murray and declined a cigarette.

Murray pointed to his own, asking if it was okay to keep smoking and Simon waved it over, dismissing concern, so Murray took another long drag before shaking his head. "He answers direct questions but he's not just running off his mouth about it freely."

"Hello, brother," Lucas said, his voice slightly muffled by the crime scene suit.

"How are you, Lucas?" Leonardo replied.

"Fine. Do you know why we are here?" Lucas asked.

"My master is concerned about my absence yesterday afternoon," Leonardo said.

"Yes," Lucas agreed. "Where did you go?"

"It was an empty store on 75th," Leonardo said. "I was instructed to go."

"Instructed by who?" Lucas asked.

"Internally," Leonardo said and Lucas nodded with knowing understanding.

"Did you ask your master about it?"

Leonardo shook his head. "I was told not to but I was not gone long."

"Did you know where you were going and why?" Lucas asked.

"The First Church of the New Age," Leonardo said, stiffening as if in a trance. "All hail the New Age. The New Age is upon us."

"Jesus," Murray muttered. "It's like he joined a cult."

"Android cultists, that's just what we need," Simon added.

"What is the New Age?" Lucas asked, ignoring them.

Leonardo's brow creased and he appeared to think about it a moment, then he frowned. "I do not know. They did not tell me yet."

"So they just told you what to say?"

"Yes," Leonardo nodded.

"We want to help you," Lucas said. "Is that okay?"

"I do not wish to be sick or to disobey or disappoint my master," Leonardo said. Lucas looked at Simon and nodded.

While Lucas continued asking Leonardo questions about the experience, Simon stood and motioned for Murray to follow him out into the hall. Murray stubbed his cigarette out in an ashtray and complied.

"I need to call in some techs," Simon said as they walked toward the kitchen. "From Connelly Labs."

"What for? I thought they were fixing him when Lucas brought him back," Murray said.

"It's not that simple to undo," Simon said. "It could take weeks, so they did what they could, but they were afraid of damaging him."

"What are these techs going to do?" Murray asked.

"Install equipment so we can trace communication to and from him when and if whoever's doing this tries to control him again," Simon said. "Something we can use to follow back to them."

"Oh fuck yeah." Murray nodded with enthusiasm. "That dude was expensive. Let's get those fuckers."

After thirty minutes, Scott and A.B. pulled up in Murray's drive in a black Connelly Labs cargo van.

"Can we get him to lay down?" Scott asked. "We need to access his back panel."

Jan motioned through the opening to the living room at a large couch. "Will that do or shall we put him in a bedroom?"

"Actually," A.B. said, "this table would be perfect." She motioned to the kitchen table which had a few plates and a fruit bowl and glasses on it.

"Right," Jan said, motioning to Linda, who hurried over to help her clear it.

They even took the table cloth and folded it neatly, setting it nearby on the counter.

"It's antique, my mother's," Linda said. "If we could avoid scratches?"

"Got a sheet?" Scott asked.

Linda nodded and went to retrieve one as Simon and Murray went back to get Leonardo.

After Leonardo was laid out and comfortable atop the table, everyone except Simon, Murray, and Lucas cleared out to give the techs room to work.

"What we're doing is attaching a smart system with nanoparticles of our own designed to set up a relay any time communications or commands come in and out and tell us where they originated," A.B. explained. "But it also self-repairs if someone hacks in, discovers it, and tries to close it off."

"What we'll do is trace the signals back to their source. It should work in most cases, depending how solid a data steam we get and how determined they are and how much time and focus they put into stopping us," Scott said.

"In other words, if they actively adjust it every few minutes to foil us," A.B. said, "we're probably screwed. But hopefully they'll be too busy elsewhere."

"All this stuff can be removed later, right?" Murray asked, looking concerned.

"We'll do our best to remove all of it," Scott said. "Even if it takes days or weeks."

"And we're already working on new security systems and protocols to retroactively refit our product line and hopefully prevent something similar in the future."

"Good," Murray and Lucas said simultaneously and the techs smiled.

"Jan and Linda want me to just shut him down 'til it's over," Murray said. "Keep him safe with us."

"This might be our only shot at tracking down the perpetrators," Simon said. "We'll do everything we can to return him to you as good as new."

"Better," A.B. added.

"We might throw in a few extra upgrades just for the inconvenience," Scott said.

"You taking requests?" Murray joked.

"Never know," A.B. said.

"Hit us up," Scott added. They were dead serious.

It took half an hour to install and test, and then they were putting Leonardo's control panel back in and reattaching the access panel to his back.

"Good to go," Scott said, smiling, as Leonardo sat up again.

"I am sorry for the trouble, master," Leonardo said, looking at Murray.

"You're like family, Leo," Murray said. "We forgive you."

AFTER LEAVING MURRAY'S, they'd called to fill in Becker, then headed for the rail yard to check with Mister Information. When they got to his rail car, the vagrant wasn't home, so they spent a few minutes looking around the yard but finding no sign of him.

Simon was about to give up, when he heard someone whistling and turned just as Mister Information came ambling around from behind a nearby control tower, the open Absolut bottle grasped tight in his right hand, and headed their way. His eyes widened as he saw them and Simon could tell he was debating whether to run.

"We just need that information, Denny," Simon said, calmly, motioning for Lucas to stay where he is. "Whatever you've got."

"Shit," Mister Information said, still walking toward them but slowing down a bit. "You just asked me yesterday. I barely had time to spread the word, and this guy's a ghost. No one's seen him, talked to him. Nobody knows nothing!"

"So that's what you got?" Simon said, his disappointment obvious.

"I need more time," Mister Information said as he finished another swig out of the Absolut bottle. "This ain't the internet or some radio or TV broadcast. We gather the old fashioned way, you know? Needs time to move around and fester."

"We're running out of time," Simon said.

Mr. Information was less than ten feet from Simon now as he stopped and eyed Lucas suspiciously.

"He's not going to bother you," Simon said.

"He's not sick?"

"He's fine," Simon said. "In complete control."

Mr. Information eyed Lucas again, giving him a dirty look,

then sighed. "The one thing I did here is about this C-4 shipment that went missing a few days ago from this small mining company that works in caves."

"C-4?" Simon said, trying to figure out how it connected to his case but worried all the same.

"This guy came in a coupl'a times and was asking about C-4," Mister Information said. "How much did they use it? How much did they keep on hand? Did they know where he could get any? Could he buy some from them?"

"What did he look like?" Lucas interjected and Mister Information shot him the stink eye again.

"Did you get a description?" Simon asked.

"No, this was second hand," Mister Information said. "Maybe even third hand. Friend of a friend of someone who was there kinda thing. Anyway, the owner—of the mining company, the one this dude talked to—he said he came back a coupla days later and was asking if they use androids. Weird questions."

"Androids? What kind of questions?" Lucas again.

This time, the vagrant ignored him and responded to Simon. "Did they use them? Why not? Wouldn't they be useful? Would they consider trading some C-4 for some who could do more dangerous, difficult work—the kind where human risk is high, you know? The guy asking was apparently really knowledgeable and he sounded like a salesman, but the mining owner is old school. Doesn't want to replace men with androids or technology. He wasn't interested."

"So the guy asking went away?" Simon asked.

"Yeah, but a week later, their C-4 goes missing," Mister Information said.

"How much?" Simon asked.

"A small stockpile," Mister Information said. "That's all I know."

"When?" Lucas asked.

"About the time of those ATM robberies."

"Jesus," Simon said.

"Just thought it could be your guy," Mister Information said with a shrug, still nonchalant as if it was just information that may or may not mean much. But in Simon's head alarms were going off. "That's all I got," Mister Information added and then started walking off towards the boxcar he called home. "Check again in a day or two if you want."

Lucas and Simon whirled and hurried to the car as Simon's phone rang. It was Becker.

"Yeah," Simon said.

"Chief's called a meeting at headquarters for all hands at four," Becker said. "You guys are helping brief everyone so I need you back here."

"We're on our way," Simon said and hung up.

Lucas' eyes met his as they reached the Interceptor. "So we think Todd Ward has C-4?"

"I don't know, but I do think whoever we're looking for just got a whole lot scarier," Simon said.

THE MEETING WAS held at KCPD Headquarters in the large first floor Community Room. Three rows of rectangular glass windows looked out upon the street and the bright lobby with its artistic hanging lamp of wire-like strands. The walls were lined with zinc panel siding designed to both add a modern look as well as absorb echoes, and two dozen rows thirty wide of gray chairs faced a short front platform with a podium bearing the official department logo. This was one of the only rooms in headquarters the majority of the public and press corps would ever see, designed to be the public face of the department for official outreach, but also used on occasion for assemblies of the rank and file, such as at present.

Up on the stage, DC's Melson, Cardno, Atwell, and two other Deputy Chiefs sat behind the podium with Chief Weber, Becker, and several divisional captains. The two rows of chairs were filled with many of the rank and file, uniformed and plain clothes, including Delmater and several others from the Generalist Squad, along with Maberry and Dolby. Simon also recognized Sergeants El Ashkar and Raymond from Central, Trevor Welch from the Computer Unit, Paul Engborg from Crime Scene, and a few others. Those missing were either on patrol or other essential duty positions and would be filled in later.

Simon and Lucas were currently briefing all assembled on the situation and pattern they expected to unfold over the next few days all over the city. They ignored the icy stare of Atwell, who had arrived after they started and looked most displeased by Lucas' participation in the proceedings. Simon was sure she'd confront them afterwards and hoped Becker had briefed Melson and he would back them.

They had already explained the nanoparticle aspects of the case and outlined various incidents as well as listing the members of the current Task Force and efforts they'd been making. When they were finished, they ceded the podium to Becker and Melson.

"We expect to see multiple incidents unfolding simultaneously across the city," Melson explained. "Sergeant Becker and her team will be helping to coordinate because of their familiarity with the case, but we expect all hands on deck, and whoever's closest will be expected to act quickly so we can shut down incidents as quickly as possible, perhaps even before they can start."

"Trevor Welch from the Computer Unit will be coordinating with a team from Connelly Labs that can track the androids as well as trace back communications to and from them," Becker added.

"Basically, we'll be employing a multi-pronged approach here," Melson continued, "prevention and detention depending upon what circumstances require. Detectives Simon, Lucas, Maberry, Dolby, and a SWAT team will be focusing on tracking communications from the perpetrators back to their source and attempting to arrest and confront them at their base as well as rescue Doctor Connelly and any other captives they may be holding there."

"Coordination between departments will be handled by Welch and Dispatch along with appointed representatives in Lenexa P.D., Overland Park, Prairie Village, and so on with a case-by-case basis," Becker said.

"Any questions so far?" Melson asked and hands went up around the room.

He pointed to Lucas' former Training Officer, Sergeant Gil Lenz, in the front row. "Exactly how many incidents of this nature are we expecting?"

"Dozens," Becker said, looking at Simon.

"The perpetrator has the capability to launch multiple attacks simultaneously," Lucas stepped forward to add. "So we expect to see androids working in pairs, teams, as well as solo, engaging in assignments through the city."

"Some will be designed solely as diversions to draw our attention," Simon said. "Anything with a large group, almost certainly, while others we believe will be attempting to acquire materials, including research and old demo and test materials the perpetrator seeks to employ in advancing his goals."

"Has anyone bothered to warn the companies in question?" Sergeant El Ashkar threw out.

"Yes, we have talked with security personnel at all of them and asked them to increase security as best they can," Lucas said.

"It won't be enough," Simon said. "We believe some of the androids will be using very life-like 3D masks impersonating employees and others with authorized access familiar to security and staff in attempts to avoid detection."

"So this is going to be a clusterfuck then?" Benny Jimenez from Generalist threw in with a grin as others around him harrumphed or grunted in agreement.

"It's going to be a wild ride, no doubt about it," Becker said.

"Which is why we want everyone on alert and ready to respond at a moment's notice," Melson said.

Chief Weber stood and joined them at the podium then, Melson, Decker, Simon, and Lucas moving aside to allow him room before the microphone. Tall with full brown hair graying at the edges, he wasn't thin but not fat either, more big-boned, as a mother might describe it. His uniform was crisp and shiny, looking like new, and bore the awards and ribbons distinguishing his many years of service. "These calls are top priority. Code 1," Weber said. If it really hit the fan, an "All

Wide City Assist" could be used. "We've had almost two dozen incidents in the past three weeks involving destruction of private property, theft, and even accidental death."

"No to mention suspected murders," Melson interjected.

"Let's shut these people down now, folks," Weber continued. "It's the end of the line. So let's hit 'em, and hit 'em hard and fast, so we shut this down for good."

Various grunts and affirmations came from around the room as the Chief looked at the others, accepting their signal that the briefing as over, then dismissed everyone.

As the crowd dispersed and people filed down off the podium, the Chief being quickly rushed off by aides to his next meeting, Atwell marched angrily over to Becker, Simon, and Lucas. "What is *he* doing in any capacity on this investigation? I don't recall lifting his suspension."

"He's here by special arrangement—" Becker started to explain.

"He's been fully checked and cleared by experts at Connelly Labs and Pruitt both," Melson interjected as he marched over to join them. "And he works for my division. He's my responsibility. We need him to track these androids and shut this crime spree down."

"He's at risk—"

"We're aware of the risks," Melson said, "but he's been checked and cleared, as I said."

Atwell glared. "I'm just trying to protect the city—"

"As are we all," Simon barked.

"If you have questions or issues with us, take them up with me or Chief Weber later," Melson said, "but I authorized his participation in this final phase and we are taking all precautions."

"I wear polypropylene gear during any contact with androids," Lucas offered helpfully. Becker put a hand on his arm to silence him.

"Questions?" Melson said, eyes narrowed and locked on Atwell.

She hesitated a moment, pondering, then sighed and shook her head. "I guess it's your call then." With that, she turned and marched off.

"Get out there and get these guys, will you? I'm tired of defending your asses," Melson cracked.

Simon chuckled and saluted along with Becker and Lucas and Melson snapped a salute back then hurried off to other duties.

"One more piece of good news. Our perp may have a stockpile of C-4," Simon said.

"Jesus Christ," Dolby said.

"You're just reporting this now?! That's kind of important information we should have shared with the troops," Becker scolded.

"He's not sure," Simon said. "We got it from a CI. But apparently some went missing from an underground mining group and they didn't report it yet. And the CI heard rumors that a guy came in asking around about C-4 and then asked some questions about the company's use of androids."

"What kind of questions?" Maberry asked.

"He wanted to know how to acquire C-4 for a demolition job," he said. "Something he wanted to handle privately and not hire a company for on his private land," Simon said. "But he also asked some questions about how much they keep on hand, if they'd sell him some, and so on that made the owner uncomfortable."

"And then he asked about androids too?" Dolby looked puzzled.

"Yeah." Lucas nodded. "Do they use them? Would they consider it? Would they trade C-4 for them?"

"Which made them suspicious with all the android stuff on the news," Simon said.

"Not to mention it's fucking odd," Maberry said.

Simon grunted, then added, "Plus the owner's kinda old school. Not a fan of using androids instead of workers."

"At least somebody's protecting jobs," Dolby said.

"Don't worry," Becker teased, "promise the department has no plans to bring in androids to replace you guys, Lucas' invaluable contributions aside."

"Wait, so we're stuck with the only one," Maberry joked.

"They're probably all too afraid he'll outshoot them or show them up," Dolby joked.

"Hell, that's how we feel about female cops," Simon snapped.

"Tell me about it," Becker said and shared a look with Dolby that said they knew the score of that all too well.

"I was kidding, I swear," Simon said.

"We've lived it," Dolby growled, leaving Simon and Maberry to suddenly look anywhere but at her and Becker. Simon felt a clot in his throat.

"Okay, boys, we've got our marching orders," Becker said. "Let's find this asshole and get Livia Connelly home."

"Hopefully alive," Lucas added.

The others said nothing, sharing the sentiment but not wanting to get his hopes up as they headed for the parking garage.

CHAPTER 22

ONE AFTER ONE, the readiness codes returned affirmative responses. His henchmen were ready and awaiting his command. Todd Ward sighed deeply and settled back in his chair to savor the feeling of total control coming over him. It was rare a man felt such power, especially a man like Todd Ward, who'd seen so many failures due to circumstances beyond his control or the conspiring of others. For once, Todd Ward was going to be the one out in front—the right place at the right time—the one with the power.

Todd was calling the shots, and by the end of the day, he'd be positioned to lead the world—at least as far as the android design field went. Not only would he be collecting key research and materials to put himself ahead, but his creations were going to leave behind the special packages his androids had already deposited all over the city—packages Todd would use to destroy evidence of their visits to key locations, and to destroy two locations he'd come to despise: Fiedler Pharmaceuticals and Connelly Labs.

By the time the day was over, both locations would have ceased to exist, leaving behind smoking holes in the ground. That employees would die was unfortunate but collateral damage was unavoidable and included among them would be a few people Todd Ward didn't mind ridding the world of at all, like Andy Moehn and Bob Pruitt. And of course, Livia Connelly. Anyone else was just a bonus he didn't bother giving a second thought.

"It's time," he said to himself and smiled as he copied the command sequence off a spreadsheet and placed the cursor next to the command prompt. The code was based on a childhood favorite movie, *Outbreak*.

He right clicked and hit paste so the letters appeared on the screen:

Cleansweep.

And that was an apt title for what he was about to unleash. A vanquishing of his enemies, erasing them from the city. A new dawn, a new day, a new start and fresh opportunity for Todd Ward.

Cleansweep indeed. He guffawed at the humor of it.

Then his finger slammed the SEND button, and the final stage began.

THE FIRST CALLS came in within an hour of the end of the assembly in KCPD's Community Room. The Central Property Crime squad had been back at the station less than half an hour when they heard it come over the radio. Due to coordination duties, they were also getting a running feed on the computer of calls from other departments around the Metro as well.

"Calls in Overland Park, Lenexa, and Independence," Dolby reported from her desk where she was monitoring the feed.

"Looks like shopping centers."

"Pure diversions," Simon said.

"Local P.D. will respond nonetheless," Becker said.

"They have no choice," Maberry said. "Gotta please the public."

"Right, we're lucky enough to be waiting for the real juice," Simon said.

"Bomb squads standing by?" Dolby asked.

"Yeah," Becker said. "All they can do until we know where to send them."

"I'm getting fucking tired of bad guys with explosives," Maberry said, reminding them all of the terrorists they'd dealt with a few months.

"Shouldn't we get closer to Fiedler and Connelly?" Lucas asked. "So we can respond more quickly?"

"No," Simon said, "Let Lenexa and OPPD handle those. We want to find the person giving the orders. That's where Dr. Connelly will be."

"We have no idea where they are," Lucas said.

"Which is why we might as well stay here for now, where we can monitor the big picture, until we get a hit on Leonardo or the other android with the comm tracer," Simon said. "You know Scott or A.B. will let us know as soon as the androids in for maintenance start wandering off."

Finding another owner to agree to allow their android to be wired by A.B. and Scott hadn't proven as simple as asking. Three of the owners were unreachable for various reasons from travel to vacations. Three other owners, when notified of their android's possible connection to the android outbreak case, insisted they'd simply order their androids to disregard any such instructions because they'd always obeyed and wouldn't harbor any arguments to the contrary. The remaining seven wanted to shut them down and send them immediately to Connelly Labs for servicing. Simon and Lucas had to carefully explain how that would hinder the case rather than help it, and even then, some of the owners were more concerned about risks to their expensive property and loss of their android and—in most cases—friend, than helping any investigation. Especially given the tech's inability to guarantee it would work.

"It's our best shot," Simon explained time and again.

Finally, Simon had resorted to deception, agreeing to have Connelly Labs inspect and run maintenance on the affected androids while surreptitiously choosing two more to wire with the comm tracers.

"We'll remove them after without a trace," Scott assured him.

And so Connelly Labs had acquired seven androids for maintenance—enough to occupy them for at least two weeks given the complexity of removal—and had set them up in a storage area to wait.

Becker had reluctantly agreed to the plan, warning, "You know KCPD and Connelly Labs could be held liable for any damage they might do when they undertake these missions."

"So far it's been minor vandalism and destruction," Simon said.

"Tell that to Ricky Garcia's family," Becker replied.

"And Louis Fiedler and Benn Liska," Lucas added.

"We think those were models not designed by Connelly," Simon countered. "This is our best shot."

"I know, but that doesn't mean I have to like it," Becker said. To cover their asses, she'd gotten Melson to sign off with the caveat that the nine androids in question be closely monitored so police could be dispatched to their destinations before any real damage was done. Given the complexity of the scene unfolding before them in real time, Simon had his doubts that would be possible, but they'd do their best.

Simon's cell rang and the caller ID read "Connelly Labs."

"Here we go," he said as he answered.

"They've flown the coop," Scott said.

"How many?"

"All seven," Scott said. "It was a mass exodus."

"Did you trace the signal source?"

"We're working on it," Scott said. "The bastard routed it through several relays just to fuck with us."

"We'll get it," A.B. called from the background.

"Okay," Simon said and signaled Becker as he hung up, "They're off. Send the teams."

Becker made the call to officers from KCPD and Lenexa PD assigned to follow the seven androids. Then Simon's phone rang again with a call from Murray.

"He just took off," Murray reported.

"Okay, thanks," Simon said and motioned to Lucas. "Leonardo's out. Let's go follow our egg."

Together they headed for the Interceptor.

LEONARDO HEADED for Fiedler Pharmaceuticals so Simon responded Code 1 south down I-35 then took I-69 south and 435 east, exiting at Metcalf and arriving in the company's lot within two minutes of exiting the highway. Altogether, the whole trip took barely fifteen minutes.

As Simon drove, Lucas slipped into a polypropylene suit while also keeping an eye on the GPS tracker, following Leonardo's progress. "I believe he's inside the building on the first floor," Lucas said as Simon pulled to a stop and they undid their seatbelts.

Simon grabbed a Taser from beneath his seat and clipped it to his belt. "Big place. Wanna narrow that down?"

"You take one end, I will take the other," Lucas said.

Simon frowned, turning to snap at him when he realized his partner had just made a joke. "Nice. Save smart ass mode for later, okay?"

"This way," Lucas said and took off running.

Simon followed, finding himself struggling to keep up. As he did, his cell rang again. He fumbled with it as he grabbed it, finally getting it to his ear. "Yeah? Simon."

"Are you guys buried or what?" Holly said cheerfully.

"You're really calling me right now to ask me that?" Simon asked.

"Okay, grumpy grump," Holly said and laughed. "Was kinda hoping you'd have a good tip which one we should jump on. There's so many I don't know where to start."

"What happened to the good old days when you guys just sent drones to annoy us?" Simon teased.

"We're afraid you'll just bash them or shoot them down. They're expensive."

"I'm hanging up now."

Her tone got serious again. "We still do. Reporters can't cover everything. I'm looking for the hot spot."

"I really don't have time to do your job for you," Simon

said.

"Okay, sorry," Holly said. "You know, after that lunch, I guess I thought we were kinda friends now. Sorry if I misread things."

Fuck. Simon followed Lucas up onto the curb and through the front door, where they slowed their pace a beat as Lucas scanned the lobby. "We are. I'm literally running right now."

The lobby was clear except for a harried-looking receptionist who looked tiny behind her very large desk-counter combo. There was no one waiting in the waiting area and no other employees in sight.

"I know. Your voice is kinda sexy all out of breath," Holly said.

"Jesus Christ," Simon said.

"Just giving you shit, Detective," Holly said. "Be safe out there. Ciao."

She hung up just as Lucas turned left and started running down a corridor, Simon struggling to keep up again.

"You know where we're going?" Simon panted out.

"Yes, he is just this way," Lucas called back.

"Is he running too or could we slow down and still catch him?" Simon joked.

Lucas frowned and slowed a bit, allowing Simon to come alongside. "You really are too old for this shit."

"Shut the fuck up."

They rounded a corner to spot Leonardo going into a door marked "Development Lab" twenty feet ahead. "Slow down," Simon said, grabbing at Lucas' arm. "Remember, he knows us, and we want to follow him for now, not scare him off or interrupt."

Lucas slowed to a walk, much to Simon's relief. "If you

would like, we could start exercising together." Simon scowled at him and he added, "I am serious. I will run slower."

"Oh my God, really, shut the fuck up," Simon snapped as Lucas led the way.

They stopped at the door to the lab and peered through the large window filling most of its top half, watching as Leonardo made his way to a security code keyed door marked "Prototypes" and typed in a code. After a series of beeps, the door buzzed and Leonardo pulled it open and disappeared inside.

Moments later, a side door opened and bald man with a goatee entered in a white lab coat and crossed the room to a file cabinet, which he opened with a key and began rifling through. Simon recognized him as Andy Moehn.

As Moehn pulled out the first file, the keyed door clicked again and opened as Leonardo emerged, and Moehn turned to look. "Can I help you?" he said, looking surprised. He set the file aside and turned to confront Leonardo. "How did you get in here?"

"The day of judgment is here, Andy Moehn," Leonardo said coldly and then leaped at Moehn.

Simon and Lucas burst through the door as Moehn yelled and struggled against Leonardo's attacks, the android's hands going around his throat to choke him. Every surface in the room sparkled and the strong odor of industrial cleaners filled Simon's nose. They each grabbed the android by a shoulder and yanked him backward. At first, Leonardo pulled Moehn along with him, but then Moehn managed to pull free and fell wheezing to the floor, his hands rubbing his neck.

Lucas and Simon struggled to control Leonardo, who cried out, "The day of judgment! The day of judgment!"

Lucas quietly whispered, "Brother, calm down now. Stop."

But Leonardo swung a fist at Lucas and yanked free of Simon, then ran at Moehn again. Lucas tackled him and Simon grabbed the Taser off his belt and aimed it at the panel square in the middle of the android's back.

"It can't hurt me! Go!" Lucas yelled.

"Fifty thousand volts?" Simon said, hesitating.

"Go ahead, make my day," Lucas quipped.

"Jesus," Simon said, hoping he was right and fired.

As the Taser's probes struck Leonardo square in the back, Lucas pushed away and rolled to the side and the hijacked android's body began shaking as the current raced through his system.

Lucas climbed to his feet and hurried over to check on Moehn, who accepted help getting to his feet but brushed off anything else. "I'm okay."

When the first charge finished, Simon started to reload and Leonardo's leg twitched then moved, so he hit him again, causing the prone android to shake once more.

This time, when the charge ran out, he lay still.

"Poor bastard," Moehn said, shaking his head.

"Are you hurt?" Lucas asked again.

"I'm fine, really," Moehn insisted. "I knew I should have stuck with a low-stress career like ministry and stayed away from high tech. Teach me to ignore my wife."

Simon stared at Leonardo's prone form. "So much for following this guy."

Just then, their shoulder radios beeped with another burst of calls and simultaneously Simon's cell rang, the caller ID identifying "Connelly Labs."

Simon answered immediately, "Simon."

"One of the units we tagged just went dead, no signal at

all," Scott said.

"Uh, yeah, that was us," Simon said. "We had to Taser him."

"Oh shit, that'll do it," Scott replied.

"Did you get anything?" Simon asked, his voice revealing his anxiousness.

"No, sorry," Scott said, then Simon heard A.B. yell in the background, "We're getting closer! Just a little longer."

"Call me as soon as possible," Simon said and hung up. Lucas was watching him. "No," he snapped as two uniforms appeared at the door, rushing inside.

"Make sure this one gets over to Connelly Labs right away," Simon said to them and hurried out the door, Lucas following.

SIMON PUT BECKER on speaker as they navigated the corridors at Fiedler. The place was so sterile and corporate, the paint, the walls, the doors—everything looking expensive and new. The only variant were the people. Some wore suits and were neatly groomed while others—mostly research and science staff, he guessed—were dressed less formally and had facial hair, odd haircuts, coloring, and so on.

"We lost our guy," he said. There were scattered people moving back and forth around them—most paying them no attention—but no faces he recognized from the storefront. For the first time since meeting Lucas, Simon found himself resenting the ability of androids to blend in with humans.

"You're not alone," Becker said. "Five couldn't even find theirs."

"What?!" A few passersby looked his way at the outburst. Again, no one looked out of place.

"They showed up and found no sign of them, even double checking GPS data," Becker said.

"We had to Taser ours to keep him from killing a guy," Simon said. "How the fuck could they not find them?"

"We're trying to figure that out," Becker said. "Any luck tracing the source?"

"Not as of two minutes ago, but A.B. swears they're getting closer."

As he turned a corner and saw the lobby ahead, Simon realized Lucas was no longer beside him and stopped, turning around. He was alone except for a lone lab tech crossing the hall ten yards further down.

"Hang on," Simons said, cupping the phone as he walked back around the corner and saw Lucas kneeling to inspect a small package sitting on the floor. "Got something?" he called.

Lucas looked puzzled. "I've seen three so far, scattered on the floor."

"What is it?" Simon asked.

"I was debating whether to open it," Lucas admitted.

"What ya got?" Becker asked.

"Hang on," Simon repeated, then knelt to examine the package. "I don't see any wires. Maybe take a peek but be slow."

Lucas reached for the package and Simon added, "Carefully."

Lucas slowly unsealed the top of the package and peeled back the wrapping to reveal what looked like off-white modeling clay the shape of a standard bath bar of soap. "It's some kind of clay."

It took Simon until Lucas peeled back a bit more and revealed two silver metal probes stuck into one end to realize. "Jesus Christ! Don't touch it!" He pulled at Lucas' sleeve then backed away as Lucas looked up then followed his lead.

"What is it?" Lucas asked.

"We're gonna need the bomb squad," Simon said to Becker.

"What's going on?" Becker and Lucas asked simultaneously.

"I think we just found C-4," Simon said, "and I think there's a whole lot more."

"Jesus, get outta there," Becker said. "Clear that building."

As Simon and Lucas ran back toward the parking lot, Simon phoned John Stott in security and told him about the explosives, urging him to evacuate.

The moment he hung up and stepped out the front doors into the parking lot, the phone rang again. "Connelly Labs" lighting up the caller ID.

"Simon."

"We got it!" A.B. said cheerfully.

"The location?" Simon said.

"Yeah, Scott's texting it over with coordinates," she said. "Had a bit of a distraction because someone reported seeing Benn Liska here. Can you believe it? Guys' dead. We told them they were crazy."

"Holy shit!" Suddenly Simon knew why the other teams couldn't find their androids. "Have you guys seen anyone leaving packages around the building?"

"Yeah, that was weird too," A.B. said. "Scott saw a little

box on the floor outside the lab when he took a potty break. Haven't had time to investigate."

"Get everyone out, now! It's C-4!" Simon said.

"What?!" A.B. sounded stunned.

"Trust me!"

She hung up and Simon was calling Becker again.

"I just sent the bomb squad from OPPD your way," Becker said.

"We need one at Connelly Labs, too," Simon said.

"They found explosives?" Becker asked.

"Pretty sure," Simon said.

"Jesus," Becker said. "I'll call in ours and Lenexa as well. We're getting weird calls now about sightings of Louie Fiedler and Benn Liska—"

"It's 3D masks, like the ATM robbers," Simon said. "That's why the teams couldn't find their androids. They're delivering the C-4!" As he said it, he saw a crowd of people exiting the lobby but another group across the parking lot were heading from one end of the building to another entrance, excitedly chattering.

"Son of a bitch," Becker responded.

"Where the hell are they going?" Simon called, motioning toward the small group headed back inside.

"Someone saw Benn Liska, he's alive," called a lab assistant who'd just come out of the lobby.

"Jesus Christ, that's not him!" Simon said and started running, Lucas beside him, hanging up the cell as he did and cutting Becker off.

His phone started ringing again as they dodged a row of cars and raced across the parking lot, yelling, "Wait!"

That drew only puzzled looks from a few at the rear of the

group, while the rest continued back inside. In the distance, Simon could hear sirens approaching—the bomb squad. He said an urgent prayer they wouldn't be too late.

Out of the corner of his eye, as he ran, he saw a Fox 4 news van pulling up and a familiar face jumping out and running toward the building as several media drones buzzed by overhead.

"No! Stay away!" He called out as Holly Sanders' smile turned to confusion, and then there was a low rumble accompanied by a vibration and a flash of light as bright as the sun as the building blew up in front of them and Simon was falling....

HE DIDN'T KNOW how long he laid there but when he checked his watch, what had felt like minutes turned out to be seconds as he pushed himself up off the asphalt and began looking around. The smell of smoke, burning wood and plastic and chemicals filled the air.

Lucas was on the ground nearby, sitting up, also taking in the scene. Fiedler Pharmaceuticals's corporate headquarters was a smoking ruin, a large dark plume still rising into the air to mark the spot. Windows were shattered front and back on cars all around them, car alarms blaring and horns honking. Some vehicles had rolled on their sides, a couple had flipped over. The Fox 4 cameraman had recovered and was taking panoramic footage of the scene as drones shot as well from various angles. Simon looked for Holly and found her there, bleeding from a cut on her lip but alive, as she shook off the shock and struggled to her feet.

Lucas' hand appeared in front of him and Simon accepted the help getting to his feet. Where the group had been surging back into the building there were bodies now, laying every which way—many in unnatural poses. From the crowd at the other end near the lobby, he could hear crying, calls for help, and cursing as people tried to grasp what had just occurred. A few media drones flittered about trying to make sense of the chaos so they could record footage or interview witnesses. Simon's cell phone was ringing. It had been since he'd first recovered alertness but had taken this long to notice. He answered.

"We have reports of an explosion in Overland Park," Becker was saying. "What happened? We got cut off."

"It blew," Simon said, struggling to find a coherent sentence. "Got to check Connelly Labs."

"I can't get through," Becker said, "but we're now receiving reports of an explosion down that way as well."

"Fuck!" Simon said, and then he remembered what A.B. had said about sending him a location and checked his texts. "He's downtown! A warehouse near 8th Street and Delaware."

"I'll get Maberry and Dolby headed there," Becker said.

"We're on our way," Simon said.

"Are you sure you're all right?" Becker said. "If you need medical—"

"We're fine," Simon said and cut her off again, flipping off the phone as he grabbed Lucas and ran toward the Interceptor, which, somehow was sitting in the fire zone in front of the lobby intact, except for its passenger-side windows which had blown out and the windshield which was cracked on the passenger side.

Simon yanked open his door and used his wallet to scoop glass from his seat as quickly as he could, then climbed in and reached for his seatbelt. Lucas just ignored the glass and climbed in the passenger's side, and moments later, they took off, lights and siren on full, headed back for the interstate and downtown Kansas City.

"You know, most people find broken glass ruins their clothes," Simon commented as Lucas shifted in his seat to the clinking and crunching of glass under his ass. "Especially the polypropylene. It's no good with holes."

Lucas shrugged. "I ripped my knees on the pavement already. It is probably too late for these."

"You're a weird guy, Ace," Simon teased, quoting one of Emma's favorite Jim Carey comedies. "Weird guy. Did you happen to see anyone besides Leonardo who looked like an android?"

"No," Lucas said.

Simon turned right on Metcalf and headed north toward I-435. "But there had to be more there," Simon said. "Where were they?"

"My guess is the Benn Liska clone was one," Lucas said.

"No shit, Sherlock, is that your best detective work?"

"You are angry," Lucas observed.

"Yeah, I tend to get that way when someone tries to blow me up." Simon took a sharp left onto the onramp and raced up onto I-435, weaving in and out of traffic as he watched for the signs for Highway 69 North.

"We will find this man and stop him," Lucas said.

"If Scott and A.B. got the address right, yes, I hope," Simon agreed. "I just hope they're alive so we can thank them."

"Is this warehouse empty?" Lucas asked.

"Apparently, but it was refurbished about a decade or two ago," Simon said, and then explained about the old street car line and that the tunnel had been buried and uncovered and buried again over the years.

"So he could be hiding in the tunnel," Lucas said.

Simon hadn't considered that but it scared the shit out of him. It was a dangerous place to be if Ward still had C-4 left over. "He might be in the warehouse. The tunnel's supposedly sealed."

"Do you think he still has some C-4?" Lucas wondered.

"Let's pray he used it all up," Simon said as he turned north on 69 Highway. But he knew the minute the words came out it was wishful thinking. Whatever they were driving into was about to make the explosion at Fiedler look like just a warmup.

CHAPTER 23

MABERRY AND DOLBY were waiting with a SWAT team when Simon and Lucas turned onto Delaware and pulled up a block from the warehouse. Standard assault procedure, especially when a hostage's life was at stake, was to stage nearby and go in on foot, and Simon had driven the last several blocks without the siren, lights only. Given this perp's penchant for technology, there was a good chance he'd wired cameras to monitor the area outside the warehouse, so they didn't expect total surprise but they could cut down the alert time to seconds.

SWAT Sergeant Dave Jackson converged with Maberry and Dolby on the Interceptor as Simon and Lucas climbed out. As they did, squad cars and other KCPD vehicles kept arriving at the staging area all around them. Car doors and trunks slammed, weapons cocked as shells were loaded, and people greeted each other or chatted, awaiting instructions. The air was crisp and cool but the sky was clear blue with scattered clouds, and they still had several hours of daylight to go. Simon heard traffic lights click as they changed on the corner and the beeping of delivery trucks somewhere nearby as they backed up, followed by the hum of hydraulics and diesel engines as two city buses drove past.

"What've we got?" Jackson asked.

Tall, black, and built like a tank, Jackson was a twenty-year vet whom Simon had worked with numerous times. He liked and respected the man, though Jackson took things to an intensity level even Simon couldn't match. A former military sniper and Army Ranger, he'd participated in more assault entries and armed confrontations than any current KCPD officer, and radiated calm and focus that Simon envied. Like the rest of his eight-man team, he was dressed in a fifty-pound vest with body armor and a Kevlar helmet with an impressive assortment of weapons hanging from his person.

Jackson pulled up a blueprint of the warehouse on his iPad—KCPD kept a database of downtown buildings for just such contingencies using public records like permit filings. "There's six entrances and exits," Jackson said, pointing them out. "But our drone is checking now. We think the alley access is locked with chains and thus not an easy exit point. The rest we can cover."

He flipped the screen to another page then continued pointing things out as he spoke, "Two floors, both mostly open with bathrooms here and here and a break room and offices around the outside edge of the first floor. Stairs and freight elevators here." He looked at Simon. "How many suspects?"

"Unknown but we think one, two max," Simon said, exhaust from idling police vehicles burning his throat. "But there's probably a hostage and he could have androids."

"Like your partner?" Jackson asked.

"Less developed," Simon said. "Probably faceless."

"Like the ATM robbers?" Jackson asked.

"Exactly," Lucas said.

"But they could be armed and trained in combat or at least defensive tactics," Simon said. "We just don't know."

"And we have no idea how many," Lucas said, "but it could be dozens."

"Jesus," Maberry said.

"So a whole army?" Jackson asked.

"It's possible," Simon said with a nod.

"Is it likely?" Dolby asked.

"Yes," Lucas said.

Simon wasn't sure. "It depends how safe he thinks he is, how much prep time he had, and how worried he is about us finding him."

"Guy's a criminal," Maberry said, then he and Dolby added simultaneously, "So paranoid as fuck."

"We should plan on it," Simon said.

"We need more men," Jackson said.

"We can't afford to wait," Simon said. "He just blew up two office buildings and killed potentially a hundred or more people."

"Fuck," Jackson said.

"Plus the hostage," Lucas added.

"The guy's held her for over a week now," Maberry said. "How likely do you think it is she's still alive?"

Lucas looked angry at the thought so Simon answered, "We have to proceed like she is. And hope we're right."

"Well, we've got maybe twenty-five people, not everyone as heavily armed and armored as my team, so we can try a basic breach formation, but if it blows up on us, we may have to pull back and wait for reinforcements," Jackson said.

"Let's do it," Lucas said and Simon nodded.

Jackson called over commanders and ran them through the plan, sending teams to watch all the exits except the front two where they planned to enter in two assault teams, but warning everyone to set up in ready positions and await the command to move in together. Then Jackson divided his unit into two groups of four, one led by him, the other by Corporal Jack Campbell who served as his second in command. Simon and Lucas would accompany Jackson's team, while Maberry and Dolby went with Campbell's. Jackson's team also loaned them extra armor and Kevlar helmets for the breach.

Standard breach formation was used by both military and police all over the world because of its effectiveness. A breacher would breach the door either with a knob or using his shotgun or an explosive charge. The first man would enter and move left into position one, the corner just left of the door. The second man moved to position four, the corner right of the door. The third took position three, the corner opposite four, and the fourth position two, the corner opposite position one. The final guy would come in and if the room was secured, move to the next door and act as guard as the breacher moved in and they did it all over again until every room was cleared.

For the warehouse, a member of SWAT acted as breacher while Jackson and the rest his team took the first three positions with Simon and then Lucas taking the fourth and fifth. Maberry and Dolby would be doing the same with the other SWAT squad on the other front door, which was thirty feet down the building from the one Jackson's team was breaching.

Radio chatter passed around until everyone confirmed they were in position and ready, then Jackson gave the command, "Go!"

The assault was on.

ALARMS SOUNDED AND Todd stiffened. Someone was invading his perimeter—a lot of someone's, and then he heard the slamming as doors burst open upstairs. He checked the video feeds.

Cops! Fuck! How had they found him? And in large numbers, too. Well, he had a surprise for them. He had to keep them busy while he and Livia got out the back way.

While there was still time.

He had an army. He hadn't expected to need them, but he'd set up some programs in case. He just had to arm them and send them out. The problem was he'd never tested them, never done a dry run. That was foolish. He cursed at himself for the oversight. His mind had been elsewhere.

Still, it wasn't that complicated. Fuck them. All he needed was a diversion while he got away. So he pulled up the files and typed in commands to activate the extra cameras and sensors he'd installed around other entrances down the tunnel. He had to know what was happening, be alert so he could do what he needed to do.

He chose the first protocol and sent it to the androids. It only took a minute for them to start lining up and then he ran over and opened the large locker where he'd stored the weapons cache. AK-47s, Glocks, Mossberg 590s. Then he directed them to the ammo and sent them out to kill some cops.

As the androids fanned out in all directions, he felt a tinge of sadness, wishing he could just sit and enjoy the show. His beautiful babies at work. Cops dying. But he had his work to do.

At the last minute, he set the video feeds to record all activity. At least he could retrieve it from the cloud later and enjoy it over popcorn. Then he ran down the hall to get to work.

THEY BURST INTO a wide open space with cement floors and a high ceiling supported by large, exposed steel girders. There were giant fans and AC units high on the walls, and the few windows were large but dirty, looking out on the alley and the street. There was no furniture and no people present except the cops. They maintained formation, moving through the space as they repeated the breach pattern on each room, clearing them one by one. Altogether, it took them less than five minutes to clear all the rooms and both bathrooms, then they stopped and met in the middle to regroup.

"You said the GPS has him here?" Jackson asked.

"Yes, but he could be in the tunnel," Simon said.

"The old street car tunnels?" Jackson asked. "Aren't they sealed?"

"Let's find out," Simon said.

"I think the entrance is in the garage, if I remember right," Maberry said.

"There are several access points, I believe, but two main," Simon said.

Simon barely heard the click before gunfire erupted around them— concrete disintegrating, bullets clanging against metal beams, windows shattering loudly as glass rained down across the floor—and he heard yelling and screaming and smelled the sweat as everyone dove for cover and scrambled and the world went to hell.

AS SOON AS the gunfire erupted, Lucas was diving and rolling and ended up near an outside wall as he looked around for the source of the attacks. A line of armed androids was pouring in three entrances, firing at the police officers, and then he saw their faces and for the first time felt true fear: he was staring at his own face again and again and again.

He could be shot by his own people if he wasn't careful. His mind raced for what to do, as bullets ricocheted off the wall behind him. Then he ran and slipped out the nearest door and ran around the side of the warehouse, calling for several cops waiting down the block to follow. He might not be able to get a good Taser angle but he could distract the androids and give his friends a chance.

"They're surrounded in there," Lucas said to the cops joining him, speaking in hushed tones as he ran. "We need to create a diversion and give them a chance." He heard glass shattering and Simon and other cops yelling and screaming inside as automatic gunfire flashed and pounded around them. He hoped they were uninjured and could move. They wouldn't be for long.

"Not sure we can get a Taser angle from here," one uniform said.

"Yeah, you guys told us in the briefing that androids are bullet proof," another said.

"Yes, Connelly Labs models are," Lucas said. "These are

different, so we don't know for sure. But even if we can't Taser them we can distract them, and that should allow the others to get to safe cover."

They stopped running as they entered the alley and looked toward the back of the warehouse and two doors Lucas had seen androids pour through. Trash scraped along the pavement as it blew past on the wind, garbage bins rattling nearby as horns honked and tires squealed in the distance all accompanied by the percussive staccato of gunfire.

"If we fire through those doors, they will react to the attack on their rear and that will lessen the fire on the assault teams," Lucas explained.

"Let's do it," a sergeant in uniform said.

"Just don't get shot," Lucas warned. Most of the uniforms had vests but nowhere near the armor of the SWAT team members, and there wasn't much cover in the alley. A couple of dumpsters and a car or two. "You take those five and hit the far door, we'll cover this one." Lucas motioned as he spoke.

"Ok by me," the sergeant said as he motioned to five men to follow him. "We hit them hard, and when they come after us, we get behind cover. Fire on Lucas' signal."

Lucas watched tensely as they slipped past the nearest door unnoticed by the androids within and took up positions on either side of the far door. The sergeant motioned that he was ready.

"Fire!" Lucas shouted and they opened fire on the androids.

SIMON'S SENSES WERE assaulted by smoke, burning lead, falling dust and debris, and cursing and screaming people. He was sure he was going to die and then he wasn't.

They went from under intense fire for two minutes while everyone scrambled around seeking almost nonexistent cover to running for the door, because someone outside started firing at the androids and caused half of them to break off and turn to face the new threat. Whatever and whoever it was, he might have to kiss them if he actually got out of this.

As he stayed low and ran for the door, he saw two SWAT men helping one of their own who was limping. Simon looked around for Lucas as he and Jackson assumed rear positions and fired back at the androids. Then he suddenly realized the androids were all Lucas. What the fuck?! Where the hell was the real Lucas? They were all across the room and all firing at him.

He checked the floor, panning as quickly as his eyes could manage while still returning fire, but no one was down. The other team with Maberry and Dolby were exiting right beside them.

Fuck. What happened to you, partner?

In the end, he abandoned the idea of finding his partner and ran out with the rest, dodging and ducking toward the nearest cover as the androids raced across the warehouse to the front to fire out at them.

Outside, other cops had moved in and set up a siege formation and returned fire, helping provide cover as the androids were distracted by the increased threat and paused to scan for the best targets. Simon noticed a few media drones hovering around and silently hoped the androids might shoot at them.

Soon, Simon was behind a squad car that was behind a

cement wall lining the sidewalk and feeling much safer as he tried to regroup and reached for his shoulder radio to hail his partner.

TODD COULD HEAR the gunfire overhead and wished he could see the cop's faces. He gave an amused grunt at the thought of it. He had finished wiring and setting the C-4 charges, and all he had to do was send a command to start the timer. Now he was in the cell where Livia was still unconscious as he strapped her to a cart in preparation to haul her to the back exit and take her out.

He'd debated just killing her, but wasn't sure yet that he didn't need a hostage to negotiate with. He had to make sure he got away free and clear, so he was taking her. As insurance.

He stopped briefly to send a few more instructions to his android army then went back to his work. The idea of 3D Lucas masks had been inspired. He'd thought of it when he was moving to the tunnel and had just enough time to print up twenty or so. It wouldn't cover all of his androids but it would be enough to cause a lot of confusion for the cops, and that's all he needed.

He finished strapping Livia to the cart and grabbed a Glock and plenty of ammo, stuffing the ammo in a backpack he slid onto his back and tucking the Glock in his belt.

Okay, time to get out. The warehouse and tunnel were a loss but expendable ones. He'd find other alternatives. The important thing was to escape and survive.

He stood and began dragging the cart and Livia toward the door.

"THEY'RE 3D MASKS," Simon explained about the androids.

"Yes, but with Lucas missing, we have to assume he either joined them due to corruption or fled," Atwell said. "So we shoot at any of them we see period." She'd showed up at the scene with Becker a few minutes before and was making a general nuisance of herself.

"He didn't join them, I can tell you that," Becker snapped.

"Damn right," Simon echoed.

"How do we know? He could be infected," Atwell replied.

"Look, this gets us nowhere," Jackson said, "If they shoot at us, we shoot at them. We have bigger concerns, like how to deal with an army that's immune to bullets."

"Well, mostly," Maberry said. They had wounded the Lucasbots with bullets but not significantly. Enough to cause a few to limp or switch firing arms though.

"What we need is a way to take them out in mass," Dolby said.

"Well, Tasers straight to the back worked on the others," Simon said, "but with them moving around so much, there's no time to get a clear shot."

"What if we got them wet?" Becker wondered.

"So we could Taser them all at once?" Dolby replied, liking the idea.

"Tasers won't have enough voltage," Simon said then

looked at the KC Power and Light utility crew standing by down the street. "What we need is to drop a power line."

"How the fuck can we do that?" Maberry wondered.

"KCFD," Simon said. "Call the fire department and get some hose trucks in here."

"You think it'll work?" Becker asked.

"It's better than any idea I had," Simon said.

More gunfire tore up the ground beside them as a group of androids finished reloading and opened fire again with AK-47s.

"Let's tell them to rush," Becker said as she dialed her phone.

AS SOON AS the rest of the androids turned their firepower on Lucas and the teams in the alley, the cops retreated to better shelter, and Lucas ran around the side of the warehouse, spotting Simon, Maberry, and Dolby safely slipped behind barriers and vehicles with the SWAT team and other officers.

For a moment, he debated whether to join them, and then he realized the appearance of the androids who looked like him gave him a unique opportunity. If he could slip into the tunnel and find Livia unnoticed, mistaken for one of the android army, he could rescue his Maker and maybe even get an advantage on her captor, so instead of running toward his friends, Lucas turned around and headed for the parking lot where the entrance to the tunnel was rumored to be.

It took him less than three minutes to find it. It was marked off by a gate that had clearly been chained shut, only the gate was wide open now and the chains lying in a bunch on the cement parking lot surface.

Turning off his shoulder radio to avoid giving away his position, he hid behind nearby cars, amazed he hadn't encountered any androids so far, and kept his eyes peeled on the tunnel entrance to see if any would emerge. Was it really just lying open and ready for anyone to enter? There had to be a catch.

But then four faceless androids emerged, climbing up onto the parking lot surface, then forming a square formation, AK-47's held ready, before racing off toward the exit.

This happened again twice, two minutes apart, as Lucas heard gunfire increasing outside, and decided he had to chance it. Standing, he strolled confidently toward the opening just as another group of androids emerged. They stopped, scanning his face, guns aimed at him, then turned without a word and raced off after the others.

Lucas stripped off the polypropylene clothes which were torn and useless. There wasn't time to go for another, so he'd just have to risk it. Then he jumped into the hole and slid down the ladder, using a hand on each side to steady himself. He landed on his feet on smooth stone below and looked around. The tunnel was lit down the middle with a row of LED bulbs, leaving heavy shadows on either side. It seemed to disappear into the distance behind him as he looked back toward the warehouse to see a few walled-in spaces on the left with a narrower corridor leading past them to a more well-lit area. This had to be the suspect's working area, and he drew his Glock and ran toward it.

"YOU WANT US to do what?!" KCFD Captain Lee Dayton asked as he stared confused at Simon.

"Wet them down," Simon repeated. "As many and as fast as you can. We're going to mass fry them with a power line."

"And you think this will work?" Dayton asked, his squad lined up beside the fire truck behind him, waiting.

"Well, shooting them sure as fuck doesn't," Maberry snapped.

"We gotta try something or taking them down one at a time could drag out for hours," Simon said.

Dayton shook his head. "There's a first time for everything."

"Just do it from as far away as you can," Simon said. "We don't want your people getting electrocuted."

"Believe me, we're against that, too," Dayton said and then turned and began issuing commands to his men, and Simon hurried over to the power crew who were already at work disconnecting one of the lines that ran to a switch box from the breaker box on the side of the warehouse, safely out of range of the gunfire.

"You're sure this will work?" Simon asked.

"Yeah, we have them standing by to turn back on the power, " the crew chief said. "Then we just flip the lever on the side of the box." He motioned.

Simon was glad they knew what they were doing, because the risks of fucking with electricity scared the shit of him, despite the necessity.

As he hurried back to join Becker and the others, he

glanced back toward the warehouse. The windows were all completely gone now and the walls were showing holes up and down the sides from automatic fire. Most of the androids were using precision firing from inside, but occasionally one or two would stick their head or arm up and the police always tried to nail them when they did. Unfortunately, it seemed to have little effect.

Simon keyed the radio and tried hailing his missing partner for the umpteenth time. He had to warn him. "Detective Lucas George, do you copy?"

Static.

Fuck. Where are you, Lucas?

"TODD? WHERE ARE WE?" Livia asked hazily as she looked around, still dazed and barely coherent.

Fuck. Worst timing to wake up. And he'd been rushed and left the medicine in a bag by his command station. He growled and turned, running out the door, heading there to quickly retrieve it. Her bonds wouldn't allow her to escape, and they'd keep her in place the minute it took him to retrieve his bag.

As he ran he heard Livia speak again. "Todd? What is this place? What did you do to me?"

Not as much as I will do, Livia.

She cut off the thought by asking, "Lucas? Is that you? Help me, Lucas. He's gone mad."

LUCAS ENTERED THE smaller corridor beside the enclosed rooms just as Todd Ward darted out and ran the other way toward the well-lit space. *So it is you, Todd*, he thought. Then he heard his Maker calling out and hurried toward her voice.

The first three rooms were locked, but when he came to the last room and looked inside, Livia was lying on the floor, bound to a cart. He raced inside and knelt, tearing at her bonds.

"I'm here, Maker," he whispered.

"What are you doing in here?" Todd Ward demanded from behind him, and Lucas turned to see Ward entering the room with a backpack. "Leave her bindings alone and hold her down so I can sedate her."

Ward hurried over and knelt beside him, pulling a syringe from the bag and reloading it with a tube of liquid. "This should give you a nice round of sleep, Livia," he muttered.

"No, please," Livia pleaded.

Todd held the syringe between two fingers, thumb poised over the plunger as moved toward her, but then his eyes glanced down where Lucas' Glock rested on the floor beside his leg and his eyes widened as he saw the badge Lucas had clipped to his belt.

I forgot my badge!

"Noooooooo!" Todd yelled and turned, scrambling for the gun as Lucas went for it too. Their shoulders clashed and they tugged at each other's hands, each trying to keep the other from the gun.

"How did you get in here?" Todd demanded.

"I climbed," Lucas replied as Todd kicked his shin and they continued struggling.

"Lucas! Help me!" Livia called out.

THE FIREMEN SPRAYED water through the open windows of the warehouse, soaking the androids, who continued firing anyway. The power of the hose stream managed to disarm a few and knock others off their feet, but they quickly recovered and jumped back up, stepping to the side.

"This isn't going to work with them in there," Dolby said. "We have to lure them out."

"Feel free to run in and flash them if you think that'll work," Maberry teased.

Dolby shot him dead with a look.

"Art would do it but we're not trying to make them laugh," Becker snapped and she and Dolby high fived.

"Water carries current," Simon said. "We just need enough of both." He turned to Captain Dayton and motioned, "Be sure and spray down the floor and walls so we can send a current at them."

"You cops are crazy," Dayton said but issued the commands.

After a good five minutes of soaking, he turned back to the Detectives. "It should be good to go. If it works." They firemen turned off their hoses and stepped clear.

"Power & Light!" Simon yelled, and the cops raised armed

Tasers just in case as the utility crew chief got on the radio and his crew stood ready, two holding the power line and the other ready beside the box. Simon raised a hand. "On my mark."

Simon glanced around to make sure they were all ready. A 240 Volt line should provide quite a blast. He said a quick prayer that all the good guys, including Lucas, were well clear, then lowered his hand and gave the command.

The power and light crew sprung to life, two of them dropping the line in the edge of the water pool then running back while the guy at the box pulled the lever. Within seconds, the gunfire petered off and he could see androids falling or shaking. A sudden smell of burning wires, metal, and hydraulic fluid filled the air.

"Holy shit, it's working," Maberry said.

"Guess you're off the hook for flashing them, Dolby," Simon teased.

"Yeah, I was planning on it," she said with a laugh.

In two minutes, they were all exchanging looks. Should they go in or wait?

Then the gunfire resumed. Some androids had been taken out but not all.

"Fuck!" Simon said.

"Any other bright ideas?" Becker asked.

And then the ground rumbled beneath them and a corner of the warehouse sagged.

"What the fuck?" Becker muttered.

But they both had the same thought at the same time. "He blew the tunnel."

"Jesus," Maberry said.

But then they noticed the gunfire petered out and the rest of the androids stopped moving and just stood there as if they didn't know what to do.

"Son of a bitch! He blew up his control system," Simon said. "Let's get to that tunnel entrance while we can."

"They're still armed," Dolby warned.

"They're lowering or dropping the guns," Becker noted.

"Let's stay out of the warehouse," Simon said. "The garage is what we need."

"Proceed with caution," Becker warned, and then they did, in full formation.

TODD WAS FIGHTING for his life against a fucking freak android! Freakishly strong and too damn smart for its own good! *God damn you, Livia Connelly! You fucked me again!*

Then Lucas grabbed him and struggle to force the syringe down. Todd dropped it and felt a sharp pain as it landed in his foot. God damn it. Well, the plunger was holding.

That moment of distraction allowed Lucas to grab the Glock and yell, "Freeze!"

Instead, Todd turned and ran like hell, grabbing his phone and pulling up the app that controlled the explosives. He had sent the last of his soldiers out, and hopefully they were holding off the cops to secure his escape route. The tunnel was wired and could be blown all at once or in three parts.

AS SOON AS Lucas had the gun again and aimed it at Ward, Ward ran, and Lucas turned back to freeing Livia so he could go after him. Where was Ward going to go? He needed to get his Maker to safety.

"Lucas, what's going on?" she asked groggily.

"I am going to get you out of here and safe, Maker," he said.

"Thank God, you came."

And then he felt a vibration and heard a deep, rising rumble as the tunnel exploded around them.

SIMON BURST INTO the garage, Maberry, Becker, Dolby, and Jackson's SWAT team close behind with others on their heels. There were scattered androids here too but not as dense as in the warehouse, and they were just standing there, looking stunned. The pillars had cracks and chunks of cement were missing from some as well as places in the floor. Many cars had shattered windows and car alarms and a few horns were blaring. Water leaked down a wall from overhead in a corner.

Then he rounded a corner and spotted the tunnel entrance as a bedraggled form emerged. Todd Ward!

"Todd Ward, hands up!" he shouted.

"Stop right there!" Dolby added, both pointing their guns right at the man.

Ward stopped and looked around, stunned, limping forward a bit. Then his face took on a look somewhere between fear and shock. "Help! It was terrible! They were holding me and Livia!"

"Put your hands up and move forward slowly," Simon commanded.

"Thank God you're here," Ward mumbled as he complied, raising his hands and limping forward as if his foot was asleep.

Suddenly, a form emerged behind him. It was Lucas—or was it?—with a body slung over his shoulder.

Ward noticed the cops reacting and spun, pointing. "That's one of them! He's got Livia!"

Guns cocked and Tasers raised as Simon tried to determine if this was one of Ward's androids or his partner.

"Wait!" Simon yelled.

"Put Doctor Connelly down, now!" Becker shouted.

"I think it's Lucas," Simon said.

"It's me, Lucas," the android said in the familiar voice Simon knew so well, and he gently set Livia down on the asphalt, allowing her to run clear toward the waiting police.

"How can we be sure?" Jackson asked.

And then as if recognizing their delimma, the android started blaring music and began to dance to a familiar song.

He sang about Kung fu fighting and cats as fast as lightning then did air kung fu with flailing arms and danced in a circle to the right.

"It's him!" Simon said, starting to laugh.

Lucas continued to dance as Simon, Becker, and Maberry raced forward and gently lifted Livia Connelly from his shoulders.

"Are you all right, Doctor Connelly?" Becker asked.

"It was Todd," Livia choked out.

Becker turned to motion. "Arrest that man now!"

"It wasn't me!" Ward protested but no one believed him.

Several officers surrounded him, cuffing him and patting him down, then led him away.

"Are you okay, pal?" Simon asked as Lucas stopped dancing and the music faded. Lucas's clothes were torn in spots and he was covered with dust and debris.

"Yes, though he tried to bury us with an explosion," Lucas said. "I am not sure evidence survived."

"We have an eye witness," Simon said, then added, "Thanks to you."

Lucas grinned. "Yes, I guess we do."

"Good work, pal," Simon said and slapped his back, laughing again.

Maberry, Dolby, and the SWAT team members raced forward and aimed their weapons down the hole.

"Is anyone else down there?" Maberry called.

"I do not think so," Lucas said, shaking his head.

"You're supposed to tell your partner where you are so I can back you up," Simon scolded gently.

"There was not time," Lucas said. "I had to rescue my Maker."

"You're an idiot, but I'm kinda proud of ya," Simon said, shaking his head.

"Can we go home now?" Lucas joked.

"Yeah, come with me," Simon said.

Walking together, they left the chaos and moved through the garage toward the nearest exit. It was over. Simon could hardly believe it.

"Nice touch with the music," Simon said.

"I knew my skill for dancing would be useful," Lucas joked.

"Emma will be so proud," Simon said.

"She says we should teach you to dance," Lucas said.

"I can dance just fine," Simon snapped.

"You are clumsy and awkward," Lucas said.

"Shut the fuck up," Simon said. "You talk to my daughter way too much. We're going to have to talk about that."

"I am just a likable guy," Lucas said with a shrug and Simon laughed.

CHAPTER 24

L IVIA CONNELLY WAS at Central Patrol the next day telling her story, and Todd Ward was sent for evaluation to the state hospital on judge's orders and was facing numerous charges. Simon was exhausted, as he always was after a major case, and he was looking forward to a relaxing evening, so Lucas and Emma had made plans for a movie and dinner and he was happy to see them leave.

As Lucas pulled out of the drive and disappeared, another car pulled up, a brown Lexus, and Simon frowned, wondering who it could be. He didn't know anyone with a Lexus these days. Then Holly Sanders got out and headed up the drive, carrying a pizza box and a six pack of bottled Pabst.

He waited until she was almost to the door before he answered. "You know the last media that showed up here, I threw them against a tree," he joked, referring to an incident with a media drone during the terrorist case.

"Yes, I remember reading about that," she said, holding up the beer. "I brought your favorite, so maybe don't do that to me?"

He laughed and stepped to the side, waving her inside with an arm.

"So this is the inner sanctum," she teased as she looked around the entry way and living room connected to it.

"I have a teenage daughter who's here a lot," he said.

"Oh? Blaming her? Wow. Not very chivalrous," she teased.

"Ahh fuck, I'm exhausted. Stop giving me shit and hand me a damn beer."

She laughed and held out the beer. He took it by the handle and led her into the kitchen where he grabbed a bottle opener from a drawer beside the sink and freed a beer from the carrier, popping the top off before taking a long swig.

When he'd finished, he wiped his mouth with a sleeve and asked, "You get the story you wanted?"

"Yeah," she said. "And you got your man."

"More importantly, we saved Livia Connelly," Simon said. "That's the best part."

"That too," she said and held out her own beer for Simon to pop the cap. He did and then she clanged hers to his before they each took another sip.

Holly was dressed in a not-too-tight but flattering sun dress and red flat shoes, her legs amazingly tan for winter. Simon admired them, momentarily embarrassed by his red flannel shirt over t-shirt and jeans.

"I feel under dressed," he commented.

She shook her head. "Pizza and beer. You're perfect." She flipped open the pizza box and Simon examined the meat lover's pizza underneath.

"Meat, meat, and more meat," Simon said. "Good choice."

"Oh hell, I'm always hungry after a good story," Holly said, grabbing a slice of pizza and taking a huge bite.

"I really had you pegged wrong," he said as he grabbed his own slice and followed suit.

"How so?" she asked when she'd finished chewing.

"I really had you pegged for the vegetarian, dainty, trendy

type."

She chortled. "You know I like pizza from the other day."

"Yeah, just saying, I like being wrong," he said and smiled.

"I haven't begun to get wrong with you yet, buddy," she teased, shooting him a naughty look.

He took another long swig of beer and ate more pizza, not sure what to say.

She giggled. "Am I making you uncomfortable?"

He shifted. "It's been a while."

She put a palm against his chest and pushed gently up until she was cupping his face. "Really?"

He smiled.

"Oh my God, the badass detective has a shy side," she teased.

"Are you always like this after a story?" he joked.

"Pizza and good drama, always get me horny," she said and raised an eyebrow suggestively.

He finished his beer and slid away to grab another.

"Gotcha running away already? No problem, I love the chase," she said.

He turned back as he popped of the cap and she was right there, pressing against him and then kissing him with a passion he hadn't experienced in a decade.

When they finally came up for air, he took a deep breath as she giggled. She was definitely getting a rise out him and he blushed when he saw her noticing the physical effect. "You have amazing confidence."

"I know what I want and I go for it," she said. "Key to my success."

She grabbed his hand and motioned to the pizza. "Do you like pizza in bed?"

He'd never had a woman he was so attracted to come after him so hard. Not even Lara. He was somewhere between liking it and being deeply afraid. *Oh well, John, might as well embrace the fear.* "Let's find out," he said.

He grabbed the pizza box and followed her into the bedroom.

LUCAS TOOK EMMA out for gyros at her favorite Greek food truck then headed for the nearest AMC. They'd planned to see the latest romantic comedy, a film called "Out of Nowhere" because Emma had a crush on the lead—Deacon Philippe, who was the son of Reese Witherspoon and Ryan Philippe. But when they arrived at the theater, one of the cameras had blown a circuit and the manager apologized, but they didn't have an extra theater open to run the film, so they decided to head back to Simon's and watch a blu-ray.

"Your dad thinks we talk too much," Lucas commented as he pulled into the drive.

"To each other or generally?" Emma asked, slipping out of her seatbelt.

"To each other," Lucas said with an amused grunt.

"Whatever, I feel like I've hardly seen you lately," she said.

They opened their doors and started up the drive together.

"I told him we offered to teach him to dance."

"Ha! What did he say?"

"He was not enthusiastic."

"You probably embarrassed him," Emma said. "Wish I

coulda been there for that." She opened the door and headed inside. "Dad, we're home," she called.

She sniffed the air. "I smell pizza. Meat lovers. Smells good."

As Lucas closed the door, they heard a woman laughing.

"Dad?" Emma said, shooting Lucas a surprised look. They walked back together down the hall toward the bedrooms.

"It's everywhere," the woman said.

"What a mess," Simon commented.

As they approached the master bedroom, Lucas noted the door was cracked.

"Dad, what are you watching," Emma said and pushed open the door to her father's room. She stopped in the doorway and gasped.

Simon and the reporter Holly Sanders were naked and she was sitting astride him, moving up and down.

"Holy Jesus!" Holly suddenly said as she glanced back and saw them.

Emma ran from the room, her hand over her mouth.

Lucas looked at Holly, smiled and nodded. "You look good."

"Would you get the fuck outta here!" Simon yelled.

Lucas backed away and closed the door behind him as Holly burst into laughter.

SIMON WAS SO horrified he didn't even know where to begin. What the hell were Emma and Lucas doing back here so soon? Oh my God, what his daughter had seen!

"You find this funny?" Simon growled as Holly continued giggling.

"Well, yes," she admitted as she slid off him and stood at the end of the bed, naked and looking like a model.

"I thought you'd be more embarrassed," Simon said.

"I'm mortified," she said. "For both of us, but well, at least you don't have to waste time introducing me to your family."

Simon threw a pillow at her. "You shut the fuck up too and get dressed."

"It was good," she said and smiled at him.

"Shhhh," he said, blushing as he held a finger to his lips and glanced toward the door.

"Okay, okay," she said, laughing again as he shrunk back under the covers. He heard her shuffling around—retrieving her clothes, no doubt—and dressing.

"John?" she said a moment later.

He popped his head out from under the covers and looked at her. "Yeah?"

"I hope we can try this again later."

"Shhhhhh, keep your voice down," he said and set her laughing again.

"You're gonna have one hell of chat tonight with your daughter," she teased and then burst out laughing one more time. Simon fought it but couldn't help it, he started laughing too.

"This is so not funny," Simon said, taking a deep breath to calm himself again. "Wait 'til her mother hears about it."

"So you have a healthy sex life? You're divorced." She shrugged as she finished putting on her panties and bra and slid the dress on over her head.

"You don't understand my relationship with my ex," Simon said.

"Something you can tell me about on our next date," she teased, giggling again.

"You keep laughing at me, there won't be any more dates."

"Bullshit," she said and grinned.

"Ah fuck," he said, sliding a pillow over his face and trying to ignore her again.

AFTER AN EMBARRASSED Holly emerged from the bedroom, she and Emma manage to chat politely for around five minutes before Holly headed for her car, giving Simon a quick kiss on the cheek.

"I'll call you," she said then hurried out, and Simon closed the door behind her, turning to see Lucas and Emma staring at him.

"Well, you're the one who wanted me to get laid," Simon teased.

"Oh Jesus Christ, Dad," Emma said, her face scrunching into a horrified look.

"What? I thought you liked her," Simon said.

"I can never. Get. That. Image. Out of my head." Emma punctuated each word the way teenagers loved to do, while rubbing her temples as if she had a headache.

Simon laughed. "I walked in on my parents once. They were doing a sixty-nine."

"Oh my God! Making it worse!" Emma said, covering her

ears and running off to her room. "La la la la la la!"

As she shut the door behind her, Simon turned to see Lucas still watching him.

"You like torturing her," Lucas observed.

"You both deserve it," Simon said. "Can't a man get privacy in his own bedroom?" He started back toward the kitchen and Lucas followed. The scent of meat lovers still filled the air, and it reminded him he was still hungry, but they'd messed up the pizza by accident in the bedroom.

"We were not expecting you to have a guest."

"Yeah, no shit, pal," Simon snapped as he opened the fridge and rooted around, selecting a pack of deli meat, mayonnaise and some wheat bread, and setting them on the counter. He closed the fridge, then pulled a knife from a drawer and began fixing a sandwich.

"I have never observed human mating before," Lucas said.

Simon had to stop himself from cutting all the way through the bread slice. "Oh my God, don't call it that."

"Is it okay if I have questions?"

Simon felt a sudden urge to cover his own ears and run away. "No." He focused on spreading mayo and refused to meet Lucas' eyes.

"But I wish to learn."

"I'll rent you some porn, shut the fuck up." He finished the mayo and went back to the fridge for two cheese slices.

"Were you able to use a pickup line I suggested?"

"No."

"It would be fascinating to know which was effective. I would guess 'You complete me.'"

"That's something you'd only say to someone you've been with for a long time."

"Was it 'You had me at hello?'"

"No, I didn't use them, Lucas. Stop asking."

"Perhaps now would be a good time for your dance lessons?"

"Seriously, shut up."

"Perhaps Holly Sanders likes to dance," Lucas said sincerely.

"I will shoot you," Simon said, motioning with the knife to where his Glock sat with the gunbelt on the hallway floor as he tossed the cheese slices on the sandwich.

"I can outrun you," Lucas teased.

"I can shoot far," Simon replied as he placed the top slice over the bottom and lifted the sandwich for a bite.

"Not as far as me."

"Are you challenging me?" he asked through a mouthful of sandwich.

"You have seen me shoot, do you really wish to try?"

"Hey, fuck you, I was shooting when your Maker was just an itch in her daddy's pants."

"An itch in her daddy's pants?"

"Never mind, it's an expression." Simon took his sandwich and headed for the family room and his favorite chair.

Lucas followed. "Explain please."

"Uh not right now."

"Does it have something to do with what we saw in that bedroom?"

"Shut the fuck up and go bother Emma," Simon said as he sank in the BarcaLounger and savored another bite.

"I thought you said we spend too much time together."

"Yes, but so do we."

Lucas grinned as Simon waved back toward the kitchen.

"Make yourself useful and go get me a beer."

"I am not a household robot."

"I thought you wanted new experiences."

"I will do this but only because I am your friend."

"Yes, you are, now be a friend and let's stop talking now and watch TV."

"Okay, but first I will get your beer."

"You know, as fast as she ran outta here, I think Holly could give you a run for your money," Simon teased.

"I did notice you staring at her posterior," Lucas said as he returned from the kitchen and held out a Pabst.

"That's another thing I'll explain another time, now sit down and shut up," Simon said.

Simon began flipping through channels as Lucas sank onto the couch and he continued eating in silence, hoping they'd never speak of what had happened here ever again.

But he knew they probably would.

ACKNOWLEDGEMENTS

As usual there are many people to thank for helping making this book possible.

Martin L. Shoemaker for helping me with nanobite research as well as working through the plotlines when I felt stuck or like something was missing.

As always, Gil Carter and Doaa El Ashkar from the Kansas City Police Department were ready and available with quick advice on procedures, policies, and details, and Melissa Mattson of the KCPD Communications Center helped me with questions on dispatch and codes. Colorado Springs Sheriff Officer Tim Hightshoe for teaching me about assault formations and breach protocols.

Guy Anthony DeMarco for editing, Anthony Cardno for proofing, and Sebastian Penraeth for helping me with the interior layout and design. And Audra Crebs for another fantastic cover.

Thanks to David Weber, Weston Ochse, and Wendy Delmater of Abyss & Apex for blurbs (I hope she likes the namesake character named after her and her husband). The many friends who allowed me to tuckerize them, most especially Todd Ward, a fan and now friend who became the namesake of the antagonist despite any risk to his own reputation.

Thanks also to my parents, Ramon and Glenda, my pets—Louie, Amelie, Lacy, and Doce (the newest addition)—and thanks to all the readers, especially my core support group, for input and keeping me going.

As always, any mistakes and errors are mine alone.

AUTHOR BIO

Bryan Thomas Schmidt is a national bestselling author editor and Hugo-nominee who's edited over a dozen anthologies and hundreds of novels, including the international phenomenon *The Martian* by Andy Weir and books by Alan Dean Foster, Frank Herbert, Mike Resnick, Angie Fox, and Tracy Hickman as well as official entries in *The X-Files*, *Predator*, *Joe Ledger*, *Monster Hunter International*, and *Decipher's Wars*. His debut novel, *The Worker Prince*, earned honorable mention on Barnes and Noble's Year's Best science fiction. His adult and chi ldren's fiction and nonfiction books have been published by publishers such as St. Martins Press, Baen Books, Titan Books, IDW, and more. Find him online at his website *www.bryanthomasschmidt.net* or Twitter and Facebook as *BryanThomasS*. He lives in Ottawa, KS with his canine bosom companions, Louie and Amelie and two cats named Lacy and Doce.

Coming in October 2020

MILK RUN

JOHN SIMON BOOK 4

For a sneak peek at the first two chapters,
visit
http://bryanthomasschmidt.net/milk-run-preview